FINAL EVOLUTION

Final Evolution

Jasenn Zaejian

Related Publishing
http://relatedness.org
Huntington Beach, California

Jasenn Zaejian, a former clinical psychologist, is the author of four non-fiction works on Critical Psychology. Following a revelation that his profession was supporting and advising on torture for the government, he realized he no longer wanted to be associated with a profession who endorses such practice and left the field to devote his time to writing fiction.

Related Publishing
Huntington Beach, California
http://relatedness.org
©2015 Jasenn Zaejian
All rights reserved. Published 2015

ISBN Digital 9780983066057
ISBN Paper 9780983066064

Prologue

The constellation survey ship Nova 4 dropped out of supralight in auto-response to an incoming holo. It was Solar Command at Terra base. Ang Vessad's awareness slowly returned from cryosleep. Having been interstellar travelers for the past few millenniums, Ang's species had evolved to sense velocity changes. He immediately adjusted the cryo volumes to wake the Commander.

Ang was one of the few non-hostile extraterrestrial creatures who recently allied with humans. Since his rescue by a Solar Command battleship from the prison satellite of the Volars, a sadistic breed of furry creatures, Ang vowed to dedicate his life to assist his human saviors as they explored the surrounding galaxies.

The Volars were from a cold, dark planet just at the boundary that could sustain life, orbiting Proxima Centauri. Ang's first contact with humans began when the battleship, Patanjali, on an exploratory mission from Terra, responded to a cry for help from a captured human on the Volar prison satellite. First blocking all communication, Solar marines rapidly took over the poorly staffed satellite, liberating all the prisoners, many from different worlds. They destroyed the satellite and what remained of the Volars. The Volar home world never discovered what happened. To express his gratitude, Ang offered to join the Solar Confederation's mining exploration company and contribute his superior knowledge of the surrounding star systems. With his knowledge of advanced technology beyond current human understanding, and his demonstrated loyalty, he was rapidly promoted to the position of master starship pilot. Ang's superior intellectual skills enabled him to rapidly learn most human languages. He not only excelled as a starship pilot with human vessels, he graciously provided valuable engineering advances to their more primitive light drives. He hoped to locate other Crespians, lucky enough to flee the home world during the Volar invasion.

Crespar was once a Terra-like peaceful planet with a flourishing society orbiting Alpha Centauri B. It was destroyed by the Volars during an unexpected invasion. While the Crespians were technologically superior to Terra and Solar system dwellers they were unprepared for hostilities, having never experienced aggression from other planetary civilizations.

"Colonel...wake up...Come on, wake up, damn it," shouted Ang over the commander's personal holo. "Colonel you must rise." He increased the oxygen levels in the cryo chamber.

Colonel Derral Priestly, rolled over and pressed the red button above his head, opening the cryonic hibernation chamber. "Are we in the solar system already? I must have really been out."

"We have an incoming, marked urgent, from Solar Intelligence," said Ang.

The commander called up the course chart on the chamber holo. "Ang, we're not even half way there. I didn't think they could contact us this far out."

"Seems like they can, Colonel. It's a direct comlink from the Chief's office," said Ang.

"What the hell does he want with us? We finished our resource survey of the Pleades system and transmitted all the data," said the Colonel.

"I don't know but looks like they've been buzzing us for the last few hours. The final buzz engaged the auto return function and dropped us out. That's what woke me up," said Ang.

"Okay, tell him I just got out of cryo and need a minute or two," said Colonel Priestly.

"It's not a him, it's a her."

"Who would that be?"

"I don't know commander. But she appears to know you."

"Okay, I'll take it on the bridge."

Derral took the conduit to the bridge. "Okay, lets see what this is

2

about," he said, as he materialized in front of the view holos. "Stay here at the controls," said Derral.

He opened the holocom. "This is Commander Derral Priestly of the constellation survey ship Nova 4. What can we do for you?"

The holo image cleared of static. "Derral, I miss you," said his life partner.

"Wow... Susan? What a surprise. How could you...I mean, I miss you too. How were you able to get a hold of us from SIS?" said Derral.

"I called your old friend Robert. I'm in his office now. There are some new developments we need to talk about. First of all, I finished my coursework, with the exception of a few minor details. And then, I received a holo from pater, this morning. He wants to arrange for us to be one of the few couples to visit with our new friends, the Da'yoni. They have some special transport that spans the galaxies in a matter of minutes. Pater said they installed a station for our use and the use of about a dozen other people, selected by the Holders. There may be some complications that Robert wants to talk to you about. I just wanted to let you know. I have to go and turn in a final paper before tonight to get full credit and graduate. We'll talk when you get back...And by the way, when will that be?" said Susan.

Derral looked towards Ang. "Who the hell are the Da'yoni?"

"A very mysterious species. They once visited our system, many years ago. You'll find out for yourself," said Ang with what passed as a smile. They have developed an almost instantaneous transport system..."

"Tell me about them later," said Derral.

"Susan...almost-Doctor Susan...sorry for the interruption. Meet my mate, Ang, one of our Crespian associates."

Ang waved his five appendages as he moved to the control panel.

"You heard Ang's assessment? We'll likely be there in a few weeks, now that we dropped out of light and need to crank it up again."

"Okay, I can't wait...but listen to Robert...as he worries me. And after the morrow you can let go of the "almost Doctor." And by the way you'll be coming home to the newest scientist at the Xtrabio Research Unit. My thesis advisor got me the gig and Pater arranged to postpone it until after we come back from Da'yoni. Hello Ang. Please drop by for dinner when you return. We'll see if we can find some Crespian recipes in the database."

"I'd be honored mam...err, almost Doctor, mam..."

"Susan, please, Ang. I only insist that Derral refer to me by my new or almost new professional title, as he did nothing but bug me to not procrastinate over the last 5 years. He'd even send sardonic texts from distant galaxies asking me if I turned in this or that assignment. Not unlike my pater, until I got so angry at him that I threatened to end the relationship,...But he knows I appreciated every minute of his irritation," said Susan, smiling.

"Yes, Susan...but I doubt you'll find any Crespian recipes, I'll transmit some from my neural storage...that's if they let me off the base...and I don't ever know that I'll fully understand the nuances of human communication... you're angry but threaten to leave your life partner, but appreciate what he did to cause your anger?" said Ang with what appeared to be a smile.

"We'll teach you when you visit. And you teach us about some of your nuances. It's not difficult...at least I think it's not," said Susan.

"I'm looking forward to it," said Ang.

Derral's childhood friend, Robert, stepped to the foreground."Going off base won't be a problem anymore, Ang. You have gained our trust."

"Thank you sir," said Ang.

"Derral, wha's up bro?" said Robert Laing, the Chief of Solar Intelligence Services.

"I hope no one heard you talk like that, old buddy. It would ruin your image," said Derral.

"Don't worry about that, this holo is secure...and for good reason," said Robert.

Derral and Robert had continued their close relationship, beginning in childhood, but cemented in loyal friendship when they both entered the Galactic Academy. After graduation, Robert was the commander of the first Galactic cruiser Derral sailed on, in his shakedown exploratory cruise to the rim system. In college they were both activists, wearing t-shirts with holograms of the Wobblies, a socialist labor movement existing many centuries ago, promoting true equality and worker owned factories, now almost forgotten. They studied ancient economists who seemed to see through the mainstream leader's rhetoric pointing towards the domination and exploitation of the populace for profit, while acting as if poverty and hunger were an individual's own creation. In the following years, both of them embraced what was to become their life-long careers, Derral became absorbed in astrophysics, while Robert drifted towards history and political science, eventually immersing himself in the study of how society is manipulated by the government.

"You look serious, my old friend. Did we do something wrong when we visited the Pleades system?"

"No, it's not about that. Since the Secretary nominated you and Susan to be one of the travelers to Da'yoni and announced it on the public holos, we intercepted some feeds from one of those Solar centric crazies. In one message they talked about intercepting your returning ship and taking you hostage so you don't land back on Terra. They figure this would cancel the Secretary's plans."

"Oh boy...and I thought this was going to be an easy cruise back. We just about exhausted our weapons last week We had a little skirmish with the Placons, you know those fish scale uglies. They said we were traversing through their system boundaries. Fortunately, their weapon systems were a bit more primitive than ours. We wasted a few of their robotic attack craft and they backed off."

"What do you have left?" said Robert.

"You look concerned. That scares me, as I know you're not a bullshit artist like most of the government officials. We have about enough charge for a few pulses and one torpedo left. We also have our fore and aft laser cannons with full charges, as we didn't have to use them," said Derral.

"I see on the galactic map that you're about two weeks out at light. I'm thinking we should send out a combat frigate to back you up, just in case," said Robert.

"By the time it gets to us, we'll be in the system. But I'd hate to be caught without any defense, in the event we are attacked," said Derral.

"Don't worry, my man. I'll take a ride out with our upgraded supralight frigate. The commander will keep the com opened, just in case you need to send a quick burst alerting us of an approaching attack. Something for your ears only...our latest upgrade includes a multiplexer we obtained from one of our trading partners. We can multiply light speed infinitely, as long as we have two fixed start and stop points. We'll track your vessel as a stop point. In the event you see an incoming attack we can get there in a matter of minutes, regardless of where we are. Some new drive physics I don't entirely understand, but it works. I was on the test run with the prototype a few weeks ago. We got from a moon orbit to Neptune in seconds with no issues," said Robert.

"I can't wait to try it. Sure beats this slow tub," said Derral.

"It is highly classified, as of now. I'll arrange for a test run for the interstellar fleet commanders, once you get back. But remember, it is highly classified. That goes for your ship mate, too," said Robert.

Ang moved into the foreground. "Yes sir, Chief. I have full clearance."

"I know Lieutenant. We had you checked out a while ago, before you joined my old friend as his second," said Robert.

The skin of Ang's face wrinkled and he raised his appendages, in response.

"Lieutenant, we do that with all personnel. That's the main job of SIS...and the law says we don't have to notify you when we are verifying. That's for your protection and for ours."

"Oh, that's a great relief. I wonder what else..."

"Ang, remember who you're talking to, even though he's a few light weeks away," said Derral with a sly look and wink at Robert's holo.

"Yes sir, boss. I just came out of cryo...is my excuse," said Ang, smiling.

"As you were, boys," said Robert. "I know you're solid to our cause. You've proven your loyalty, Ang. See you both in a few. Lieutenant, as I need an update of your security clearance because of what you just heard, stop by my office after you get settled back on the planet. It should only take a brief moment to reprogram your secure chip." The holo blinked off.

Ang looked chagrined. "I hate that. The human says a few words and I have to get my chip reprogrammed. That's one of the things I miss from home. We had virtually no paranoia, like you have with your people. A definite pain in the tentacle."

"Well...yes. But didn't the Patanjali find you on that prison satellite? You were there, not by choice, right?" said Derral with a deadpan look.

"You got me boss. Probably if we did have a little paranoia we would have been prepped for the invasion that destroyed my home world," said

6

Ang as he put his tentacles over his forward eyes, looking like what could pass for embarrassment and sadness.

"...Tell me, exactly what the hell is a 'pain in the tentacle?' Is that like what we refer to as a pain in the ass? said Derral.

"Yes, Colonel. We use our fifth appendage for intercourse, not different than your fifth, but with more uses, as an additional arm with our sixth," said Ang, still looking embarrassed.

"Jeez, Ang,"said Derral as he laughed.

"Yes, we're just as modest as your race, if not more so about sex and sex talk," said Ang, still covering his eyes.

"That's good to know. Our realistic paranoia is from centuries of experience with adversaries. Don't worry about meeting with Robert. He's one of the most honest people I know. I'll come with you. It'll give me a reason to visit outside of any surveillance from my partner's biologue."

"What do you mean, Colonel? He has you under surveillance just because you live with her?"

"Yeah. That started a few months ago. Actually it was Robert who alerted me to it. He gave us a device to use to transmit a loop of past behavior, if we wanted privacy. Talk about a pain in the "tentacle" or ass as the case may be. But I guess that's the consequence of living with the Secretary's biologue. We kind of got used to it. Susan told me he covertly surveilled her mother when she was alive...and her when she was a teenager. When she started grad school, she confronted him about it and he stopped. He's a lovely, trusting pater. If you know what I mean."

"Colonel, forgive me for asking an embarrassing personal question, excusing that my species is inquisitive. I often don't understand your sarcasm" said Ang.

"Don't worry about it," said Derral, smiling. "I think you got this one, if your know what I mean."

"I see. Another human peculiarity. I learn a new one every day. Why does talk of tentacles and asses call for laughter?" said Ang.

"Well, I guess I laughed out of embarrassment. Humans don't feel comfortable talking about evacuations or sex, much like you said about your people."

"I see," said Ang looking puzzled. "You're a peculiar but familiar species. What do we do now, stay awake for two weeks or go back to cryo after we jump back to light?".

"We should probably get back to sleep to save our energy in the event we're intercepted. Set the auto alarm to wake us of any approaching ship within a half hour of contact...a human half hour."

"Okay boss, no worry. I always use your time reference, not mine," said Ang as he programmed the jump. "We're ready to cryo."

"See you on the other end," said the Colonel.

They returned to the cryo tubes. Ang's sleep was image free. Derral lapsed into a disturbed sleep. Almost immediately, he began to dream of giant bug like creatures, similar to those they had encountered but doubled in size. The bugs were moving across a planet surface following him. Susan was with him. He did not know what to do. He looked at Susan in the dream and started trembling with fear. His physical alarm buzzed him awake. This was a safety feature installed in the cryo chambers to prevent being overwhelmed by any dreams stimulated by the cryo features. After lying there and staring at the inside of the chamber for a few minutes, he closed his eyes and was immediately transported to a dreamscape of luxurious scents and a flowerscape of images. The cryos were programmed to neurally stimulate this if the alarm were to arouse the occupant.

At that same moment Robert Laing and his staff were actively scanning the exit orbit lanes.

"Chief, I have an unscheduled blip on the lunar exit orbit. Looks like two combat needles with no e-signature."

"Okay. Put a tracker on their coordinates. If they set an intercept course with Derral, notify me immediately and arrange for me to be on the launch of the maxlight.

"Okay chief. Will do."

Robert Laing lay back, floating in his zero grav chair, and watched the lunar exit orbit tracking visual on his holo. His thoughts drifted to an earlier time when his friend Derral grabbed him at the last moment as he started to fall out of the solar wind racer during a rounding maneuver as they tacked back to Terra from around the moon. He had forgotten to hook his suit up to the safety rail. They won that race, one of many in the under 18 class.

Maybe this will be an opportunity for repayment, my friend, he thought. This had troubled him throughout most of the last 20 years. He didn't like feeling indebted to anyone, even his life long friend.

***

Derral was awakened by the pulsing alarm. He took the conduit to the control and saw 2 blips appearing on the sensors, about a half hour out at sub light. The signatures from the vessels indicated they just dropped out of light and uncloaked.

Ang appeared out of the tube stretching his appendages. "I hope this isn't what the Chief was talking about."

"We'll see in a few minutes. They are not on any scheduled transit. Ang, get on the weapons systems, just in case," said Derral.

"Yes sir." A holopanel dropped down in front of him with highlighted targeting information. "I have the two vessels in our fire command, Colonel. Say the word and we'll see how secure their shields are."

"As you were Ang. Wait until they are about five minutes out and hail them. If they don't answer, give them a laser shot across the bow to see how they respond," said the Colonel.

"I'd be delighted, Colonel," said Ang with what passed for a smile across his Crespian features.

Derral watched Ang's movements on the holo panel. "Amazing, Ang. I don't see how you can move so fast. Your arms are just a blur."

"Practice, Colonel. What does your species say? 'Practice makes perfect?' And I do have an extra tentacle."

"I don't know if I'll ever get used to that word to describe a limb. Tell me something, Ang. How did you so quickly grasp our culture?"

"I used the subliminal sleep learning my species developed centuries ago. For months, I played all media from your language and other Terra languages during my sleep. I scanned most of your science and engineering libraries. We are particularly attuned to that kind of learning, by our genetics. Most of our education is done during sleep where we have near perfect recall. What you call schools we used as a kind of social assembly for social learning. Most of our conscious time is devoted to creating and pleasurable pursuits, unlike your compulsive working environment," said Ang.

"In the few years since we've partnered, you never cease to amaze me," said Derral.

"Well, since meeting your species, I always wondered why so much of your time is spent on serious, goal directed activities. It doesn't seem to be a healthy life style. Perhaps that is why we exceed your specie's longevity by some 175 of your Terra years," said Ang.

"...Okay, Ang. We need to pay attention now, like compulsive attention," said the Colonel.

"Yes, Commander, I've been watching them from my chamber for the past ten minutes," said Ang.

"The Needles, dropped out of hyper and uncloaked about 20 minutes out from weapons range. They're slowly moving towards us on our starboard. They haven't charged any weapons...Wait a second. Correction, the first Needle just charged its weapons," said Ang.

"Target them both, but don't fire," said Derral.

"What's our status now Ang?" said Derral.

"I have them lit up on our covert targeting systems, invisible to them. What should I do, Commander?"

"Hold steady Ang. What is their weaponry?" said Derral.

"They have four mag guns between them. Pretty primitive," said Ang, as he rapidly changed settings on the targeting system.

"Okay. Looks like a few of our old surplus Needles. Let them see our targeting system and demand that they shift course and power down their weapons," said Derral.

"Okay boss. But to avoid any problems I could vaporize them with our laser cannons, now," said Ang.

"No, remember, our signature says we're just a survey vessel. If they keep coming, then we take action."

"Okay...unidentified vessels in this matrix, what are your intentions?" said Ang.

"No response. So tell them to change course or we will assume they are hostile," said Derral.

"Unidentified vessels, please identify yourselves and change course. If you do not, we will assume you are hostile."

"Full shields, Ang. The other one just powered up their weapons. Give them one more 5 second warning and then hit them with our lasers," said

Derral.

"Unidentified vessels, please change course or we will be forced to defend ourselves. We out power you and will destroy you if you do not cooperate...Boss. The other one just let go a torpedo," said Ang.

"Destroy the torpedo and target that vessel with a few laser pulses and disable it. Make all our weapons visible and notify the other one that will be their fate if they don't back off," said Derral.

Ang engaged the laser pulses, broadside to the engine compartment of the ship. It started spinning out of control, as it lost power. The other ship stabilized it with a mag grapple.

"Talk to us, said Derral over the holocom. We know you came from the Solar system. We will destroy you if you continue your hostile actions."

The ship responded. A holo appeared. "We misjudged your weaponry, Colonel. We know who you are and wanted to send a message to Solar Command, given our opposition to your forthcoming trip to Da'yoni."

"We were warned. Now back off or we'll vaporize you both."

"Yes Colonel. But you need to know that it is a dangerous proposition for you to go with your partner to Da'yoni. We believe they have ulterior motives for our species.

"Listen, whoever you are...we were warned about you from Solar Intelligence. If you have an argument against our trip, which I just found out about, make that argument to Robert Laing, the Chief of Solar Intelligence... and don't try any of this shit again. One thing I learned in my stellar travels is that dialog is far superior to weaponry. Identify yourselves and I will send a com to Major General Laing to expect you. But don't expect to avoid consequences. However, I will tell him you did no harm but powered up your weapons and dispensed one harmless torpedo. Okay?"

There was a long silence.

"Yes, Commander. We apologize. This is Chance Newland of the Solar Centric Society. We will await your further contact."

"Stay in this vector and give me your vessel's signature. I will put you in touch with Major Laing. In fact he is on his way here to assist. Again, if you do not cooperate we will destroy you," said Derral as he ended the holo. "Ang, send a burst to see if we can contact Robert."

"Aye, Commander," said Ang as he opened the holo channel. Robert

11

answered immediately.

"How are you doing, Derral? In trouble again, I see. I don't know what we're to do with you. We're about to jump out of light, just between you and the aggressors. Our sensors detected laser bursts in your vicinity and what looked like a proton torpedo blast. Do we need to come in hot?" said Robert Laing as his holo appeared.

"Well, that was pretty quick, Chief. I think we have it under control. Can't wait to get a ride in your new boat. We're okay. As you warned us we were attacked by two needles from the Solar system. A guy identified himself as a Chance says he's from the Solar Centric Society. That was our burst. We disabled one vessel and wasted a torpedo they fired on us. We made a deal with the other one to contact you and they'd receive leniency as they didn't hit us. Ang's superior tracking took care of that. I'm sending you their signature. I directed them to stay in that sector for your directions."

"You mean they cooperated with you, my man?" said Robert.

"They had no choice as Ang had their drives targeted and I told them if they did not want to cooperate we'd turn them into space dust. When we made our systems visible in their scanners, they fortunately realized we out gunned them," said Derral.

Robert's ship materialized off their port side. "Okay, my old friend. We'll take care of it from here," said Robert.

"That's a pretty slick vessel you got there. We'll see you in a few weeks when we get home. Thanks."

"No, thank you guys...alright if I call you 'guy,' Ang? said Robert, grinning in the holo.

"Either sex is appropriate, Chief, as our species converts every few years. Much like some of your lower creatures sheds their skin."

"I don't want to go there, Lieutenant. We don't know each other that well, yet. We'll meet when you get to Terra," said Robert as he closed the holo.

Ang turned to Derral, appearing puzzled. "What does he mean 'he doesn't want to go there?' I thought we were prudish. You humans have a thing about even talking about it. How can you stand it?" said Ang.

"Let's wait until we get back and you come over for dinner and you can talk about that with Susan present. She'll give you her perspective. Okay?"

12

"Sure, Commander. I can't wait to hear it," said Ang.

Derral rolled his eyes. "That should be a good one...you'll see...and we are a prudish species. Never got over that from many centuries ago."

"Your species may be prudish in some things, but from what I've experienced so far, we have our own issues you call prudish, developed over eons," said Ang.

Chapter One

2484 Beginnings - Inconceivable Plans

The sun light fractured into rainbow patterns as it passed through the translucent ceiling of the zero gravity stim chamber.

"Let's stay in for the rest of the day," said Susan Priestly, to her life partner, Derral. They were suspended in mid-air, embracing each other.

Derral's eyes were closed. He appeared lost in thoughts of pleasure. This was his first day back from the six month journey with a multi armed alien of advanced intelligence as his only company.

"You know, in a few days it will be New Years Eve, 2484. It's the first New Years we'll be together in five years. You can't imagine how nice it is to be with a beautiful...you, again," said Derral in a dreamy tone, "even if you're not as smart as my Crespian pilot."

Susan released her grip to float away. His attempt at satire recalled her irritation at his long absences. Looking back, she suppressed a smile at his athletic figure. It was at these times she felt that melting sensation, overcoming any irritation. Susan inched back, wrapping her arms around him.

"Yes," she said with a tinge of sarcasm. "You and your star travels, all for enriching the oligarchs. And what do you mean, 'not as smart as your pilot?'"

"That was a bad attempt at humor. You do know, though, that he is likely the smartest being on the planet, right now. When he joined with us and became a pilot, we discovered that his intellectual skills could not be measured, as we don't have the means, yet. Ang said he could retrieve some instruments to accomplish this if he were to ever locate his planet mates."

"Thank you for the clarification, my dear," said Susan, with a scowl. "...But for what purpose do you continue to risk your life? The natural resources you mine only goes to feed the coffers of the moneyed few and the greedy patrons of the Holders. Also, I was beginning to wonder if you had some kinky thing going on with your alien partner. You know if it weren't for your great bod, I'd ask pater to call up the corporation head and have you permanently stationed on a rim planet, maybe your alien buddy can keep you company. You know, that pisses me off, Derral. I just got my degree and that required all my effort...all my intelligence."

"Ow. That hurt. You know I have the utmost regard for your intelligence...far more intelligent than me. I don't understand half of what you know about astrophysics, even though I command a star ship. How many times have I said that? Besides, Ang is a stimulating source of knowledge. You'll see when he comes to dinner...But, is that all you think of me...a piece of meat? On the other hand, I don't think your great biologue, the honorable Secretary, would comply with your wish, my friend. Especially since last year's explorations in the Canopus system netted the company, the Secretary, and his band of Holder criminals enough platinum to sustain them forever."

"That's all the more reason for him to honor my request...so watch out star man," said Susan.

Derral feigned seriousness. "Talk about domination and control. You tell me when I was not even back in the solar system, that we befriended the Da'yoni and your pater managed to arrange a visit, your first opportunity for interstellar travel, jeez. As if I had no say in the matter. Besides, Ang is a hermaphrodite and has no interest in sex with humans or other species, as far as I can tell. If fact, I don't even know how he does sex. We never had that conversation. I didn't want to embarrass him to ask."

Susan stretched. The abrupt motion propelled them across the chamber to bounce off the containment field. "Well that's comforting," she said. They floated back together, laughing.

"You know, I was totally surprised that pater selected us for the Da'yoni visit. I wonder about his ulterior motives," she said, stroking his cheek with her free hand while holding his weightless body close to her. "We were never that close, given mater's animosity towards him from his sexist ways. "Besides, I'm a little leery about going, especially the danger in teleportation over such a long distance. We don't yet understand the physics of the system they gave us. Perhaps your buddy Ang can shed some

15

light on it. When the Institute was opening a dialogue about their science, the Da'yonis were vague, saying that we would have to fully understand their physics, before they can adequately explain distance teleportation to us, far different than our short term teleport tech. It was hard put to say they weren't condescending to us inferior beings."

Derral was slow to respond. He opened his eyes. "I think Ang can clarify that. I know there was never any problem with shorter journeys. Da'yoni is relatively close to Boötes, about 44 light years beyond our system. It is one of a string of planets around the red giant, Arcturus...but you know that," said Derral, blushing. He covered his face with his hands at another condescending slip.

"I'll ignore that one my dear. At least you're learning," said Susan.

He continued. "I know we don't fully understand what the risk is, especially within the gravitational and EMF matrix of a red giant and the four other stars. Ang said his species had prior contact with the Da'yoni and said we'd be pleasantly surprised. The climate is semi-tropical. He said they were quite friendly with the Crespians, but that was many years ago. They mutually benefited with the tech sharing. But we have no idea of the effects of such exposure to their gravitational matrix other than the varying degrees of amnesia experienced by the probe crews. It took them five years to get there and 5 seconds to come back. If you read the workup I sent to your chip last week. When they returned, the ship atmosphere was triple the oxygen content, right at the borderline of harmful. That's likely why the memories of all the returnees are foggy. That increase could have been acquired when they landed on Da'yoni. Or, it happened during the technological miracle of whatever they did to compress the time and distance, when they returned. We checked. The tech was unknown to any of the galactic societies we communicate with, other than the Crespians. The Da'yoni introduced their sophistication to us with this singular feat. Some speculated they were putting us on notice. They may well have been more honest with the Crespians, as they are far more advanced than our species, but Ang says they're pretty straight forward."

"I vaguely remember you mentioning that," said Susan, in a sleepy voice. "I didn't pay much attention at the time, as I was studying for my Exobiology exams to get into the Institute."

"So now you're interested? Boy, shows how insignificant I am. Is that a female thing, or just you?" He reached over and stroked her long, curly chartreuse hair, silently noting that it didn't seem to fit with her stunning features. "But I still love you," he said with a sardonic grin. Susan pushed away from him.

"Ang assured me they are relatively peaceful. He'll fill us in when he comes to dinner. He said he can dig up some mem holos of his visit there, many years ago," said Derral.

One of his incompetent attempts to make peace after another insult, thought Susan. "Sometimes. I don't think we'd be together if I was right, most of the time, right?" said Susan.

"Well, you finally admit that, my dear...long time in coming," said Derral.

"Take a break from that, will you?" she said, wincing. "You know whenever you do that, it turns my stomach. I learned something from your absences. I put up with a lot of sexist crap from you, thinking that your income and support for school made up for it. Now that I'm finished school, I realize it doesn't...it's irritating, as usual," said Susan.

"As you wish, my dear. Women get their way, always. That's been an historical fact for millenniums."

Susan playfully shoved him against the chamber. "Come on, Derral. Stop with the "dear" crap and the demeaning sexism. I need to know more to make a decision. I'm skeptical and a bit afraid. I haven't been following any of it with school and all. And I need to know, in your heart, you don't believe this sexist shit, right?"

"Guilty about the sexist part. As I mostly traveled with male crew until Ang...and I'm not quite sure which sex or both he identifies with. I tend to forget that intelligent women are offended. But I know...you're right to be wary. Since the Da'yoni began sharing some of their technological advances in exchange for silica we started to trust them. It's odd their planet is mostly metallic rock and soil. Our people returning from the first visit said their soil is mostly decomposed organic matter, but very little silica. We're actually lucky as sand is a good exchange that we have plenty of."

"Thanks Derral. That's one of your best qualities, you admit when you're wrong," said Susan.

"Not all the time," he said. But to continue about the Da'yoni, since we learned more about them, word has it that they always seemed to have been forthright. As a species, they claimed to be genetically programmed for the truth. Robert and Ang independently confirmed they either never heard or experienced anything to the contrary. They tell us altruism is their primary motive for interacting with other species. You gotta wonder about that, given our history of being deceived by other species. The first travelers said they could barely suppress a laugh when the Da'yoni leadership told them that. But, all experiences with them seems to support their claim. At least so far. Needless to say, the solar confederation welcomed the economic arrangement, without question. Our sand for their tech. When Ang comes over remember to ask him for details."

"Well, if we go, we'll see," said Susan, looking suspicious. "By the way, how many times has this teleportation chamber been used?" said Susan, sitting erect in mid air.

Derral hesitated as he watched her, wondering how she could remain in that posture with such limited zero grav experience.

"Come on. Stay on the topic," said Susan, as if she could read his mind.

"You're an amazing character...I can't help myself...Okay. Since you alerted me on the way back, I stayed awake for a while and searched our historic holos. This past solar year saw the Da'yoni receiving their first nonmilitary, diplomatic guests to further the trade relationship. The journey offered by the Da'yoni were for a few individuals at a time, They specified it to be all Holder's relatives, for some mysterious reason. No one ever questioned that, even Robert. The first group all came back, unscathed. Although Robert was puzzled with the aftereffect. He told me, upon return many of them either migrated to barren but habitable planets outside the solar system and cut off all communication with members of the Solar Confederation or, stayed on Terra to lead a monastic-like existence, rarely communicating with anyone outside of their genetic clan. Almost to a person, they shunned virtual-media interviews. It was as if they were programmed as a group to avoid contact with others. Aside from what the Da'yoni have provided in virtual simulations, very little is known. Robert's service monitors the health status of the returnees. Each one had a monitoring chip embedded for security purposes. I spoke with him this

18

morning. He says they all seem to be in superb health."

Derral and Robert never forgot what they learned from their early activist studies. Robert Laing's subsequent career took him to leadership in the rarefied atmosphere of the most secretive agency in the Solar System, Solar Intelligence. After that promotion, they continued to communicate. But their communications were always by code to preserve their friendship outside of the politic. Mostly at locations or times selected by Robert. As their relationship existed before both came into government service, they were outside of Holder's suspicions. It was in those contacts, sometimes lasting throughout the evening, that Derral learned the extremes the Holders were capable of, as a group. At first, he wouldn't accept that their benevolent-seeming government would ever be capable of the intrigue and murderous, sometimes genocidal behavior or threats frequently invoked to maintain control of the masses. Derral began to see the picture following numerous discussions and holovid evidence from fly bots Robert shared.

Susan frowned. "Derral...Derral. Where did you go?"

"I was just thinking about what Robert told me, sorry."

"What did he learn when he interviewed them?" said Susan.

"He was able to interview a few of them before they refused contact and became hermits. They told of Da'yoni being a lush planet with a higher oxygen content than ours, and 5 suns, with consistently mild and pleasant weather. It's a semitropical climate like the Southwest territory or the Southern Euro climate was until the Great Catastrophe. The flora appears similar with many unusually strange and beautiful variations. It only rains at night. There are about 75 degrees of equal daylight and darkness between the rising suns. Seventy five degrees of our solar revolution, of course, or 5 of what we once called hours in my great, great, great grandpater's time reference."

Even though degrees had been used by ocean ship navigators for eons. One of the more positive things the Holder's accomplished was to embrace degrees as a universal time standard, far more accurate, as Terra travels in a consistent arc around the sun. But it does contribute confusion when traveling in another system.

Derral continued. "The circumference of Da'yoni is about 2/3 of our planet so the movement between day and night is relatively quick. The galactic physicists said that may be why there is such unusual physical feeling on the planet. The returnees all reported they felt an unusually pleasurable sensation at planetside. All described it as 'strange' and wondered why. At most the strongest pull from the red giant, Arcturus, is about 1/6 of ours. Kind of like being on our moon, but with a perfect climate. The rapid rise and setting of the suns along with the high oxygen content maintains a stable climate. Normally, in a system with more than 2 suns, the planetary bodies are in upheaval, all the time. Most peculiar, the position of Da'yoni within this five star cluster centered around Arcturus moderates their gravitational matrices..." Derral floated closer to Susan, as the timer went off on the stim bath. Susan turned and brushed Derral's lips with a kiss.

"Well, I almost got lucky," said Derral.

"Oh, cut it out. That gives me some reassurance, though," she said. "I gotta tell you...I've been thinking of not going. I ran into my exobiology professor the other day and discussed the Da'yoni trip with her. She expressed concern at the teleportation distance and the time on their planet with the unusual atmosphere and gravity configurations. I need to think some more about it. Let's eat. I'm starved. What do you think the odds are that I'll make it to the kitchen?" she said, playfully.

"Let's see," said Derral. "My money is on you. I need a bit more time."

"Adjusting to Terra grav is kind of tiring after where you've been for the last few moon cycles, right?" she said, stroking his cheek. She held his weightless body close to her, with her free hand. Derral responded with a long sigh. Gravity slowly returned.

"We haven't eaten anything since last night. So hurry up." She wriggled out of his grip and ran to the door, looking back with a coquettish grin. "I'll take payment after I eat, thank you very much."

"You can't get blood out of a stone. I don't have any pockets. Look!" said Derral. He turned up the stim and got lost in thought, again.

"Oh well, cheat if you must. But I'll take the money in your uniform pocket.

"No luck, my dear. That's probably mining colony chits, worthless here." Derral turned away and saw the recent past as if in a holo.

On many long transports to other systems, to defeat boredom, he studied Terra's historical records in the suspension chamber holos, with sleep learning. He became an expert at manipulating the holograms, programming them to record events on his personal chip that his neural link favored. He limited the recordings to what he believed were predictive of future trends. To try to get a sense of what direction he wanted to move towards, he replayed the recorded holos. He was feeling unsure about his relationship with Susan. Turning up the anti-grav to zero, he directed the historical holo record to begin playing back through his neural link. He realized, along with his growing dissatisfaction with their relationship, that he had no direction. "Or maybe its just a recognition, from studying history, that led me to this," he whispered to himself. He thought, maybe its all me and has nothing to do with Susan.

The holo began in the 22nd Century. Self aggrandizement and greed had risen from the ashes of defeat in earlier eras. Derral settled in to watch the historical images and media events, in silence.

Subtle manipulation of the citizenry became a prevailing media art used by the wealthy, having less than altruistic goals. There were wars, mostly from competing religious factions. In reaction, the Constitutionalist movement grew. The citizenry awakened to the false promises, the token vacations offered to induce long hours of labor throughout the year, with bare minimum remuneration for the laborers relative to that acquired for the owners or profiteers. The common citizen was used as labor fodder, to extract more and more profit under increasingly sophisticated deceptions. "And to think that I ignored this as I was earning a good living being associated with these criminals," he said through tight lips. "And I continue to work for them, Guess I'm not much different."

His thoughts drifted to the Great Catastrophe and how the planet fared before that. He scanned the headlines and images. In 2210, a massive explosion occurred on Terra's moon. This was a direct result of the mining operations, designed to extract the moon's mineral wealth. The same thing I'm doing in other star systems, he thought. Before Terra could mobilize defenses to destroy it, a massive piece, almost a quarter of the moon's surface, broke off and was propelled out of orbit into a collision course with Terra. The chunk rapidly gained speed. When it struck, most of the eastern and central portion of the United States was wiped out. The resulting tidal wave rapidly devastated what remained of the eastern coastal areas of North America and devastated the coasts of the European, and African continents. The eastern shoreline was now the eastern slope of the Continental Divide. Whole countries were wiped out. The British Isles now lay at the bottom of the Atlantic Ocean The European and African shore lines were pushed inward, about 500 miles from their origins. Holland was saved as a result of their superior dikes and sea walls, perfected over the centuries. The Pacific Ocean was relatively unaffected.

Derral slapped his palms to his forehead. He was becoming overwhelmed with a feeling he just couldn't identify. Guilt, despair, he thought. As he scanned the record, the more frequent was his uneasiness when he compared his job to what the lunar miners had done. This never occurred to him until he began to view the history holos on his trips.

He focused on an article he had saved from *Earth*, a progressive astrophysical scientific journal. Prior to the Catastrophe, in the U.S., the source of most manufactured nuclear material had been maintained east of the Continental Divide. California and the Pacific coastal region had outlawed the use of polluting nuclear fuels and power plants, some 20 years before the collision. The U.S. lost most of its nuclear stores. "That was certainly a relief," he chortled.

The immediate aftermath of the Catastrophe was ten years of darkness. The sun was blocked by the debris cloud. In that decade, crop failures had risen to a magnitude where there was beginning speculation that the planet must be abandoned. Worldwide efforts were quickly underway to build massive vehicles to transport as many people as possible into orbit around the planet, a technologically impossible task, given the billions of citizens. The prevailing thinking was that most of the population would die off if not relocated.

At the end of that decade, there was not enough manufactured food to sustain the population. Famines returned. The historical records talked of a great solar flare sending out solar winds that impacted Terra, severely affecting communication systems. Once communication was restored, the planet's citizens erupted with glee, as all the debris blocking the sun had been swept outside the solar system by the EMF stream from the solar winds. The elimination of the collision dust was a miracle to say the least.

The planet, or what was left of it, recovered over the ensuing years.

The shocked citizenry remaining alive entered an era of a return to natural life. Fearing another catastrophe may again destroy what remained of the power grid, an intense ubiquitous focus on developing biological alternatives to machines and computers took precedent over other industrial and scientific accomplishments. Every machine or computer, previously developed with sophisticated electronics, had its counterpart in a natural biological or plant resource. Alternative machines and computers were grown, using biological substrates. Within a decade, biological substrate-based machines eventually came to replace all electronic devices. The tech experts began experimenting with integrating the biological machines into human brain.

Two hundred years later, Denver, the mile high city, developed into a major Atlantic Ocean beach resort community and world city, replacing New York, at the bottom of the Atlantic for the last two centuries, as a world commerce and government hub. The United States had become a 1400 mile wide peninsula.

Just prior to the Great Catastrophe the country politic and philosophy had been captivated by radical conservative thinking, driven by the oligarchs. The majority of the progressive Constitutionalists, especially those associated with universities and academic positions began settling in the more liberal territories west of the Continental Divide. After the Catastrophe, the Constitutionalists were all that remained of a majority in the continental government. We lucked out, thought Derral as he sat erect in the chamber.

The Constitutionalist political movement spread throughout the remaining world territories. The Africasian territory became the predominant territorial democracy encompassing what was formerly called Europe, Africa and Asia. Their rule, was dominated by the "Committee," a group of citizens that fairly distributed the massive new wealth to all citizens. The Catastrophe and what some believed to be the divine intervention of the solar winds united all people. Every family on the planet now had a moderately appointed dwelling with modern conveniences. All those over the age of 18 could choose one of five paths: public service, music or the arts, literature, science and research, or agronomy. University education was free as was living expenses. Work, while not mandatory, was expected by development of personal interest. While each citizen was expected to complete at least 4 hours of work in the area of their choice from the primary paths, the rest of their day was given to pursue creative interests, leisure or, if they so desired, to continue working in their area of interest or an alternative area of interest. As the population had been greatly reduced and the resources increased by orders of magnitude, pleasurable life thrived. Not since the dawn of civilization and the rise of capitalism, have humans been free to choose. There was no more attempts at government or corporate deceit for personal or political advantage. The Committee was devoid of graft or personal gain. While policy change was a burdensome task, as all members of the Committee must agree on any change, a new era of positive communication in government was developed. Committee members represented sections of the planet. The proliferation of mandated and integrated biocomputers enabled all citizens to instantaneously vote on any policy. Each Committee member was bound to represent the ¾ majority opinion of the residents in their section. If there was disagreement with other Committee member's sections, a new vote was taken, clearly explaining the opposition points of each Committee member. Maximizing every citizen's welfare was the prevailing ethic of all Committee members and the populace. The Catastrophe made the planet's citizens clearly aware of how personal and corporate interest had left the planet unable to effect a quick recovery. The initial government experiments by the Committee proved that joining in a mutual endeavor of cooperation was far more effective and efficient, than the history of factional disputes, corporatism, and wars of the past.

The citizenry embraced this mutual focus in their voting. Regional conflicts were absent for the first time in history. All members of the Committee were chosen for the degree of altruism they demonstrated in their lives. The establishment of a universally agreed-upon parenting process, based on a scientifically validated educational model, was recognized as essential to society. Parenting was well defined by schooling. Those desiring to raise children were required to attend 3 years of pre-birth schooling that taught parenting skills designed to maximize the intellectual and altruistic potential of their future prodigies. Prior to conception, potential parents were subjected to a sophisticated analysis of three months of constant daily recordings of their lives to determine if they had integrated and practiced the necessary skills to bring to their parenting. All potential parents agreed because all knew this system virtually eliminated the crime and exploitation among the populace that was rampant in pre-GC eras. Those failing the review were given instructions on how to meet the goal and then reviewed within 3 months or at a time of their choosing. This was the dawning of a new age.

Derral mused aloud to himself. "Having other interests, I guess I never paid much attention to history. Probably most people are like that...and is why society has such short memories and always repeats past mistakes."

Physical pregnancy ended. Couples desiring a child had their DNA combined and cloned. The cloned cells developed in a perfect nutrient rich environment inside a transparent container developed for home use, enabling parents to clearly see and monitor the fetal development of their children. Women could now choose to be freed of the burden of child birth.

The Africasia developments spread throughout the planet for the next 100 years.

But unfortunately, basic human greed had not evolved out of human society. There was a time after the Great Catastrophe, when the visitations from other worlds evoked interest, not greed. That was just after the evolution of capitalist democracy into the galactic unification. The unification gave way, in the 24th Century, to the formation of the Holder government. They replaced the Committee. It was thought that human civilization, one civilization among many in the new galactic consortium, needed a centralized, clearly identified governing body to negotiate the many trade agreements, technology exchange, and emigration of other-world beings to this planet, as well as our own migration outward among the stars. For the first hundred years, the spirit of the original founders of the Holder movement was the foundation of all decision making. The spirit embraced fairness, honesty and, what was the most beneficial for the whole, not just a partition of the planet. The philosophy of the Committee was the guiding model for the Holders. The remembrance of past failures and the destructiveness of a civilization based on political machinations sustained the evolving Holder movement. As we progressed into the 25th Century, historical memory appeared to fade.

The beginning of the end of a good thing, thought Derral as he wrapped his arms around himself for comfort.

A changing environment, the availability of unheard of techno advances, and the stabilization of the world economy occurred. Poverty had been eliminated for the second time in history. The reign of the Committee saw the first relief from world poverty. Wealth and prosperity became abundant through intergalactic exchange of technology.

As years went by, a subtle change in the original Holders consciousness began to surface. Recently appointed Holders began to rationalize and consider their self-importance as leaders as a justification for their own greed, a character trait that was thought to have become obsolete. The solar confederation environment began to change. This prompted those with the original consciousness to regress to archaic defenses that were dormant for the past few hundred years. The Confederation government devolved. In 2460, the committee of Holders, through political manipulations, evaded the pre-birth and consciousness tests, previously required before appointment as a Holder. They set up the planet's people by resorting to what they had discovered in historical vaults to be the mind control procedures existing in past centuries. The world's consciousness regressed. The Holders continued as the Solar Confederation government, albeit now with a completely different focus. The recent ones were appointed by those few families who controlled most of the economic interests on the planet. They were not elected. Democracy was abandoned. The Holders manipulated the citizenry to believe that centralized control was the wave of the future by comparing this to another civilization that existed only as a fictional creation of the Holders. There was no way to contrast this, as it was claimed that this civilization was too many light years away...but had been visited and studied by a Committee commission, just prior to the change to Holder government. The planet's citizens became immersed in the authoritarianism hearkening back to another bygone era that precipitated World War II, many centuries before. The Holders, by and large, subtly disguising themselves under a mystical veil, using mind-control techniques, became the extant committee that determined the fate of humanity. There seemed to be no way out now, no hope.

26

***

"Derral, It's about time...what the hell are you doing in there, playing with yourself?," said Susan.

"If thinking is playing with myself, I guess I'm playing with myself," said Derral as he opened the stim chamber.

"I apologize. You know I get aggravated when I'm hungry," said Susan addressing the food module. "I'll have a Jupiter's palate, hold the ketchup and Derral will have his usual Solarian health breakfast. Two large glasses of Caliopus OJ, two cups of Africasia coffee, one with and one without cream."

The food module responded in a feminine, French accented voice: "Will there be anything else for you two naked love birds?"

"Yes, just lay off the sarcasm today, will you Michelle." She turned to Derral. "God, what a ridiculous name for a domestic bot. How did we ever come up with that?"

"I think it was your idea, buddy. After we came back from that French colony on Saturn.."

Susan grimaced. "I remember. Well, I guess it lost its glamour. We'll have to come up with another name, don't you think?"

"Right, but I kind of like Michelle. It's like getting served by a sexy Europa-Franco chef."

"Thank you Derral, said the computer. I feel likewise. I guess it may be a woman thing between me and the madam. At least that is what a Freudian of the 21st Century would think?"

"If we want an analysis with our meal, we'd order one up, Michelle," said Susan, with a smirk, as if she was talking to a real person.

"Oui, madame. I guess I slid a bit out of line. Your breakfast is served." The center of the kitchen table shimmered and both meals materialized.

"Thank you Michelle," said Susan.

"It is my singular duty to serve you humans. Praise will not a better meal get...only better programming," said the computer.

"God, you never quit, do you..?"

"I am only the sum total of my programming, madame. And if I'm not mistaken, are you not my creator?"

"Yeah, well. Sometimes I'd like to create something else and wipe your AI circuits. Go to sleep now, until further notice," said Susan.

"Your wish is my existence, madame," said the bot as it powered down.

"You know," said Derral with a feigned seriousness. "I think you have a real knack with biomachines. Did you ever think of going on the road with that act?"

Susan rolled her eyes. "Derral, you're worse than her...or it. I'm convinced that you snuck in and enhanced her logic circuits, when I wasn't around."

"Not me," said Derral in mock surprise.

"Never you, my innocent... So what were you thinking about?"

"Oh, about our history and what we've come to or degenerated into. Did you know the Committee, the group before the Holders, when formed, were totally centered on what was best for the citizens?"

"I seem to recall something about that from my political history classes, when I wasn't totally hypnotized by the teaching assistant," said Susan.

"What do you mean, hypnotized?" asked Derral.

"Uh Oh, got your male possessiveness up, did I?...Hypnotized by her boring drone."

"No, just my curiosity. By the way, I almost forgot to tell you, I received a feed from Robert, yesterday. Some additional reading about Da'yoni. It seems the Da'yonis were far superior in culture and war making ability than any other civilization we've encountered," said Derral. "However, they haven't engaged in conflict with any other system in more than 1000 years."

"Gee, that makes me feel much better. Makes me want to just jump up there today. How do they do it? I mean, why are their defenses so superior... no conflict for a millennium?"

Derral paused, as if he were calculating his response. "Well, it seems, some time ago, along with the EMF formation they created this ability to transmutate into any species or form. Something to do with evolving under the light gravitational matrix and meson particle distribution from five different suns. They were gracious enough to give the visiting Federation crew vid disks showing some invasions they repelled in a matter of hours or days, with virtually no casualties. Their warriors have the special ability to meld with any being and change their thinking, en masse. On one vid

28

disk we actually can see them doing this with a weird species looking like upright bugs. They melded with the invading army officers and government officials. It seems that species could instantaneously communicate to their troops over some sort of "bug" vibration. That's what facilitated their inter species aggression and conquests. The vid illustrates the effect on the invaders."

"Then what's to prevent them from doing that with us?"

"…Well, other than their word, we really don't know. I thought that would raise your suspicions. They had translated the language on the disks into solar standard so we'd have no difficulty comprehending the message." Susan frowned. "Some gift! More like a subtle warning to indicate what might happen if we ever got the idea to invade or harm any of their populace."

Derral ignored her comment and continued. "The bugs, fierce looking with a history of many conquests, were, in a matter of minutes after the enjoinment, reduced to compliant beings that began to give away their possessions and weapons to the Da'yoni, including the fuel cells from their ships. Of course the Da'yoni refused the cells, asking in return that they leave for their home world and not return. Before they left, the Da'yoni wiped all traces of the contact from the bugs computer files and cortical memories. At least that is what the vid says."

"Wonderful. Just what I need. Total amnesia."

Derral sighed with impatience. "I don't think there's anything to worry about. We have too many valuable resources they want. It's apparently all true, as the Da'yoni are genetically incapable of lying, according to their records. One of the cardinal features that endeared our crews to the Da'yoni were the direct and forthright attitudes that never wavered, even when minor disagreements and squabbles between us and them occurred regarding the taking of some unusual mineral samples back to the Solar labs. Our people maintained a congeniality with them. In consideration for the friendly respect we showed them, they gave us the invitation and technology to visit. If you decide, we'll be the 12th and 13th party to go through what they call their vortexa chamber for the journey, as they closely control the limit on such visits. From what we've been able to learn it's more like a chamber that enables wormhole travel. The physics is not yet understood by our people. If you don't want to take the risk, I'll not go either." He looked the

29

other way, pressing his lips together in disappointment.

"That warms my heart…that's another reason I love you and stay with you, in spite of it all and your distant travels." She reached across the table for his hand. "I'll go. Maybe it will improve the relationship we have with Pater, even though I never liked him, especially the sight of his androgynous body."

"Being a newly minted exobiologist, I thought it was your desire," he said smiling broadly. I'm surprised that you didn't seem to be following the news holos given your interests."

"Derral, I've been totally consumed with meeting my degree requirements. I lost track of what day it was. I'm glad that's over."

"You do know, this will be a once in a lifetime opportunity. You can't imagine how lousy it is traveling on those star ships," said Derral. "It would take about five years to get there by our usual galactic vessels." His thoughts drifted to speculating what would happen if they did part with each other, but consciously decided to table that consideration until after their return from Da'yoni.

"Derral, are you there? Looks like you drifted off some place."

"Uh, no, I was just thinking about some things," said Derral.

"Not to change the subject, heaven forbid," she said. "But let's play the Da'yoni feeds, while we sleep tonight, so I can get caught up. That sleep-learn chip, you got from Robert, takes the frustration out of our joint endeavors. It's a great time saver. Do you want anything else?" said Susan, as she paused before waving her hand to clear the table.

"Nothing that the table can give me, madame. Let's sit by the faux fire and plug in," said Derral, smiling with his usual sardonic grin.

"Just for a few minutes. I have to finish the cartographic representations of the civilizations on Neptune, before I go in tomorrow. I have to present at the Holders meeting," said Susan, yawning.

"Take a break from seriousness, will you? I don't think the Holders will be miffed, if you're a bit late. After all they do nothing but spend their credits and attend a few meetings a month," said Derral, continuing his sarcasm.

"Be that as it may, my dear. Aside from Pater, they're responsible for granting us the permission to be the only couple to travel to Da'yoni on

New Year's Eve. If it were not that I made a number of presentations and gained their respect, I doubt we would have gotten permission for the trip, regardless of my genetic endowment. So hush up. One of the Holder's microflys may be hovering outside the window recording what you're saying...and it may come back to haunt us. You know they do use the microflys with people who are leaving the system to determine if they're a security risk?"

"You're right. You are certainly connected, *mon cher*. I'll also try to keep my trap shut."

She smirked. "You're starting to sound like our food bot. Do you want to take over and become a home body?"

"You're funny, too," said Derral.

They sat before the blazing holo fire place and plugged the virtual system into the needle-size portals set behind their ears. Susan darkened the windows and dimmed the lights. Derral reached for her hand. For the next 30 minutes, they were in virtual consciousness with each other.

Derral was interrupted by a signal from his holo. He released the vid plug and pressed the small protuberance under his chin. A three dimensional holograph of his friend, Robert, sitting before the Solar Intelligence Community logo, appeared. He rotated the control so that the encryption function was activated. The holo rescinded to the space just before his retina. The voice feed adjusted to his cortical communicator so that he could communicate subvocally.

"Good evening buddy, hope I'm not disturbing Eros. I see you and Susan are enjoying each other," said Robert.

"A pleasant disturbance. What does the Chief of Solar Intelligence want with us? Your new look...shaved head and all...makes you look like a real spook in one of those noir films."

"Thanks for the complement, my friend. Da'yoni is what I'm contacting you about. We've just received some interesting facts from a genetic connection of one of the folks who visited there last year and never disclosed anything. She's a SIC agent on Saturn. Says her cousin got a bit tipsy at a pentathone club, a few nights ago, and shared some of her experiences. Seems the Da'yoni are probing us, on a limited basis, for intelligence. Her cousin told of some strange dreams she had while sleeping in the gravitron matrices the Da'yonis provided to mimic a comfortable physical environment, as they claimed. At one point she recalled being aroused to consciousness, noticing a probe attached to her temporal area. She heard a soothing voice say that she was assisting their understanding of us and not to worry, as there is no need to awaken. The next thing she knew, it was morning and the first of the five suns were shining in the chamber. So, to insure our mysterious hosts don't do that with you two, I'm going to leave a microcirc tablet for you both to ingest, just before you enter their chamber. You have far more information about our military capabilities and politics. Susan has significant information about our biological evolution and our species susceptibility to exobiological contacts that is too much to risk, at this stage. They'll be in a small tissue bag in the pocket of the jump suit you'll change into for your transport. Just to be on a super safe side, the same symbol we used as kids when we had our secret Saturn club, will be on the envelope, inside the bag. I'm sure you'll remember, but don't say it aloud. The tablets will block the Da'yoni probes and remain lodged in your intestines until you reenter our gravity. They'll then decompose and you'll pass them with no trace. Perfectly safe, to say the least, given what you know of our secure little spec of the universe. By the way, you can thank the Secretary, your partner's not-so- favorite genetic pater, for pushing through the legislation to allow distribution of pentathone in licensed clubs, a few months ago. Just between you and me, if the truth be told, not entirely a pun, I think the Secretary was not completely selfless. Having the upper levels of the Holders temporarily loaded with truth drinks provides him with some good political fodder. I hear tell he discretely positions a few of his inner circle around the clubs, each time a Holder's entourage enters. A good source of intelligence for him, and us. As you might have guessed, we insert microfly drones at the bars and tables, whenever an official is in such a public place. They're all linked to our SIC holo, so we get instant, discreet confirmation of any disclosures. That's very QT, by the way,...not to be repeated, even to Susan.

Derral rubbed his eyes, looking startled. He responded subvocally. "I'll say one thing for you Robert, while our contacts have been less frequent these past few years, when we do connect, you spin me. I mean, what a trip this is. How about having breakfast with us tomorrow morning so you can tell me more?"

"No that wouldn't be too prudent, right now. I don't want to draw attention to our relationship. I just met with your ship mate, Ang for his security upgrade. He said you invited him over. Tomorrow would be a good time to meet with him. Contact him and ask for suggestions for the first meal of the day. He or she will surprise you. He has good info about the Da'yoni. We know the whereabouts of the Da'yoni ambassador's staff, but we may not know the identity of other agents they could have easily inserted in human form. Maybe when you come back next week, if everything goes okay," said Robert as he looked down at his desk and moved some triangular shapes around.

"Robert, that doesn't sound too consoling. Would we be in any danger there?

"No, Derral, we don't think so. I'd certainly tell you if I thought you would. I think the microcirc tabs will keep you from being scanned and interfered with. The effects will transfer to you when in the Da'yoni EMF forms. The Da'yoni won't be able to discover what's wrong with their equipment until you're back home. And even then, they won't be sure. The microcirc looks like an intestinal polyp by any known technology, including what we have been able to piece together about the Da'yoni techs. We developed it from our bartered knowledge with the Capazoid folk in the Regulus system. Remember that we stumbled on them a few years ago? They needed silicon wafers. We bartered them for advanced technology in exchange for a few billion tons of sand. They're just about a level below the Da'yoni in sophistication. Just enjoy the experience there. I understand, from our intel reports, it's ecstatic."

"Well they could always cut us open and autopsy us...Okay? Even though that makes me a little nervous, I suppose we'll be alright," said Derral, frowning. "Susan only just reluctantly agreed."

Robert interrupted. "Don't worry my friend. If they do cut you open the tab will dissolve before they see it. But they won't risk cutting you open, especially you two. You both really need to talk with Ang. We have something they're in dire need of. They also have a deficiency of silicon on their world. We take it for granted here, with all our beaches and ocean floors. And old buddy, do work a bit on your trust. Just don't let anyone know about the details of our contact, including Susan or any of your bots. I shared some SIC intelligence that could get me in a black hole if it got out, especially the microcirc deal. Please tell Susan it has something to do with the vortexa chamber. Of course, when you return you can tell her the truth. The less she knows the better position she'll be in if something does happen," said Robert.

Still frowning, Derral replied, "What *could* happen Robert. I get the distinct feeling that there is more to this."

"Well, Derral, while I'm being as straight as I can with you, given the circumstances, I must admit that we're not all that sure. However, as far as there being any danger, I think that's minimal. To further minimize any thing occurring, as we speak, I'm arranging the EMF cycle linkage to transmit a hypno signal at the end of this message that will erase your memory of this conversation, but maintain the memory of the microcirc tab ingestion as a standard procedure for intergalactic travel, so if anything does happen you too will be safe. Remember, I'll leave it in the pocket of the white suit you'll wear. You'll need to inform Susan before hand, so she knows to take it, discreetly, before putting on the suit. You might tell her it's extra protection that we don't want the Da'yoni to be aware of. But, when you do tell her, make sure you are in a shielded location like a stim bath. You'll then seem to be exactly who you are: New Years Eve tourists out for an ecstatic time on Da'yoni. No one or thing will be able to discover anything different, as no reference of it will be in your conscious mind. We'll transmit another hypno signal after you take the tab. Know that your safety is relatively assured given your relationship to our Secretary. Okay? Uhh. Listen, I gotta go...am receiving a holo from one of my operatives.."

"I want you to speak with Susan and tell her directly, on this secure signal. She's nervous about it, too, okay? I'll call you right back after I get her on."

"Okay. I'll transmit the hypno signal to both of you, after that call."

Derral touched his chin and disconnected. He plugged the vid back in and interacted with her. "Susan, that was Robert I just spoke with. Let's talk"

"What is it?" she said, disconnecting her portal.

"He wants to talk to both of us about the Da'yoni venture. I'll get him

34

right back in a few degrees, in a conference call, okay?"

"Sure. Is everything all right."

"Yes. He just wants to share some details with us on a secure transmission."

Derral touched his chin and initiated the secure call to his old friend. Robert repeated his concerns and the details to both of them with notification of the hypno signal.

"Robert, I was a little nervous about this before. What you said makes it more disturbing. But I guess for the sake of the Confederation and what we'll gain, I agree," said Susan, subvocally through their secure holo.

"Good. There is minimal danger, as we hold the high cards. It is crucial to their survival that they find an open source of silica. Now, when Derral ends the call, I'll transmit the signal. I'll restore the details of this to you after you return from your journey." But record this mem note. Meet with Derral's shipmate, Ang, for breakfast tomorrow. I'll transmit some Crespian recipes after I disconnect. He will enlighten you further.

As Derral tapped his chin to end the call a blue holo field appeared in front of them followed by a second of static.

Susan looked at Derral, wondering why they were both disconnected from the virtual. They reconnected and resumed, falling asleep on the couch. They awakened the next day by the mem note to have Ang over for breakfast. He connected the holo with Ang who readily accepted the invitation for his first human social invite.

Derral entered the exercise room and settled in to the virtual program. Susan was still asleep. The virtualiciser increased the load as he thought about what the immediate future will bring. Dr. Ling, his old anthropology professor, would be thrilled, he thought. I'll give him a call. The program level flashed on Derral's retinal holo, asking if he wanted to increase the intensity. He signaled the maximum intensity level. Five minutes later he was sweating profusely as the program ended.

Susan stood in the doorway. "I hope you're finished. I'm going to exercise for the first time since finishing my dissertation.?"

"Just finished. I'm going to call Hsu Ling, to see if he has any suggestions. You know, my old anthropology professor. He's the confederation's leading expert on the outer galactic," said Derral.

35

"Yeah. I met him last year at the Galactic Society Science meeting. You were on one of your jaunts to some star system. He told me how obstreperous you were in his class," said Susan.

"I was just argumentative and asked a lot of questions," said Derral standing in the sealed portal of the oxygen enhanced exercise chamber, grimacing.

Susan turned around. "You're going to go like that, naked?...Dr. Ling was just jesting, by the way. He said you were one of his best students."

"Let's hurry up," said Derral, turning away and smiling. "I contacted Ang. He should be over soon, for breakfast. Robert transmitted some Crespian recipes to our wonderful food bot."

"Derral, you didn't even tell me. This place is a mess" said Susan.

"I know...sorry about that but Robert's mem reminded me on awakening and I called him right away. Don't worry. He's as casual as can be, once you get used to his appearance," said Derral.

Chapter Two

Pecksniffian Or Sociopath?

Secretary Nathan Priestly's voice boomed over the din to each personal holo chip of the 150,000 delegates present. "The 100th annual meeting of the post G.C. Solar Confederation, in the year 2484 A.C.E., will come to order." The rustling in the huge meeting hall quieted. The 12 Holders, the ruling body of the Solar Confederation sat around a transparent table suspended 20 feet above the floor. The Secretary stood on an elevated platform before the Holder's table. The delegates were clustered around similar transparent tables but at a lower level, across this great hall. A live holo of the Secretary's androgynous form flashed on the center of each table.

"I am not pleased to say that my words are sorrowful. Some quadrant leaders, right here on our very home planet, have been sowing seeds of disaffection amongst the other members. A bit of history will assist your understanding of what I'm about to say.

As you know, when the Confederation was established, in the final years of the 21st Century, we saw a period of unlimited growth and contact with other civilizations, along with a few severely crippling wars. Were it not for the Great Catastrophe, the final wars during the beginning of the 23rd Century may likely have eliminated Terra civilization as a whole. Following the solidification of the Confederation after the Great Catastrophe, no longer did our home planet bear the burden of regional disputes, conflicts among groups of differing spiritual beliefs, or the economic downturns resulting from financially incompetent governing bodies of what were then referred to as countries. The Committee was formed to establish guidelines and rules for the planet as a whole, grounded in the spirit of altruism and all inclusive democracy. The Committee was successful, beyond imagination, for 172 years. We saw the end of wars on Terra.

The Holders developed, as a diplomatic need arose for a central body other than the loosely formed Committee, to carry on relationships with neighboring civilizations and govern the expanding migration to the other Solar planets. The Holders followed the original Committee design, but reached out to different galactic civilizations in peace. As you know, our civilizations derived magnificent trade benefits, from the Holder's outreach. Terra's citizens have all benefited.

While each quadrant of the planet was no longer considered as separate, but part of the governing whole, all resources from the Holder's diplomatic efforts were equally distributed. There was no separation of powers as any decision made at the Central government was a result of the neural communication tech, thanks to one of our galactic partners. This has enabled input from all citizens, and affected all quadrants. This system of governing continues to this day. As we all know, elected representatives from each quadrant function mainly as advisors with major decision making in the providence of the Holders.

For those of you who forget, this particular day of the solar year marks the day, 100 years ago, of the ending of what was then known as Committee rule and the beginning of the new age of human civilization, managed by the Holders. Resources expanded as contact with other species grew, and continued to be equally distributed. Terran citizens successfully expanded to settle the outer planets, and in some instances, other galaxies. This was only possible as a result of the combination of our continuing unification as a people, and the technological advances we graciously accepted from our contact with those from other star systems at the beginning of our current century. In return for their technology we bartered with our vast wealth of mineral deposits, unique to every planet in our Solar Confederation. Many of our galactic neighbors lacked essential minerals, abundant on all Confederation planets. This was our good fortune, because technological bartering advanced our civilization to heights that one could never have imagined. We owe this legacy, in part, to the development of friendly trading relationships, established by the Holders."

Two of the Holders shifted in their seats and opened up private holo channels with each other. "If he wasn't so charming, we could have gotten away with eliminating him years ago. Too bad, don't you think?" Rakard Oice stole a glance at his table mate looking for a response.

General Urvey Suddhis lowered his head, placing his hands in the folds of his double chin, as if in prayer. He briefly glanced at Oice, feeling the usual disgust at his scaly, lizard skin tattoos, a recent fad. "We might be fortunate that we did nothing and waited. We were able to accumulate those mineral holdings on Io because he was so naive. His time is slowly drawing to a close. The problem is, we need to have someone ready to step in as chair. That's no small order given the disagreeable factions among the 12 of us, that he so conveniently minimizes. It may prove quite chaotic," said the General.

"I'm well aware of that, General. If nothing else, we need to proceed with utmost caution, from here on. Our holdings must remain in a blind trust so as not to cast any aspersions on the character of our movement. We all know that each of the Holders, for the last 50 years exploited the citizen's trust by undervaluing the technology and resource exchange we obtained from other star systems, to line each of our pockets. If this were to become public, we would all be destroyed. We'd likely see a return of the Committee, the committee of fools who set up equal distribution systems."

"I suppose you are correct, Rakard. For an extra precaution I decided to send our elite unit to discreetly place themselves in the New Europe Government Center, ready to act. When the time comes we act swiftly and contain the New Socialist tier. Once that is accomplished, if our foolish Secretary survives, he will see the light and come to us when his main support is vaporized. We can then dispense with him, too," said the General, casting a spiteful glance at the Secretary's holo.

The Secretary was concluding his speech. The delegates all rose and turned towards the Holders table, saluting them with outstretched arms, palm down, reminiscent of another time, many forgotten centuries ago.

Amidst the silent cheers, the Secretary arose and floated off the holos. "Were you able to capture any transmissions from those two?" said the Secretary to his waiting assistant.

"Yes sir, we got it. Let's meet later, in your office and you can see for yourself," said Ulemann.

The Secretary descended down to the great hall, as a ceremonial gesture, to personally say a few words to some of the delegates. When he saw an opportunity he took leave to his office where Ulemann was waiting with the holo record keyed up. They sat in silence, viewing the interception of the conversations between Rakard and the General.

"That piece of space excrement," shouted the Secretary. "I supported many of his military projects, even when I thought they were a waste of the confederation's credits, just because I felt some friendship with him. I suspected Rakard more than he. I can't believe they intend to eliminate me. If the Holder private trusts are exposed as a result, we'll all be finished. There **will** be a Confederation vote to regress back to Committee rule. Mark my words."

Ulemann looked down and didn't care to remind his boss that he had warned him of just this scenario, a few solar revolutions ago. Ulemann was a loyalist from an off world settlement. A world that produced copper skinned, very tall and spindly individuals.

"Ulemann," growled the Secretary. "I want you to arrange a 24 hour fly on those two. Dispatch more microflys to monitor all whom they contact. If any of the flys are disabled, I want another backup to immediately take its place. Use those new flys with the DNA tracers. What were you telling me last week? We've developed the technology to implant an undetectable microfly in the hair follicles? If so, use them."

"Of course, Mr. Secretary. I'll put our people on it. The system will be active within the hour. We can do it with an EMF transponder as long as we have the exact coordinates and the bio signature. And of course every Holder has a homing security implant we track. We can hone in on their implants to insure contact."

"Good, I don't need to know the details, I just want the results. I'll be in my chambers. Relay the feed to me as soon as it activates," said the Secretary as he rushed off.

Ulemann waited for the door to close before he whispered to himself. "Never ceases to amaze me how short memory becomes when one is in power. Oh well. I'm just your humble servant, Mr. Secretary." He opened the communication panel and spoke with the technicians.

Outside, in the meeting hall, many of the delegates were lingering, conversing with friends. The topic of conversation was on the Secretary and his admonition.

One of the delegates from Africasia had the attention of a group composed of delegates from all the quadrants.

"Given tone of Secretary, wondering if not time to begin discussion about return of Committee. It seems like Holders outliving their utility to Confederation. What do all think about that?" said Chin-Tsu, from the Eastern Quadrant.

"*Si*, perhaps this is the time," said Paco Zibran a delegate from the Southern Quadrant. "Yet it seems to be *muy impossible*, given *dominio completo* Holders have on all of us with rules...the *reglas constrictivos* they passed since the Secretary was appointed."

"Yes, Paco, they certainly control the military power of the Confederation," said Logo Panagobe, a dark, skinned delegate from Africasia. In soft light his skin reflected a dark purple sheen. "We don't know the extent..."

A woman suddenly approached from across the hall and interrupted. "Excuse me, Excellencies. I'm Patrice Leguna, a scientist working on the Psy project. I was one of the first Da'yoni travelers. I could not help but overhear. I need to be quick so as to avoid security detection." They all frowned, looking around for security agents or microflys. She continued. "You might know that your ideas are in sync with our discoveries, since we came back. However, before you take any action, I plead with you to wait for a while. We will be in touch with you. Our relationship will enhance your potential to accomplish your goals."

"Madame, you walk out of nowhere, startling us, saying you overheard us. How we know to trust you? How we know you are not agent of Holders?" said Chin-tsu as he fingered his long stringy chin-beard, reminiscent of his ancient relatives.

"I understand. As of now, I'm not at liberty to disclose the details. However, I'm asking that you give us a few weeks. We can then assure you. We'll be in contact, as a group, to discuss the details of our plan. I was asked by the others to approach you, at this time. There are many contradictory factions among the Holders. Some have only their own interests at hand. We believe the Committee rule, in the last century, proved itself to be the best for the confederation. Our group is in constant contact with each other. In a few days, upon return of the Secretary's biologue from Da'yoni, she and her partner will join our group."

"For some reason, Madame, I am prone to trust you. I don't know why," said Logo Panagobe.

"*Sí, igualmente*" echoed Paco Zibran.

"You say the Secretary's biologue? That is just what we need. A word in his ear of anything remotely similar to the disenchantment we are talking of and we will end up visiting the "*Welcome Center*" of the security service. Most never return from such 'welcoming' visits," said Panagobe

"I can assure you, Excellency, that the Secretary's biologue will be as deeply committed to our cause as yourself or any of the other returnees from Da'yoni. While I cannot now divulge how that will be, I can tell you that you will be assured as soon as she gets back and has the routine "debriefing" meeting that her Pater will be so eager to convene. After that we all will meet with her."

"As we have only few moments ago begun discussions about how proceed, we wait to hear further from you," said Chin-tsu as he nodded to the others.

"Thank you, your Excellencies. We will not disappoint you. But know that discretion is of the utmost importance," said Patrice.

She quickly turned and walked through the nearby exit door. The delegates looked after her without speaking.

"You know I have heard *un rumor* that the returnees retained some of the mental powers they acquired while on Da'yoni. *Me pregunto si es verdad*," said Paco Zibran. "In fact, *por un breve momento*, it felt as if I was in some sort of *estado alterado*. I vote that we wait to hear further from her…or them."

"Yes. Felt unusual, especially after she turned and left. I agree. We talking about change Solar Confederation government. May be most important to cause. Would be better if we know who 'they are' she refer to," said Chin-Tsu, with a sardonic grin.

"Yes. But I think it best we take a wait and see, hey?" said Logo Panagobe.

"*Si, hay* no need to rush, *¿Hay?*" said Paco Zibran

Chin-tsu fingered his beard to an uncomfortable silence. "Sources tell there are no plans afoot. Things proceed as usual with Holders. So we can wait until hear. I see all agree?"

42

Chapter Three

Anxiety

"You have a strange looking guest at the front portal," said the house bot.

"That must be Ang," said Derral as he opened the portal.

"Ang, I'm glad you came. Susan was wondering about her competition. Make yourself at home and please have a seat," said Derral as he gestured to the kitchen island as Susan walked in.

"Ang Vesad, this is my life partner, Susan. I'm sure you two will have a lot in common, given Susan's academic work in outer species bio structures."

Ang waved his tentacles and offered one to Susan. "My pleasure, commander. This is my first allowed visit to a human domicile. What a pleasure, indeed," said Ang as he encircled Susan's hand with a tentacle.

Susan was momentarily stunned at Ang's appearance. "I apologize at my initial reaction, Ang. I studied Crespian society and biology in my final classes at the academy and am still startled, but delighted to meet you."

"Don't worry, Susan, Ang elicits many different reactions from every human...at least since I've been traveling with him, said Derral.

"Madam, I am the one to apologize for my appearance. I thought the Commander had briefed you," said Ang.

"Oh, he did. It's not your appearance, Ang. It's just that I am astounded to finally meet an off planet being that I've been studying. And please call me Susan and the "Commander", Derral. You are our guest and we leave our formal work relationships behind, at home. Otherwise I'd be relating to him as if he were my master," said Susan, in mirth.

"Well, I think you should relate to me as your master, dear. After all I am a few years older and more experienced," said Derral.

A typical satirical response, thought Susan, as she shook her head.

Ang raised his tentacles and looked like what appeared to be frustrated. "I don't know if I'll ever get used to the Commander's...or Derral's sarcasm. Sarcasm is not so prevalent in Crespian communication. I only first learned its meaning in our many journeys together. At first I was puzzled and didn't know if I should be offended, until he explained the subtleties of human communication

Susan smiled. "Don't worry Ang, he is often sarcastic with me... especially when he is anxious or caught with his hand in the cookie jar."

"Please forgive my ignorance, Susan. You must explain what getting ones hand caught in the cookie jar implies," said Ang.

"It just means getting caught at something you should not be doing or saying. Sort of being embarrassed," said Susan.

"I see. So if I place my tentacle into a place where you do not want me to be, and you see me, the human feeling of "embarrassment" is what occurs?"

"Kind of like that," said Susan.

"Just watch where you place your tentacle, Ang. Especially your sexual tool you described on our last journey," said Derral.

Both Susan and Derral laughed. Ang waved his tentacles and made a high pitch sound, akin to a laugh.

"So you do have humor in sexual contact," said Ang. "From what Derral has conveyed to me, I thought sex was most sacred and secret among humans. In our society it is...how do you say, uninhibited. But we do have our private aspects."

"Derral was always the prudish one...and sometimes gets crazy jealous when there is no reason to...probably his own insecurities," said Susan, with a smirk.

Derral interrupted. "Let's eat. We arranged to have our replicator search a database for some Crespian delicacies and intoxicating drink. Let's have fun...enough for this serious talk. Sorry but we don't have much time to spend this afternoon, Ang, as our trip time is scheduled for the early morning hours. When we get back, we'll have you over again."

"That is acceptable. I know you humans have a thing with time. We Crespians recognize that time is an illusion and don't pay much attention to

44

it, only to schedule things," said Ang.

"We haven't quite gotten there yet, Ang. A few weeks ago, when I was rushing to complete my studies, you would have thought I was crazy," said Susan, with a wide grin.

"Well, he wouldn't have been too far off, my dear," said Derral

"My, my, humans sure have a complicated, way of communicating or joking," said Ang.

"Sometimes it is not all joking," said Susan, as she scowled at Derral.

"Oh, come on. Let's enjoy this short time together," said Derral.

The remainder of the meal was enjoyable.

"I must be getting back," said Ang. "I don't want to let the Chief down, as I told him I'd be back early, given your flight schedule."

"Okay, Ang," said Susan. But please remember you must come back and spend the day with us when we return."

"That would be most gracious of you Susan. Perhaps you can teach me more about human idiosyncrasies," said Ang.

"Sure. But I don't know if there is much more to learn about idiosyncrasies after all the time you spend with my partner, here," said Susan, poking Derral with her elbow.

"Oh boy. I guess I'm the court jester here," said Derral.

"Something like that," smiled Susan.

Ang waved his tentacles and emitted a high pitched, almost human sounding laugh. "Now I understand sarcasm. Thank you, my first human friends"

"See you on the return, Ang," said Susan, rolling her eyes at Derral.

***

Susan and Derral were feeling anxious as they arrived at the transport center, a large underground complex. The massive power in pentawatts needed for transport was provided from invisible solar power biocells in geosynchronous orbit, solely dedicated to operate the transport. An innovation provided by the Da'yonis. Ships leaving Terra orbit pass through the invisible cells without disturbance. An engineering feat that Terra scientists were still working hard to understand.

"Remember the tabs? He said he'd leave it in the package flap of the white suits they'll give us. He cautioned us to be discreet as we don't know who is watching. I'll slip you yours when we're putting on our coverings," said Derral before exiting the security of their vehicle.

"Oh boy. More to be nervous about. But Derral, do you think we embarrassed your star partner, last night?" said Susan.

"No, he's used to that banter, living with me for all those months... Just think of it as added protection during our transformation," said Derral, affectionately touching her hand to reassure her.

"I like him...or her. I hope we become good friends. But we should really come up with a pleasing pronoun, other than androgyne, to refer to him. My pater is androgynous, as offensive as he is. I don't want to refer to such a sweet being like Ang in the same way."

"How about just bisexual, like a flower, said Derral.

"We'll ask him how he feels about that, when we see him, We can trust Robert, right... I hope," she said. Susan continued trying to deflect her increasing anxiety by imagining herself in a trance that this wasn't happenning, as one of her professors suggested.

"No worry there. He has our best interests at heart. It's his risk, too. "Bisexual has no emotional charge, at least in our culture. If Ang feels okay with it. But stop worrying our journey, my best friend. Robert assures us the others had only some minor cognitive problems that only persisted for the first few minutes after they returned. Calm down," said Derral. '

"What was that?" said Susan. "I just got lost in thought."

"Forget it, then. I was just trying to reassure you about something I'm not too sure of," said Derral.

They were ushered into the Da'yoni preparation chamber, directed to strip in an outer room, and scanned for foreign objects. They entered the dressing room and donned the white suits. Derral found the envelope in his pocket and smiled at the symbol of their childhood Saturn club, a childishly sketched image of Saturn on the envelope. He bent over and took out the almost invisible clear tabs from the pocket of the bag. Both bent down to fasten the bands around their leggings.

Derral nodded towards Susan, whispering in her ear, "It's real small, be careful." He grasped her hand and said aloud, "There's nothing to be nervous about, my friend."

The tab almost slipped through Susan's fingers, but she feigned to fumble with the laces and then brushed her hair away from her mouth to take it. At the same time Derral slipped his into his mouth. After finishing donning the suits, their personal coms directed them to pass through an electromagnetic chamber that provided a complete cleansing of all Terra-born virus and bacteria.

"This is the cleanest we've ever been," joked Susan, with a tremble in her voice.

"I suppose so," said Derral, absent mindedly, as he scrutinized the gages of the chamber. He turned from the panel. "You look sexier than ever in that white leotard or whatever it is. It makes me worried about the Da'yonis coming on to you," he said, smiling.

Susan rolled her eyes at him in response. "How can they come on to me in EMF...and you know, one of the things I value in you my partner is your calming sense of humor, even at the most anxious times." she said.

"Sometime tell me what the others are, will you? It comes with practice in a lot of scary combat ops. But, who knows. We actually have no idea what will happen. We just know that the others came back quite ecstatic at the experience, but unable to be specific of the details of what happened. A peculiarity, at the least. The Da'yoni's explanation was that human forms are not capable of retaining specific memories during transformations into EMF formations. All we know is what we saw on the Da'yoni training vids," said Derral.

"I was trying not to think about that," said Susan.

"Well, at least they all came back," said Derral, as he continued his nervous inspection of the equipment. "Robert told me the Da'yoni ambassador recently posted an update. Since the first travelers, they've been able to modify the transformation process to enable memory retention. We will soon see."

A voice came over their coms: "Three minutes until transformation, Dr. & Colonel Priestly. Once we power up, you must remain perfectly still as your molecular structure is being transformed to be compatible with Da'yoni atmosphere and culture. Once the transformation is complete you will exist only as an electromagnetic field, not visible to the naked eye. While you will be able to sense your selves and others through field vibrations, communication will be solely through telepathy once the transformation is effected. That is so because, of course, you will no longer have vocal chords, lungs, and other physical manifestations. You will be pure EMF signatures. Any questions before we begin?"

Susan and Derral looked at each other, wide eyed. Susan shuddered.

"You mean this is the last time well be able to see each other until being re-transformed?" asked Derral.

"Well, not exactly. You'll be able to sense each other through vibrations...and be able to sense other organisms, vibrationally. While the sense is somewhat equivalent to vision, it is both more sensitive but more indistinct than vision. Just slightly indistinct. You will not have the crisp images similar to what appears on your retina. However, the range of perception is enhanced. For example you will be able to simultaneously perceive over a 360^0 range. This is what we've learned from the Da'yoni technicians that assisted us in developing the equipment. Even they had difficulty translating the experience in terms that we are familiar with, given the limitations of our physicality."

"Well, I suppose it'd be a bit foolish to back out now," said Susan. She was staring intently at Derral.

"We know that everyone experiencing it, came back relatively okay, aside from their subsequent social isolation. As we're together, we can isolate ourselves and still be okay. Don't you think?" asked Derral.

"I just hope well recover to the point where we'll be ourselves again," said Susan, in a hoarse whisper.

"Well, even if we do change, it will be for the better, according to the Da'yoni texts," said Derral.

"One minute to transformation," reported the disembodied voice over their coms. "Just relax. It will feel like a slight tingling, lasting about 30 seconds. Then you'll be transformed and we'll begin the orientation process. You'll have two Da'yoni technicians, the Da'yoni answer to robotics. They'll enter the chamber with you to orient your new sensory awareness. Ten seconds, nine, eight...five, four, three, two, one...transformation is beginning. Just sit very still, please."

The room took on a shimmering glow. In seconds, Derral and Susan began to see the human forms on the other side of the chamber.

Wow, this is amazing. We can see right through walls, thought Susan.

Yeah, thought Derral. I just realized…I simply thought a response to what you said…or thought…and you heard it.

Another voice seemed to emanate through the complete room as if a surround sound device was projecting it.

Welcome to the Da'yoni consciousness. From now on we will communicate in thought, not voice, as I am doing now. We are your guides. We will teach you how to orient to our consciousness. We'll be requesting you to complete some exercises, none of which will be harmful in any way. They're designed to assist you to navigate in our reality, what your culture refers to as an electromagnetic field or EMF.

Do we have a choice? thought Susan, with a tremulousness to her field.

Doctor Priestly, there is always a choice. We can bring you back at any time, thought the Da'yoni technician.

That was only a rhetorical question, out of my nervousness, thought Susan.

You know, even in this EMF form we communicate emotions, thought Derral, as he attempted to locate Susan in the field. He could not locate her but sense the anxious vibrations.

The Da'yoni tech continued. We will demonstrate how to sense each other's presence and the presence of others. It only takes a few adjustments to the EMF receptors that are automatically installed during the transformation process, thought the guide.

Well, please hurry up, thought Derral. This sudden alienation is getting a bit uncomfortable.

Susan, are you okay?

She responded in thought. I suppose…can't see anything but the view through the walls and the technicians on the other side. I can't see you. That's a bit disturbing. I'm just holding my breath…or whatever it's called without lungs in this form.

At that moment the room shimmered in a golden light. Derral and Susan looked at each other and saw essentially their human form but bathed in a shimmering light that constantly changed colors.

Why do we keep changing colors, thought Derral.

The guide responded. The color change is the changing EMF as you process different emotions. Pardon the presumption of superiority, but that is one reason why we Da'yoni are a bit more advanced in consciousness. We have done away with the human trait of disguising emotions. When you learn to read the field, you will know instantly what the other is feeling. You can perceive each other now because we increased the sensitivity of the field, for the moment. Once you adjust we will drop it back to normal...and you'll continue to perceive.

How do we learn, thought Susan.

The same way you learn in physical form...by doing, thought the guide. It takes a short time to get adjusted. After awhile you will become experts at recognizing the field changes. This will serve you, even after you return to human form, as we've found some of the sensitivity developed in the EMF state persists when re-transformation is accomplished.

The Da'yoni guides led them through a series of exercises until they were reasonably sensitive to movement and their own forms. Susan was particularly adroit at sensing and identifying the emotional shimmer in Derral. Derral was more skilled at movement. Both practiced until the technicians were satisfied.

Now we can guide you to the transport chamber, thought the Da'yoni bot. Please move through the wall on the opposite side of the technicians. You can follow me. Remember once you begin passing through an inanimate object, you must continue moving forward, as you don't want to become entangled in the molecular structure of the object. While it is not a danger, it does feel a bit uncomfortable.

Whatever you say, thought Derral. Boy, this feels as if there is no weight, no pains, no other signs that we're a body anymore.

It is a bit frightening, isn't it? thought Susan, as she rapidly shimmered with multiple colors reflecting the rapid cycling of her feelings.

Yes, but it's also a relief not to have to carry a carcass around with us. The 360^0 view ain't bad either, thought Derral, as he shimmered a fluorescent blue green. The view is a bit much...but you have to hesitate and think which direction to move.

I suppose it takes getting used to, thought Susan, matching his color.

Yes. That is correct, intoned the robotic voice of their guide. Your human aphorism, practice makes perfect, is most applicable to EMF transformation. By the time you arrive on Da'yoni, you'll have adapted

50

quite well. You see, you'll have about one of your Terra hours during the transport to practice. The transport speed is slower than the maximum, as we want to give you time to be comfortable before reaching Da'yoni. The capsule has suitable comforts so that you can move around and explore your new forms. Let us proceed to the capsule, now. Time is almost correct for the transmission.

Derral, Susan, and the two guides moved through space, invisible to the naked eye, towards the capsule at the end of a long hallway lined with shimmering metallic plates. The purpose of walking down this hallway is to repolarize your forms to ready you for transmission, instructed the guide. These walls contain large instruments similar to your electromagnets that are doing their work at the moment. You may feel a slight tingling. Some have described the feeling in your Terra born sexual terminology.

What kind of metal is this, asked Derral.

It is not a metal but a substance unknown to your world. I believe the closest equivalent would be a diamond-titanium alloy. But it is more durable than your diamonds.

Chapter Four

Conspiracy

"A cup of 20th Century Italian espresso with an inch of foam and a lemon rind," said Secretary Priestly to the nourishment console. A glass cup materialized in front of him. The holo before him chimed. "Open view," said the Secretary. Ulemann appeared on the holo.

"Mr. Secretary, the flys are in place. Should I download the feeds to your holo?"

"Yes, indeed, Ulemann. Now we'll see how destructive these so-called friends can be."

Two simultaneous views of Rakard and General Suddhis appeared on the translucent table in front of the secretary. "Record mode only. Get me Solais Cursard…and encrypt it," said the General. The holo blinked. A foreboding figure with multiple scars across his cheeks stood before the General. The butt of a gamma pistol could be seen protruding from his cloak. "Yes, I thought you'd be contacting me soon, General."

The General looked sternly at the holo. "Well, Cursard, it is time to move. I want you to install your people in the capitol building. They need to be able to move on a moment's notice. We'll need a few more weeks to get everything in order. But have them ready by the end of next week. Remember, this is crucial if you want to give up your outlaw status with the confederation and return to some semblance of normalcy, when our people are in place. I cannot emphasize that enough to you can I?"

"No, your Excellency, I am your servant," said Cursard, with a smirk and an exaggerated bow.

"Cut the crap Cursard," said the General. "You know how important this is for us. If we don't want to have the Secretary ruling forever with his half-witted, impulsive schemes 'to help society,' and pad his own bank account, then we must act."

"I understand. You must appreciate the humor in this, though: a Holder allying himself with a declared outlaw. Holders by definition are the essence of righteousness, are they not?" said Cursard, still smirking.

"Yes," said the General, flashing a look of irritation at the holo. "But if one believes the confederation is decaying, is it not a righteous to act to head off the deterioration?"

"I'm not a politician, General. I'm a thief, a grifter, and a profiteer. It may be righteous, but not as decaying as some might want the public to believe," said Cursard.

"What do you mean, Cursard? You mean to say we're being told a pack of lies by the Secretary's analysts or the Secretary himself?"

"General, I mean to say that reality is not politic reality."

"Well, damn, if it's not a politic reality than what the hell is it," snarled the General. "This is the home country of the Solar Confederation, and don't you forget it."

"Yes sir, I am well aware of that fact. You're not the only patriot," said Cursard.

"Well if you're aware of that fact, why do you speak in such cryptic fashion?"

"I don't know that you realize the true nature of the situation, General. The Secretary's hidden agenda, unbeknownced to those who might question it, is purely economic, as are most of the other Holders. They are interested in making the maximum amount of credits, regardless of whatever they must do to deceive the populace. I can identify with all of you on that level. I don't think the hidden agenda was shared with those who have shown they might give the slightest opposition. But anyone who knows anything, knows or suspects that. I know you fully understand what I'm saying, as you're on the same ship. Secretary Priestly knows the situation and covertly supports it. He is driven, mostly by greed and power, the two predominant motivations of pre-Committee human kind. However, he disguises his true motives under the camouflage of what is best for all, a true politician."

"Are you accusing me of being corrupt, Cursard?"

"Of course not your excellency. I'm merely stating what has been a fact for many years," said Cursard, through a tight lipped smile.

"For the moment, I'll ignore that you're putting me in the same category. How can you know this about the others, Cursard? I believe the Secretary is merely stupid and greedy. What evidence supports your suppositions, that he's shared his outlook with other more trusted Holders?"

"I really don't care to share that over the holo, General. There is no guarantee of security, even if it is encrypted. The Security agency can break most encryption, if they want. I'll share it with you in person, when we can get to a secure location."

"Damn you, Cursard, you are a pain in the ass. As a Holder, for me to meet a criminal type like you in private, would implicate me with you and whatever else you're up to. I can't afford to chance it."

"General, that depends on what you want to do in the future. If you meet with me, I'll provide you with factual information regarding the Secretary and his supporters, not to mention the two who are taking the trip to Da'yoni this New Years Eve, the secretary's biologue and her partner."

"Listen Cursard, the political climate is such that it would be foolish for me to meet you now. This connection is secure. Tell me what you know."

"Pardon, your Generalship, I don't agree with your assessment. The Secretary's agents are quite sophisticated. I won't risk disclosing sensitive information that could get back to him. So far, I've been safe from his forces, as I was only an opportunist and did not represent a direct threat to his regime. However this involvement with you changes the calculus. I will only meet you in the flesh, at a place and time of my choosing, mon General."

"Cursard," the General shouted at the holo. "I cannot risk my position, at this point. Find another way to communicate, but not in person, do you understand?"

"Yes, General. I will be in contact with you." The holo went blank. The General turned away with a look of disgust.

Secretary Priestly turned away from his holo. "Cursard doesn't know it yet, but he no longer has his safety net. Ulemann, what do you think we should do, given this development?"

"Forgive me Mr. Secretary, but I do not think action is called for. We must continue to accumulate information, especially about this Cursard. I'll see if our agents can locate him and implant a fly. It will be difficult, as I understand he maintains a constant high security alert, but with the new technology we acquired from the Capezoid we should be able to locate him.

We do have a match of his cellular structure, obtained last year during that fiasco at the Platinum Depository Complex."

"Ah, yes, when he bungled the break-in. I remember that one. Gave me more confidence in our security code technology," said the Secretary with a sneer.

"Yes, he failed and also left some of his body secretions. We obtained a DNA match. We can program a fly to seek out the designated DNA pattern within a click, but first we will need his general location. If the General or someone else we track will meet with him, we can make the implant. That would be the easiest way."

"How, in the Confederation can we arrange such a meeting? Cursard is an outlaw," said the Secretary. "And the General, surprisingly, is intelligent enough not to meet with him."

Ulemann lowered his voice in a conspiratorial tone. "It is possible to raise the suspicion level of the General's people so they'd arrange a visit to obtain Cursard's information," he said with a sly, toothless grin. "We might be able to enlist the aide of the General's partner-in-crime, Oice, if he believes his position is in serious jeopardy. The Service can pump up the vid media with false information attributed to an anonymous, highly placed assistant to the Holders. It may or may not work depending on how suspicious and relatively stupid he is. The Service profile suggests he is not very bright," said Ulemann.

"What are the odds that we will be associated with such an act if it turns into a debacle?"

"Slim to none," said Ulemann. "The Service can cover its tracks quite well, it will be almost impossible to discover a link. And then, even if they suspect, there will be no firm proof."

The Secretary looked solemn. "Time is crucial, I guess that is just about the only solution we have. It must be done with haste, we don't want the two scoundrels to suspect anything. Do it, Ulemann. It seems to be the only way," said the Secretary as he turned back towards the holos.

Ulemann tapped his holoset and whispered a direction. He turned towards the Secretary. "I anticipated your response, Mr. Secretary, and had my staff set up the implementation to await my order. They'll now set the stage. It should take less than a day. By the next solar light we should be receiving direct confirmation from the fly holos. If the General chooses one of his staff to meet Cursard, we will have a fly installed on that person within minutes of the General's choice."

The Secretary smiled. "This is one reason why I've kept you on the payroll all these years, Ulemann. Thank you again for your efficiency, it makes up for my inefficient political style," said the Secretary in an atypical moment of self-criticism. He turned back towards the holos and addressed the nourishment console. "Mary, an extra dry 21st Century vodka martini with a citrus cured olive and some Beluga caviar with rye toast."

I can't believe I just said that to this servant...this mechanical bot. I must be getting on in years, thought the Secretary.

The console flashed a glowing blue light. "Yes sir. Would you like a splash of vermouth?"

"No Mary, all frozen vodka."

"As you wish sir. But have caution. Remember how your system reacts." The console light changed to a glowing purple and a martini with a dish of caviar and toast materialized on a tray. The tray levitated and moved to the Secretary's desk.

"Kill the health advice, Mary. Turning to his assistant he said, "This is how our 21st Century relatives relaxed on a Sunday afternoon. At least the relatively well off ones who could afford the finer things in life."

He turned to Ulemann. "Care to join me?"

"I'm sorry sir, but what is this vodka and caviar. I'm not familiar with these concepts," said Ulemann as he sniffed the martini and caviar making a face.

"Vodka is an intoxicating drink. Somewhat like our zith. It alters the consciousness. Caviar were eggs from the sturgeon, a large fish that swam in the seas and rivers before they became polluted. The Beluga brand was prized for its size and taste, from what was known as Russia on the Caspian sea, now the great salt expanse. Caviar was served with vodka or champagne at festive occasions."

"Must I familiarize myself with this form of intoxicating beverage, Mr. Secretary?" said Ulemann.

"Of course. Mary, another martini and a plate of caviar. Don't drink it until you prepared the mission and can relax, as it is quite intoxicating."

"As you wish, sir. I'll do that now," said Ulemann as he engaged his internal com, giving directions to the personal Security staff. He then took a sip of the martini and made a face. "I don't know if I care for this beverage, sir."

"It is an acquired taste," said the Secretary, as he returned to the holo on his desk.

Ulemann turned his attention back to the holos. They watched as the General directed a staff member to make contact with Cursard. The General called up Cursard on his console. "Cursard?" said the General, as the holo appeared. "This is Lynchon, my assistant. He'll meet you in your place. You can share the information with him. He only reports to me."

"I am leery, General," said Cursard. "Although I do realize the problems with meeting me directly. I will trust your man."

"Okay Cursard. Give us the directions and he'll be there," said the General.

"I will send a coded signal to your man's personal vid. A map will be transmitted after he is on his way. The map will direct him to a location where an aquatic vehicle is programmed to take him to my location. Do not allow anyone to follow your man, as the aquatic vehicle has a device acquired from my alien travels, that surveys the surrounding area for intelligent life form signatures. If we detect any, they will be destroyed. I'll be ready for him." Cursard nodded, looking chagrined. The holo blanked.

The Secretary turned from the holos towards Ulemann. "You'll insert a fly on this Lynchon? It may be the only way to get close to Cursard and tag him, too."

Ulemann smiled. "I just gave the order, Mr. Secretary. He is now tagged. My people know this Lynchon and have been monitoring him. We'll tag him with another fly and launch it into Cursard's hair follicles when he makes the contact."

"Excellent," said the Secretary as he turned back to the holo. "Let me see this Lynchon," said the Secretary. "Can we call up his fly?"

"We can do it with ease. However to see him he must be looking in a mirror. But we have recent electronic footage I can play for you. In fact, it comes from the Generals party we monitored a few days ago."

"Okay. Bring it up on my holo. His name sounds familiar to me. I

57

usually don't forget a face," said the Secretary, turning away to the holo table.

"Yes sir. Here it is. Your Lynchon is the person to the right of the General, holding a blue synth."

"Yes. I thought so, that was the man or thing I was introduced to some months ago as the Generals personal assistant. Seem to recall he was part droid, but had a brain composed of human and Eritrean components. Those Eritrean evolved on the planet in the 4th galaxy, a slovenly bunch. Ate their own young, I'm told, at least until we invaded and took control of their civilization. As the General commanded the expedition forces, he exploited the issue, as usual, by having our galactic science department create this thing from an existing human he had in his employ. Apparently the human either was too greedy or wasn't aware of what he'd bitten off. The General offered him 3 million credits to allow the transformation." The Secretary ended the conversation with a backhand wave. Ulemann knew this gesture signaled increasing irritation and excused himself.

"Mr. Secretary, I must go and oversee the microfly implantations, in the event a command decision must be made as the events unfold. Would you like me to input the feeds as soon as they are up?"

"Yes, but I'll be on standby record. Input them to my holo chip too," replied the Secretary as he repeated the hand gesture.

"Yes sir. But you know the holo chip implants are not as secure as the desk top holos? Especially since our intelligence detected the opposition parties contact with the Capazoids and subsequent technology exchange, albeit illegal as it was. We took no action but to increase our surveillance. The Capazoid are remarkably sophisticated. Their technology is a cut above ours."

Ulemann lowered his head, feeling a bit anxious. He knew from past experience that to cast doubt on the Secretary's desires can lead to an outburst of hostility.

"Okay, then. It'll suffice to connect with my desk holo. Besides I can't monitor their every move. That is your job. Its just that I have a bad feeling about this. My feelings are rarely ever wrong. But carry on."

Ulemann smiled in relief, for the first time in weeks.

Chapter Five

Einstein Was Wrong

Derral and Susan floated past the threshold of the capsule. Their thoughts were transmitted to each other, as if they were speaking aloud. That's incredible, thought Derral. It felt like each foot we traveled evoked a weird feeling like an orgasm, but not exactly. More like a streaming of pleasure.

There was no loss of awareness, thought Susan. But, I know what you mean partner, although I don't translate it into such male sexual terms.

Too bad we don't have our bodies back. I'd like to step into a vacant room with you for a half hour or so, said Derral, with what felt like a loud cackle.

That was interesting, thought Susan. I experienced your laugh and didn't hear anything. It was like you verbalized it.

The Da'yoni droid interjected: As we mentioned, when you become adjusted to your EMF form, feelings appear as real. The EMF field has a tendency to translate a thought form with an emotional color, thought the Da'yoni tech, sounding slightly above a whisper.

Both Susan and Derral startled. Their EMF configurations shimmered brightly. They had almost forgotten the Da'yoni droid-guides were beside them. Their shimmering suggested embarrassment, almost at the same vibrational frequency.

I see why you two are together, thought the Da'yoni droid. You vibrate with the same constrictive emotions at just about the same frequency, the droid continued.

This increased their embarrassing shimmers until Derral responded to the droid. It seems as if the Da'yoni are devoid of the civilized graces that are so ingrained in our culture. The Da'yoni people, if you're a representative sample, seem to be rude at best, is that correct?

We are most apologetic, sir. That was simply an attempt at what I perceived was some human humor. Perhaps my perception was inaccurate. My synthintel system learns and grows from doing and being responded to. At present, I lack the information regarding some of the subtleties of your communication patterns. Please forgive my rudeness, sir. Da'yoni communication is always direct with no covering of intentions. I see that humans require what you confirm as "civilized graces." It won't happen again. My synth circuits are now integrated with your emotional sensitivity. We will close the capsule door now and begin transport. You will experience a slight feeling of what can best be described in two dimensional space form as nausea during acceleration beyond the speed of lumen. That is the sensation of your EM fields wanting to stay behind. But don't worry. The chamber is lined and will protect you from any disturbance, thought the Da'yoni assistant.

Both shimmered multicolored waves, as their anxiety increased. After a long pause, Derral articulated a recognizably anxious, okay, I guess we can trust your reassurances.

Susan shimmered with a hundred thoughts, going over the past 39 years of her life.

Their thoughts were punctuated by the Da'yoni assistants in tandem. Please know that the Da'yoni are incapable of conveying a false statement. We drones are programmed to mimic our creators, to the letter as you might say. We understand your fear, at this juncture. However, if you focus on your fear field and not on the pleasure of the journey, you will miss out on a most remarkable experience for your species. That vibration you feel is the capsule passing through the 1st lumen or, in your Einsteinium equation, the speed of light, doubled. As we pass through each raising of the equation to the next 10th power, we will experience a slight vibration. As we past through the second lumen we will be traveling at about four times the speed of light and so on to 100 lumens which will be our cruising speed at 107 times lumen for the last hour, in your Terra time, for our journey. We will then begin our rapid deceleration and prepare for orbit around Da'yoni. The deceleration will be similar to the feeling you experienced as you traveled through the tunnel to the capsule; what you refer to as sexual feeling. Considering traditional calculations it takes about 3 Terra days at this speed to reach Da'yoni. However due to a particular anomaly when we approach 107 times the speed of lumen, your Terra time is compressed. We have not yet been able to provide an acceptable understanding for this anomaly. Thus the total time will be, at most, a few of your Terra hours. Usually not more than that depending on the galactic winds. If you can relax and concentrate on the wall in front of you, you will be able to experience the travel through the galaxies, akin to a visual experience.

Well, I guess that is slow enough for me, thought Susan with a bright green iridescent shimmer.

You mean you can't make it any faster than that, asked Derral, with an equally bright mirthful shimmer. I don't know what I'll do with all that time sitting in this thing.

The Da'yoni droid ignored their attempt at humor, responding formally. When we are past the 3rd power, you will experience your form changing. I believe the word is stretching. Your field will stretch to the boundaries of the capsule and form what you refer to as a mobius loop back to your original form at the 7th power. It will not create any discomfort now that you know what will happen. That vibration we just passed through signaled the 3rd power passing. I will turn on the view holo so you can see the changes.

The wall of their capsule came alive, as if passing through multicolored waves of light. There were no forms discernible, just blurred streaks of colored light.

What happens if we hit something, asked Derral.

There was a pause before the droid answered. Until we surpass the 3rd power, if we hit something we would become merged with the object and not complete our journey. That is why the navigational plotting is precise to the 500th decimal in your mathematical system. After passing the 3rd. power we will simply navigate through the molecular structure of whatever we come in contact with, including any stars in our path. The transporter has an autopilot function, many times more efficient than a Da'yoni. In fact at 40 of your light years out, coming up soon, we will pass through the star you know as Arcturus. We will also pass through a few more along the way, too. When we do you will notice a bright glow on the holo and experience a vibration. If you remain relaxed you can experience the actual passing through the star.

If I didn't feel so frightened, I'd have to say this was the most beautiful light show I've ever seen, thought Susan.

Yes, we think so. It is the passing from one star system to another. If one repeats this journey a number of times, one can recognize the star systems from their light signatures. Each is different.

Derral shimmered. How close are we? Its been just about an hour, right?

We will begin our deceleration in five centares or rather 3 of your Terra minutes, reported the droid. You'll have to excuse us for a few moments, as this is the difficult part. We must concentrate or focus.

That's reassuring, thought Susan, as she shimmered in unison with Derral. They noticed a wave form change in the walls of the ship. It appeared to rapidly expand and contract as if it were breathing. At once, Derral and Susan began to shimmer in differing colour patterns.

Do not be alarmed, communicated the droid. As the deceleration process comes to a complete halt, your EMF must make an adjustment to the gravitational matrix from our five stars or suns, as you will. We must remain in orbit for a while to complete the EMF transformation to a wave form that is comfortable on Da'yoni. We will open a portal so you can view the planet. At this time of our planet's light it is particularly beautiful as the suns are lined up in what you would refer to as a pentagon shape on the other side of the planet from where our transport capsule is stabilizing. In this transit, the light emission from the suns intersect to form a most beautiful pattern.

The side of the vehicle immediately opened like an iris to reveal the sight of Da'yoni as a multicolored orb. How beautiful, she thought. Clusters of sparkling diamonds emitting every known color.

It is more than beautiful, thought Derral. Their fields shimmered and glowed with the colors of what they were perceiving.

Know that with your eyes, in human form, this sight would appear as a dull glow, reported the droid. You are not seeing the light, per se. The vibrational constant that creates the light is what you perceive.

As if on cue, a different voice was perceived. Welcome to Da'yoni, humans. You may refer to me as Eudrf. I am the central spoke of the Da'yoni consciousness. The closest Terra equivalent might be referred to as President or Secretary of the Holders. My position is somewhat similar, in your planet, to your pater's, Susan. She shimmered with anxiety.

Eudrf continued: Please do not be alarmed. As you are in EMF forms your thoughts and historical data are, shall we say, visible to all. However, before you dock at our Crennium or seat of government, the droids must train you to access this skill. It will take but 15 centares, about 10 of your Terra minutes, for you to grasp the skill to become like us. Please forgive any anxiety we have caused by our neglect in not informing you of this aspect of your new, but temporary existence. As soon as you dock and are made comfortable in your quarters, we will convene a meeting in the central hall. We would most appreciate if you were to come, as it will be an introduction to our existence as well as a view of how our government functions; much different than yours. However, we are aware that you are vacationing here, and your time is limited. We think though that an introduction in the seat of the Crennium may be a first of many valuable experiences you can bring back to your home world. As the Crennium only meets once every quinson, roughly equivalent to six of your Terra months, this will be the only opportunity to experience it in your brief stay.

We would welcome the opportunity, thought Derral. It seems that there is no fatigue in these forms, or what I know as time shift lag from interstellar light speed journeys. We are...I think I can speak for my partner, most appreciative and looking forward to honor your gracious invitation.

Eurdf instantaneously responded, as there are generally no temporal gaps between thoughts, unlike speech. We will meet again at the Crennium in two revolutions of the third star. As you will see, Da'yoni revolved around this closest and smallest of stars about once every 22 degrees or what you once referred to as 1.5 of your Terra hours. In the interim, after you dock, we suggest you stay out of the domicile so as not to miss the stellar revolutions and light change. It is stunning at this particular point in the planet's revolution.

Thank you. But, I wonder how you are so familiar with our old time keeping systems and our relatively recent transition? thought Derral.

Eurdf shimmered and responded. I'm sure this won't alarm you, but we have been tracking your human history for at least a thousand of your years through our EMF sensors. We will transmit some of our accumulated historical holos that you can view at your leisure, when you return to Terra. We initiated that once we came upon your star and saw how quickly you evolved, compared to other species

That's amazing...but thanks. We are eager to meet with your Crennium, thought Derral and Susan, simultaneously. A clicking sound was heard as the communication with Eurdf ended. Derral and Susan shimmered in unison. Did you notice, we often think the same thoughts, especially when communicating with others, thought Derral. Susan responded with a shimmer that suggested a response. Probably has something to do with us living together for so long, don't you think. I mean at least the relationship cyberdocs say that happens, thought Susan. Derral shimmered in response.

Chapter Six

Cursard And The Jovians

Ulemann watched intently as the fly unit embedded itself behind the seat in Lynchon's personal transporter.

"Once he sits down and activates the controls the fly will attach itself to a hair follicle. When this happens we should have a panoramic view, as if we were looking through his eyes. The fly will move to the hairs just above his forehead," said Char, the techno chief.

"Very well," said Ulemann as he watched intently. "Just make sure the fly is attuned to Lynchon's sensory neurons so that it will freeze operations if there is any sensation at all...and especially redirect him from scratching his head if he gets the urge."

"Yes. When he enters his transporter, the neural net will be mapped into our control center, as soon as he starts the transporter's drivers. The initial pulse will be camouflaged by the drivers field generation. Now it's just a matter of waiting until he leaves," said Char.

Ulemann's eyes brightened. "Look...he's getting ready to leave. We won't have to wait long."

Lynchon walked rapidly to his transporter. As he buckled himself into the pilots harness, the video shifted to the microfly's view, looking out over the top of his head. When he gave the command to start the drive motors, the fly moved. It flew to his forehead, hovered for a micro second and descended to a hair follicle. A bell tone sounded on the console to indicate the plant was secure and in place. Whatever Lynchon was seeing appeared on the holo. When he moved his eyes, the fly moved to track his vision. An additional panoramic view from the fly's perspective was pictured in a lower right corner of the holo.

"I need to notify the Secretary. He wanted to know as soon as we were activated," said Ulemann, as he touched his chin to engage the direct connection to his boss.

Char watched the holo and adjusted the transmission image. Lynchon was setting the geographic locater to his destination. She called up the location on another holo. It was an abandoned building from the last century in what was once the thriving space port, before the acquisition of the bartered anti-grav technology.

Lynchon pressed the synchro panel to touch down at the abandoned building. Char sent a program command to the fly units. Five were immediately dispatched to the location, arriving just as Lynchon landed. She then signaled Ulemann with an emergency burst. His face appeared on the holo.

"Sir, our carrier has arrived at the target location. The fly successfully attached to his tunic. I think your direct presence is required at this stage, as he is about to meet the target," said Char with some urgency.

"I'll be right there. Don't take any action, just monitor until I get there."

"Yes sir. It looks like it will take him a few minutes to get to the location," said Char.

Lynchon jogged across a large field from his transporter. In an instant, the field dematerialized. He was now in a submersible vessel that momentarily interfered with the field transmission. The fly holos blinked to the change of density. Char adjusted the controls.

Ulemann entered the room and hurried to the holo console. "What's he doing?"

"Apparently Lynchon passed through an EMF transform to a submersible. The submersible delivered him to the chamber. Seems Cursard has a high technical level of security, but the flys will be undetected as they're aligned to Lynchon's field."

The chamber opened to another room where Cursard stood, hands resting on the butts of his two blasters, behind two large Jovians hefting laser rifles aimed at Lynchon. Lynchon flinched. One of the Jovians, affixed a scanner to the business end of his rifle.

"Those Jovians are disgusting, They all look alike and are the same size. You can't tell the difference between them. They all look like inflated pigs with rhino skins. If you ever get close enough to smell one of them, you'd want to throw up your lunch," said Ulemann.

"The gravity on Jupiter...," Char began, but was interrupted as she worked the console. The scanner beam slowly moved from Lynchon's head to his feet.

She shut down all but one of the flys. Breathless, she said,"The remaining active fly should be shielded from scanning."

Lynchon was carefully scanned from head to toe.

"This mo clean boss," said the Jovian in the gruff, thickly accented dialect, ubiquitous with his species. He gestured with his rifle for Lynchon to step forward.

"Good afternoon Mr. Lynchon," said Cursard. "I hope this was not too alarming. But caution insures my ongoing existence. One need not be too careful nowadays. I'm sure you can understand my point."

Lynchon nodded in the affirmative. His eyes widened in fear as the other Jovian ambled across the room and leered over him.

"This one good eat boss," said the other Jovian.

"Keep your disgusting habits for off world, Grancha," growled Cursard.

"Mr. Lynchon, you are only the messenger. I bear you no ill will. Forgive my boy's manners. They have been known to eat other species. But they know to be on their good behavior here, or they don't get paid. And they certainly are a greedy bunch. So not to worry. Here is the vidcom of the Secretary speaking to the...."

The fly transmission fluttered for a second but stabilized.

"I'll play the audio, said Cursard, waving his hand over a console. The fly transmissions fluttered again. Chars holo continued the image, absent the volume. She made some adjustments, to no avail. Cursard then waved his hand over the panel.

"The first voice is the Secretary. The second is the Da'yoni ambassador," said Cursard, as he turned to a console.

Lynchon recognized the unmistakable voice of the Secretary. "Mr. Ambassador, I understand our agreement. When my daughter and her partner travel to your world, you will transfer 5 billion credits to our off-world account. This gesture will be in return for allowing your people to scan our genetic makeup. I understand you only want to do that to enhance the missing pieces of the historical records of our species, especially those connected to our governing bodies."

A synthesized voice responded. "That is essentially correct Mr. Secretary. Our...what you refer to as anthropologists will then examine the information in their ever increasing zeal to know the nature of your culture so that we can better coexist. The credit payment is done only as an incentive to allow such a scan. There will be absolutely no deleterious effects. When they're scanned, they will be in EMF form, not in your flesh and blood form. Our government or Crennium will be most grateful. We have arranged similar agreements with other Holders and their relatives."

Cursard switched off the recording and handed the holocube to Lynchon.

Char's set came back online, but fluttered again. The audio sounded as if it was being jammed.

"That is about the gist of it," said Cursard. Tell the General that he's not to make this public. To do so would compromise my sources inside the Secretary's circle. I will also give you this disabler. When you play the cube for the General, you must first turn on this disabler. The cube will not function unless the disabler is on. It will disable any listening devices or flys in the immediate vicinity. The General will have only one chance for viewing. After the first view, the cube will self erase in the secure mode. Remember, if this falls into the wrong hands it could be very unpleasant to all. My Jovian boys will take care of those responsible...in a very unpleasant way."

"As you wish, Mr. Cursard. The General will be most grateful. Now I must go quickly so as not to draw awareness of my absence. My cruiser, on your tarmac is cloaked from the sentry. The cloak can only be effective for 20 minutes at most. Thank you for seeing me. Now, how do I get out of here?"

Cursard pointed towards the Jovian who opened the inner chamber. As Lynchon stepped in, there was another blinking of the microfly transmission, now minus three. The three had implanted themselves in Cursard and his two henchmen, but were immediately disabled by Cursard's sophisticated tech. Lynchon appeared again on the surface and walked to his transporter. The fly in his hair again became active. The drive started on automatic as he approached.

Char spun around in her chair to face Ulemann. "I'm afraid we missed

68

the crucial transmission. Cursard must have had scanning and blocking devices, beyond our frequencies."

Ulemann appeared lost in confusion as he stared at the holo, whispering to himself. "I don't know what to say. I'll have to take this to the Secretary, at once. The Secretary will be very disappointed." He slipped a small transparent cube in the console and recorded the interaction with Cursard and Lynchon. "I hope it's not true…that Cursard's technology is more advanced than ours," he said with a fleeting look of desperation.

Robert Laing the Solar Intelligence Consortium (SIC) chief was eves-dropping on Chars fly transmissions. Just before the visual portion blanked, he noticed the passing of the cube to Lynchon and immediately dispatched a microsensor with the ability to extract information from media, without detection. The microsensor managed to enter Lynchon's vehicle when he got in. Robert had recently obtained this technology from his Capazoid counterpart in the Regulas system in return for a cloaking technology he provided. He had not yet informed the Secretary of this exchange. The sensor transmitted the digital media to Robert's console, without disabling the security functions of Cursard's cube.

Robert looked stunned as he watched the replay. "Incredible," he said aloud to himself. "And to think I believed the Secretary's 'doing the most good for all' rhetoric." He verified the digital holo for accuracy, tracing it to the actual holo of the meeting with the Ambassador. The SIC had implanted holorecord devices in all the Holder's offices for historical purposes. Evidently it slipped the Secretary's mind at this juncture, he thought. "Or perhaps his greed got the best of him," he said aloud.

Troubled about his loyalties, especially to his life-long friend, Robert made an immediate decision.

Chapter Seven

The Crennium

The Da'yoni droid silently entered the chamber. Derral and Susan shimmered with an unnerving vibration, as they had been involved in an intimate conversation.

Please forgive that I startled you, thought the droid. We will begin the training session. This will enable you to view all ones history from their field, as long as you are in close proximity. Emotional pictures as well as other experiences over the course of the entities existence will be discernible. I must first enter certain codes into the system for your EMF matrix. The room will do the rest. The droid floated to a small virtual console that appeared from the blank wall displaying multiple gages and dials surrounding what looked like a keypad. The droid rapidly entered data into the key pad. Now, please will Susan turn towards Derral and imagine his emotional state at six years of age.

Susan shimmered a rapid change of colors. Whoa. Amazing...I can actually see you as a little boy. You're troubled by something. You're in black. Yes, you are in a room outside your father's funeral, He was accidentally killed on an expedition to Mercury. I see your mother. She's trying to console you, but you just want to be left alone in your room... this is incredible. That's something you never talked about, Derral. If this becomes an actuality, then dishonesty would be a thing of the distant past?

The droid responded. While in theory, that is correct. Our forms have discovered subtle ways to disguise true natures. Yet the truth is the foundation of our cosmology, so most Da'yoni are truthful. Only a small minority advocate for more secrecy. The Crennium is currently debating this issue. In fact, you will soon be there to witness the debate and call of the vote. Now Derral, you turn to look at Susan in the same way. Imagine her at 5 years of age.

Derral shimmered as he turned. I don't know what to look for, he thought.

Just attempt to visualize Susan as a five year old and imagine how she responded, thought the droid.

Derral shimmered in recognition. Oh, I see. It's like a picture lights up...like a holo in place of your form. Mmhh. Your mother is helping you ride an air cycle. She has you on an invisible leash...or at least the cycle on a leash. It is going around in a circle. You're laughing with delight. Oops. You almost fell off, you were laughing so much. There now you have it. He turned to the droid. Can we see any ones history like this, simply by turning towards them and imagining?

Most certainly, responded the droid while manipulating gages and rapidly entering data on the console in front of him. When you develop the skill you can rapidly shift scenes and move through the major events of a persons life in a matter of 30 centares or about 20 of your Terra minutes. But, like everything else, it takes practice to master. I'm afraid you won't be on Da'yoni for enough revolutions to master the skill

Can this skill be carried over in our physical forms, thought Susan.

Not exactly. But during this training I have received permission, if requested by you, to transfer as much as possible into your EMF signature so that there will be a possibility of some carry over. Do you wish this to be so?

Susan and Derral shimmered. Both thought simultaneously. What will be the implications?

Derral shimmered, anxiously. I wonder if that was why the few others went into isolation after returning? Seeing the true nature in human discourse...the disengenousness and deceit. Seeing the actual truth of any dialogue.

The droid remained silent.

Susan continued Derral's thought. Imagine having this ability and playing a central part in the Holders world. One would have to adhere to the highest ethics not to abuse.

Yes, but there would be temptations, thought Derral. As we think of these issues I continue to see pictures of elements in your life where you had problems with others lying to you...and the bad feelings it created.

71

You know, as one speaks or thinks...or whatever we're doing in these forms, pictures seem to light up. Pictures similar to discourse, as if we're describing them.

The droid interjected a comment with a new tone of directness. That is correct. That is why truth holds much centrality in the Da'yoni cosmology. Know that it is I, Eurdf, who is speaking through the droid, now. I was contacted when the subject of our sensate ability arose and am interested in your introspections regarding this element in our society. We would welcome giving you this gift to take back to your world. We have given it to the few others. But sadly, on returning, they were too overwhelmed to put it to good use. You seem to be different than the others. Your vibrations are more in synchrony with our spin rate.

Both Susan and Derral shimmered in puzzlement.

Eurdf continued through the droid: You see, in this form we can differentiate each other by the rate of spin of our fields. The spin rate is a measure of what you would refer to as the relative emotional and cognitive stability of an organism. You must know though, the sensate process apparently is more subtle in your atomic molecular form. You must be well practiced in EMF. Then, when your transformation begins, you must keep the sensate process in awareness as you change back. Once back in your molecular form, you must spend many centares practicing with each other to stimulate the correct bio circuits in your controllers or what you refer to as your central nervous or neural net system. Only after many of your planets revolutions will you master the sensate system and can trust your experience with it...Enough of that for now. We must go to the Crennium so that you can experience how our society works.

Susan thought, but we have so many questions. She wished she could contact her old astrophysics professor

Derral joined: Yes, how can we transform a process like this to our forms?

Please, communicated Eurdf, we must hurry. I will respond to all your queries after you have experienced the Crennium. That experience alone, will answer many of your questions. Let us not waste another moment. There is no need to contact your human teacher, now. We will respond to all your inquiries, as he could not understand our field, yet, anyway. The assembly is about to open.

The droid rapidly entered data into the holopanel. At the next instant they found themselves in a massive crystalline structure. Both felt an unease, as if they were melting.

Please do not be alarmed, transmitted Eurdf. His form now appeared between Susan and Derral, touching them both with his field. That sensation you are experiencing is simply the transposition of your EMF fields into the Crennium where all of our organisms are present. You are feeling the communion with all. This is a common feeling that you will get used to. This will enable you to partake in the experience of the voting process, as well. I neglected to inform you that travel, while on Da'yoni, occurs almost instantaneously as there are no physical forms to move through space, only an EMF field.

Both shimmered in multiple colors, but could not seem to think any thoughts.

Once the melding process is complete, in a moment, you will be able to again communicate with individuals. Your sensation of not being able to conceptualize, momentarily, is partly because this is your first experience in melding with the Crennium.

Susan felt an increasing sense of well being. Her form shimmered in unison with the many different forms in the great hall. Derral exhibited a multicolored shimmer, partly of angst.

Slowly, they both began to see through the eyes of many others, in fact millions of others almost simultaneously. Both felt overwhelmed. Eurdf continued to reassure them, through their private channel. The Crennium is the Da'yoni answer to democracy. This is true democracy; a primary truth of existence. Every being has a vote in every decision affecting the society. We have evolved a process whereby each living organism or field senses the interconnections of what you would call their energy spirals. On star systems inhabited by humanlike species the sensation of the interconnections is lost in appearances and speculations. On your planet, since the advent of human civilization the sensation of the energic interconnections were distorted by the character armoring or neurosis that served as a defense against giving into the vast field of tenderness that pervades both yours and our species. The process of character armoring that I speak of is the chronic hardening of your striated tissue, your muscles, that prevents higher order sensations from being felt. Eons ago, when our species transmuted to EMF forms, character armor was no longer functional If only the primary truth were to be uncovered your species…

He hesitated and appeared to censor himself.

…For now, let us attend to the Crennium. It is wrong for me to be critical of your species. I was just politely admonished by a few of what you would refer to as legislators, for doing so. They caution that I convey the facts but not the judgments.

How is it that we did not experience your admonishment, thought Derral?

Just as I have opened a private channel to communicate with you out of the thought stream, I have direct contact with the legislators at all times, thought Eurdf. He exhibited a notable difference in shimmer of vibration, and now communicated in didactic generalities, devoid of personal references. Unusually prescient beings appeared throughout all epochs and all species. Through a quirk of their prenatal neural development, they exhibited a special genius and sense to detect the spiral interconnections. Some adopted the visage of religious or political figures; others developed into the role of scientists and philosophers. These group of beings devoted their lives to bringing into awareness the interconnectedness for the species. However, due to the layer of sadism and cruelty beneath the surface of the armored or neurotic layer of your physical forms, every one of these special people were castigated and shunned by the mainstream. Many were dismissed as mystics or mad. A number were killed because of their beliefs and research. The armored human character could not learn the truth about their species. Other species, having adopted similar armor, had similar problems. To learn this all embracing truth, would evoke a fear and a recognition that there are no boundaries. The species adopted or evolved artificially created cognitive walls against this recognition. These artificial boundaries have been the source of wars and other treacherous actions among your own and many other species. In the latter part of the 22nd century on Terra, we watched as your planet was almost destroyed by wars over these boundaries. There is one thing all intelligent species have in common. Those species evolving the technology to explore space evolve

74

a progressively increasing development of what you would term neural nets. With the evolving neural nets or sophistication of civilization, as you might understand it, came an equivalent evolution of means to suppress the advanced understanding. Many different species attempted solutions to the emergence of this cognitive and organismic armoring. However, only the Da'yoni succeeded by evolving into EMF signatures, foregoing the physical body.

As Susan and Derral continued experiencing the melding of consciousness, a dim awareness emerged. They both were coming to see the source of historical difficulties encountered in their species and others who have been in conflict.

Frightening at the raw truth, isn't it? thought Derral.

I'm having trouble processing it all, thought Susan. They began to settle in to this melding and total lack of protection from the thoughts and experiences of others. Do you feel this melting sensation, much like when we first made love years ago?

Yes mam, thought Derral. It's hard to admit but I almost forgot what it was like. This is like making love to thousands at the same time.

If this is what true democracy is, I can see why our civilization has been in such turmoil over the centuries, remarked Susan.

Eurdf continued. That is what most from other civilizations have concluded when experiencing the Da'yoni Crennium. Our species have existed since the initial formation of the galaxies. Our viewers or what your species refers to as astrophysicists, anthropologists and astronomers have determined that the Da'yoni were one of the first among all the galactic societies to evolve technology. As our unique forms evolved, we have been able to travel across temporal space and view most other galactic societies from their inception. Our ongoing research has enabled our society to develop the EMF form as an alternative to physicality so that we can function in this fair and egalitarian way, absent of the conflict that has pervaded other physical cultures like yours. It has also enabled us to travel the galaxies and acquire knowledge, unhindered by temporal or space constraints.

Derral thought: I believe both of us are very interested in taking back some of these amazing advances in communication to our species. We then might have an opportunity...The signature of Eurdf interrupted Derral's thought.

This is the very reason our ambassador made the agreement with your Secretary of the Holders, to have you transported here. While he did not inform the Secretary of our purpose, we all had hoped that you would request it, as you appeared to be more congruent and sensitive than many of the others of your species. Certainly more sensitive and less self-serving than your relatives or the Holders as a group.

What do you mean, agreement? We're not aware of any agreement made with my pater, thought Susan.

I beg your forgiveness. We had assumed that you were informed. It was our error. We had taken it for granted that your pater would have informed you of the transfer of the credits to his secure accounts as a gift in permitting you and your partner to be with us, said Eurdf. His thought tone had noticeably softened, as if he was experiencing sadness at having to disclose the information.

No, we were never informed, thought Derral. In fact we were notified by holo that such a trip for our New Years Eve was available, albeit it was limited to one or two people. We applied, as did many. Only later did we discover that Susan's pater had influenced the granting of the trip.

Never did we know that my pater had set this up for us to begin with, to enrich his coffers. We're certainly grateful for your information, though.

I think our sense of the character of your pater is even clearer than before, thought Derral with a constriction in his wave form.

Yes, thought Susan as she rapidly changed colors, signifying embarrassment. The Crennium members around her began to shimmer in unison. This had a soothing effect.

At times, we failed to recognize the level of deceit that pervades other species. Your pater asked for 10 billion credits. Our ambassador concluded the agreement to transfer 5 billion to his secure accounts. As we have no use for monetary value on Da'yoni, we did not appreciate the nature and extent of what was happening. However, after a recent study of your historical genetic memory and records, we recognized our error. Especially what the value of having a large amounts of credits in one's possession is. At the time our ambassador was not all that familiar with the intricacies of your society, so we did not appreciate the significance of such an arrangement, especially its effect on your government.

Well, yes, thought Derral. Five billion credits is enough to buy a major controlling interest in at least one, if not more of the major technological businesses on our planet. Once a controlling interest is gained, the person who has the interest can direct the nature of the business for his or her own political or personal ends. There are currently only a few of our species who have accumulated more than a billion credits. If you've reviewed our history, you know that one credit, in old Terra pre-Holder terms was worth a million dollars. Perhaps only a few hundred thousand of our people are wealthy enough to possess more than a few hundred credits in their personal accounts. Most of our species live out their lives, rather comfortably, with luxury lodging of their choice of what is available, free food and clothing, free education, and medical, without earning more than 1/10th credit per annum. Most invest their extra credits. Recent advances in our economy, from trading relationships permits that.

Yes, we realize that now, communicated Eurdf. While it was never our intent to interfere in the workings of your society, the transfer was made at the time of your transmission here. The error cannot now be reversed. We hope that you will have enough influence on your society when you return to prevent the injudicious use of the credits by your pater. That is why we decided to permit your retention of a fuller range of sensate ability in your human form, along with some of the more stable Holder relatives. Our technicians have recently refined the EMF transformation process and have tested it thoroughly. It should prove quite safe.

Derral's scientific curiosity was stimulated. How could you test it without one of our species as a subject? Eurdf's signature responded. We have developed specific holographic models of your species, refined to the molecular level. Our Viewers began the process when we first had contact with your exploration team, many revolutions ago. With each subsequent contact we were able to enhance the model. If you recall, when you first began the transformation process to EMF, our technician directed you to walk down the metalicized corridor. During that walk, not only were your organisms being adjusted for the EMF transformation but our sensors were storing data from your molecular structure. The latest modification was assisted with data from your own structures. So it is not just one of your species, it is an accumulation of many of your organisms that we have used to develop the process...quite safe, indeed.

Susan felt a bit squeamish, reflected in her shimmer. The group surrounding her shimmered, again, in unison. A soothing wave washed over her when she spontaneously understood that the data gained from their intrusiveness was used to help and not, as many at home would have done, used for malicious purposes. What felt like a multitude of voices now commanded their attention.

Eurdf interrupted her thought stream. Your Terran university studies on exobiology did not prepare you for this level, as our contact with your species has only just begun.

But now, we must begin the Crennium assembly, as we have important decisions to make. The assembly shimmered in unison. The first deliberation was proposed by our central spoke at last gathering. The essence of the proposal: Do we continue to share Da'yoni technology with other species, knowing that it has the potential to alter their development. Our friends from the spiral galaxy, our visitors in the current instance, will take back our sensate technology when they are transformed back into their physical natures. Our ambassador to their planet, erred in making an agreement with their leader, physically related to one of our visitors, to transfer a medium of exchange to his private seats of exchange, in exchange for us permitting a visit by our gracious visitors. Our initial analyses of their historical records had confirmed that these two of their species have evolved in a way that is slightly different from many of their species. They have developed certain beliefs in the value of truth and ethics, similar to our culture. Be that as it may, though, if we transfer the technology to their forms, it bears the potential of further altering development in their civilization. The valence of such alteration, given these two of their species, is certainly positive. But the question is, do we permit this to happen? It will represent a further intrusion into another species culture. Let us now adjust our fields for the decision.

The whole assembly shimmered, mostly in unison and at the same frequency. The feeling impression received by Derral and Susan recalled the tender melting sensations.

The same voice continued. Apparently, we still have a small segment of disagreement. But the overwhelming decision is to proceed as planned. Perhaps the Da'yoni place in the interstellar community is to promote positive change. This seems to be the direction we have been moving in, in your time concept for the past 1000 revolutions around your star, or a thousand of Terra years. The assembly shimmered in unison. Susan and Derral's thoughts were unified, now. The sensate transformation was accomplished at the instant the decision was made. They both experienced the same definitive change in their field signatures.

This feels like a further melting, almost a total opening and trusting, thought Susan.

Yes, it's like for the first time we can open up to each other...trusting that there will be no deception. Our existence is unfortunately driven by deception. Most people will speak in such a way that will maximize their opportunities. Honesty is not a top priority. We've had discussions about this before, but it never appeared as prominent a feature of existence until now, thought Derral.

Susan shimmered as she responded. I can see, now, how much of our lives were influenced by the fear of deception or mistrust of other's intentions. Our whole social experience is based on trying to discern the truth from deception. I remember pater talking about the micro fly technology. The governments use of them to eves drop on those who dissent or disagree with the mainstream...a modern version of the early 20th Century purges from different governments. I never paid it any mind.

I studied the historical holos on my work sojourns, to pass the boring travel time, thought Derral. The records indicate, one of those government leaders, Josef Stalin, murdered hundreds of thousands. Your pater, in his turn, exiled many thousands to mining planets, many for the remainder of their lives. Not unlike previous historical oppressors, he had the courts declare them as deviants, so as to labor for the Holders while earning only a bare subsistence. Centuries ago, the newly forming colonies in what was the country of America exacted similar strategies from those having a higher melanin content in their skin. They were easily identified and enslaved as workers to increase wealth. In fact, the old America was founded about 600 revolutions ago to preserve the very lucrative traffic in human beings, referred to as the slave trade, when the rest of the planet was beginning to object. Holonet reporter's investigations similarly uncovered that a percentage of profit from the mining planets went into Holder private accounts in return for the cheap labor of those exiled. The only crime of the "deviants" was that they worked at exposing the Holder greed and secret alliances. Though no proof was ever presented, as most exiles were a result of Holder fiat.

Eurdf interjected. Yes, we have seen such figures in your historical records. However, but know that with our gift to you, you both will be able to see deceit as it occurs in the thought planes of others of your species. It is not what you would refer to as a reading of the others thoughts. It is a direct knowing of what the other is thinking and planning for the long term. This is more valuable than mere thought reading. At first you will be startled at the clarity of the process. However with practice, seeing will become second nature. You will decide what to do with these gifts. Some of our visitors sought isolation. We believe you will use it wisely and discreetly. Discreetly, because we would not want others to know. It would lead to severe and unnecessary animosity. Your history teaches you what actions the mainstream took against your gifted ones. Did not your Copernicus meet his end when subjected to that barbaric ritual of being burned at the stake because he disagreed with the mystical beliefs of those in power by citing a fact derived from his own science? The Crennium debated whether to intervene, then, but decided your evolution as a species, was too important to interfere with based solely on mistaken mystical or religious beliefs and persecution. Did not your Wilhelm Reich who defined the energetic process of your being, die in prison and be declared a mad man, by those in his healing profession. They were most threatened with his correct ideas? We had a particular interest in him because of his study of bioenergy. It was unfortunate his health was compromised, as we expected him to continue his thrust into reality based research, once released. His followers, unfortunately misconstrued and distorted his discoveries. Similar beings who were advanced from the common element were accorded similar fates, were they not?

Derral thought, if you did intervene with Copernicus, a whole segment of scientific research may have advanced, more rapidly.

While that may be so, our tracking of development of human and other galactic species taught us that certain truths must take time to unfold, so that the species can readily accept them, thought Eurdf, as his tone took on a different felt seriousness and intensity.

Always be cautious. We strongly advise you not to discuss the gift or its workings, with each other aloud, unless you are absolutely assured of privacy. A component of your new sensitivity will signal you that privacy is assured. But even then, it is best to communicate only in thought. We are not sure that mutual sub-vocalization can occur in your atmosphere. That remains to be seen. If you can sub-vocalize, only discuss your new abilities on this level. We certainly advise against sharing the nature of the gift with other beings on your planet, regardless of how close you may feel with them. This will provide you a climate of maximum safety from which to negotiate your changes at the highest levels of your civilization. We are sure you both understand the full implication of what you are receiving and bringing back to your home world. We do not believe you are naive but we must caution that if you read another's thought plan, do not advise them directly of it. For if you were to do this with your species, word would soon get out that you have acquired some vision...and it would most likely be attributed to your stay on Da'yoni.

Both Susan and Derral shimmered in unity for some moments. Their thoughts, joined in synthesis with their Da'yoni EMF signatures, transcended time. They rapidly moved through their life experiences and simultaneously projected into the future. Both saw themselves arriving home but seemed blocked from proceeding further with this line of thinking.

Eurdf interjected again. I'm afraid the ability to simultaneously project into the future is limited. We purposely inserted this limitation, as we believe it transcends the boundary of our intentions. In fact only those in the higher echelons of Da'yoni community...what you would call metaphysicians... possess this ability.

Derral responded: What you have given us will radically alter the political game. We are most grateful and eager to return to Terra so we can begin. Neither of us care for the negative direction that our society has devolved into.

We have anticipated your eagerness. We know of your relationship with Derral's long term friend, the chief of Solar security. We have scanned his intentions and trust him, as do you. You may safely share what you learned with him, if you feel comfortable in doing so. The transport chamber is being primed as we communicate. We Da'yoni are indebted to you for allowing us the experience of your beings. We will be ready to transport in 200 centares...a little more than two of your Terra hours. In the meantime you can explore our world. We have taken liberty to upload a schematic of our planet into your EMF field. Remember, in EMF, you can instantaneously travel to any place on the planet by merely thinking of the location. So what you can see in 200 centares will seem like many days in normal human form. We will signal you just before the transport is ready so you can return to your chambers for the journey.

Many voices simultaneously: We all wish you good steed, knowing that you will use our gift with wisdom.

Susan and Derral also thought with one voice. But where to begin, that is the question.

The signature of Eurdf responded. You must certainly return to your normal duties. While our gift will enable you to rapidly rise into the upper echelons of power on your world, you must never push. Let your rise in power come from a natural unfolding. When our ambassador begins to make regular visits, you will find natural opportunities to meet with him. He will be able to clarify any concerns and questions. But again, you must communicate only in thought with him, never aloud, in public. In public, probably the most secure way would be to turn away from him and communicate. He will be expecting you to do so and will not feel disrespected. However his cycle of visitations will not begin for two cycles of your moon. Until then, you will be occupied with much new learning.

Susan and Derral responded with a unified shimmer. At that instant, they found themselves out on the planet's surface beneath the unusual multicolored sky. For the next few hours, they learned to hop around to different parts of the surface, noticing the strange flora and very weird looking animals, some with what looked like heads at both ends of their bodies. Some looked like hairless, upright apes with skin that shimmered in the light. Multicolored flying creatures approached them as if they were curious. They returned to their temporary quarters, when signaled.

Words could never describe this, thought Derral.

Susan shimmered at what would usually be considered an attempt at humor, but knowing Derral, he would miss it as such unless she pointed to it. She began thinking about what she always was amused at, his concrete way of viewing the world.

Now, my dear, know that I know what you are thinking. What you see as concrete is actually my approach to avoid confusion and ask for clarity. That was a style developed from many years of experience communicating with other species, without risking embarrassing them, thought Derral.

I guess I always misperceived you in that way. Since we've been together I often felt irritated at your concrete way of relating to emotional things, but have learned to become amused. I was wrong. Now, I can sense your emotional changes, much better.

Derral responded. What do you mean?

Oh, nothing much, thought Susan, feigning sarcasm. I was just thinking about what an unusual character you are and how this process makes you even more unique. I find myself wondering if this new awareness will affect us in any negative way. It's beyond imagination. We'll no longer be speculating about an individual's honesty or dishonesty. As long as we keep the ultimate goal in mind: the elimination of the Holder's deception and the reinstitution of the rule of honesty and altruism governing decisions affecting society. If Eurdf's word rings true, we can enable an overturning of the old guard within a revolution around our star, she jested. I'm even talking like them now. We can do this within a year.

I still have my reservations about believing another species like we have been led to, given experience around the different galactic personalities I've met. Believing them in opposition to our own species is something else, altogether, said Derral.

Yes, if his word is true and not just a tactic to infiltrate our system with some undetectable bio device, with us as a carrier, Susan replied with a dull vibration. I kind of don't think so, though. It all feels so right.

But then again, maybe that's just part of the deception, said Derral, with the same dull vibration in his field.

They both felt a shimmer of a different nature.

The energy of Eurdf was present. Ah, it must be the galactic spiral you are from that resists what we give you. But then again, perhaps it is just as well that you do not accept without question. But, now we must bid adieu. The chamber is prepared. The return voyage will be much quicker.

They instantaneously transferred to the transport chamber. Without a sound, they felt a tearing of their molecular structure. Their physical bodies were reformed from the EMF signatures. In what seemed like an instant, both were back in Terran space. They sat for a long time and stared at each other, speechless.

Poor Albert Einstein, if he only knew we overturned his theories a thousand times, he'd jump out of his grave thought Derral.

Chapter Eight

Returning

As the Holders commenced the traditional New Years Day transmission to the citizens, subtle changes were being made in the power structure. General Suddhis and his allies had coalesced their forces over the past few days. The Secretary was monitoring their movements. However, he was not aware of the power sharing agreement that Suddhis and his cohort, Oice, made with the Eastern quadrant. The Eastern contingent had joined Suddhis' forces and inserted themselves in government buildings surrounding the Holder's offices. Suddhis was monitoring their movements from his underground compound just east of the Holders Center.

Susan's pater was immediately notified of her arrival. He hurried to the transport station below his residence to be teleported to the galactic complex to greet them. He materialized in the chamber as technicians were opening the transport tube. Susan and Derral emerged. The Secretary rushed forward to greet them with a broad smile.

"Welcome home you two. I hope the New Year brings you new knowledge," said the Secretary.

Susan embraced her pater, as she looked over his shoulder to Derral who was silently remarking about the Secretary's disingenuous. The Secretary's immediate thoughts, they both sensed, were focused on the political fodder he could gain by their unusual visit. He hoped they would provide him with a new technology that would enable him to further aggrandize power and defeat his enemies among the other Holders. Susan, troubled at this new awareness, noticeably stiffened.

The Secretary held her at arms length. "What is the trouble Susan, my dear. Didn't the trip agree with you?"

She looked down in embarrassment, but remembered the caution from the Eurdf. "I must admit, getting back to physical form is rather strange, pater. I haven't been touched like this since we were transformed. Sorry, about my reaction," said Susan.

"Oh?...but yes my dear, that is quite all right. While I have no idea what your experience was like in that domain, I really never did, as you grew up...so what's new," said the Secretary, with a rare attempt at humor.

Susan and Derral laughed spontaneously, given the rare truth in the Secretary's expression.

"Please accompany me to my domicile. I've arranged a small reception for both your relatives and some friends," said the Secretary. Susan and Derral immediately translated his expression to: I've arranged a small reception with your relatives, friends, and a few of my agents so that we might discover details of what you learned from the Da'yoni.

Derral spoke first. "I think we would like to go to our domicile, first, so that we can get grounded again, if you know what I mean. This new transformation has been a bit stressful. We would need a few hours."

"Yes, pater," said Susan. "We don't feel like we've been alone since the start of our voyage. The Da'yoni were always with us, or could tune in on our energy transmissions at will. We never felt alone. We do need a few hours together before joining you. I hope that is not an inconvenience." They both sensed the conflicting vibrations of her pater, fluctuate between anger and frustration as he spoke the opposite.

"Why that would be quite alright. It is now 45 minutes past first light. Why not come over at 45 minutes post zenith? That would give you about six solar hours for your "grounding." I'll direct the guests to come back at that time," replied the Secretary as his demeanor exhibited only a slight irritation that he couldn't disguise. Susan and Derral saw the meaning of his expression to say that they were quite impertinent and interfering with his plans. Both nodded in the affirmative but had difficulty saying anything, due to the vast difference between his words and their true experience of the undercurrent of his meaning.

Derral spoke in deference. "Thank you sir. We really do need the time to acclimate ourselves. Later on, when we'll try to describe, how amazingly different this experience was from our normal physical forms, you'll understand why we need this time."

Susan spoke quickly to assuage the suspicious nature they both detected. "You see pater, it is so different than human experience that it is difficult to explain in words. We've tried with each other, when on Da'yoni, but lacked the words to describe it. It is much different than teleportation. Teleportation is instantaneous, with no awareness. The EMF state is continuous."

"I see," said the Secretary. "We will look forward to the details of your journey, this afternoon." He turned to leave through the entry portal and dissolved. Derral and Susan both read each others internal sigh of relief and smiled. They were both surprised that their new ability was enabled so soon. They thought it would take some time to adjust.

A holo of a technician approached Susan and Derral. "We will need you to come through our decontamination chamber. We will need you to go through our procedures prior to further contact. To allay any questions, the Secretary was shielded by his personal containment field, a security measure for high government officials. If you follow me, it will only take a minute or two." As they walked behind the technician down a long metallic tube with a gold like finish, they felt the probes. The technician led them to a portal at the end of the tube. " Please enter here. This is the final stage... an ionic shower, to remove any alien matter you may have picked up on your travels. Simply walk through the tube and exit the door on the far side. I will await you there, in real form." They walked slowly through the ionic shower.

"Ahh, a most refreshing ending to our journey," said Derral, aloud. On a subvocal level that only Susan could hear he said: You think they would inform us of the probing. At least the Da'yoni did. I'm beginning to see how very right Eurdf was about our society.

Susan similarly replied, verbally, "We should get one of these showers," but subvocally said: No wonder there is no trust...no honesty left in our world...no wonder everyone is straddling for positions of power and exploiting any other who might be of use, regardless of friendship or family ties. I'm ashamed of my pater...and ashamed of myself for being so gullible all these years.

Derral subvocally responded. We have a job now, to change all that. I think the reception, this afternoon, is an ideal starting point. I'm sure most of who is important to the Secretary will be there.

Perhaps a few of his Holder cronies, responded Susan. And maybe some of his enemies for, political reasons. This should be a good starting point to learn the truth from both sides.

Yeah, but remember Eurdf's caution, thought Derral. We must proceed very slowly and do nothing to tip our hand. We can use this first meeting as a learning experience of what is to come...and perhaps, subtly influence certain individuals to meet with us again.

They both dressed and entered the exit tube onto the tarmac. The tech directed them to their autoflyer. On the way back they sensed micro flys in the cockpit with them. They talked about the difference in the terrain and Da'yoni terrain, but subvocally continued their discussion of the nature of the society.

Susan thought, I would never have expected pater to bug his own family. But then I would never expect him to lie to us either. Not answer a question, but never would I expect him to out and out lie.

I know, thought Derral. Even with the little respect I had for him, I would never believe him to be dishonest with us. It is disturbing...and it looks like our job is cut out for us.

For the long haul, thought Susan. It's beginning to seem overwhelming already...before we even get started. The autoflyer docked in their domicile port. As it nosed up to the docking port, the grav generators stopped and their autoflyer dropped into the holding clamps. The cockpit opened to the hallway outside their residence. As they entered through the front portal, both noticed the presence of more microflys.

Susan thought, in exasperation, I wonder when we'll have a moment of relief from this intrusion. I wonder how much of this was going on before we were aware of it, she thought in anger.

Derral reminded her of the security devices he had installed, because of his work function in the mining program. When activated, these would transmit a false loop to all microfly transmission within 100 meters of their location. He waved his hand in front of the control panel and turned them on. This is a perfectly normal use of the device. No one will question it, as it was provided by the Holders for the security of the off world mining operations. Remember, I was told to activate it whenever we entered the domicile, thought Derral, with a wry smile.

If we could only get rid of them. I don't like the feeling of their disgusting presence, even if they are deactivated. I don't know if I can get use to subvocalizing with you, she thought, smiling.

We could vaporize them all. Although that would certainly raise the level of suspicion, responded Derral. Best to speak subvocally, if we have anything important to discuss.

Chapter Nine

The First Real Journey

Ulemann was absent mindedly watching the fly holos. There was first a blink and then just static. He sat bolt upright and adjusted the projection. This was followed a few seconds later by a blank holo. He adjusted the holo dials to send in others that were lingering outside the building but could no longer get a fix. "They're either jamming them or vaporized them," he said. He looked up Susan and Derral in the database to see what technology they are licensed. "Oh, shit," exclaimed Ulemann, as he saw Derral's name appear with a license to block transmission and vaporize microfly devices from Confederation Mining.

He immediately called his boss. Secretary Priestly appeared on the holo, looking annoyed.

"What is it, Ulemann. I am busy preparing for the reception of my two important family members."

"I am sorry to bother you sir, but I wanted to alert you that Derral is licensed to block and vaporize fly technology, as a result of his association with Confederation Mining."

"Why the hell is he licensed for that?" snapped the Secretary.

"As you know, sir, his work for Confederation requires that he handle very sensitive data regarding our off world mining operations. That is a legitimate reason, I'm sorry to say. He just blocked the flys as they entered, but did not vaporize them."

"Well, that's just wonderful. Fortunately, I'll be able to induce him to speak about his discoveries, as an interested family member. Both he and Susan's liberal bent includes a trust of all those close to them. Sorry to use them this way, but my future is at stake, as you know. Now, get back to work monitoring the others who are not licensed. And work on a way of rescinding his license without his knowledge. Report to me before 13:00. I want to know what to expect before my little reception begins."

"As you wish sir." The transmission ended. Ulemann busied himself calling up other data sets and live holos. The Secretary turned towards his security bot, Ronald. "I want you to scan everyone that enters today, so that there are no recording devices. Also scan for flys. By now we're probably not the only faction to have this technology. When my daughter and her mate appear, see to it that they are never without drinks. If they won't drink alcohol, then offer them some with sativa, that herb. Their liberal persuasions will not permit them to turn that down. I want them to be as loose as possible. There will also be some folk from the Solar Intelligence Community here. Keep an eye on them. They'll all have recorders. But I want you to tell them to check them at the door, due to the presence of the Holders. Keep your recorder open. Record all conversations with my daughter and her mate. Also record the movements of the Intelligence folk.

The Secretary holoed Ulemann again. As he appeared in holo, the Secretary said, Bring your escort, your artificial sex partner.

"What?" I tried to keep that secret, Mr. Secretary, as it was a private thing."

"Well, my good man, I found out about that when I transported to your domicile one evening, to discuss a pressing issue, and heard strange sounds, as I was about to request entrance. After that I asked our Intelligence Service to ascertain what you do in your off hours. I know she is a mode 15 security bot, a perfect human replica. Program her to monitor the other Holders conversations, as she blends in. You needn't pay attention to them."

"Forgive that I take offense, sir, but I..."

"Listen, Ulemann, don't worry about it. I value your experience, in spite of your strange morals," said the Secretary, with a wry grin.

"Well, okay sir. I can accept that, said Ulemann, but his thoughts were very different.

***

Susan and Derral were in the stim bath. At that moment, Derral's holocon alerted him. His ret viewer visualized Robert. Pressing the small protuberance under his chin to encrypt the transmission, Derral nudged Susan to also tune in.

"Well, hello my friend, said Robert Laing. I hope your journey finds you well and the Da'yoni were unable to detect the bio anti-scanning device?"

"I don't know what they detected, to tell you the truth. They never mentioned a thing. But what are you talking about, my friend."

"Oh. I'm sorry. I'll transmit the hypno signal to restore your memory. Give me a sec." The holo depixelated for the briefest moment

"I see now. But what an amazing experience. We were actually living as EMF signatures for a few days. We can't find the words to describe it."

Robert laughed. "That's what the others said. However, you seem to be faring a lot better than they were. I'll be at your reception in my official capacity as Intelligence Community Chief. I don't think the Secretary or his allies are aware of our relationship. So I'll be quite formal. Make like it is the first time we met. I'll ask if you and Susan would like to tour our facility...and of course you will agree. It will give us an opportunity for a few drinks and talk about old times. I couldn't risk it, at this point, without that premise."

Susan sub-vocalized to Derral. Don't you want to tell him about some of the details?

Derral responded: No. As good a friend as he is, he is still susceptible to interrogation. In fact if he doesn't know, that will be the best cover for us, regardless of what the Da'yoni said about his trustworthiness. We don't want to compromise him, at least not yet.

Robert looked puzzled at the silence.

"Seems like you two are lost in each other. I'm sorry for bothering at this time. I'll see you at the party. Bye Susan."

Susan adjusted her retinal viewer. "Bye Robert. Thanks for being sensitive to us. Yes, I'll see you then." The retinal viewers blanked.

Derral continued sub-vocalizing. It makes me feel real bad to not trust one of my most trusted friends.

Susan responded. It's not that you don't trust him. What we've been given will hopefully change the tenor of our times, for the better. Eurdf cautioned us against disclosure. That was the contract we made. We're just honoring our agreement to the Da'yoni.

I suppose so, said Derral, as he audibly sighed.

"Lets get moving, as pater will be annoyed if we're too late, Okay?" said Susan.

"I'm ready, my dear. It's you who needs to have the bot check and redo your makeover. I'm just a natural kind of guy, you know...no frills?"

"Derral, please. No frills? Then why do you often stand in front of the biosym for untold minutes, watching your cellular structure fluctuate and change? It's as if you are looking for a cell that is out of place."

"I do that because I want to continue to be healthy to match your superior feminine structure...dear," said Derral, with a touch of sarcasm.

"All right...let's get out of this mode," said Susan. She continued, subvocally. Did you realize that we switched back and forth between sub-vocalizing.

It's becoming so natural and effortless I didn't realize I was, thought Derral. I think we need to be careful in public so that we don't lapse into that without realizing it. Both you and I make facial expressions, as if we are talking. If someone were to be watching us, they'd probably think we're both crazy. Besides, we need to concentrate on always interspacing it with supercilious talk. If anyone was watching they'd just think we're too boring to listen to. There sure will be a lot of people watching us, this afternoon...a lot of people with all sorts of agendas and intentions.

At least now we'll know what they are, thought Derral, subvocally, as he turned off the biosym. This will be our first real journey...be interesting to see if we don't get jammed up with all the incoming discrepancies with the true impressions.

Susan stepped in front of Derral and turned the biosym on. Her cellular structure was projected into the life sized holo before them. "Sorry to interrupt but, not too bad, for an old hag, wouldn't you say?"

Not too bad, thought Derral. His thoughts drifted to another plane where he believed Susan could not follow...his sanctuary. He thought in images. Arcane images from his travels to the system of multicolored planets around Hamal in Aries where he thought he'd like to live. He dreamed of this frequently. It was when he was most dissatisfied with Susan's banter that he went there.

So that's what you do, thought Susan. I wondered. I know I have a tendency to talk a lot. But now you can't get away. They both laughed.

"Woman certainly have a way of framing things," joked Derral.

"Just be careful where you're going with that, big boy," said Susan. They turned towards each other and hugged. Both felt the same melting sensation experienced in the EMF form.

Wow, I thought we could only experience that in EMF. Another unrealized benefit.

Yeah, but don't say that out loud, my dear. I felt it and also felt your feeling of it, too.

Amazing. Must be some carryover with the consciousness transform. Probably has something to do with the way the Da'yonis make love, if they do engage in that primitive activity, thought Susan, with a wry smile.

You know, they never mentioned anything about that, did you notice? said Derral.

Yeah. I wondered, but did not feel comfortable prying too much, said Susan.

"Lets get a move on. We must not make Daddy angry," said Derral.

"Daddy?" Susan look puzzled. "Daddy? I haven't heard that expression since mater passed."

Derral smiled. "I know. I wondered why you never used it. I know it's an artifact. I read everything in the cyber archives about our past history and watched all the old vids up until the present, during my travels to the mining planets. Nothing else to do."

"Hmm. You never mentioned that," said Susan. "Each time you returned from a long journey, we got occupied in other things. Is that why?"

"I suppose. After being away from you for a few weeks or so, those other things became paramount. Just never thought it would interest you... as I did it to stave off the boredom when not suspended," said Derral.

"Just when I think I know all there is to know about you, including your thoughts, there's always something new that comes along. But enough for the mushy stuff," said Susan.

"Lets move, my dear. I'll get the transport ready. Your pater said we would need a military escort coming in, for security purposes. I'll call and let him know we're about ready to leave," said Derral.

94

They entered the transport and signaled the central virtual databank of their destination. The transport slowly backed out of the building notch and entered the flow of traffic. As soon as they reached the traffic speed, they were signaled.

The transmission was audible, only. "Good afternoon. I'm Major Dennings, I was assigned to escort you to the Secretary at the Capital Towers complex. I'll be to your starboard all the way." Both Susan and Derral looked to their right and waved at the Major. Derral was surprised to see a class Five, heavily armed atmospheric fighter.

"Thanks, Major," said Derral. "Pretty serious vessel you have there, a Five. Should we be concerned?"

"I don't think so Colonel Priestly. But we do take precautions. I see you know your military configs?"

"Yes, I piloted an Eight astral fighter, in the Venusian conflict, many years ago. Remember about those mineral rights which we claim?"

"How could I forget?" said the Major.

"About how long, given the patterns at this time of day, Major? We're not used to traveling to that part of town," said Derral

"Oh, we should be there within the half. I'll contact you again, just before we come out of pattern," said the Major. And by the way, Colonel, I also piloted an Eight in that action, with the fleet. I'm surprised we don't know each other. What a bunch of disorganized idiots they were."

"You got that right...good for our side. I jumped to Venus from the Moon and was not assigned to the fleet, but ran quick strikes. See you there," said Derral, as the holo image blinked off.

Chapter Ten

The Illusion of A Plot

General Suddhis paced back and forth in front of his blank holo. Rakard Oice sat in the corner of the room looking at the live holomap of their fly distributions.

"Well, what do you find, Oice," grumbled the General. "Do we have a go or do we fail again?"

"It appears that Cursard was right," replied Oice, looking up from the holo in front of him.

"Wait before you say any more, you imbecile. Activate that disabler he gave us so Priestly's flys don't pick us up, if they're here."

Oice grimaced and moved towards the console. He waved his hand to activate the device and made some adjustments. "There, now we can talk, your excellency."

"Give up the sarcasm or I'll transfer you to one of my mines in the outer rim," said the General.

"As you wish sir. It appears that Cursard's vid was accurate. The Secretary had 5 billion credits deposited in a numbered Venusian account by an anonymous donor, just after he met with the Da'yoni Ambassador and arranged to have his bio child travel to Da'yoni with that seething liberal lifemate of hers. I don't even know why they allowed him in the service. His beliefs are so out of touch with our time. You can bet our honorable Secretary will use every means to extract whatever it is they learned from that visit. Perhaps we can befriend them, after all. I mean we were invited to their reception, an ideal time to extend an invitation," said Oice.

"It is fortunate, for you, that you have skills. You're not as much of a fool as you seem sometimes, Oice. I think we need to focus on your strategy. We also have our own agents at that reception. They might be able to provide some assistance in that direction, by planting ideas in the young couple regarding our sincerity. Those agents are respected professors from the University, just like the Secretary's biologue. Amazing how one can even buy off "ethical" academics with a few well placed credits for their pet projects. People whom a liberal would trust without question. In fact they might even know her," said General Suddhis, with a smirk.

"Thank you General," said Oice, with an exaggerated deference. "Sometimes I react poorly when you insult me. I know you don't mean it. We should begin to alert our plants in the Holder Center. The Eastern contingent, if running as planned, should be in place and waiting for activation. We'll need a few more weeks to firm things up. Then we'll release the data on the Secretary. After that, you must convene an emergency Holders commune to discuss the fate of our beloved Secretary."

"I can't wait," responded the General, rubbing his palms. "When we get that idiot out of there...no more problems with decision making and power. We'll have all the power and make all the decisions. Besides, prior to his exit, we'll make a motion in the Holders commune to demand the 5 billion credits he accepted from the Da'yoni and distribute it to public works projects to gain the people's confidence. Of course the projects will be assigned to our private holdings for construction. Oh, I just can't wait for this. It's just too good..."

Oice interrupted. "That may be so, sir. But, we must be as careful as always, to maintain our discrete distance from such projects. If word of that were to reach the public, I wouldn't want to imagine the consequences. It could mean a one way trip to a Corrections asteroid in the Andromeda system, at the very least."

"Yes Oice, you...I'm well aware of that. I wasn't born yesterday. If we don't talk, there'll be no record. The credits from our current holdings go right into sham corporation accounts, 100 times removed from any trace to us. We need to keep your big mouth shut, don't we?" said the General.

"Thank you for withholding another insult, my General," said Oice.

The General smirked and looked back at the blank holo viewer, signaling the console with a hand gesture. "Where in the underworld is that criminal Cursard. He was supposed to secure a transmission, well over an hour ago."

At that moment, Solais Cursard was hunched over a large holoboard, making adjustments. His Jovians were standing by the door, blaster rifles at the ready. "Just a few more minutes, boys. Then well be able to tune in at will. Keep an eye out your viewport. If any one enters the outer portal vaporize them."

"Ho boss. Be right nice to see last flicker in vape," said Grancha, the larger of the two Jovians.

"Me breathe it in, Gro. Last two revs ago," said Bocha.

"Too long," said Grancha as he smacked his foot wide lips.

"Just don't get trigger happy, boys. If we aren't detected here, the more credits well get from those morons, Suddhis and Oice. Just a few moments... There. Lets get out of here."

The three came together in the center of the room in the basement of the Secretary's complex. The bots, usually occupying the room, were engaged in preparing for the Secretary's gathering in the domicile. Cursard activated the transporter. The three materialized in Cursard's secure complex at the abandoned space port.

"We did good boys. Now, when those dolts speak in there, where they think they're secure, well record every moment. Good for some street cred."

"Mo, boss," said the Jovians, simultaneously, as they both smacked their lip flaps.

"You know boys, you remind me of some others on our planet. Centuries ago we had primitive aboriginals who put plates in their lips. I always thought that was pretty ugly."

"What you say boss. That insult? We dis way because grav on Jup," said Grancha.

"Okay," said Cursard. "I was only trying to make a joke. Sensitive aren't we?"

"We vape insultors, wouldn't be first time," said Bocha.

"I'm sorry boys. Lighten up will you? Remember, if you vape me you're out...how many credits?" snickered Cursard.

At that moment, the General and Oice came back into the Generals office. The General gestured over the panel to activate the security console, as Cursard watched through his holo. He sat back in his chair and smiled. "Ah the wonders of Grametian technology. I'm so glad to have run into those uglies in our last galactic search. It's consistent with the general stupidity that the Confederation has not had much to do with the Grametes. Passed over them because they were too offensive looking. Little did they know how evolved their technos were."

"They mo stunk," boss, said the Jovian.

"Yes, but it was well worth it to wear nose filters for a few days, wasn't it now?" replied Cursard, with a smile as he fine tuned the system to take in the whole of the Generals office.

"Mo right boss."

Cursard waved a hand in front of his holoviewer, the General's face appeared. "Sorry, I didn't connect earlier, General. We had some work to take care of. So, I'm hoping you viewed the disc I sent?"

"Very well Cursard. Are you certain this link is secure?" said the General.

"The most secure link on the planet, General. Just to be on the safe side, don't speak any specifics. What you were asking for is in place. But that's going to cost you some more credits. We took a big risk just installing it. We can move whenever you deposit the "fee" and give the word. But, we must have a go in the next few revolutions. The moon cycle changes to new in five revs. The personnel are automatically rotated," said Cursard, with a feigned air of seriousness.

"I resent you trying to bleed us, Cursard," said the General.

Cursard smirked. "Having a link into the Secretary's security is not worth a few thousand credits? If not I'm sure we can find another willing buyer. Perhaps one of your Holder enemies."

"Cursard, you're scum."

"Thank you for the complement, General. That's what you're paying me for, isn't it? So when do we go?"

"I'm not sure we can move that fast, said Oice, looking over the General's shoulder We must prepare the public news release and then wait for the reaction. Depending on what the Secretary's reaction is, will determine how quick we can move."

The General turned away from the holo to Oice. "Look...I don't care what you need to do. We have to coordinate this before the cycle changes or we'll have no one in place."

"As you wish General. I will do what I can to set it up," said Oice.

"Do what you can? What do you mean...do what you can? You will have it ready to go. Or else...you'll find yourself back on Jupiter with no gravsuit," said the General, as he turned back to Cursard in the holo.

"Maybe you can use one of my boys to tune up your boy," said Cursard, with a snicker. He pointed at Grancha standing behind him.

"Cursard, this is not funny. I will let you know when everything is in place."

"The next contact will be 1 rev before our surprise event," said Cursard, with an exaggerated bow as the holo disappeared.

"Oice, get out of here and give me some time alone. I need to refurbish myself," said the General, with his usual irritation.

"As you wish, General," said Oice, bowing and turning towards the entrance portal with a flourish. As he went through the portal, he looked over his shoulder at the General getting ready for a holosex session. Oice shook his head in disgust.

"Begin holosex sim with Deva and Nia," he commanded the home bot. Two naked female holobots appeared before him, as he laid on the couch.

They spoke in unison: "How can we please you today, General?"

The General smiled. "You can remove my clothes, give me a massage and then the works."

"As you wish General." They moved to each side of the couch and began slowly removing the General's clothes. Virtual sim had developed the technology of inserting tactual experience in sims. When engaged in something as intense as an erotic experience, one could hardly tell the difference between sim and reality.

After a few hours, the General was found by his assistant fast asleep and naked on the couch.

"General...General Suddhis," said Rakard Oice, looking down in disgust. He nudged the General's shoulder.

"Mmumph," the General replied and opened his eyes, staring at his assistant, as if he were a stranger.

"Oice, do you remember a few years ago when representatives from my sector traveled to the outer rim to those planets in that Cluster. I don't recall the name...

Oice interjected: "The Omega Cluster. The inhabitants call themselves

100

the Shallice."

"Very well," continued the General, with an air of irritation at being once again shown up.

"Yes, the Shallician. Do you recall they shared a technology that enabled one to access the records of our genetic forebearers...and assemble a gene profile of our strong and weak points. Whatever happened to that holochip that enabled our holovids to do that?"

"I think you stored a copy of it in your personal files, General. I remember attempting to understand how to operate it and getting frustrated," said Oice, with what he perceived was the appropriate deference to take the edge off the General's irritability. It was actually the General who became frustrated and gave up.

"That holobit should still be in my files. I want to access it. I have an idea that might assist us. I need to know my genetic influences so that I can determine what I can bring forth in our plan to assume influence over the remaining Holders...after we dispense with the Secretary, of course. Find that and get out and leave me alone. I need to do some planning."

Oice found the holobit on the General's console, bowed and backed out towards the entryway. After it closed behind him, he made a hand gesture towards the portal, one he saw in old twentieth century records, with the forefinger and little finger extended with hand held sideways. The gesture, from the culture of what was once called Italy, meaning death. As much as he hated to have to relate to the general with deference, he was grateful for his assistance in his rise to a position as a Holder. What hurt him more than anything was the General's relative stupidity. Oice knew, from the start, that he was far more knowledgeable and able. The General achieved Holder status, after a series of fortuitous military actions he commanded, not from any innate intelligence. At a crucial moment in each, the worm hole to the enemies home planet collapsed, preventing them from replenishing their forces. The collapse of the dimension was one of those temporary anomalies. It was as if too much of one plane randomly leaked over into another. However, at two crucial moments it happened and favored the General's ships as they were about to be overtaken by superior fire power and the superior technology of the invading forces from a distant galaxy. Sheer luck. After this defeat, the Krakes decided to move on to other parts of the galactic cluster to make their forays for essential minerals. If they were to come back, they would surely have won the encounter. But they wrongly interpreted the almost simultaneous random dimensional collapsing as having something to do with an unknown technology possessed by the Confederation forces.

The General rose from his couch and sat before the holovid panel.

"Holo," he commanded. "Open that program from the Shallice...the psychoeugenic vid."

"As you wish, Sir," said a pleasing female voice from the holovid. The holo appeared with unrecognized language markings.

"Translate that into Solar normal, you idiot," shouted the General at the holovid.

"As you wish Sir. The holo changed to recognizable figures, directing the user to insert a piece of their hair into a tray that appeared on the table before the vid. The General took a strand of his hair and placed it on the tray.

"Thank you sir, said the holo. This will take about 15 degrees to assemble. Once assembled, sir can request any holo from genetic time to see which historical figure contained a string that evolved to your present genetic status. Please forgive the short delay, but we must assemble the records from various sources. Thank you."

"Make it quick."The General walked to the simulator. "Make me a Saturnian ringer," he said. A glass of luminescent purple sparkling liquid appeared in the simulator. "Ahh," said the General to himself, as he took a long draft of the liquid. The colors in the room become brighter. After his second sip he dozed off, awakening abruptly 45 minutes later. "Now to see if I can navigate this damn alien holo. Holo, begin projecting my genesis, whenever..."

"Yes sir, a moment more. It seems we've been able to take you back to Precambrian times.

"No," shouted the General. "I just want to know about those since civilization."

"Yes sir. Your first genic trace is found in Meletus of the Grecian City State called Athens around 399 Before the Common Era. Records are sparse. For that period we have only historical accounts. The holos you see were constructed from the historical records and are deemed as accurate as was possible for historical records of that time. As you can see in the holo, your trace, along with two of his associates accused a 70 year old citizen, named Socrates, a stonecutter by trade, of corrupting the youth of the city and professing disbelief in the ancestral gods that were worshiped by those humans. In reality, the records find the charges were a result of no wrong doing from entity Socrates. His only act was to readily express his philosophical opinions at any public occasion. He believed that it was important to focus on making the best out of living, not to focus on the differing philosophies that found disagreement among many. Meletus, your trace, was a poet. Socrates often referred to that profession with disdain. The charges against Socrates brought by Meletus and his associates were suspected to be copied from a play by another Greek, Aristophanes, occurring 20 years earlier, called *The Clouds.* That play also had a character named Socrates who was a sophist. Plato's Socrates was against the sophists. Although in the actual trial he was accused of being one. Socrates, by his unique dialectical questioning, showed up Meletus to be a fool in the trial. Socrates went on to make a mockery of the trial. The assembly narrowly convicts as a result of his mockery, not that he was guilty of anything. Socrates is sentenced to death mostly for making a mockery of the trial.

The General looked on in chagrined silence. Another case in which a genetic kin was shown up to be a fool, not unlike his current experiences, he thought.

The General grumbled, "Even fools win...go ahead."

"The next significant genic trace in our records is found a few thousand years later..."

The General interrupted. "Why did it take so long in between?"

"Well sir," said the holovid, "for the next few thousand years, your genic traces were absorbed in mundane activities and with commoners with no apparent input into any component of history. They were mostly ignorant people who followed the herd mentality."

"How dare you insult me," sputtered the General.

"I am gravely sorry sir, but you are asking for the historical truth. However at the end of century 19 after the Common Era, there is some significant interaction. There was a movement in a section of the planet then known as the Middle East. There was a country by the name of Iraq. The trace brings you to a dictator in that region, named Hussein. He virtually held the world hostage, for years. He was a very clever and devious man. However the western powers eventually captured and executed him. Following an extended religious war, lasting longer than the previous World Wars, Iraq became a model of democracy in that region, for the next few hundred years."

The General scowled. "That's enough. They're all either fools or end up dead. I don't want to see any more."

"As you wish sir. But some had a cleverness threshold, not to be overlooked. Even the Greek got what he wanted, Socrate's death."

"Yes, yes...I see that. Perhaps my destiny is to take whatever qualities I can use to my full advantage."

Chapter Eleven

The Real

"There's pater's complex," said Susan as their transport pulled out of the air lane and slowed.

"Amazing! The towers on the periphery shimmer with surveillance modules and pulse guns. We'll be safe in there, I suppose...at least for the time being," said Derral.

The com link interrupted. "Okay folks, Major Dennings again. I'm arranging for clearance to dock in the Secretaries private port. It'll just take a moment. I'll see you again when you leave. The Secretary asked for you to be escorted back, too...as this is a publicly announced activity. You may know there are some militant solar centrist groups who strongly objected to your contact with the Da'yoni civilization and threatened retaliation."

"Not really, Major," said Susan and Derral, almost simultaneously.

"We weren't told that. Nor have we tuned in to the media since our return. What's that about?" said Derral.

"It seems like some of the spiritual factions felt that your journey and EMF transformation violated some moral imperative, as well as their prohibition against contact outside the solar system. I don't know any other details other than that I am assigned to insure your security," said the Major as both cruisers decelerated and turned towards the towers.

There's the Major on our portside, thought Derral.

I'm glad for the security then, thought Susan.

As they banked, two more cruisers pulled out of the traffic lanes and climbed to a few hundred feet above them. The Major banked sharply to position himself between their vehicle and the other two. The com link crackled.

"Looks like we have a few uninvited guests," said the Major. "I'll maintain control of your vehicle and give you instructions."

"Major, even though I left for greener pastures, I haven't forgotten my combat skills. I could pace your wing if you want to give back the controls."

"There is little concern, Colonel, I have laser locks on both vehicles. If my sensors pick up a hostile intent, they're dead in the air. But I'll return your controls, just in case."

Just then the two vehicles banked in opposite directions deploying a large holo of the Da'yoni ambassador and the Secretary. The caption below read: "The Beginning of the End. Priestly Is A Traitor To The Human Race."

The com link crackled. "I hope that's all they wanted…to make a statement," said the Major. They pulled back into the traffic lanes. "I'll take back control and remote you into the Secretary's station, now." Derral made quick finger gestures to hand over the control panel. The vehicle lurched slightly and then banked upward to the level of the penthouse. They decelerated and headed straight towards the side of the building. When they were a few feet from the building, a section illuminated with a flash. The port doors receded to permit entry. Inside the port were uniformed bots waiting with arms crossed and flashers protruding from their utility belts.

"Looks like pater has some extra help," said Susan.

The com crackled. "Don't be concerned about the bots. They're programmed to recognize your DNA structure, and that of the other guests," said the Major."This is one of the precautions needed today, because of the many virtual threats that came over the com system…like those flyers. You'll note the portals. They all scan. By the time you reach the main dining room, you'll have been scanned about six times."

I wonder why they're scanning us, thought Susan.

Derral responded silently. That is likely your loving pater's wish. They can easily deactivate those scanners when we pass through.

I know, thought Susan. They visualized the Secretary watching the scene. The technicians were explaining the data to him. The Secretary was just then sitting in a darkened room with a tech watching the scanners as people came through. They focused on the holos before the tech. In addition to the DNA sequence, an iris scan and facial structure was compared to the main holobank.

Derral continued subvocalizing. Susan, I don't think we paid much attention to this before. When I was in the military I found out some

106

interesting tidbits about how free our society really is. Every registered citizen has a holo record. The Holders passed a confidential fiat, a few decades ago. That fiat requires the citizen to update every five revolutions with a new holo. Remember when you renewed your university teaching credential last year? That is one of the ways it is accomplished. Transport license renewals; galactic passports, school admissions for children, etc. This is one of the ironies of a one government planet. While it provides relative freedoms in some areas, personal privacy is non-existent. All privacies are eroded. In fact with children, for many centuries they have been offering parents a micro implant so that they can track the children. A decade ago, the Holders convened a discrete conference with planetary educators and demanded that every child has it. When they reach age 20, they can have it removed. But by that time most people had forgotten about it. We didn't have much cause to think of these things, until now.

Yes, I had a class on that, just before I received my degree. But there was no mention of a mandate. I recall the professor saying it was at the preference of the parent, thought Susan.

Yeah, thought Derral. That was one of the problems. The Holders swore the educators to secrecy. The implants are done when the child has his first visit to a school health screen bot. It is about the size of a pore, so the parents rarely notice the injection site. The child is told he is just getting the routine vaccinations. It has gotten out of hand. Any official, or other individual with access to the holo files can instantly access a citizens profile and history, as well as any child's location and physical data, if they were born after the implementation date, around 2474. The Holder rule and their control was renewed each decade, based on this singularly silent principle of a minimum of public disagreement. If one were to question even at the highest level, the response is always identical, a trip to the Solar Intelligence complex for a review. All officials used the system to one degree or another. A few revolutions ago, a group of pedophiles led by an official that had been terminated for embezzlement, were caught by authorities accessing children's location data. Fortunately the Security service had a fly monitoring their activities. They moved to arrest them before they could harm any of the children. The citizen has no privacy, even down to their DNA. It could be sampled at any of thousands of intersections, building entrances, and certain streets where there are air samplers for breath and normally shedded skin particle molecules, as well as iris analyzers. In essence, a person's genetic fingerprint can be followed from street to street in most sections of the city.

Susan momentarily glanced at Derral, as he continued. That invasion of our privacies became standard practice in the 21st. Century, with the increasing sophistication in electronic tech. Citizens don't even give it a thought, anymore. We didn't pay much attention to such things before, but now they're crucial.

That should be the first change we can implement: do away with invasive tech, thought Susan, as they walked down the corridor to the main living quarters.

Well, let's not jump the gun, thought Derral, as he turned and smiled. We have a number of stages to accomplish, first. And some of that tech is good for security, given the crazy elements in the Confederation. At least they passed laws to prevent sensors from reading neuronal patterns.

Those are laws. I wonder what the actual practice is, thought Susan.

They walked into the main living area. As they entered all faces turned towards them. The chatter stopped abruptly. Most of the Holders were present, as were many of the sycophants associated with them. General Suddhis approached them with a wide grin.

"Welcome to our famous travelers from the realm of formlessness. You must tell us immediately of your experience. We're all waiting to hear with baited breath. We understand that you had quite a time with the Da'yoni, much more than the few previous travelers. Pray tell my good people."

Derral and Susan read his intention. So he wants to use what he learns from us to further his taking over of the Secretariat. His plans include people in place at the government centers…and he's allied with the Eastern faction. We need to tell pater, in some way, thought Susan.

Derral thought: I'm not so sure….I know he's your pater…yet we don't know what his intentions are in all this. Wait until we see what your pater has to say before we interfere. Remember what the Da'yoni caution was. Do nothing to interfere unless we can insure that no one will be able to have even the remotest suspicion of our involvement. So it is best to continue to accumulate information, now, don't you think? thought Derral, with a slight grin.

Susan looked at him and smiled, but did not respond in any way that Derral could perceive. He turned to her with a puzzled look. Looks like I've learned to disguise my thought...that wasn't too difficult, she thought.

He looked at her and she was smiling widely. Derral responded. Well, I guess I lost the advantage. Let's be sociable with the guests. It will open our eyes, I'm sure, thought Derral.

Shouting was heard from the main room. All eyes turned towards the door. Susan and Derral were standing just around the corner and moved into the room. They saw Ulemann taking a protective stance before the Secretary as Oice was shouting loudly at him.

"You have no consideration for the commoner, Mr. Secretary. They are languishing in the cities, satiated on your social welfare. Anyone with any intelligence higher than a Venusian snail, knows that your social welfare programs are all designed to control the populace so that you will remain in office," said Oice. His face was turning purple. The veins in his neck were so swollen that they cast a shadow as he turned toward the light. At that moment the Secretary's chief bot unobtrusively streamed behind the Secretary.

The Secretary pursed his lips into a tight grin, speaking through his teeth.

"Are you thinking of challenging me, Mr. Oice? If so, then I suggest you begin your campaign, for I believe the commoner, as you so demeaningly refer to them, surely remembers your previous exploits during the late 80's. It ran on the holos for most of that year. Didn't my sources inform me that it was you who led a group of galactic fighters into the death trap set up by the Krakavarians from the Epsilon system...and you did so because of your greed...as they promised to increase your credits at their mining bases? And, oh, I almost forgot...weren't you and your wing man the only fighters to return of the 15 to go into that fiasco. While we don't have definitive proof, my people monitored the suspicious communications between yourself and the Krakavarian ambassador, a few revolutions before the attack. The Krakavarians were able to use the details you shared with the ambassador to defeat and destroy a confederation fighter wing. The commoners, as you refer to the fine people of our confederation, would be just begging to know the details of that engagement. They will certainly be well informed, if you choose to challenge my position as Secretary."

The Secretary looked over his shoulder at his chief bot. "Did you record all that Chief?"

"Yes sir, I believe we have the complete exchange," said the bot.

Oice stammered. "Are you attempting to blackmail me into silence, Mr. Secretary?"

"On the contrary, Mr. Oice. I am simply imparting some information so that you can be better informed. When one is better informed, the decisions one makes are more in the service of one's interest, are they not?. By the way Chief," he said over his shoulder. "Prepare that vid for instant transmission to the networks in the event that Mr. Oice doesn't seem to get the point. His past behavior on the Holders tends to indicate he does suffer a bit from a deficiency of foresight."

Oice's face turned purple with rage. He stomped out of the room to the subdued chuckle of those surrounding the Secretary. General Suddhis was the exception. He stood quietly to the side, looking grim, clenching his fists. This did not escape the notice of Ulemann who was now intensely scanning the onlookers surrounding the Secretary.

Susan broke the ensuing silence. "I propose a toast to my pater, the Secretary. May he remain in office until he chooses a successor."

"Here! Here!" The shouts in the now crowded room were exhilarating to the Secretary. However, Susan and Derral picked up his underlying feelings: I wonder what her intent is...or her partner's, thought the Secretary. Susan was about to respond to the thought, when she felt Derral's arm on hers. As she turned, she noticed his forbidding look.

Derral thought, Be careful, my dear...You almost slipped. Remember, he just thought that.

I know, thought Susan. How could my own pater believe that I have something other than honorable intentions? I was astounded that he would be so mistrustful. I've never shown him anything other than respect and honesty...until now.

I think his misperceptions of your intentions says more about him than it does you, thought Derral.

Yes, I see that. Pater's chief mode of operation is to externalize onto

110

others what he does not want to see in himself. That was his primary mode of relating to mater, thought Susan.

Doesn't that give us an alert to what will happen to us? Even you...his prodigy, if he finds that we are interfering with his operations or political goals. His greed seems thicker than blood. Perhaps we can find some way to support his healthy focus on giving more power to the common folk of the planet, so that his suspicions of our motives will be quelled, thought Derral.

That depends on how he receives our intention. He may just perceive it as another manipulative strategy to gain some favor. That appears to be how he receives most of my overtures, though, I didn't know how consistent he was, until now, thought Susan.

If we're embarking on this journey, it won't be just the Secretary's suspiciousness we'll be dealing with. When I was on those month long interstellar journeys I read about historical figures...geniuses who changed the planetary consciousness. Most of them isolated themselves from their followers. The followers were afraid of the change. Detractors created a public animosity against them. This was not unique to just a few. Throughout history, any advanced thinker, and I mean any, without exception, became the recipient of character assassinations and attacks designed to destroy them. Many were destroyed, put to death or imprisoned, thought Derral.

The Secretary interrupted their silent communication. He approached with a smile. "I hope you weren't too disturbed by that outburst. Oice has been on our watch list for quite some time. He has not been a kindred sole. Are you enjoying yourself, my dear? I see that you have adjusted well to your old form. Quite an experience with the Da'yoni, was it not?"

"Yes, pater. We were almost lost in ourselves, at first...when we were transformed. It was a frightening experience...the first time without a physical body. However, we soon adjusted to the experience. Our Da'yoni guides facilitated our adjustment by coaching us through our fears, until we became familiar with our forms and how to navigate," said Susan.

General Suddhis interrupted. "Excuse me Mr. Secretary, I was about to have a conversation with your delightful and intelligent bio, before we were rudely interrupted by Oice's outburst."

"One more question General, then you can have her," said the Secretary.

"What was your experience when you arrived on their planet? I'm told that the government is quite different than ours."

"Yes, answered Derral. Radically different. We experienced many simultaneous communications, overwhelming to us. The guides helped to filter out the chaotic voices so we could communicate with individuals. The President of the Crennium, their governing body, often addressed us. We were invited to one of their Crennium meetings...a meeting of all the beings on the planet. We were initially beleaguered by the multitude of voices but were able to filter out the noise and focus on the major communication."

The Secretary took on a puzzled look. "What did you learn of their civilization?"

"It appears," said Susan, "that all decisions are made after a vote is taken. As they exist in EMF form, the vote is instantaneous. Everyone either votes or decides to abstain. Abstentions are not considered oppositions, but merely a desire not to express an opinion on a particular issue. We were amazed at how quickly vast amounts of information are communicated to all the beings. This is the epitome of a true democracy. All citizens vote or abstain on every decision, instantaneously. Eighty to ninety percent of the citizens vote, with few abstentions. All votes are cast in thought form through the EMF field, so there is no delay or actual effort to vote. Unlike our culture and most other democratically aligned civilizations there are no back room dealings."

"Yes, so I have heard," said the Secretary. "Did you learn anything about their motives for giving us the technology to travel to their world?"

"Yes," said Susan. "They provided us with the technology so they can expand their knowledge of our culture. They are a curious lot, much like anthropologists, to learn about other worlds and how they work. I believe their only motive is curiosity, as they are far superior to our culture, they need nothing from us aside from a request for trade of silica."

Be careful, thought Derral. Susan turned towards him with a quick smile and reached for his hand.

"That may be what they told you, my dear," said the Secretary. "Being that you are a citizen and not an official, I'm sure they did not communicate their real motive. Our galactic partners tell us they are in dire need of silica. Perhaps we will never know other motives. But I'm very suspicious, as a number of people came back to us from the transformation. Only a few remained relatively sane or wanted to relate to others. It seems that most were too frightened at what they saw to remain in contact with people."

"Yes, I was concerned after hearing that. While we both enjoyed the EMF existence, I didn't think I'd want to live without a physical existence for too long. We enjoyed the solace and perceptual benefits of the EMF, but didn't feel any need to isolate when we came back. I don't understand what happened to the others," said Susan.

The Secretary pursed his lips, rubbing his chin between thumb and forefinger. "Perhaps you were treated differently, my dear, given your relationship with me. I suppose that is something we won't be privy to. Yet, I still find it difficult to trust such openness from a civilization that is superior to ours in every technological way, but has need of our most abundant mineral."

Derral interjected. "I know, sir. However they seemed to be above board with us in every way. We took a quick, unaccompanied tour around the planet. There was no sand on their beaches. The soil appeared as decomposed organic matter. We didn't notice any rock or mineralized surfaces, even when the land was elevated or in areas where there appeared to be excavations. Our first contact vessal took soundings and discoverd a hardened core, but directly in the center of the planet, too deep to be susceptable to mining operations with any known technology."

One of our trainers did verify that when we asked," said Susan.

Derral continued. "They invited us to an open government forum where their whole civilization was present and voted on various issues. We were able to experience most all of that, as our EMF signatures were made to sync with theirs. They did not appear to censor anything. In fact, we were permitted to listen into one faction that sought to expand their civilization by taking over other planets like ours, that could support their culture. This was unanimously voted down during the Crennium session. I believe we were able to experience the complete debate on both sides. The vast majority of Da'yonis were not wanting to intrude in other planets or cultures. They wanted only to act in an advisory capacity to many of the less evolved civilizations, with limits, and to learn from their observations. They made it very clear about not wanting to interfere with the natural evolution of other civilizations. They embraced this non-interference policy for many millennium. It seems that the Da'yonis are a compassionate civilization, far more ancient than ours. Compassion appeared to have evolved to a centralized trait, as a result of their experience."

"Yes, thank you son," said the Secretary with an air of impatience. "I'm sure they have many of their kind who are strict isolationists, given the relative superiority of their technology among the galactic community. Yet, I will not so readily accept that their only motive is altruism. I'm certain that there is more than meets the eye. Time will tell, as always," said the Secretary. At that moment the chief bot leaned forward and whispered into the Secretary's ear.

The Secretary broadcast his voice to all present. "Yes, people, my bot just reminded me, we are here in celebration of this event. Let us not get so serious, now. Have pleasure today, for there is a lot of work to do in the forthcoming days. Come, my dears, let me introduce you to the other Holders."

General Suddhis approached them again. "I couldn't help but overhear. That must have been a fascinating experience. I will see if I can use my influence with our partners close to the Boötes system to take a voyage there, as a state visit."

"I don't think that will be possible, General, said the Secretary. The Da'yoni ambassador recently informed me that they are sending a contingent here to enter discussions on establishing full diplomatic relationships."

"Oh?" said the General, deflated at being outranked by the Secretary.

The Secretary ignored the response and personally introduced Derral and Susan, to each of his guests. They were the focus of many questions from different groups, throughout the afternoon.

Susan was most taken aback by the dissenting voices in the minds of the Holders. While pleasant and social on the surface, the majority had one scheme or another they were contemplating. Most were centered around how to aggrandize their own power base and replace her pater.

Let's get out of here. I can't take much more, she thought.

Yes, thought Derral. Tell his Excellency, you're exhausted and want to rest.

Susan found the Secretary in an adjoining room joking with friends.

"Pater, I'm afraid I didn't realize how exhausting this would be. It must take a period of adjustment. I'm about ready to collapse. I think we should leave, if it would not be too much of an imposition. I'm sorry we couldn't have done this a few more revolutions from now when we'd be more rested. Please forgive."

"I understand perfectly, my dear," said the Secretary, turning to the small group. "People, hold the rest of that story, while I say good bye to our luminaries."

"Thank you pater."

"I'll notify the Major that you'll be leaving. Perhaps we can meet in a few days for a small private gathering so that you can fill us in on the details. I can imagine the transformation was an ordeal, given what happened to some of the others." He nodded to the chief bot who came beside Susan and Derral to escort them to their vehicle.

"Madame," said the bot. "Please follow me. I will have your vehicle ready at the portal. Your escort is notified."

"I was honored to be here, Mr. Secretary, said Derral. I hope we can return the favor and you'll come to our home for that private gathering, at least for dinner next week."

"Yes, that would be marvelous, a first for me in many years. Isn't that right my dear? Not since mater's passing, the poor dear."

Susan and Derral read the actual animosity he had for Susan's mater, regardless of his words. Amazing how clever he is in disguising his true feelings, thought Susan. I would have never believed it. Even with his deceptions, though, I feel uncomfortable being dishonest with him.

Yes, thought Derral. We need to never lose sight of his deceptive nature.

The Secretary continued. "I will have to verify my schedule and let Susan know when I am available." He appeared to warm at the invitation. Both Derral and Susan picked up his intention of the dinner invitation as an opportunity to probe them further.

"Goodbye pater. Let us know. We'll see you then. I'll see to it that your most favored dish is served," said Susan, as she embraced him.

"How do you know I haven't changed my tastes in the years since, my dear," said the Secretary with a devilish look.

"Pater, since I learned how to talk, you have never expressed a desire for anything else at celebratory occasions, other than those steamed Pleadian giant plumlike things that taste like Octopus. We'll have some transported in this week from the galactic rim."

The Secretary grinned. "Please, my dear. You learned to talk at about age 1. I can eat just plain old Terran food. It is the rare delight to be with my offspring that excites me more than food."

"No pater, I insist. Your favorite treat, is my treat."

That's good, buddy. Disarming the Secretary of the Holders. You'd make a great diplomat, thought Derral. Susan gave him a side glance.

"Very well, I will have Ulemann contact you with my available schedule, tomorrow at the zenith. Good day my dear...and Derral. Have a safe trip home. The Major will serve you well."

"Thank you sir," said Derral. Susan blew him a kiss and turned to follow the bot to the portal.

As they entered the staging area of the portal, the Major hurried towards them and spoke directly to Derral, with an intensity. "Colonel, I don't want to disturb you. But, we must take a more circuitous route to your home, sir. There is some activity we need to hopefully avoid. I've taken the liberty of having your personal cruiser towed to your home portal. I replaced it with an atmospheric fighter like mine, with a field generator and pulse weapon, in the event we are attacked. We've intercepted an encrypted communication from someone at the Secretaries gathering, ordering a dissident faction to track you when leaving. You're military training should enable you to quickly acclimate yourself to the weaponry"

"Yes Major, but how serious is the danger to us?"

"It is probably nothing to worry about...just someone who was disturbed by the Secretary...one of the Holders. We are just taking all precautions," said the Major."

Susan and Derral immediately thought of the interaction with Oice, the Holder, and General Suddhis' reaction. Susan started to speak, but hesitated. This is absurd, she thought. We need to get to the bottom of what Oice or the General is planning.

Yes, thought Derral. But remember, it just may be your pater who has a more negative effect by his actions. We don't know yet. So, let's not jump to conclusions or say anything to betray our hand.

"Is there something the matter?"asked the Major, in reaction to their silence.

"Ah, no Major. I was just shocked that we took a vacation, and are now targets for some lunatic, as a result."

"Yes," said Susan. "Likewise."

"Will you give me a brief refresher on class 5 weapons," said Derral, with a hint of anxiety, as they entered the cockpit.

"It is not much different than the weapons and shielding on the astral class fighter you flew to the outer planets, Colonel. The control panel requires the same gestures and eye glances to activate the shields and fire the weapons. The tracking and firing mechanisms are in your helmet and can be engaged by the red panel on your arm rest. It's best to manually engage it rather than the cortical helmet control, as that would take getting used to. As soon as we leave the complex, I'll take you on a dry run while we're still in the security zone."

"Very well Major. Lets get going," said Derral, sounding more official than Susan had experienced him. Both vessels immediately gained altitude to the ionosphere to test the weapons. Following the test, they took a course around the outskirts of the city, outside of the regular traffic zone.

As they approached their home building, the Major interrupted. "Sir, there is a double blip on the holo approaching fast. Please activate your shields." The Colonel drew his hand across the panel.

"I was keeping an eye on that Major. I'm powering up weapon systems."

"I can't believe this," said Susan. "You mean we're being attacked?"

"Not quite, yet. But you see these blips on the holo. They'll be within range in a moment or two. That's when we'll know. I'm scanning their weapon systems....Oooh boy. See those red flashing lights to the right. That means they're arming their pulse weapons. Looks like we're on Major," said Derral, as he engaged the full thrusters to gain altitude.

The Major kept tight on his wing. "I see you haven't lost your touch, Colonel. If they come in any closer, I'll try to decommission them with a pulse. Come in on my port wing. In the event I miss, get behind them and put a mag up their tail thrusters. They're powering up. Here we go."

As he spoke, the Major broke rapidly to starboard. Derral followed. They were now above the attackers. The light trail of the pulse weapon followed to their targets. Derral punched in a visual. Just as the pulse was about to hit they broke formation. Derral followed one, missing with his first pulse. The Major hit the other dead on. It rapidly decelerated, out of commission. The second maneuvered behind Derral. Before they got a lock, Derral took the fighter towards the ground at high speed and pulled up sharply, looping behind the attacker.

"Holy shit," yelled Susan clutching at her harness. Derral's sight lit up the target and fired two pulses. Both hit and disabled the vessel. They could hear the Major calling for a pickup vessel. In what seemed like a few moments, a large vessel appeared on the horizon, rapidly approaching. It coupled the disabled attackers together and drew them into the bay.

"I'd take you for my wing man any day, Colonel. Good shooting. That was an old fashion dogfight maneuver...an Immelman loop you pulled, was it not, Colonel? Haven't seen one of those since cadet school.

"Yes, thanks to you too, Major. I remembered my air history lessons. That wasn't the first time that worked for me. But I'd rather resume my peaceful existence. I thought I saw the last of such business in the Pleades last year. We had to hold off a whole navy there. Fortunately, their weapons were not too sophisticated. That was touch and go, there for a while," said Derral.

"Shit, Derral, I never saw you in action like this. You never mentioned anything about that," said Susan, trembling. "Why not?"

"I didn't want to trouble you," said Derral. "Besides, it was only a minor incident."

"Minor? I don't call being attacked by an alien navy a minor incident," said Susan.

"Well, I didn't want to alarm you. We came out unscathed anyway," said Derral.

"...Major, I don't see any others. Is it OK to dock at our bay?" said Derral into the com

"Not yet, Colonel. Looks like we have some more uninvited company, coming in hot off starboard. My scanner is more sensitive than yours. In a moment you'll see 4 blips."

"I have a visual, Major. That's some big firepower, I don't recognize the configuration"

"Looks like they're alien craft...piloted by humans" said the Major.

"Let's split up and see what they do," said Derral.

"Okay. But it will be some time until our backup arrives," said the Major.

They separated and rapidly accelerated to the outer atmosphere.

"Major, looks like 3 are on me. One on you." I'll see if I can get behind them. Good speed in taking yours out.

Derral rapidly decreased his thrust in the thin atmosphere, spinning around, horizontally. He was now pointing directly at the attackers.

"Jeez, Derral. They're coming right at us. I hope I can hold my lunch in all this, if I don't start screaming.

"Don't worry. These guys don't seem that sophisticated or they would have outmaneuvered me. This gives me direct canon shots at their cabins." Derral fired three canon bursts. One of the intruders was destroyed. Another was hit in the tail and started spinning. The third continued on, firing pulses.

"Derral, I'm about to shit in my pants. We're getting hit."

"Yes, he thought. But our shields are holding. Watch this one...and hold on. If you pass out, don't worry, it will just be a momentary blackout from the maneuver."

"But what if you pass out, too?" said Susan, trembling with fear.

"Don't worry, my dear. I've done this hundreds of times. My body is used to it"

He made a high speed ellipse that took him far from the attacker's sight and then dove back in the atmosphere beneath him. The rapid deceleration blacked Susan out. Derral held his breath and maintained. His sight lit up the target and he fired a series of canon bursts. One went up the tailpipe and exploded the target.

"Major, how we doing back there? I just took our friends out."

"I was hit in my rudder and am ejecting in the outer atmosphere, as I can't control a landing. That was right after I launched the kill shot on my attacker. Our back up arrived...a little late. They'll magcouple my capsule and take me on board. I think I'm okay...other than being embarrassed."

"Nothing to be embarrassed about Major. I lost my ship and had to eject a number of times in one of our little interstellar wars, just after I got my flight certification."

"Well, I had my certification for years now, Colonel...that's what embarrasses me. I just received the com that one of those you hit, crashed. They're at the recovery now. We'll learn exactly who attacked us and just where they got those craft. The crew's escape capsule was maglocked in position by our backup, before they landed. I'll be going directly to the interrogation when they get their asses up here to pick me up. Want to sit in on the interrogation, Colonel?"

"Major, I see you on my holo. Want me to grapple your escape pod and take it in?"

"No. Thanks Colonel. But our back up, the Aristes class have special docking for taking on a hitchhiker. Your ship can only grapple me to your hull...and that's a little dangerous for both of us.

"That was quick...mobilizing an Aristes wing. That's something you don't forget from the academy, as you well know. I had the opportunity to train in one of those, some years ago. They're quick, agile, and nasty."

"That they are Colonel. They can take out anything about halfway around the planet, at any time, as long as they have another body to beam their protons off of."

"Yes, I always wondered why they don't use the same weapons guidance in all our fighters and cruisers."

"I think it is a matter of economics, Colonel. I understand the weapons guidance alone costs more than a billion credits to manufacture. And it must be manufactured on a negative gravity body, of which there are only a few within a month's journey."

"Why, negative gravity," asked the Major.

It has to do with the protometric fields that sense the targets. They cannot be constructed in zero gravity. It must be some factor of negative gravity to get them to sight right...at least that's what I know about them."

"Okay, boys, perhaps we can invite the Major over for a continuation of your man talk, dear. I'm about to puke and still trembling...lets get out of here and back in normal gravity," said Susan.

"I'm sorry Ms. Priestly, I got a little carried away...I enjoy talking to your partner."

"Thanks, Major. Come over for brunch, some day. We make a mean Venusian pastiche."

"A what?" said the Major.

"You'll experience it for yourself when you come. Bring your partner too," said Susan.

"I'm looking forward to it, said the Major. Leave the fighter in your auxiliary port and we'll send someone over to pick it up."

"We'll be seeing you," said Derral. We'll call in a few revolutions to set the date.

"Thanks for your protection," said Susan.

Derral pulled up and turned towards their complex. As they docked, Susan leaned over and kissed him on the cheek. "My hero, Colonel Derral," she said, as she ran to the bathroom.

Derral smiled. "You too, honey. My co-pilot. Exciting wasn't it?"

"Yes, but I can think of many more safer ways to get excited...and less nauseating," she shouted back through the entrance portal.

The night was pleasant.

Chapter Twelve

Tuning Up The General

General Urvey Suddhis sat before the holo console talking to Cursard.

"We need to spread those rumors of the Secretary, now. This is the first stage or our power grab. We must discredit him. When a substantial proportion of the populace believes this, we will then launch your people. They're still in place, I hope?"

Cursard rolled his eyes. "They're still in place. However it costs me extra to keep them loyal and in place, doing nothing. I need 100 more creds by the next rev...or the deal is off."

"Listen Cursard, this is the most crucial time. I don't like you squeezing me, you criminal psychopath. I can't get that amount to you by the morrow. You know that. It would be traceable. If you can't keep them in place, I'll expose you and all the foul deeds you perpetrated against the Holders over the past few solar revs. Who will they believe, me a decorated war hero or you a galactic criminal?"

"Well, General, if you put it that way, understand I took precautions against just such a threat. I think you've underestimated me. Do you recall those meetings with your Lynchon. That was all recorded for posterity, as was our talks, including this one. You'll learn, if you haven't yet already, I'm no fool."

The General turned towards Oice and smirked. "I didn't think so, Cursard, that's why I wanted you to join us. But, let us get real here. I'll get you the credits, but not when you want. If you pull out on me, you're finished. You might as well go to another star system, as your deceit and murderousness will be broadcast throughout this system, in an instant. Let that be the final word. I will talk to you on the morrow." The General ended the comlink.

Cursard continued to stare at the lingering image. "You know," he said to the Jovian in a slow drawl, "I think its time to call in our options. I'm not going to be threatened by this phony piece of space junk."

"Mhh boss," said the Jovian, "You wan me and Grancha to get man to bat him and his peep?"

"No, but I want you both to use your cloaking devices and follow him until you catch him in an isolated place," said Cursard. "Then appear before him and remind him to ask Lynchon who you work for. Show him your neutron blade, crackle it a bit before his eyes and then walk away and cloak yourselves as you leave. That should tune him up a bit. In case he doesn't look frightened when you crackle your blade, tell him what the blade could do to his vital parts...and mention that he was easy to locate, even with his security forces. Make sure that delicate flower Oice is with him. Then the fool could not blame it on the synth he's always drinking. If either of them goes for a weapon, cut their hand off, but hand it back to them so they can get it reattached. That way we won't get the attention of the security forces."

"Me gotcha boss," said the Jovian. "We be done it right. After me and Grancha meet with General, he no want to resist no more. We fright him good. He dribbling when we through."

"Yes, Bocha, but don't harm him unless you have to...remember we still want him to pay us. We just want to show him he can't threaten me and get away with it, in spite of who he thinks he is. To make sure he knows you're on my team, mention that I know his phony "war hero" status is a cover for his cowardice...that I know it was from a piece of luck that closed a wormhole, just in time, when he was running from the Krakes," said Cursard.

"Okay, Boss," said Bocha. "Me and Grancha like don this right. No hurt if no fight. Chop, chop if tuh mudder fight....Chop, chop...me like a boss...but no if no fight. Me and Grancha see morrow you. Okay?"

"Bocha, just stick with the plan and don't get creative. But do emphasize that I know he was a coward because the Krakes are one of my business partners and are still agitated about his lucky escape. With a look of seriousness, Cursard mused that the Jovians didn't always follow details...love to see human blood...something to do with their roots and the invasion into their hidden civilization before we got whacked by the moon chunk. With the General if there's a misstep, I might as well kiss this planet goodbye, he thought, reaching into the desk drawer and taking out a small pen like instrument. As Bocha and Grancha walked down the hallway, he aimed the device at each of them and pressed a lever. Each simultaneously slapped at their backs as if they were swatting a flea. With their body hair, not an unlikely possibility.

That should do it, thought Cursard with a wry smile. I'll watch through the fly scanners. If they get rough, I'll dispense the knockout charge and then come to the General's rescue as a hero.

The Jovians took a skiff to the General's location and waited. They immediately picked up on Lynchon's energy configuration. Jovians can sense and differentiate the energy fields of most creatures.

Just in front of him walked the General.

"Mmhhh we be on dem target, Grancha."

"Mmmbay, Boch...we got rid of tail first. Me go turn down street here un wait for him...easy pull in alley."

"Okay...Me go straight for target General. Trees up dere. Get him in trees."

Bocha ran, twice as fast as a human, despite his size. He waited behind some trees and scrub brush. The General approached at a fast walk. Boncha leaped in front of him. The General reached in his coat and Boncha grabbed his wrist. "No. No, boss. You be good man and every now OK."

"What do you want," said the General. "You can have all my credits. Please they're in this." He held out a holo card. The Jovian grunted a deep retching sound that the General felt as if it were inside his own body.

"No boss. No need credits. Need you to no threaten Master Cursard, no mo. Me and Grancha..."

Grancha came around the corner with his arm encircling Lynchon's neck, literally carrying him. The General startled.

Boncha reached for his long curved knife...the curve neatly fit around one's waste. He slapped the flat side against the General's chest, the blade inches from his neck. "Dis favorite blade. Take head off easy short swing. Gotcha, boss?"

"I've got your meaning," said the General. "I won't be threatening him again."

"Mmh," growled Boncha. "M boss know you phony shit. Fake war hero. Boss do business with Krakes and know you get away by luck. Krakes still pissed."

Boncha and Grancha quickly departed and cloaked, out of sight, around the corner. The General felt the dampness in his trousers. Lynchon picked himself off the ground looking frightened and embarrassed.

"I'm sorry your Excellency. There was nothing I could do."

"What about the weapon you had you damn fool. Didn't it matter when you saw me getting attacked. Or were you just too cowardly, dammit?" growled the General, as he looked down at his soaked pants He shook his head and stormed off.

"I'm very sorry, General. He surprised me. He just appeared. I didn't have time to..." His voice trailed off as he ran to keep pace.

The General walked quickly in the direction of his tower

Chapter Thirteen

Trust, Maybe?

Derral awakened at first light from a fitful sleep and slipped out to the dining space. Susan remained curled up in the low gravity sleeping space.

"A large, strong cap, Michelle," he said.

"Your wish is my command," said the replicator.

Derral sat at the breakfast bar. He was thinking of the last time they had taken any time off. A few years ago, when they went up to the high mountain range in the California province, they delighted at being alone with no other people around. He remembered the pleasurable experiences of waking up in the morning to a brief snow shower...

Susan interrupted him with a thought. Why don't we just take the cruiser up there. We have nothing to do for the next few weeks. And I'll be glad to get away from all these mini-interrogations.

"I thought you were asleep, buddy"

"I was but awakened at the pleasure of your thoughts, my dear. If we go, I wonder what the Major will say? He is our security detail," said Susan.

Be careful what you say, thought Derral. If we let him know where we're going, then your loving pater will know. I don't know if that's such a good idea. If he knows where we are, he can send his microflys around to spy on us. I just want us to be alone in the mountains. Perhaps Robert might be able to advise us as to how to slip away unnoticed.

Yes, thought Susan, you trust him as much as anyone. You said you'd call him when we got back, anyway.

He said we probably shouldn't have any contact, given the nature of our trip to Da'yoni. Now that we're back, he might be OK with it. I'll contact him on our secure link, thought Derral.

Derral pressed the link connection beneath his chin. The logo of the solar security federation appeared before his eyes. The image dissolved into Robert Laing."Hello my old friend. What do I owe this pleasure to?" said Robert.

"Hello Robert. I hope I'm not disturbing you...too much. I have a dilemma."

"Well my friend that's the usual reason you contact me."

"Robert. I know we should have contacted you sooner, but we've been quite busy since we've come back," said Derral.

"Oh, I know. The Secretary has me keeping tabs on your movements."

"That's not surprising. Robert, would it be at all possible for us to meet?"

"Yes, of course Derral. We haven't talked in years. Let me call you back from my personal holo this afternoon. You know you got me at work. We will be pretty busy here for the next few hours. I'll talk with you when we wind up this current project."

"Years? Has it been that long? I'll look forward to hearing from you," said Derral, with a wry smile.

Robert feigned a neutral response. "I'll call you..."

Well it looks like will have to wait awhile for an answer. Seems like he's being monitored, too, thought Derral.

I hope he can help us. I don't want us to have to deal with bots and whatever other devices they came up with to plant around us. Unfortunately pater appears to have too much invested to let us go on unobserved. We also need some protection from the nit wits out there. Perhaps Robert can help with both problems, thought Susan.

"We'll see," said Derral.

You are slipping my dear, thinking aloud. You must be tired, thought Susan.

You caught me again, thought Derral. My military senses are making me nervous, given our recent attack. To go up there without any security, at the present time, is taking a risk that I feel very uncomfortable taking. So, we'll wait to see what Robert has to suggest. In the meantime, let's take a bath, thought Derral, smiling.

"Something new," said Susan. "We haven't shared that experience since last year. Michelle, get the stim bath ready."

In as sensual a voice as her circuit's could muster, the computer responded. "Your very desire is my command, Mademoiselle."

"Oh my god Derral, how did you teach it to be so disgustingly sappy?"

"Well it just took a little recording, discreetly, from your voice on occasion. Do you notice the similarity?"

"Similarity? You've got to be kidding," said Susan.

Derral smiled. "Listen carefully to the intonation."

"Later for that," said Susan, as she entered the stim chamber shaking her head.

They stayed in the stim bath, for the next hour until Derral was aroused by a holo call. It was Robert.

"Hello again, my friend," said Robert.

"Hey old buddy. We thought we might invite you over..."

Robert interrupted."I think it better that I invite you two over here. I owe you a dinner, anyway. I'll start the cooking. Can you be over in a few hours?"

"Yes, we can make it then...right Susan?" Susan nodded.

"I see you're just as beautiful as when I first met you, Susan," said Robert, leering.

Susan pulled the robe up to cover her nakedness and flushed. "Thank you...I think," she said.

"You're quite welcome," said Robert, still leering.

Derral laughed. "You're still an old degenerate in spite of it all, huh?"

"Well," said Robert. "Not really a degenerate...but an admirer of fine beauty."

"I think the word is still out on that," said Derral.

"Whatever it is, you'll be over shortly?" said Robert.

"Yes, I think we can get it together. See you then," said Derral, as he ended the com

Susan thought, if he is a degenerate, as you say, we should have some fun.

Robert is always fun. And I think he's just about the only person we can trust. But even with him, I'm reluctant. I wonder why he rushed this, for one. To be on the safe side, perhaps we just better keep our secret to ourselves. After all, he does work for the government. I hate to say this about my old childhood friend but to betray this gift to anyone but him would be pretty stupid, and now I'm wondering about him. We wouldn't know who else is listening around him. And it would end any possibility of us having an impact on this sick, destructive society, thought Derral.

Susan remained silent. Her thoughts were transparent. She thought of how burdened they are now as a result of the Da'yoni gift. Before, they had friends they could freely share anything with. Now, they can only trust themselves.

At least until the politic changed, thought Derral. The trouble is irrelevant. We have a serious obligation we fell into, he thought, looking visibly agitated while pacing back and forth.

Susan reached for Derral's hand. I know you're right. Perhaps a side effect is that I'm becoming impatient. I want this class to be over. I don't want to keep up the masquerade. Come to think of it, we never did sit down and discuss the specific goals. It's as if we're improvising as we go along.

Derral's agitation resolved into a smile. I have this vague remembrance of our guide on Da'yoni. He said that it would take a few weeks or months to adjust to this existence. Perhaps we're just completing the adjustment phase.

Susan responded. Probably right. I was so befuddled when I started to pick up other's thoughts, especially the negative thoughts that I would never have suspected. She put her arm around Derral and hugged him tightly. A vacation is what we need.

"Yeah. We can start planning...but after we get...," said Derral, aloud.

Dear, thought Susan, interrupting with a wry smile. We must just get some control here. At least you didn't disclose our plan of travel. She switched to voice. "Yes, dear. We both need to get back to our normal routine in the next week or so. I have a lot of work piling up at the institute. Have you been contacted for any more sorties amongst the stars?"

"Yes, as a matter of fact," Derral said looking surprised. "Just this morning I received word they're considering a galactic rim run, again. Something about prospecting for that new element discovered in the asteroid belt. It's much like uranium but not dirty. It has a unique proton configuration. Something about the spin canceling any proton or neutron radiation. When refined, it produces clean energy, unlike uranium. If we can mine substantial quantities of this, we might revive the nuclear technology that was outlawed centuries ago… At least that was what the company said on the announcement feed."

"And you trust the company propaganda?" I mean why would we even want to turn back history. Didn't we almost destroy the planet at that time? Why even try to generate that technology, when we're so far advanced, now? said Susan, looking chagrined.

"It's all about politics and economics. I hear a rumor that some of the Holders have large investments hedging on the return of this technology. The old nuclear plants of the 20th Century are still intact, as they were too hot to dismantle…and needed a thousand years to achieve the half life where they would not be a danger. A few of the Holders bought up all the plants existing on the planet, some years ago. That was common knowledge. Most people considered it to be a foolish investment. However, this newly discovered element, because of its peculiar molecular structure, is reported to neutralize alpha particles and gamma radiation. So perhaps the Holders stumbled onto a gift they can use to decontaminate their nuclear plants. We'll see what happens," said Derral, shaking his head in despair of what could transpire.

He thought: Those lunatics were joined at the hip with your pater. I think he also invested in the endeavor. In fact, when you went to the bathroom, the other day at his place, he asked me if I heard about the plans. At that time I hadn't. I'm sure that's why I was called. I'm going to plead ill, though. My physician at the agency did say I had some bone density problems from my last extended travel. He advised that I hold off on any long term travel. That won't raise any red flags when we suddenly disappear. I'm hoping that Robert…" The zenith holo feed flashed. "Whoops, we need to leave to get to Robert's. Let's hurry."

Susan replied in a sultry tone, as she slinked out of the bedroom wearing her sexiest tight black jump suit. "I certainly am, babe. I'm looking forward to being with your degenerate friend."

Derral laughed. "Well, let's hope he's developed some social skills. Recall the last time we were together. He got a bit tipsy and knelt down after the theater, in the lobby with hundreds of people on their way out, and proposed to you."

" I sure do. So watch it, buddy," she said as she slinked around him, brushing his cheek with a kiss.

"Wow, I guess even the thought of the possibilities of this rendezvous excites you. I wonder what will happen when Robert comes further out of his closet."

"We'll see, dear," said Susan, smiling demurely.

They walked silently to the docking port, exchanging thoughts about the possibilities. That even turns you on a bit, doesn't it, thought Susan.

The security bots noticed. "Is there anything wrong, sir and madam. Might we be of some service," said the chief bot.

"Oh, nothing's wrong, Chief. What made you think so?" said Derral, anxiously.

"This is the first time that you both were so silent, when coming to the portal. You are usually engaged in conversation," said the Chief.

"Can we not think, Chief?" said Derral.

"Of course sir, I apologize. I was only inquiring..."

"I'm joking with you Chief....but we can just think and not talk, right?"

"Right sir. I won't inquire that way again. Sorry," said the bot.

"Please continue to inquire, Chief. You never know if something might be actually wrong."

"As you wish sir. Pardon my saying so, but you biologues are certainly complicated."

"As you were, Chief," said Derral, feigning an offended look.

Looks like we'll have to be more careful and talk some, thought Susan.

Derral responded: Yeah. I'm hoping that the bots are the only ones that noticed. It's hard catching on to a balance.

"I'll drive. You can work on your balance," said Susan.

Derral shot her a side glance as they entered the anti-grav vehicle. Susan programmed it to Robert's house and engaged the autopilot. The portal opened and they entered the swift moving traffic. In a few more minutes, the security holo popped up on their vid displays. A synthetic voice, sounding somewhat like their friend said, "You are programmed to enter my security area. Please send your ID signal."

Susan waved her hand over the console transmitting their encrypted security ID from the DNA sensor. The security holo in their vids momentarily flashed. Robert appeared on the holo in apron, grinning. "Just in time.

Release your controls to my system and you'll automatically be taken in."

"Hi," said Susan, disengaging the controls. Their vehicle moved sideways a few feet and then accelerated towards a tree lined slope. It slowed and navigated through the trees to Robert's house.

"Amazing. The Colonel lets you drive. He must be getting old, maybe too old for such a ravishing beauty," said Robert, leering.

"Derral was right, you are an old degenerate. But, I have to say, Robert, after living in our mega building, to come here is a relief, fresh air, green, and all, said Susan.

"I'm hungry," said Derral.

"Thanks, I hope your hunger is sufficient to ignore my cooking skills. As you take the turn to my portal, look off to your left and notice, just in front of the deck, my newly formed pond. I had that put in a few months ago. It's stocked with a lineage of Japanese carp from the 16th Century. We found some skeletons with intact DNA, and cloned them. Pretty to watch, especially with a round of synth, unless you have something else on your minds."

"Robert, you gotta control yourself. Susan is my partner...and we prefer monogamy....at least I think," said Derral, looking quizzical.

"Mmhh," said Susan, playfully. "I don't know. Perhaps after we are romanced by your wonderful cooking and a few rounds of synth, who knows what can transpire."

Derral feigned a look of despair. "Well, I guess the old adage about a woman's dalliance raises its head, here."

Robert played along."One can never know...can one? I'm breaking off so I don't burn the appetizers. See you in a few."

Come on Derral, you can't be serious. I was only joking, thought Susan.

"Well?" replied Derral. "Does it sound like I was?...I was."

Susan poked him in the arm and laughed. "You have this clever way about sounding serious...you always catch me, my friend."

Derral looked at her with a fake scowl. They both laughed.

The vehicle swung down through the trees and slowed as it connected to the portal seal. On entering the portal, Robert met them with a bottle of wine and two glasses.

"Welcome my good friends," said Robert, as he embraced both of them. He made a subtle hand gesture towards Derral.

Derral instantly recalled this from their childhood. It was the gesture they had adopted to warn each other that their parents were watching them on the home security holo. Derral smiled and thought: Susan, be careful what we say. Did you see that gesture Robert gave us? We used it as kids to indicate that we were being monitored by our parents.

Wow a spy being spied on. Imagine that. Pater's wonderful trusting nature, perhaps? she thought.

We'll soon find out, thought Derral.

As Robert poured out a glass he quickly said, "Let me show you the house. I've changed it since you're been here last. Follow me." They stepped through a portal and materialized some stories below ground.

"Now, this place...wait a minute..." He passed his hand in front of a panel. "Ah, yes there were a few left...micro flys on you. They were disrupted when we entered the portal. I'm sure you knew your goings and comings are a real source of curiosity to some of the holders. These particular bugs were from your pater's crew, Susan. Now we're free to talk."

"We suspected he might be tracking our movements since we returned," said Susan.

"This is one of the reasons I wanted to speak with you in private," said Derral. "We want to go to the mountains in the northern part of the California province, but do so without being traced. We thought you might be able to help us get there. What do you think?"

Robert paused for a moment and rubbed his goatee. "I might be able to help. We'd have to create a facsimile of your energy patterns and a running holo at your place. We could start with a drama that you'd want to just stay inside for a few weeks. Work on some personal projects, etc. We could then provide a feed to any fly in the area that would mimic your presence. In the mean time, I could take you in one of our secure vehicles...that can't be traced by any signal...and drop you off where you want to stay. When you're ready to return, you'd just have to call me and I'd pick you up. I'm assuming you have a place to stay there."

"Not really, we thought you'd help us with that, too, as any place we would usually go to may likely be monitored," said Susan.

Robert thought for a moment. "There is a place just south of the

Mammoth Lakes crater. I've used it in the past. It's a small underground cottage at the 9,000 foot level, between two lakes. Usually no one is ever seen there, as it takes about 3 days to hike up to that level from the port near Bishop. If you'd like to rough it you can hike it. Otherwise, our secure vehicle can slip past the sensors. There is no vehicle traffic permitted at that level or around that part of the mountains, due to the environmental laws. We wouldn't be dropping any pollutants, anyway. The secure vehicle emits no traces of matter."

"I think we'd rather take the ride," said Derral, as he turned and smiled at Susan.

"Don't look at me," she said, playfully. "I could just as easily hike up there, as long as we have an anti-grav device to lug our belongings." They laughed.

"Now let's get on to more current and pressing matters. I'll do that for you. Next Monday, okay? That will give us time to record a facsimile staying at home bit."

"Yes, we can be ready by then," said Susan.

"Notice this wine is about 6 centuries old. From organically grown grapes in the old California province. I was able to program my simulator with some tech we received from one of the outer rim civilizations. It projects back in time and generates a profile of the soil samples and weather conditions for any crop. Then, generates the product."

"Wine is great. But what about food, said Susan. Take us to your kitchen and we can get drunk while watching you work."

Chapter Fourteen

Suspicion

The Secretary was standing over his holos. They flashed brightly and the holo went blank. The view from Susan and Derral's microflys embedded in their clothing, disappeared from the holo.

"Shit," shouted the Secretary, "The son of a bitch activated his security system. Well, as the chief of my intelligence service, I suppose he is merely doing his job. Too bad, looked like they were getting into something interesting. Oh well. It's not like they're some arch enemy like the idiotic General and his blithering crony, Oice."

"Yes Mr. Secretary," said Ulemann, with some hesitancy.

"Susan's my blood relative...bedding down with that star jockey as a life partner. Why do I suspect they're up to something? She's much different since coming back from her New Year's journey. Why do they go to one of my Intelligence people. Records have Derral and the Chief growing up in the same Common, so they must have known each other. The space man and the spook. But I can't seem to get over that they're up to something," said the Secretary, partly to himself while absentmindedly working his console.

"Perhaps, Mr. Secretary, it is just that...a lasting childhood friendship and nothing more," said Ulemann, sheepishly.

"No!" the Secretary shouted. It just doesn't make sense. My intuition has rarely been wrong, even about people whom I hardly know. I just don't feel right about this."

"Perhaps sir, that your intuition is more accurate with people whom you do not know so well, as you have little history and the cues are not so intertwined with what your experience is. As we know, experience is not always the most accurate predictor. Many in our circles are quite skilled in acting out false personas to set up a certain mind set."

"Oh, cut the bullshit, Ulemann. I know you're usually right about these things...that's why I retain you as my confident...but still, it grates on me...I know they're up to something and I want to know what it is. Send more flys out to their location," said the Secretary as he abruptly turned to leave the room.

Ulemann called after him. "We already attempted to insert more flies, Mr. Secretary. But Major Laing appears to have an excellent security system. None could get beyond his outer perimeter. An attempt was made to put back-tracers on our flys to discern their origin. I'm sorry sir."

"What the hell do you mean, back-tracers...do you mean they can trace them to our command center here?" The Secretary spun around and stormed back across the room until he was standing over Ulemann with his hands on his hips, looking down as if he about to admonish a small child.

"Not exactly sir...to back trace the exact location is not totally impossible. But we've identified the back-trace signal at the 1 billion gigahertz range and blocked it. However that took some seconds to accomplish. In that time, the back-tracers could have identified our center as the originating focus, but not you specifically. There is no way of determining that, now. However, our techs assured me that the next set of back-tracers will be tracked to a bogus system they set up and identified as coming from there, someplace in Africasia."

"Ulemann!" shouted the Secretary. "Why didn't the techs have that set up to begin with? What are we running here, a third rate operation? This is the office of the Secretary of the Solar Confederation, for shit sakes. We are supposed to have the most up-to-date technology for protection of the Confederation, not commoner drek. Why? ...Tell me why?"

"I'm sorry your excellency. I asked them that same question. They told me they could not tag a tracking signal at first reception, only after it was identified as a tracker, could they then program their modules to track subsequent signals."

"Well, get rid of the whole damn section and get me some people who are suitable. I don't believe that bullshit...Did you?"

"Not really sir. I asked them why. They said it was beyond their capability, the standard response from techs when they've been duped."

"Who is running that section...that Char woman. I thought she was good. Get rid of her, too."

"I'm sorry sir, but she was on vacation over the past month. Her seconds are in charge.

So give her another chance, but get rid of her seconds. Call her back from vacation and demand that she get some techs who keep up with the latest innovations...that won't just give us a bunch of crap, will you. There is too much at stake here to play with sensitive egos. Give them a life pension...but get rid of them. Thank them for their service, for me. But hint that their failure to keep their end up in this operation was the proverbial straw. But only do so when they're on the doorstep. We wouldn't want them to sabotage any equipment. Tell them the life pension is dependent on their silence and discretion. And you tell Char to warn them if they have sabotaged anything, their pensions will be revoked and we'll send them to the outer rim colony for treason. Make sure you tell Char to let them know this is coming from me...and I'm very concerned about this lapse. Of course they'll likely be quite happy to be pensioned. They'll just become more of the otiose majority supported by the Confederation for doing nothing."

"Yes sir." Ulemann long ago learned to respond as little as possible when the Secretary was in such a state. But he took a chance. "I'm afraid Char will be quite disappointed, as she nurtured these techs..."

The Secretary abruptly cut him off. "Well you can tell Char to choose between her disappointment and her position here. That's all I want to hear about it. Contact my Intelligence Chief and see if we can do anything about the tracers, so we don't get any more. Oh. That is Laing, what a mess of Plutonian snail shit this is..."

"I'm afraid I've contacted his third in command, loyal only to you. She checked that with her techs. They said there was nothing they could do but to put a back-track signal on the spectrum. That would enable identification of any other tracers by embedding a photon in any signal. She was surprised that Char hadn't already had that enabled. Char's techs said they were having problems with the photon emitter, and left it disabled until she came back, in a few revolutions."

"Oh shit, shit...snail shit," proclaimed the Secretary. "Tell those mindless idiots that they're lucky they're even getting a pension after that. They're lucky I need support from the populace, now more than ever...but don't you dare tell them that."

At the same moment General Suddhis was in his command room

with Rakard Oice, peering over Lynchon's shoulder at the holo display. It suddenly went blank.

"Lynchon," screamed, the General. "What happened? And whatever happened you better make it good, you fool..."

"It seemed as if the flys we had on the Secretary's genetic daughter were destroyed. It's not surprising as they're at Major General Laing's house. He was associated with Derral Priestly in his boyhood. Probably just friends. But Laing is the SIC Chief...maybe there's more to it."

"Is there anyway we can get some more in there. Our operation depends on what they've obtained from the Da'yoni's. We don't even know what they ate there, yet...or how they ate with no bodies." said Rakard Oice, frowning.

"Yes," said the General, becoming increasingly agitated, pacing back and forth. "Listen, you little piece of a black hole for a brain, get that fixed so we can get some more flies in there...or I'll have you skinned alive."

Lynchon began to tremble. "I...I'm afraid that we most likely will not be able to. Laing has the latest SIC proprietary security. We can't decipher that, General, sir. I've tried to send more in but they were destroyed at the periphery of his security perimeter. But there is one possibility."

"Well do it you fool...or else," said the General as he and Oice hurriedly stepped through the room portal.

Chapter Fifteen

Shared Pleasures

"Robert, how did you ever get such a contraption...that's a gas stove from the 21st Century isn't it? I've seen pictures of them in historical records," said Derral," as he turned a knob and a burner crackled to life. They both jumped back. What did I do, he said.

"You just lit the burner. I had that fabricated from an historical holo record," said Robert as he took the lid off one of the pots.

"That smells delicious...what is it?" said Susan, as she peered over Derral's shoulder.

"It's my own special spaghetti sauce...food from the Southern European Province...also from centuries ago. I'm certain you've never seen this food, unless you had a replicator that was programmed to create it...but not the same as really cooked. Yes, gas is the only way to cook real food. Notice these pots and pans are fabricated from ancient stainless steel and iron, metals that we no longer use. It was difficult finding a fabricator to make these....but these are the best to cook with. Have a taste," said Robert, dipping a spoon and offering it.

"Wow. This tastes a bit like an Andromedean sauce I had when I visited one of their small planets in that system a few years ago. Makes me hungrier," said Derral.

"Maybe the Andromedeans had some Italian blood. I've tasted their sauce, too. Do you know they make it from a fruit, not unlike the Italian tomato. But the Andromedean fruit is the size of a watermelon. It also grows on a vine like the tomato. I have some tomatoes planted out back, right outside the back deck if you want to take a look," said Robert as he gestured towards the portal behind Susan.

She stepped to the portal and materialized on the other side.

Robert started to whisper to Derral, but stopped as Susan came back in.

"What a beautiful view. Those vines...those large red berry's. That's what tomatoes are?" said Susan.

"Yes. Those are the only ones I know of on the planet. The plant is considered to be extinct. I grew those from some seeds found in an excavation site, discovered during one of our operations. They were preserved in a large container of oil that tested to be about 500 years old. I used some of that oil to make the sauce. It's olive oil. We still have olives growing on wild trees in the more moderate climates. Hey Derral, can you hand me that bottle of wine over there. This needs a bit more," said Robert, as he stirred the sauce.

"Can I do anything to help?" said Susan.

"Sure...see if that water is boiling. If it is, put a few spoonfuls of the white stuff from that box over there, in it." Robert gestured with his chin. "That's salt. Also something that's no longer produced. I distilled it from the ocean water. Then dump the contents of that bowl...fresh pasta...I made that this morning...into the boiling water. Derral, you can take that large round wok...the round pot with the wooden handle...put some oil in it and some of that garlic...the crushed tan material in that dish over there...and then, when it heats up, place the bowl of seafood....that was from my replicator, unfortunately....in the wok and brown it...cook it by swishing it around until it browns. When it browns take some of that green stuff in the two small dishes by the stove...that's parsley and oregano, place half in the sauce and the rest over the seafood. Toss it...mix it up with the seafood. When the pasta is done in a couple of minutes, we can eat."

"This is amazing. What odors and flavors...but what work. Nothing like a replicator," said Derral.

"Yes, but you'll see the difference when we eat...and you can't smell the cooking from the replicator. That's part of the pleasure," said Robert. "Let's sit down, have another glass of wine, and wait a few minutes."

Sitting at the round table in the kitchen, Robert refilled their glasses. "Cheers," he said.

Susan looked around, taking a sip. "Robert this kitchen looks so old fashioned. How did you do it?"

"I hired some local craftsman, researched kitchen designs going back to the early 20th Century, and gave them the plans. They used the trees

140

around the property for the cabinet wood, and locally mined quartz to fashion the countertops. A local metal smith fashioned the plumbing and hardware. The smith also fashioned the stove from some plans I discovered in an old database. He is probably the last of his kind, as he was the only one around the area I could locate. Unfortunately, the gas is not like the natural stuff that was used. That was mined from the planet, something that is now against the Solar Confederation laws for personal use. I had a replicator create it and stored it in some tanks out back. Let's talk about your request, before the food is done. We're secure here.

Derral responded. "We'd like to arrange a transport up to the mountains for a vacation from Susan's watchful father and his microflys. Now they're ubiquitous, especially in our living space. Can you help us?"

"What you're asking for, my friends, can get me in a lot of trouble with your pater, Susan, for one," said Robert, with a sly grin.

"What could he actually do. Doesn't the SIC charter direct that it is an arm of the people, not just the Holders or the Secretary? That's what most people believe," said Susan.

"Yes, that's true, in a way," said Robert. "But the reality is we still report directly to the Holders through the Secretary's office. If he finds out about such a deception, I'll likely be in hot water with my Chief, the SIC Cabinet minister to the Secretary. And if the Secretary is notified, I could lose my position and have to move in with you for a place to live. I could no longer afford the expense of this place. As you know it's now fully covered by the Holders. We're not supposed to use SIC transports for public or even political use."

"It's not that you'd be using it for the public," said Derral. "After all the publicity, since we came back from Da'yoni...and the hologs following our every move in hopes to get something they can display on the evening uploads...and especially since the attack on our life that was unsuccessful thanks to Major Dennings, our military escort. After that, I think you can justify use of this little deception to take us to the mountains, don't you think? ...You know this wine is...it's a bit like intoxica."

"Attack on your life? I wasn't privy to that information. I've recently been occupied with another project and haven't kept up with the holo uploads," said Robert, looking puzzled as he refilled their glasses. "This wine does have the same effect as intoxica. The ancients referred to it as spirits....as in raising one's spirits. Intoxica is a sublingual of real wine... takes all the pleasure away from drinking it."

"I don't think our adventure got on the holos," said Susan. "Fortunately, Major Dennings anticipated such an attack and exchanged our personal carrier with an atmospheric fighter, before we left pater's gathering. The Major thought it best not to publicize it. But on our return to our place from paters, we were attacked by a few heavily armed atmospheric fighters with pulse weapons and who knows what else. They tried to disable us. But thanks to my brave hero Colonel Derral and the Major's excellent, but scary air combat maneuvers that scared the crap out of me, we were able to disable their fighters and take them into custody. The Major later told us they were from a dissident jingoistic faction promoting isolationism. They wanted to kidnap us and hold us as hostages while demanding concessions from the Holders. The concession being to cut off relationships with other stellar communities and return to the planet-centric days of the 23rd Century."

"Doesn't that make a difference," said Derral humbly smiling, as he gave the secret hand gesture of their childhood club, four crossed fingers.

Robert laughed. "Well, my friend, I guess that certainly does make a difference. Our story will be that you came to me to help you get away for a while, as you both were sick of being in the public eye...and the danger of that. That should cover it with my boss, if he asks. But, as I said, I'll need a week to prepare. It will be just between us, but that is a good cover. I'll set up some flies that will record your moves about your place over the week. That will be the feed we'll use to randomize and send back through to whoever is monitoring you. You'll be replaced by realistic holos that no one could tell apart, even if they were standing in front of you, unless they reached out to shake your hand or something. We'll fabricate an illness that you, Derral, contracted from one of your galactic trips...one that calls for isolation for a few weeks. That way, no one will dare come to your door. Every incoming transmission will be voice-channeled to your location. You will answer in voice and the holo will simulate your gestures for the holocom. For starters let's see who those flies we just dismantled were sent from." A holo panel appeared before Robert. He made a few finger gestures.

A stream of pulses appeared in front of them, then a synthesized voice:

"The microflys were from two sources. One emanated from the Secretary Priestly's complex, the others from General Urvey Suddhis' control room. Both have tried to re-establish but were blocked by security perimeter."

"I wonder what interest that brain trust Suddhis has with you two. I can see the Secretary's interest, but Suddhis must have something in mind to risk this infraction. If he were identified as the originator of the tracking flies, he would be dismissed from the Holders for violating a citizen's privacy. On the other hand, the Secretary can justify his violation in the interest of security. I'll have to look into that. It may just mean he's doing his usual bumbling. But I don't think even he's stupid enough to take this kind of a risk. So something must be up. At least we have the tracer evidence on him, now...Let's eat or mangia, as they used to say in the Italian protectorate."

Chapter Sixteen

Beginning Plans

Over the next week, the Secretary reestablished his microflys, as did Suddhis. Upon leaving Robert's compound they reinserted themselves in Susan and Derral's clothing. They were careful not to speak about anything that might betray their plans. Towards the end of the week, Derral went to the medspec set up by Robert. He was diagnosed with a highly contagious form of cross-species Cerulian disease supposedly contracted from his last work experience at the outer rim planet of Cerulia. As it was a viral parasitic disease, it took a month to manifest symptoms. Both he and Susan were quarantined in their domicile. The server bots were not to have any direct contact, only through vid, as there was a concern they would pick up some of the virus on their artificial skin and transmit it to humans. They put on a pretty convincing act of boredom, being so confined. The only symptom displayed by Derral was fatigue. He feigned to sleep and read a lot over the next few days. They were contacted by secure holocom at the end of the week. Robert said he was ready to reprogram the flies in their quarters. They were to sit at the table eating and talking about Derral's fatigue. The fly transmission exhibited a momentary flicker, noticed by Ulemann on the Secretary's holo. At the point the fake holos took, Susan and Derral grabbed their cases and met Robert at the portal. They had given their server bots the afternoon to recharge. No one was around to see the portal open. The vessel materialized once the portal closed. Robert was at the controls. Susan and Derral hurriedly entered. The vessel became invisible, the portal opened, and they were off.

Ulemann, sat staring at the holo. He called the Secretary. "Mr. Secretary, I just detected an unusual flicker in the fly transmission from your bio and her husband. Perhaps we should investigate?"

"Get them on the holo and watch the fly holo as they answer, ordered the Secretary.

Ulemann opened a channel and contacted them. The audio of Susan's holo alerted her. "Uhh. Robert, I think the Secretary is trying to contact me. What do I do?" said Susan.

"Just answer as we rehearsed. Watch the feedback on the holo from the flys at your domicile. Perfectly in sync with your voice," said Robert as he activated the com link to the holos.

"Yes, pater," said Susan, with a surprised tone. Susan's facsimile reflected a surprised look on the holo before them.

"Just calling to see how you two are, my dear. I'm sure being isolated isn't something that you prefer," said the Secretary.

"You can say that again, pater. While Derral's been a bit under the weather, I'm fine. But I guess we'll have to remain isolated for the next few weeks, according to the medspec."

"Ah. So I'm told, my dear. If there is anything I can send you, please feel free to ask."

"I'm afraid not pater. We can't even have direct contact with the bots, as the medspec was concerned that we'd transmit some of the virus to their artificial skin. Fortunately, as it only became active and contagious the other day, we didn't infect anyone else we met since our return. We were told that such a virus, if left untreated, can become quite complicated. It's an alien cross-specie virus we have no immunity for. I guess all we have to do is wait it out. We were even advised to not accept any outside packages or envelopes, as that risks interfering with the treatment by introducing other organisms."

"Very well, my dear. I'll check in with you every few days to see how you're doing. It's not something you picked up from Da'yoni, is it dear?"

Susan hesitated for a brief moment. "No pater, we don't think so. The medspec identified it as a Cerulian virus, specific only to that system. That was where Derral was last working, just before we left for Da'yoni. The Med said it takes about a month to manifest the first symptoms. The only thing we can do is take the prescription and follow the Med's direction. He guaranteed that we'd be able to move out and about within a lunar cycle or so, as that is when we should begin, or rather Derral...should begin to test negative for the presence. Thus far, I don't seem to have contracted it. I may have started taking the medicine in time, according to the Spec."

"I'm disappointed that will disrupt our dining plans. But, perhaps after you get the clearance. Okay, I have many things to do today. I'll be talking with you in a few days, dear. Good by...and get well soon...Oh, by the way give me the name of the medspec and I'll verify he's the best for you."

"Oh, his first name is Lascott. He was recommended by your Intelligence Chief, Robert. We didn't meet him face to face, as he examined us over holo. You can check with Robert for his full name."

"Okay, my dear. Get well soon." The holo closed to the seal of the Secretary.

Susan turned to Derral. Well I hoped we passed that test, she thought.

Derral responded aloud. "Remember who is also here my dear. How did pater sound?"

"He sounded his usual but I sensed he wasn't actually believing us, but had nothing to base his suspicion on. He asked for the name of the medspec to verify his credentials. I referred him to Robert. What do you think, Robert?"

"That was a great performance," said Robert. "Even a pro couldn't have done better. Don't worry, I'll send a feed through the flies that will convince your father and anyone else monitoring your holos, that the small disruption in the transmission at the switch, was the result of a recent solar flare. The next step, in our grand deception, is for Derral to develop some gastric distress...and you'll be concerned to call the med spec. Of course your pater will be recording the whole bit. He'll never suspect a thing."

Robert banked the craft and pointed. "Look down there. We're coming over the Bakersfield quadrant. We should be over the Bishop protectorate in a few moments. And the best part is that we're invisible to any sig detection. We're flying at about 15 K Kilos per 15 degrees of solar arc. Your pater's fastest, aside from other SIC craft, couldn't touch us, even if they could see us."

"How do we keep from burning up," said Derral. "Any conventional craft would be glowing and breaking apart at that speed in the atmosphere."

"The invisibility also minimizes atmospheric friction. Special skin on the outer hull," said Robert as he passed his hand over the panel, decreasing their speed.

146

"Are those the lakes area down there?" asked Susan.

"Yup. That's it. See that small dome structure, barely visible on the middle lake? That's your home for the next few weeks. We can pull the craft right inside it's portal. If anyone is watching...which is highly unlikely... all they'll see is the portal opening and closing. The bots are programmed to communicate they're testing the portal, in case anyone is watching or listening. Then you're on your own for the next few weeks. I have to get this thing back to dock it, so it's not missed."

Robert set a glide pattern. The craft slowed and glided towards the blank wall. The portal opened momentarily and closed behind them.

"Here we are folks. I'm afraid I can't stay. But it's fully stocked, even with some simulated wine and some of that Italian protectorate food I cooked for you, in the cold fusion area. Enjoy your selves. Feel free to walk and hike about. We set up an invisible net so that any passing satellite or cruiser will not be able to see through it. To them it will look like an uninhabited dome and surrounding forest. The net is set up to nullify any infra-red signature from human bodies. Animals will be picked up, but no humans."

"How about people around here," said Derral.

"I checked that out. The only people around here are some mountain folk, living off the land. While they're a bit shy, they'd probably like to host a new face. They're right over the ridge of the upper lake, if you get a hankering for some company, check them out. I'm sure you'd be welcomed. But don't tell them who you are. If you run into any trouble...which you shouldn't, call me right away. Have a pleasant vacation."

"Thanks old friend. I can't express how appreciative we are for this," said Derral, as he hugged him.

"Susan kissed Robert on the cheek. "Yes, thank you Robert. This should wash the stress away."

"Remember, though, as long as your wrist sensor is green, no one can listen. Every 30 solar degrees I have to let the net down, as it would be detected if left up all the time. A few seconds before it's down, your wrist sensor will flash a yellow and beep you. When that happens, don't talk about anything other than general issues, especially don't use your names... as it is only the audio sensor net that we have to let down, Okay?" said

Robert.

"Okay, said Susan and Derral, simultaneously. "We'll be watchful of the signal, continued Susan.

"You don't have to be too watchful. As I'd only have to do it if we sense other craft in the vicinity...so it will be either every 30 degrees, on schedule, or shorter if something is sensed." He waved to them and closed the hatch behind them. They turned and the craft became invisible. The portal opened and closed for the briefest moment.

"Wow...we're on vacation," said Susan. They embraced. "We can do anything we like. Let's build a fire in the fireplace if there is one. Robert told me the smoke and body heat is contained and scrubbed to avoid detection."

They walked into the living quarters. "You got your wish," said Derral, looking around the dome. "This must have been furnished from another era from the distant past. No polymers. All the furniture is made of wood. The bedrooms had real beds, unlike the anti-grav beds. I hope we can sleep in them."

"Don't worry about that. Hiking at this altitude will make us sleep like babies," said Derral.

Susan looked for the controls to the fire place. "Derral, I can't find how to light this," she said.

Derral laughed. "Looks like we'll have to get some exercise chopping wood and lighting our own fire, my dear. I noticed a real axe in the corner as we entered. Look here though." He lifted a wooden panel in the wall. It was stacked with wood and kindling. "There's enough to last a few weeks... so maybe we won't have to work."

Susan expertly piled up some kindling and logs.

"How did you ever learn to do that?" said Derral.

"I was at summer camp as a Galactic Scout, when I was a kid. I know more than you give me credit for." She took out her small pulsar and lit the kindling.

"That's no fair, said Derral. You have to use what is here...the natural way. He pointed to the matches over the mantle piece."

"Well, that's okay for a start. Later for the fire sticks."

" How about a bottle of wine before the fire? Imagine that, a real fire," said Derral.

They awoke the next morning to a scratching noise at the portal.

Susan was already at the control panel in the bedroom attempting to figure out how to activate the outdoor holos so she could see who or what was there.

Derral watched from the bed.

"Why don't you try that slider on the left," saidDerral. He got out of bed and stood beside her.

Susan did and the holo flickered for a moment and then displayed a map of the surrounding property with highlighted points for viewing angles. Susan touched the nearest viewpoint to the front door. They both jumped back as a large brown bear with cubs stood on it's hind legs in front of the vid, just outside the front door.

"What do we do now," said Susan. "I've only seen the likes of those in a zoo. How can we leave here with that girl and her family at the front door?"

Derral grinned. "Look at the help holo and search for bear and safety."

Susan commanded the help holo. A list of instructions scrolled in front of her. It showed the EMF pulsing weapons in a closet that were guaranteed to drive a bear away. Also there was a central pulsing around the perimeter with a highlighted switch. Susan touched the switch and was directed to another series of commands. She touched the command sending an EMF, non-harmful pulse within 100 meters of the property and watched the results. The bear and her cubs reared on their hind legs, growled and then ran into the woods.

"That was easy," said Susan."I guess we won't be leaving the house without those weapons in the closet. Let's see." She crossed the room to the closet and retrieved two small EMF pulse pistols.

"Wow, these look serious. Here's a stun gun with a few degrees of disabling settings...and a help holo." She pressed the help button and a rotating holo image of the weapon appeared before them. She pressed it again and the holo demonstrated the different settings and effects.

"Mmhh," said Derral. "Looks like we could seriously hurt someone with this set on maximum. The stun setting will alter an animals consciousness and put them to sleep for 2 minutes; an animal as large as our bear friend."

A warning flashed in red on the holo. *Can cause heart stoppage if set above 5 for humans.*

"Well, I hope we don't have to use it even though it feels good to have it. Just be careful you don't shoot yourself in the foot, my dear. Use the safety when it's in your pocket," said Derral, as he examined the other pistol. "We should lock it on stun 3, so it will stun a bear and we won't kill anything or ourselves by mistake. We'll have the Environmental Police up here if we did, I'm sure. Robert told me this is a nature preserve, maintained by the Confederation Ecology Fund. All the animals have sensor chips. That's all we need is to be investigated by them...and our private vacation is over."

"In my final year of classes," said Susan, "I learned The Confederation Ecology Fund was set up by a group of Holders, a decade or so before, ostensibly to protect the environment. However, some believe it was set up to protect any sub-surface mineral rights the Holders had secretly purchased years ago. I recall having this conversation with pater, but he said that was absurd. Most of the diamond producing areas in the Africasia, are no longer mined. This region was bought up by one of the Holders in the Ecology Fund consortium, as were some mineral rich areas in the polar regions of the planet and beneath the seas. Around the turn of the 22nd Century, the world government...a pre-Holder government, passed a planetary treaty to permit private ownership of the sea floors. While some took advantage of the opportunity, the treaty was largely ignored until a group of Holders discovered it when researching the archives."

"Yeah, on one of my long, boring trips I read the history," said Derral. "For the past 200 years, there was no interest in sea floor property because there was no cost-effective technology to farm or mine it. Now, with the advent of visits to other star systems, the Confederation acquired technology that can easily be adapted to ocean depths. From some of the rim galaxies, pioneers brought back tech that can nullify the pressure of the depths. One can easily work at 10,000 feet depths, now, as easily as one can work on the surface, whether it be through water or rock. Before the pioneers even returned to the planet, the Holders group had jumped at the possibility and filed owner certificates on many thousands of acres of sea beds and mountain ranges, where there were concentrations of minerals. They manipulated planetary media so that when the Holder purchases were leaked to investigative reporters, the holos were occupied for weeks with humorous anecdotes about the idiocy of the Holders and their purchase of these useless certificates. The Holders maintained silence on the matter. They were at least wise enough to stay out of the debate. The publicity gradually subsided, as there was only a one sided attack in the news holos. As the reign of the Holders became more prominent in planetary affairs, the few that had invested in the seabed and mineral rights established the faux Confederation Ecology Fund, ostensibly to protect the ecological resources. The Fund was another Holder deception used to keep watch over their privately owned seabeds and mountain ranges containing rare minerals and other means of wealth."

"These are one of the ranges, monitored by the Ecology Fund?" asked Susan.

"Robert told me this one was secretly owned by General Suddhis, Rakard Oice, along with a few other equally deviously minded Holders. Fortunately, this was only a minor part of their investment, one which was forgotten, but still monitored by the salaried employees of the Ecology Fund. The monitors were stationary satellites with sensors that captured any large discharge of EMF or energy that would detect any mining or prospecting operations. That's why Robert had shields installed, I guess," said Derral.

It's so beautiful out here, thought Susan, as she opened the door to the fresh pine scented breeze blowing up the slope from the south. The cabin dome was just below the tree line.

Derral joined her and took a deep breath. Yeah, clean, clear air, unlike the city. I'm surprised we didn't notice this when we were dropped off, yesterday.

"Our noses were probably still clogged with the dirt of the city," said Susan, as she primly covered her mouth in a gesture that mimed an "Oops," when she realized she slipped and switched to vocal from thought.

Derral thought: You know that's not so bad here, especially since we're having a mundane conversation. Robert did say there were others living up here. But you know...

Yes, Yes, Yes... Daddy, thought Susan, as she elbowed him in the ribs. He picked up a handful of the newly fallen snow and threw it at her. She ducked. They had a snowball fight, laughing heartedly.

You know that's the first time we really laughed since we came back, thought Derral.

Yeah. We need to have more fun...but it's hard to do knowing the seriousness of our mission, thought Susan.

Derral reached out for her hand. Let's take a hike up to the lake above and see what's there. Should only take a few hours. We don't even need to take water, up here. It's above human habitats. We can just follow the falls and the stream. Hear it off in the distance? Sounds like wind whispering through the pines...almost like one of the rim planets I worked on for a while. I almost forgot what nature is all about.

Yes, thought Susan. Wait a minute, I'll get a small pack and some snacks from the replicator. She went back in the dome for a few minutes. Derral stood outside gazing into the woods, thinking: I hope we do the right thing with this...I act like I know...but am just as frightened as she is.

Susan picked up his thoughts from inside and responded. I knew you were just a softie, dear...you didn't fool me with all that machismo stuff. He could hear her laughing through the door.

I know...I guess I can't keep anything to myself, anymore. But you know, I just wish we had some way to stay in contact with the Da'yoni for advice. I mean they kind of dumped this on us and left us out in the cold.

Susan came out and locked the door. "Just in case any more hungry bears come by," she said. They started to walk in silence, up the switchbacks leading out of the trees and stopped about half way up to the next lake for a break.

I didn't think I was in this bad of shape, thought Susan, as she caught her breath. She bent over the rushing stream, dipping her cup to take a drink. These cups are pretty cool, she said as she held out the stainless steel cup for Derral.

Yeah, that's why they're called Sierra cups, from a long time ago when hiking was a popular activity...a few hundred years ago...Since that time, hiking went the way of other enjoyable activities. People got lazy with the new conveniences. I was surprised they even had some in the cabin. Must be one of Robert's contributions, thought Derral.

As Derral drank from the stream, Susan closed off her thoughts to him, looked up the mountain and visualized a future, two divergent paths. One path led to a place where most all the Holders were dismissed by the populace, including her pater, after their deceit was discovered, using their position to accumulate hidden wealth. The two Holders who were not dismissed were from the Africasian quadrant, were ethical and spiritually oriented. While they maintained their candor, they did not have access to the technology possessed by the others. And because they held personal ethics over material goods, they found themselves actually excluded from the other subgroup of Holders. Those two have been contacted by the Da'yoni Ambassador, in private. He engaged in ongoing dialogue with them. Just prior to his trip back to the home planet. Our Da'yoni guide mentioned we might contact and trust these two, alone of all the other Holders. Something to keep in mind to minimize conflict when we act...

Susan...Susan...where did you go, thought Derral, as he stood in front of her.

She shook her head seeming to come out of a reverie. I was just... thinking...about where this will all lead us.

Derral, she thought. Those two spiritual Holders from Africasia, the Da'yoni mentioned just before we came home? Perhaps we should contact them, at some point.

Do you think we should do this so soon? thought Derral. I think we have some more ground to travel before we ally ourselves with anyone from the Holders. The only thing we know is that these two Holders have been in private contact with the Da'yoni. I'd wait a while. We need to make more contact with the remaining Holders before we develop alliances. We don't know that there aren't others who are relatively untainted. When we get back we should try to contact the Da'yoni ambassador and ask him.

Whatever, let's enjoy this vacation and not get so serious. You're right, thought Susan. She reached for his hand and they started walking up the steep trail.

"I didn't realize I was in such bad shape. Too much leisure time," said Susan, as she sat on a rock, gasping.

"Well, this is about 10,000 feet up, dear. I'm having a bit of trouble, too. Take one of these oxy tabs," he said, reaching in his pocket to hand her a packaged tablet.

"What'll this do?" she said.

"It's something they gave us on one of the rim planets when we had to climb against the gravity. It increases the oxygen absorption 50%. It takes about 5 minutes to start working."

She unwrapped the tablet, went over to the stream and took a cup of water to wash it down.

Maybe we should sit down for five minutes, then, thought Susan. They leaned against a boulder and listened to the fast moving stream, in silence.

Chapter Seventeen

Suspiceon Or Delusion?

The Secretary was huddled with Char and Ulemann over a holo of Derral & Susan's dwelling.

"It seems all they've been doing is sleeping, eating, and reading over the past five days," said the Secretary. "They haven't left their dwelling. It's almost too good to be true. Are you sure the flies are intact at their place?" He turned to Char who looked puzzled.

She hesitated. "Yes sir. They are intact. I've been running checks every few moments. All came back clean. It seems like your bio leads a dull life, especially when confined to their home."

"Yes...perhaps, my suspicion is just because this is the first time I ever monitored them this intensely. Just keep on with the monitoring. Anything unusual, report to me immediately. I'll call her to see if anything is different." The Secretary went to the holo and dialed in Derral and Susan's code. The holo blinked for a few moments and Susan appeared. He looked over at the holo to confirm the image.

Susan was actually taking the call by the stream. "Yes Pater," she said with a smile. Her voice was synced with the holo at their domicile. The background noise from the stream was filtered out.

Hello, my dear. I just thought I'd call and touch base. I haven't heard from you in a while," said the Secretary.

"We just wanted some down time with our quarantine and all, Pater. I'm sure you can understand...especially after all the publicity following our trip. We're just sort of staying around," she added, hesitating for the briefest moment.

"Well, my dear, when are we going to see you again. When can we have dinner together."

"Thank you Pater. I'll talk with Derral and get back with you. While

Derral feels fine, we probably wouldn't want to do anything for the next fortnight or so. We'd have to get clearance from the Med to have visitors. I'll call and let you know. We'll be sure to have those Rim delicacies. We loved them the last time we dined together."

"I'm looking forward to it. Feel free to call me anytime. You're my only family, you know."

"Of course, pater. We'll be in touch." Susan ended the call and thought she felt kind of sad for him.

She turned to Derral. "You know his bio partner was murdered a few years ago in a coup attempt by an unknown party. They were aiming for him but she stepped in the way at a large gala. They never did identify the shooter. A long range pulse weapon was used. The shot came from about five clicks away. Before the sensors backtracked to the spot, whoever did it had disappeared. The only people who had possession of such weapons were the military. They had just recently been acquired from one of the rim planets. They don't think it was an alien, as there were no alien signatures within 10 clicks along the sight path, either before or after the killing."

"Your pater hasn't had it easy. Sounds like it may have been one of his military connected Holders," said Derral. "As he is one of the more straight-forward Holders, he has acquired many enemies." He continued in thought: Surprising he is also so deceitful and self-aggrandizing.

Let's not bad mouth pater, thought Susan. He has done a lot for me as I grew up. If it weren't for him, we would never have had the opportunity to go to Da'yoni.

Derral silently responded: I'm sorry, my best friend. I know. He put his arm around her waist. They resumed the steep climb.

The Secretary continued to look at the blank holocom. "I don't know Ulemann. Something doesn't seem right here. She's not the same. There's something different here, I can't put my finger on it. Char, run an analysis of the transmission during that holo with my bio," said the Secretary.

"Yes sir. It should only take a few secs," said Char, as the call analyzer holo appeared. "It seems okay sir. The only unusual thing was a microsecond flicker at the beginning. However, that is not uncommon, especially if the band width is heavily used. This time of day is a time of heavy usage."

"Okay, maybe I'm being too cautious. But I was sure there was a difference in her mood."

"Perhaps you disturbed them in an intimate moment, Sir," offered Ulemann.

"Don't be disgusting, Ulemann. But you're probably right. Perhaps we should focus on what my real enemies are up to, rather than my only relative. Go to the General's site and see what he's cooking up."

"Yes, sir," said Char. She directed the console to a holo of the General's office. The General was sitting at his console with Lynchon, looking at a holo of Susan and Derral's dwelling.

"Well, that son of a bitch," cried the Secretary. "Ulemann, first see if he's monitoring our flys or using his own…and send troopers out there to arrest him and suspend him in a neurofield box for a few days until I see him. I love those boxes. All neurofunctions are suspended except consciousness. See if he likes that, watching his own waste accumulate with no control. That is the highest violation of privacy, my god…my own biologue."

Ulemann turned towards the secretary with a sheepish look. "Mr. Secretary, that is what we are doing, too. If we arrest them, that fact will surely come up in any legal proceeding."

"I suppose you're right," said the Secretary. "Can we withdraw our flys and then have him arrested?"

"That could be traced, unless we insert a fly to do it from the inside and then self-destruct. The fly would have to circumvent their defenses, though. That might take a while. But it could still be traced by the field residuals. We would have to direct a bot to go to the General's dwelling and shut down their power for a second or two. They would be very suspicious after that. They might be able to trace it back. However the chance of them doing so is pretty slim."

"Do it then. If we are traced, I'll claim I discovered him by intercepting his transmission in a random security holo…and my flys were used to monitor the health concerns of my daughter, given the recent infection of her partner. As Secretary, I certainly am entitled to do random security checks through our public agency."

"As you wish, sir. It should take less than a cycle. We should be able to complete it by first light on the morrow."

General Suddhis abruptly rose to his feet and began to pace back and forth in front of the holocom platform. Susan and Derral were on the holo.

Chapter Eighteen

Revelation

They continued climbing the steep trail in silence, breathing heavily. Susan thought about her pater, as they climbed. They were now above the tree line and stopped beside the stream. How did our first simulation go? thought Derral. Did our con work?

You don't have to put it like that, thought Susan. But yes, he didn't seem to suspect anything. Perhaps when we speak again, I won't be so nervous at deceiving or being deceived.

Yes, thought Derral. All you have to do is keep your awareness on the fact that Pater treats you like any other political threat. He uses his technology to keep an eye on you, especially since our vacation to Da'yoni. He has no consideration for you as his biolog, nor does he have any feeling for you. He will use you to his own advantage. This is not exactly like a 25th century pater-daughter relationship...

Derral, please stop, thought Susan. I have a hard time dealing with these, even if they are facts. To me, a genetic connection is meaningful, regardless if it is to him or not. It just upsets me to hear you tell me of what the *reality* is...that's if there is one. All my life, I yearned for a family like I read about in the historical records. So, at least with this, let me keep to my fantasies. I'll be cautious...don't worry. Now lets get moving. I don't want to have to come down in the dark.

OK, thought Derral, as he reached in the pack for his locator. I think we only have another 15 degrees...an hour or so until we reach the topmost lake. Let's move through this scrub over here. The trail goes away from the stream for a while, but it's more direct. See?

He held up the locater. Their position was marked by a flashing x. He pressed a button and a holo formed in front of them. Derral pressed his finger on the third lake and asked the device: "How long will it take to get to the lake here, given our rate of travel."

The device responded in a soft, feminine voice: "If you begin now and don't stop, you will achieve your goal in a 15 degree arc of your star."

Well, thought Susan. Just an hour to go. I hope you can keep up. She spun around and ran up the steep trail. Derral followed.

As they reached the upmost ledge before the plateau, the locater softly chimed, notifying them of the presence of other people, within 500 meters. As they climbed over the top, they walked into a gathering of 10 people. The 10 appeared momentarily startled. The person who was addressing the group paused and greeted them by name. Derral and Susan were immediately fearful. They formally acknowledged the greeting by bowing their heads with outstretched palms. The person responded, but not vocally. He communicated in thought. Welcome to our fifth gathering of the Cogito formed by the remaining members of those who survived a visit to Da'yoni, with the exception of one who is in committee with the Holders.

They hesitated, momentarily speechless at this sudden intrusion. Do you mean, good sir, thought Derral, that everyone here are the only others on the planet who visited Da'yoni? This must be an extremely fortuitous meeting, as we too have just returned from the Da'yonians.

The lecturer, Genine Overlitch, responded in thought. Not fortuitous, my friends. When our group began meeting a revolution ago. We sent a signal to your unconscious designed to bring you here. However, to have this occur right now was a bit startling to all of us. All of us have been taught the Da'yoni mode of thought communication. We find that when we link, we can communicate around the globe with any person. If that person's awareness has evolved, an ongoing dialogue with the group begins, regardless of their location relative to ours. But timing is a bit beyond our current abilities. Our representative will be meeting with the Da'yoni Ambassador to seek out how we can refine the timing. That's why we were as startled as you.

Susan looked towards Derral and thought, this has to be some sort of set up.

The speaker ceded the discussion to Arturo Centinel, from Susan and Derral's, neighborhood. Welcome, you know we live in the same complex and have occasionally seen each other.

160

Yes. I recall when we gossiped on a few occasions, thought Susan, smiling.

Not a set up, as you can see we can also read your thoughts. We have all, including yourselves, realized the potential to enable the return of our culture to a truly representative democracy, much to the chagrin of the Holders. We now have the 13 needed to begin the transition. We have a representative speaking at the Holders annual convention in Amsterdam, at this moment. She has a linkage from all of us. She has begun to utilize the synergy of the linkage to influence the Holders of the necessity for abandoning their life granted positions and deciding on a truly representative government. You have met the Holders on your return and scanned their true intentions. This was a component of our plan, suggested to us by the Da'yonis. We influenced your pater, Susan, to grant you the trip. We, apologetically, influenced your interest in the trip. Our motives are the establishment of the end to the return of the ancient fascism by the Holders and an end to the manipulation of the populace. This increase in fascism, is the singular element that was noticed by the Da'yoni, when it emerged. They monitor many galactic civilizations for such trends. They then followed the development and decided to intervene, as they respect our species and do not want us to enslave ourselves, as in some past historical epochs, or destroy ourselves. To end such an authoritarian hold by a group whose zeitgeist is focused on the manipulation of the public to believe that they are making free choice, requires that we also manipulate. This will be one of the few bloodless and hopefully seamless revolutions in history. The scope encompasses the whole planet and all its peoples. In a few lunar cycles we will begin the final phase of change. Just prior to the change, our agent will arrange a meeting with us and the Holders, in one secure location. That will enable the last stroke of influence. Following the disbanding of the Holders, we will all vow to never use this power of influence again. Our Da'yoni tech indicated they have some tech to remove our special abilities and cause amnesia for the event. We haven't yet decided on what to do about that. The Da'yoni Ambassador, in a secret meeting with some of us, while you were on their planet, promised to introduce us to a biotechnology they developed that helped them subdue a continuously aggressive and hostile civilization in a distant galaxy. The civilization was at the point of destroying itself through wars and internecine conflicts, not unlike ours. That civilization is now a thriving benevolent democracy, dedicated to an unwavering enhancement of all of their lives. The elimination of hostility and aggression between social and regional factions was a lasting accomplishment through the use of the Da'yoni biotech. We all viewed a holo of the transformation and were enabled to contact the committee leading that rim civilization, to our satisfaction. While they still have the force to defend themselves against attacks from other civilizations, theirs is a productive and peaceful series of planets. The Ambassador will arrange a meeting with us again, at our location, here, to provide us with the technology and instructions regarding how to employ it.

What technology can accomplish that? Surely not anything we have discovered. Or in fact, any of the civilizations we now trade with, thought Derral.

We will show you the holos of our contact with the other rim civilizations. We do not yet know what the tech is. However, we were able to verify the altruistic nature of Da'yoni intentions when we contacted other civilizations they influenced, answered Genine, silently.

Chapter Nineteen

First Experiment

As the craft landed in stealth mode, 10 miles outside of New Amsterdam the local news was broadcasting a significant moment in the Dutch parliament. Holland, given the culturally ingrained independence of its people, was the only country that preserved their own identity, refusing merger into the Africasian quadrant. Other European countries were either destroyed by the tidal wave and ocean elevation caused by the Great Catastrophe, or greatly diminished in size and population. Holland was spared as a result of its sophisticated drainage and water transport system. A century ago, the major coastal cities below or near sea level were all raised on floating platforms that elevated and lowered with the tide. The original architecture and canals were able to be maintained. The canals were all bounded with an EMF field that provided flow of clean water in from the sea and flow of contaminants out. All the canals were crystal clear, a marked change from previous historical epochs of the dank canals and mosquito infested cities.

A few of their citizens returned from Da'yoni along with a technological offering of a special microholo. This influenced the Dutch protectorate and its parliament to undertake discussions of an experiment to dissolve and replace themselves by a radical democracy. Each citizen voted on every government action. The Da'yoni tech was rapidly developed and distributed such that each person in the Netherlands was now connected to a personal holo via a microscopic infusion of a holo device through their pores. All the Dutch agreed to the infusion when the government issued a guaranteed assurance regarding the safety, security, and ability to personally turn off the locator function. These biochips, about the size of a red blood cell, under strict usage guidelines can only be accessed if the bearer gives explicit permission. This is set in the tech and cannot be controlled or changed by the government or others. As another precaution, an irrevocable clause is written in the Dutch Constitution that it is the primary duty of the government to protect the public from unauthorized use. When in front of a desk holo, the holo cell connects when a personal code is entered. The holocells are fraud proof as they are tied to each individual's DNA and particular cell structure. Once the possibilities were fully explained to the citizenry, the initial experiments in democratic voting produced successful results, with more than 90% of the population responding to each measure put forth. The Dutch had just concluded the first solar revolution in this novel form of experimental democracy. Every citizen was now connected. Voting on all issues was announced with time parameters given within which to cast ones vote. Certain issues required a 2/3 majority for passage; other's required 51 %, depending on the nature of the issues and degree of seriousness for each. The degree of seriousness was assigned a percentage rank by a large committee. The committee members, appointed by a 75% majority of all citizens for one five year term, included statisticians, economists, philosophers, theoretical mathematicians, agronomists, ecologists, architects, scientists of every persuasion, and psychosociologists. Psychosociology had replaced the disciplines psychiatry and psychology, banned towards the end of the twenty first century, along with the concomitant banning of all psychological research. It had been established that psychiatry and psychology were based on mostly unproven theoretical constructs manipulated by politics and industry, minimizing citizen health interests.

The final discussions on full implementation of the new government were now underway. The final vote would come within a lunar revolution or two. The parliament wanted a vote from the citizenry regarding dissolution before they proceeded. The meeting of the Dutch Parliament coincided with the Holder's convention, held in New Amsterdam for the first time.

The campaign laws of the Holland Protectorate, established decades ago, prohibits the use of media for campaign purposes. This resulted in candidate's creative attempts to have themselves positioned on news coverage. The rules for strategies of attempts to gain coverage had been passed by the citizen vote of 2/3 majority in the mid-twenty fourth century.

Candidates were restricted with campaign attempts limited by direct contact with the public, including, lectures, neighborhood meetings, and personal holo contact. With the new holo tech, spamming was also prohibited, requiring candidates to research personal facts concerning those whom they contact, citing this personal information in the body of the holomail campaign letter. The requirements for the nature and degree of personal information was also legislated by a 2/3 majority citizen vote, renewable every five years.

Derral piloted the transport accompanied by Susan and the other 11. As they arrived Derral, Susan, and the others were greeted by the majordomo droid. "Welcome to New Amsterdam," said the droid in a marvelously articulate speech with perfect diction. He repeated the same in each of the primary languages of the group.

Susan was silently nominated to be the spoke's person for the group.

She responded, "Thank you. I think we might be a few minutes too early?"

The majordomo bowed slightly and responded, "Not at all. In fact I just now received notice that they have finished the congress and are ready to see you. If you come with me in the transport, we will be there instantaneously."

"Thank you," said Susan.

"No need for politeness, I am merely carrying out my instructions from Chairperson Priestly," said the droid as he smiled mischievously.

A few minutes later, they walked through the transport chamber and sat on the pedestals. The chamber took to the air and in what seemed no longer than a moment, landed at the entrance to a hall. A table occupied the center of the hall. At the center sat the Holders. Susan and their contingent entered.

The Holder's ceremoniously stood at their places, heads lowered, palms outstretched in the newly adopted tradition from the Dutch. Susan, Derral and their group returned the greeting. They were ushered to their places at the table. As they sat, a holo menu appeared announcing refreshments. Each chose by looking at a selection on the menu.

The Chairman stood at his place at the end of the table. "Welcome, my dear and Derral. The last time we met was not such a pleasant feeling.

I welcome the advisory committee. All of you have successfully returned from Da'yoni with tales to tell. While we've interviewed all of you, individually, we welcome anything of value and interest you would care to share, as a group."

Derral and the others imperceptibly shifted position to physically touch each other. Susan spoke for the group. "As you know, beloved pater and Holders, the experiment with representative democracy, here in the Netherlands is about to conclude. Our scientists announced the major findings. In essence, the society would be best served to adopt their decision making process on all determinate matters. Our recommendation is to set up a subgroup to develop the procedure replacing the Holder's with a citizen vote."

The General and Oice immediately stood up looking angry, as did the Secretary. The combined influence of the Dozen, kept them from speaking. All the Holders looked puzzled.

Susan continued. "…The success for this process, seen in the past year, proved productive to the citizenry in all dimensions. Services improved. The Dutch economy grew at a rate of 35%, as citizens realized, for the first time they were provided with free choice, absent politics. The taxes, formerly utilized to pay for the massive government bureaucracy to manage the society were returned to the citizens. Prices were reduced on all goods to 75% less than previously required to generate the profit margin running the competitive industries. Now, here in the Netherlands, competition is based on providing the lowest cost to the consumer, rather than, in previous times, the maximum profit to the producer or business owner. Advertising was simplified. Each company deciding to market, had to limit their simplified advertising to announcement of bottom line price and product description based on experimental data collected by independent scientists, only. Rules governing the use and maintenance of the environment, including land, water, and subterranean use, decreased pollution by 60% in the span of just one revolution around our star…"

Chairman Priestly interrupted. "My dear, I guess you do not realize that we have considered all these matters and discussed them amongst ourselves. It was our conclusion, reached within the past few days, to implement a similar system across the world's populace, with some revisions. We have just this day sent an emissary to the Dutch Parliament to enlighten us on how to initiate such an endeavor. We now have a microcellular chip available for distribution. There are some subgroups who initially rejected it, based on privacy concerns. However we have directed our techs to develop a system to protect individual privacy. Once the detractors realize their vote will not be counted, they will likely agree to join with the rest of us. Our surveyors assure us of this fact. We only need to decide on the distribution system. Whether it will be ubiquitous through the atmosphere, or by individual choice is the question. There will soon be a Holder's vote taken as to which distribution system we will choose."

"Yes, pater, we know that. However, the system you recommended is able to be manipulated by special interests. The Dutch system has built in protections, against such manipulation."

The General, still standing, sputtered, "We could never do this. It would be too much of a burden on society."

Derral responded. "The burden, General Suddhis, is far offset by the benefit. Your own government research team deduced that."

"How do you know what the government research concluded? Mr. Secretary, did you inform your biologue?" demanded the General.

"Of course not, but she is accurately portraying our researcher's conclusion," said the Secretary with a look of surprise at his own candid reply.

The Dozen looked at each other and smiled. It worked, thought Susan. They all concurred.

***

At that same moment, Solais Cursard was sitting before a console at his secluded underground dwelling. He was watching a live holo of the Holder's meeting through the retinal vid of his newly allied colleague, General Suddhis. Lynchon, come in here and watch this. Tell me if you suspect the Holders have somehow been influenced by a force outside of the awareness of your General Suddhis and Oice.

Lynchon entered from the antechamber and sat before the holovid. He watched for a few moments. "The General suspected they were up to something, weeks ago. This might provide us with an opportunity to take control, sooner than expected. How are your techs progressing in developing the software to hack into the chips?"

Cursard suddenly appeared flustered. "They've been able to hack into and implant messages in singular chips, as long as they have a schematic of the exact bio pathways of the individual chip. Thus far, the only way to get a schematic is to actually possess the chip, after it integrates with an individual biosystem and run it through a scanner. Each chip differs based on the owners EMF signature. So far, this is impossible for the population, as a whole. Our group has been attempting to hack into the Holder database to seek the individual codes. So far, they've been unsuccessful. Each attempt has been followed by a tracer. Our group in the New Washington province just missed capture. But we are moving forward, thanks to a greedy Shallacian I met in one of my sorties to that system. He supplied us with a new technology that can scan a crowd and record the biocellular energetic signatures of any installed chips. We're working on adapting it to the human cellular system. It should take another moon phase cycle when we'll be able to go into production."

"Does the General know of this lack of progress? The last time we spoke he was assured you will be ready in a much shorter time. Now you're saying that what you got from the Shallacian will take years to implement, on a planetary basis? Is that what you're saying, Cursard?"

Lynchon turned away with a disdainful smirk. He initially resisted being placed with such a deceitful criminal element, until the General assured him that it was for the good of their mission.

"You can tell your General that we're progressing. As this is a completely unique techno leap...and the Holder's are maintaining such high security, we must proceed with the utmost caution, or we'll all be shipped to a prison asteroid on the outer rim."

***

Susan, Derral, and the others exchanged quick glances. Their group persuasion appeared to be flawless. As of a week ago, this idea was remote or non-existent in the Holders consciousness. In fact, just last week, prior to the opening of the Parliamentary convention, they produced statements on the media holos demeaning the simplistic conclusions from the Dutch experiment, suggesting they were biased and tainted by preconceived notions for a political advantage for one of their factions.

Derral stepped forward. "Have you been able to establish a date of implementation?" He stepped back, subtly touching those beside them. The group visualized a date at the next full moon.

Secretary Priestly and the others suddenly appeared agitated. The Holders whispered to each other, across the table.

"We've chosen a target date, 1 lunar cycle from now, said the Secretary. We will then hold the first mass citizen vote after we proceed with the dissolution of the Holders."

"Thank you for receiving us, pater. I'm sure we will have many more productive meetings. If we can be of further help, please let us know," said Susan.

"Yes, my dear, we will," said the Secretary, looking puzzled. The Holders arose and gave their newly traditional gesture. The visitors mirrored their gestures.

As they turned to go through the door to the portal, the General thought to himself: If Cursard can pull this off, we will control the vote and retain our power.

The Secretary was lost in his own musings, wondering how they had all agreed to make this change, ultimately resulting in their loss of power.

Susan turned to look at the General and the Secretary, as she picked up their thoughts.

The General and Secretary simultaneously felt anxious, but could not understand why. The Secretary's mind raced to something Susan's mater once said to him, in anger. She told him it was a waste of energy to attempt to disguise his thoughts that he chooses not to share, as each thought was manifested in his gesture, body position, tone...and could easily be understood by a sensitive or one who was trained to be a sensitive. He noticed Susan, out of the corner of his eye, shaking her head affirmatively.

The group of 13 departed in silence, though active in thought.

Did you pick up the General's and pater's last thought, Susan thought-projected to the group.

They responded in unison. Yes. We see how devious both are.

Roberla Stone overrode their group thought transmission.

I know this Cursard. We had some dealings with him before Da'yoni. He's an arch criminal and terrorist-for-hire. He'll do anything for credits, regardless of the consequences. He was implicated in the decimation of New Vegas by bio-weapons a decade ago. However, the proof was never forthcoming. All those connected with him were eliminated. There was also some talk of his involvement in the helo-bombing of the deca mines on Venus, a few revolutions ago. It was suspected, but never proven, that the company hired him to murder the majority of the miners who were advocating for unionization. Most of those miners were Galacians, from the outer rim planet of Gala, as they were impervious to the high levels of radiation in those mines. They never made a big deal about it because most of them were undocumented or unregistered so they could avoid paying the Solar tax.

Well if that's the case, we should attempt to seek him out and have one of us locate near him so we can get a fix on his deviousness, thought Derral to the group.

That would not be easy, thought Roberla Stone. I understand he has been able to avoid detection all these years by using technology he bartered from a contact in the Shallacian system. The technology insulates his whereabouts from any current EMF field detection system. We would first have to locate him. Unfortunately, EMF detection is the epitome of our current tech.

Not so, thought Susan. We now know who his connection is with the Holders. We only need to position one of us within proximity to Oice or General Suddhis to establish a link with him when he contacts them. Once the link is established, we can trace him and his thoughts using our 'group mind,' or whatever we want to call it.

The others responded, simultaneously. That is certainly a possibility. While it may generate publicity, Susan and Derral, you might give up your current dwelling and move into the building occupied by the General. It's an equivalent but more central location. It is also closer to your pater. You can use that to defuse suspicion. Who knows, you and the General might come to be best friend-neighbors. But let us never forget we are being equivalently devious.

The group silently laughed but betrayed no observable emotion.

170

We had better speak aloud, thought Saulian Bellan. I can sense the microfly presence.

Derral resumed a conversation. "This is incredible that your pater has considered the adoption of the Netherlands experiment. I'm sorry, but I must have misjudged him."

"Yes," said Susan. "Pater has accomplished many things for the people since he became chair of the Holders. I remember mater telling me of his good heart." And, she thought, the deceitful and evil ways in which he terrorized her.

"Perhaps we can assist him with some of the things the Da'yoni taught us," said Roberla. "We might provide seminars for those whom the Holders designate as ubiquitous communication coordinators or u-coms for short." They all smiled in response to the acronym. She continued in thought. We can teach them how to conduct a mass communication through the chip. Let's silently instruct the Holders to appoint one u-com per region. I think we've learned enough from the Da'yoni experience to be helpful, don't you think?

"Good idea," said Derral. He elaborated in thought: When we connect to the u-coms, we will be able to communicate, subconsciously, to all those integrated into the system. That includes most everyone on the planet. At that point, we may be able to selectively communicate and leave the Holders and their primary's out of the less subtle and more direct communications. The only way they'll find out is through heresay. They will always suspect others associated with their inner circle. General Suddhis and his chief surrogate, Oice, are great targets for suspicion. We can implant a suggestion that can push the Holders in that direction.

I don't know about that, thought Susan. This may be stretching the ethics of our mission.

Chapter Twenty

Jovian Demise

"I don't think it will be a wise idea for you to meet me, General. This personal policy has kept me free since I began my...shall we say, unique business." Solias Cursard looked pleased with himself, at his new found 'diplomatic' style, picked up from studying his implanted holos.

"Listen, Cursard," said General Suddhis in a high pitched, irritable voice. "We have to act in a few revolutions. I told you there is something funny going on. I don't know what it is, but it has something to do with those who traveled to Da'yoni. We need to take control of those chips, now. You said you had the contact with the Shallacians. Get me what I want and you'll be wealthier than your wildest dreams."

"That's fine, General, but I'm wealthy now. I will not compromise my security to meet with you. I have a particular distaste of the prison complex on the rim, as I once resided there. I will make contact with my Shallacian operative and notify you of the details...but only through this secure holovid. If I see a need to set up a device to intercede with the chips, we can set it up here, in my place. I don't know what it will take, but I'll let you know as soon as I find out. First, though, you need to supply me with a biochip that I can give the Shallacian so they can determine if they can do a mass scan and hack it. Think about how you're going to get one without arousing suspicion by killing someone. Then give me a call."

Cursard waved his palm across the com panel, ending the call. He slowly turned in his chair. The Jovians were sitting on the floor by the door, eating some disgusting Jovian preparation, as usual. It smelled like rotten eggs. They had a need to consume foods and gases rich in hydrogen and helium, to enable their metabolisms to continue to function in an oxygen rich atmosphere.

"Listen, you two big slobs, can you eat that vomit in another room, please. I can't stand the smell. More important, I want you to use your invisible cloaks and begin to follow the General around. I'm not sure what he's up to but I don't trust him. Only communicate with me over the secure link. If you observe him to be anything but real regarding his promises with me, let me know and I'll give you the order to complete his existence... but do nothing until you first contact me, even if he threatens you. You can leave after my meeting with this Shallacian thing."

"Yo boss. What you mean by slob? We just eating. Me and Bocha do good wit dis. But before we vapor his hi, can we have sex wit him?"

"You're both fucking perverts. Okay. If it'll keep you happy. But don't do anything until I give you the order...and the order has to come over the secure link. If you get any other communication, not on the secure link, put a tracer on it, and, if it's the right people, you can get it on with them, before you vape them."

"Me no know what perverts, boss. Boncha no know either. But we like idea of sex with humans. After do them we like eat their stuff. Then we vape them. Stuff taste good.

"Okay, okay. Don't talk about it any more. It makes me sick to my stomach. You can do it. But only after you get my word. That's most important. We don't want someone setting me up, now. You'll lose your supply of that disgusting mess you consume, if that happens."

Grancha spoke for the first time. "Boss, we do want what. We do what."

"Okay. Now get out of here and do your job," said Cursard, cringing with disgust.

"Be right, boss," said Boncha. "We see on return. But you need respect us. We just people, too."

"Right," said Cursard, as he nodded and turned away from them. They got up and lumbered through the door.

He spoke aloud to himself. "If those goons find something, that'll be the end of a potentially profitable relationship. If they don't, looks like there's more credits to be had."

Cursard directed the com panel to his Shallacian contact.

The vid appeared of a diminutive human.

Cursard waved his hand again. "Kratur, this is Cursard, don't waste

173

your energy to put on that persona. I need to know some important things about our agreement."

The image on the holo morphed into a being that appeared to be more spider-like in nature, with a mouth and eyes appearing almost human. "What can I do for you, Cursard," said the creature. Its voice sounded as if it was holo-synthesized.

"I need to know if you folks can access the universal chips, used to implant in the human population. Especially if you have the technology to reconfigure them. I have a billion tons of aquafir available, on a moon of one of the solar planets, that will be shipped to your planet, if you can help me."

"We do need aquafir to stimulate the plant growth on our planet. To finally end the pollution caused by, your friends, the invaders, centuries ago. We need more to complete the transition. We are willing to do whatever we can to seal the agreement," said the spider-like creature.

"I don't want to know what you need, get it? I have the stuff. If you can supply me with what I want, you get it. If not, I'll sell it to one of your rivals, bottom line. I don't give a shit about your pollution or anything else. I need the information and that's all. Can you hack into the chips?"

"We may be able to, but we'd need a sample to verify."

"You'll be getting one shortly," said Cursard, as he closed off the communication.

As soon as the Jovians left, another Shallacian materialized through the rear portal behind the com center. Cursard turned as the Shallacian took form. "Seems like your friend will come through."

The creature responded with a different synthetic voice, now of the opposite sex. "We are an honest race. When we make a commitment we feel quite obliged to complete our obligation. We have what you humans would call a code of ethics that preclude lying."

"Then, how is it that you associate with the likes of me, a known rim crim and exploiter?"said Cursard.

"We may be totally honest, but we also like the finer aspects that credits can provide. We see the value in acquiring what you humans call... capital. Our civilization were credit traders since the origin of the nova that spawned this planet. We trade. In spite of your misguided ways, you have something that we want, and we trade. Even though what you do with what we give you is against all of our precepts, you will not be invoking the dishonesty on our civilization, only your own inferior species. That way we can trade," said the Shallacian as he brushed his trembling appendages before his proboscis.

Cursard glared at him. "Seems like your evolution skipped a step. But I don't give a shit. You give me what I want and you get your aquifer. A deal is a deal."

"Very well," said the alien in a dark male voice, as he twitched his appendages to accent his words.

Cursard responded with the sarcasm that had become his trademark among the trading races: "Now that we have an understanding, can I show you to the transport to take you back to your lair...or is it a den? And I wish you'd stop switching sexes in my presence...that flips me."

"I'm not certain of your meaning honorable Cursard,"said the alien.

"Just as well. Forget it. Do you want a lift back to your place of residence? My boys can take you back under their invisibility cloaks, at least until you get away from here. It just keeps things more honest."

"As you wish, even though I am concerned at being in the same space with Jovian thugs," said the Shallacian with a note of cheerfulness in his synthetic voice.

Cursard pressed the com unit to signal the Jovians. "I need you back here. I got a job for you."

"We jus outside boss...finish eating."

They appeared at the portal. "Take this...being...to where he wants to go, but do it using your cloaks. Make sure he enters and leaves, cloaked. One of you can accompany him to his residence and bring back the cloak after he's safely inside.

"K boss. Lookum good snack."

"Sorry fellas, no snacking this time," said Cursard.

Except for a slight twinge of his proboscis, the Shallacian didn't seem to understand what they were talking about. Is this my transportation?" he said, with what sounded like disgust as he clicked his lips

Cursard, sounding annoyed, responded. "Yeah they're your transportation. They'll take you inside your domicile in full invisibility."

He waved them off; through the portal.

"Boss you want other job after we drop off?"

"Yes, let me know how you progress on the secure com."

"We good boss." The three stepped through the portal.

Cursard returned to the console and directed a view from one of his flys. The General appeared in the holo, talking with his aide Lynchon and his colleague Oice. "Amazing...these flys," mumbled Cursard to himself.

"General, I don't see how we can trust this sleazy criminal Cursard. He's been implicated in many deceitful actions, in the recent past. He's a murderer and liar," said Lynchon.

"I'll show you the kind of murderer I am when I sic the Jovians on your ugly ass," mumbled Cursard to himself.

The General finished a long sip from his iridescent purplish drink. "Sometimes, those are the traits that can be most useful to accomplish our goals. He said he'd procure the technology to hack into the biochips. Once we have that we can implant suggestions in well over half the populace. I'll be the next Secretary..."

"That's if he's not doing one of his cons on you. You don't know who else is paying him," said Oice, with a scowl. "He has less ethics than we do, and that's saying something. He'll negotiate for the highest bidder. The other side will never know they've underpaid him...and he'll be setting them up."

"That's if we don't know. I told you the last time you brought this up. I have my people, some friends from military intelligence, keeping an eye on his comings and goings and who he's in contact with. Since I gave him the first installment there's been no chatter, it's been quiet, said the General, with impatience.

Cursard turned away from the holo, smiling, thinking of how smart he was to insist the Jovians use their cloaks with each entrance and departure. "Pretty slick, if I don't say so myself," mused Cursard to himself, as he turned back to the holovid. "Mmhh, maybe here's a few for the boys to fulfill their sexual urges with..this little crap head Oice."

As Lynchon left through the entrance portal, Oice turned to the General. "Are you sure we can trust your aide, he said, nodding in his direction."

"Implicitly. Lynchon has been with me through 3 battles, when I was younger. I saved his family from certain vaping by tipping him off to our plans to end the last battle on that small planet in the Pegasus system. He was able to get them off before we acted. He is a deeply grateful, loyal aide... for life, as he once told me. Are you questioning my judgment Oice?"

"Certainly not General. But we're playing with fire here. I want to insure we're taking all precautions. If we're suspected, as you are well aware, we will end up spending the rest of our lives on one of the Jovian moons, digging in the mines, or in the rim prison colony. Neither of which I would want for you or anyone. If you recall, I set up the prison colony and the Jovian prison mines for the Holders, back when we thought we could have an advantage," said Oice, with severity.

"Very well. We won't end up there unless we are incredibly stupid or this filthy criminal finds another buyer who has more cash. Based on what we offered him, I don't think there is another buyer on the planet that could match it. Besides, after we're in control of the chips, he will have the market cornered on all nefarious activities, especially the gambling concessions. That was part of the deal I promised him," said General Suddice, with a barely noticeable twinge of anxiety in his voice.

"That's my hope, sir. Now, I must bid you adieu. I need to attend to some family matters," said Oice, abruptly turning and leaving through the portal.

General Suddice looked after him, puzzled and thinking, he doesn't have any family, as far as I know. He waved his hand in front of the holo panel. "Lynchon, has Oice left the outer office?"

"The portal just closed, sir," said Lynchon.

"Lynchon, Oice said he had to attend to family matters. I want you to contact Lieutenant General Armitage over at Intel and ask him to do a complete bio for me on Oice, especially focusing on the remaining family members, if any. He owes me a few. Ask him, when he gets it, to transmit it to me over my secure com, as soon as possible. I don't want to leave any stone unturned in this operation, if you follow me," said the General with severity.

"I'll do that right away, sir. Can I be of any other service today, General?"

"No, that's quite all right. I'm going to my portal. After you make the request you too are free to leave for the afternoon. I'll be in at 10, tomorrow," said the General, using the historical time reference.

"Thank you sir..."

Cursard terminated the com and spoke aloud to his reflection in the blank holo. "Well, I guess the old bastard doesn't trust me. He thinks he's clever. I suppose he shouldn't, though. But it looks like he's right. No one has come forth with a counter offer. So all we need to do is..."

An alarm tone over the holo interrupted. Grancha appeared, speaking excitedly: "Boss, that spider shit...kill Bocha in back seat. I see it. He stuck his nose in Bocha's ear after Bocha try to get friends wit him. Bocha just shrunk in nanos. The spider, he get out and ran inside his house after that. He was no invisible, boss. What you do want, boss?"

Cursard looked stunned. "You mean that bug went out of the car into his house? Was the car cloaked?"

"No boss. It be not. We no see reason if he be invisible when he leaves, but Bocha had cloak."

Cursard was now on his feet. "Well, shit. We'd be lucky if he wasn't spotted..."

"But boss, Bocha best friend...What you want me do with him. I want blast his bug ass to vapor."

Cursard responded with his usual callousness. "I'm sorry about Bocha. But we need to use this creep to get us the technology we need. After that I don't care what you do with him. In fact you can vape his home world, for all I care...But we can't do anything until..." He was interrupted, again, by an incoming holo. It was the Shallacian. His limbs were twitching severely. "Bocha, I gotta go and take this...it's the bug. Come on in and we'll decide how to handle this."

He spoke in a deep male voice. "Cursard, if you want me to follow through with this deal, we don't want any other of your Jovian thugs to attempt anything more with us...or you can find the technology elsewhere and we'll seek another source for the aquifer. In your primitive terminology: do you get it?"

"I get it your excellency. I just got off the vid with his partner. He said he was only trying to be friends with you, said Cursard.

Friends? the Shallacian shouted in a screeching female voice. He
178

stroked my organ that conceives. Is your mind the size of a piece of space dust? The only one who touches that is my partner....and only if I want her to. That could have put me in a coma, you nit-wit. You should be glad I didn't kill his partner, too. Where do you get these ugly pieces of dirt, Cursard? If I have any more dealings with you, I don't want to see any of them. Get it?

Yes sir, or mam, as the case may be. From now on you won't see any of them. I'll get rid of them all."

Chapter Twenty One

Opening Move

General Suddhis' vehicle approached the docking port to his office. As soon as the maglocks connected he noticed an alert from General Armitage.

He ran to his office and opened the com link. Emmanual, good to see you again. It's been a while.

Yes Urvey, it has been. Not long enough though. These requests you made. Both of them can get me fired or executed by the Secretary if he finds I'm using our intel apparatus for your own purposes.

Suddhis interrupted: No mind, Emmanuel. No one will find out. What do you have for me?

Armitage responded with a frown. "We have a visual from a flyby of a Shallacian exiting a transport owned by a known criminal, Cursard. The vehicle was piloted by one of Cursard's Jovian associates. It's strange, though. We back traced the visual to the departure point and have no one entering. It was as if the drivers and passangers were in the vehicle for the longest time, before it left. The satellite we were using had a momentary power shift about an hour before the departure, so we lost about 10 minutes or so. But still, they must have been in the vehicle for at least an hour."

"As for your other request, we did a comprehensive historical analysis on your Oice. He seems clean aside from two recent, brief contacts with the Secretary's son-in-law. One was only momentary, when both were alone at Kennedy Spaceport during a gathering of those who came back from Da'yoni. The fly transmission was sketchy as there was a lot of background noise from nearby departing vehicles. The other was at a dining port. He stopped by the young man's table where he was dining with the Secretary's daughter to exchange greetings. At that one, he and the Secretary's son-in-law shook hands. Our flys were not positioned to see if anything was exchanged. Their field transmission was blocked for some reason. He does have some family members living in the mountains, outside of New Denver.

He visits them occasionally. But they are distant relatives, not immediate family

General Suddis looked away from the holo, shaking his head. "My wish is that you had a more precise operation. May the galaxy help us if we had any real problems and needed good intelligence..."

General Armitage's head snapped around, scowling. "General, I resent your implications. While I may owe you one, we do the best we can with what we have here."

Suddhis smiled wryly: "You still owe me one. I thought I could get some good intel. What you have is about the level of my 12 year old nephew's searches. Don't worry, I'll be calling on you again. Perhaps in the meantime, you can upgrade your systems." He ended the communication.

General Suddhis pressed the comlink. "Lynchon, get me Cursard over a secure link."

"Yes sir," responded Lynchon with his usual deference.

Cursard appeared in the holo before the General. "Cursard, as much as I don't want to be observed talking with you, I'll get right to the point, quickly. What were you or your goons doing with that Shallacian bug. Have they offered you more than what we agreed? If so, I'll up it."

"General, I'm surprised at your intel. I must confess we had a problem. It was the Shallacian who was going to supply us with the technology to hack the biochip. One of my Jovians took a little sexual advantage of his high bugness and was killed. However, they still want to deal...typical of these disgusting creatures."

"Well you close the damn deal, Cursard, quickly," said the General. "We don't have much time. I'm looking for other sources. I'd contact the Shallacian's directly, but they hate me for vaping one of their smaller sattelite moons and about a million of those cockroaches, in our last skirmish on the rim. So get on with it."

"Yes General. Soon, we'll get you what you want. It takes three lunar revolutions to ship from the bug world on the rim. The com will come at hyperlight, their latest, faster than light communication buffer. He last said he placed the order, yesterday. And they don't know you'll be the end user. All they're interested in is the payment."

"Just like a cockroach. That's why we vaped them," said the General.

"Don't you dare let on who it's for, as they'll likely renege on the deal."

"As you wish, General," said Cursard, ending the com.

***

The Dozen concentrated their energy and manipulated the real estate agent, permitting Susan to move ahead in line for a dwelling. When she walked through the portal, the agent appeared to ignore her, looking bored.

She tapped the counter to get his attention."Can we see the dwelling on the B side of the 14th floor."

"Why that one. This one is more reasonable in price, on a higher level and a few hundred more square feet,"said the agent.

"We like the South facing window. The light, you know. The only one on that side of the building, available, is it not?"

"Well, yes, as a matter of fact. You'll have some nice neighbors. General Suddice, you know...one of the Holders, lives in the dwelling directly above this one. Secretary Priestly lives in the adjacent building."

"Yes, we know. The Secretary is my pater," said Susan.

The stunned agent snapped to attention, becoming quite solicitous. "Please forgive me Ms. Priestly. Whatever I might do to encourage your living here, please let me know. It would be an honor to have you as a resident. We have the latest security bots."

"Dr. Priestly, sir...We know the General from some recent gatherings. This one with the south facing window will do. We have just arranged sale of our current dwelling, at Lucent city. I'll have the proceeds transferred directly to your account, to settle our agreement. We will be paying in full. The transfer should be completed by the morrow. When you receive it, inform us of the balance due and we'll have it immediately transferred."

"Yes, mam. It is a pleasure doing business with you, albeit a bit unusual...as most folks finance through an institution," said the realtor, unable to conceal his glee.

"We have two incomes, sir, said Susan. My partner's income all went to his savings account for the 3 years he was off world with the military. That's how we do business. Another thing: we need utmost secrecy and security, given my relationship to the Secretary. That's why we chose this building. This is a confidential transaction with no records. If anything is leaked you will have to deal with the Secretary's security service...I must be going. Have some appointments to take care of. I'll expect we can move in on the first of next week?"

"Of course, Doctor. We'll have it swept and resealed by the end of this week. We are very discreet, as we have many high end clients like yourselves. Here are your temporary ident cards so that you can get into the building. After you move in we will extract your pattern and issue a permanent ident chip that can be implanted if you wish, for convenience."

"No, Derral and I prefer portable chips. He's in the Solar guard reserves, and I am an attorney and an exobiologist. We both work in areas, too sensitive for permanent ident chips that can be tracked."

"Very well, mam. I'm sure you will enjoy your presence in our little community,"he said with a feigned smile.

"Okay. Thank you very much. We'll be seeing you next week," said Susan, with a hint of irritability as she turned to leave through the portal.

Calling up the Da'yoni network, Susan thought-linked with Derral.

Well, we're good. We move in next week. Should be an interesting experience. I dropped the hint that we're moving to be closer to pater. The sales agent was taken aback. While, there I was able to pick up snatches of a comlink call from the General to his spy agency peer, Armitage. I was too distracted to focus on it, as the sales agent kept intruding on my pattern, but it was something about a Shallacian and Solias Cursard.

Derral responded with a marked change in tone. That's the guy that Roberla communicated about. After the mining explosions, our security investigations traced Cursard's whereabouts to about 1 light-click from the site, just before the explosion, then we lost his trail. So we had nothing to get him on.

Susan thought: I'm not sure. We should get more information after we move in next week. I do know the Shallicians have developed some hacking devices that are capable of detecting the signatures and transmissions from biochips placed in their own race. I wouldn't be surprised if that's the connection. The General would greatly increase his standing if he were able to pluck information at random with that tech.

Roberla Stone interrupted the thought communication: Yes, when I was in the employ of Armitage, we had a tracer on him, as he was suspected in a number of murderous intrigues for profit. He's a clever operator. If he's involved, you can be assured General Suddice is out on a string. This Cursard always has something on any one he does business with. It wouldn't be the first time he was employed by a Holder to do some dirty work.

Derral responded: So how do you think we should play this? I'm asking for a consensus.

The thought transmission hesitated for a few moments. Then it sounded almost as if a voice was actually speaking: We need to not mention this to anyone, nor speak of it, aloud, amongst ourselves. Especially with Susan and Derral moving to the same building as the General. We may not know if there are any flys around. We just need to insure that no one begins to suspect our newly developed abilities.

Following a brief moment of silence, the group continued: With Susan and Derral ideally suited, we must never disclose what we've learned, aloud, even to ourselves. Nor must we act on what we've learned until we can decide upon a final moment. We cannot emphasize that enough. For us to succeed in our mission to transform the societal rules and eliminate deceit, discretion is paramount.

A little paradoxical isn't it, thought the group, unanimously. The group acquiesced. We must meet as a group at our original retreat in the Sierra's. There is enough natural geomagnetic interference at that particular level in the mountain to render any attempt to view the meeting useless. We've all been going up in that area for years, even before Da'yoni, except Susan and Derrick. Whether it was destined or coincidence, it worked out to our advantage. That way, when we leave no one will suspect our gathering. Thanks to our Da'yoni friend's recent offer of soft holo facsimiles and the stealth vessel tech, we can throw anyone off the scent regardless of how sophisticated their technology is. Going at the end of this lunar period, in two revolutions, should give us sufficient time to arrive there and cover our tracks. Make sure you all use the Da'yoni stealth mode starting before you open and leave your portals to travel in your vehicles. You can leave the facsimile in your home ports. Program the facsimiles to do a number of mundane activities like shopping, attending lectures, etc. No one will suspect we even left the city.

Derral and I do not have the stealth mode. We used the cloaked vessel of a friend to get there, when we first met. How can we obtain that to use on our own vessel? thought Susan, looking puzzled.

You have it now, thought Roberla. We just transmitted it to your chip. You only need to download it into your vessel's configuration. It is a secure download as it is disguised within the EMF propulsion system routine update.

Susan walked to her vehicle. As she entered she noticed a microfly light on the corner of the roof. She did nothing but turn on the universal newscom, turning up the volume to irritate whoever is listening through the fly. She communicated what was occurring to Derral.

Derral thought: Looks like what just happened to me a few moments ago. Perhaps this Cursard and/or the General suspects our motives. We should just go about our routines, doing the usual boring things. They'll eventually tire of watching. I'll meet you back at our new residence so you can show it to me.

Okay, thought Susan. I'll just go back in and wait in the agents office. How long will you be.

Probably just a nano or two. I'm approaching the quadrant, now.

Susan feigned looking in her bag for a few moments, then quickly left her vehicle to return to the agents office to wait for Derral.

They didn't then know that it was Susan's father's assistant, Char who was sitting before a dual console watching the transmissions from the flies. She was in hololink with the Secretary.

"They are clear, sir. Her link is transmitting from the vehicle, while her partner comes from their home in Lucent city."

"Okay, thank you Char. Just to be on the safe side, keep monitoring them until they move in. Their move was a big surprise I was not expecting, as Susan and her partner seemed so distant from me. Yet the agent told us this was the reason they initiated their move e.g., to be closer to a relative. Keep an eye on them. I'll have Ulemann relieve you from time to time. I'll be in my private portal. Check on them at least once every 15 degrees or so. If they are in any discussion, at all, make sure you turn on the recorders."

"As you wish, Mr. Secretary. But sir, can I be free to express my sentiments?"

"Go right ahead, Char."

"Well sir, this is your biochild and her mate. She is an outstanding member of the bar and an exobiology honors graduate from the Institute, a lawyer and a scientist, to boot. He has equivalent honors in the military service. Why do you suspect them...and what do you suspect them of?"

"Char, suffice it to say that I noted a change since they returned from their little excursion to Da'yoni. Something I can't put my finger on. Susan actually confronted me for the first time, shortly after...something about one of my political positions. That was highly unusual, especially since she has had little to do with me after her twenty first birthday and her self-declared emancipation. We have many forces trying to bring me down. Not that she is one of them, but I want to be on the safe side. Especially, I want to know what she is doing with the information I provide her."

"Very well sir. I will keep you posted on the secure comlink, especially if anything of significance occurs."

"Thank you Char. That's why I pay you those big credits." The Secretary smiled and closed the link.

The Secretary turned to Ulemann. "What do you think, my old friend? Am I overreacting to this?"

Ulemann turned from his own console and spoke gravely. "I would not say you are over reacting, sir. I would say your cautious nature is one of your best assets, especially in this climate of backstabbing and intrigue among the Holders. Besides, you never did have much to do with your biochild, even when she was growing up. Her mater saw to it that you kept your distance. One never knows what that sort of influence can have on a biochild against the other parent...and we certainly don't know what messages her mater implanted in her during those years when you were in conflict."

"I suppose you're correct, Ulemann. I just have a hard time admitting it to myself. I guess, after all, there is a part of me who would liked to have had a solid family relationship. But the business at hand, over the past cycles, precluded any involvement. Especially in this power grabbing environment...the past ten cycles, since the last elections." Sardonicly, he continued with a lilting tone. "Oh, if people were only simpler and less complex, we could be honest and tell everyone that I desire to continue in this position through any means, as it is lucrative, beyond all imagination, especially when dealing with offworld contracts for our business holdings. Yet, smart history says we must remain ruthless and deceitful to succeed. against the ruthless and deceitful adversaries that would have my position"

They were interrupted by Char on the secure link. "Sir, your bio hadn't yet left the building. It looks like she's returning to the agents office. Her husband changed his course and is only a few clicks away. I'll switch channels to the agents fly to see what they might be up to."

"Very well, Char. Keep me posted."

At that same moment Susan walked through the door to the agents office. "Sorry to bother you again, but my partner is coming over to see the place. I hope you don't mind."

The agent looked up from the console. "No, of course not. I'll be occupied with another property viewing. Here, you can use my chip to enter. There may be some workers doing last minute prep, but don't mind them. Tell them you are the new owners, and show them this chip card. I'm going to leave now. Have a seat. If you need anything, ask the bot, Margaret. She will take care of your needs. I have to rush."

"Thank you, much appreciated," said Susan. She called up Derral on her thought linkage.

The agent handed Susan the key and disappeared though an inner office portal.

Derral, just dock in the guest portal and ask the bot to escort you to the agents office. I'll be waiting for you there, thought Susan.

Great. Can't wait to see our new home. I'm docking now, thought Derral, as he maneuvered into the portal. His thought displayed an unusual irony.

Just be careful of your allusions, my dear. Pater has very intelligent people working for him. People who are absolutely paranoid by nature. As we know, intelligence and paranoia are dangerous qualities, together.

Got you, thought Derral, smiling. I'll watch my p's and q's. I guess we're learning to detect emotion in this new silent communication deal.

***

The Secretary was focused on the link to the fly that Char provided. He turned to Ulemann.

"It looks like nothing unusual. She just wants to show him the place. He turned to his own comlink. It seems odd, Char, but did you intercept their plans to meet back at the new domicile?"

"No sir. But there was a few nano's delay when the flys were getting into place. They may have linked up then. I'll see if I can retrieve the hololink data. But I may not be able to because both of their link data are secured by the nature of their positions: From the laws protecting lawyers for her; his from his military status. While you can hack it as it is occurring and record it, playback of unrecorded sequences is impossible."

"Well, that's okay Char. But play back the communication from Derral to Susan about coming to the new building. Perhaps I'm over thinking it, a bit," said the Secretary as he turned to smile at Ulemann. "Perhaps I am, don't you think, my friend."

"I don't know sir. We'll see how this all shakes out."

***

Derral entered the real estate office. They wordlessly embraced.

Susan responded to Derral's thought. I just discovered dear pater is the person who is having us tracked. I was hoping that wasn't true, but I did tune to his conversation, just now. This location is apparently close enough. Derral nodded in agreement. I also was able to catch the final words, as I entered the approach pattern to the building portal. I'm sorry.

I am too, Susan wordlessly replied, as she clenched his hand. Yet it certainly clarifies the relationship. I'd like to be able to know when he began his mistrust.

Both paused, as if they were listening to a distant voice.

Well, there it is, Susan thought, as she tuned into more of the conversation between her pater and Ulemann. He suspected us since we came from Da'yoni. I guess we weren't able to hide our changes very well.

Derral paused and replied in thought. Yes. But always bear in mind that it is only supposition…and we can never let on that we know.

That realization brought home what you had lacked with your pater; what you so dearly missed.

Susan looked at Derral wide-eyed and spoke aloud. "That is the sad truth."

"What," asked Derral, realizing Susan had responded to a thought.

188

She recovered: "Oh, I was just thinking about what I had missed in life. another time for that discussion though. Let's take a look at our new home."

Derral and Susan entered the transport. They were at the front portal in an instant. Susan passed the chip in front of the reader. The lock clicked, almost silently. They entered and startled the workers.

"We didn't mean to startle you," said Susan, contritely. "The agent gave us the chip. We're the new owners and thought we'd take a look. I hope you don't mind, gentlemen."

The foreman was gruff, but friendly. "Okay. So long as you don't get in the way. We're on a tight schedule today. I'm short handed. Damn union work rules."

"Thanks, we won't be long. We just wanted to look around," said Derral.

Susan went to the large picture window. "Look, Derral, that's Pater's just up there to the right, at the corner, about 10 floors down from the roof."

"We'll have to keep our windows darkened," said Derral with a mocked seriousness. They both laughed.

Susan thought: That's good, my dear. I hope he was listening.

Derral responded: I'm sure he was, as the flies are still inserted in the material of our tops. Derral, non-chalantly patted her shoulder where the fly was located. It's in the same place on me, too.

Susan and Derral froze, listening to something, intently. They were picking up General Suddice's thoughts, as his portal was not far from theirs.

Derral directed a thought to Susan: Seems like the General is true to form.

Yes, thought Susan. But lets not miss anything.

General Suddice was sitting in a neutral grav chair, floating by the window, as he spoke to his assistant, who was standing at attention against the far wall, just inside the portal.

"We need to find a way to monitor this scum, Cursard before he sells us down the galactic stream for his retirement credits. He seems to be impervious to our flys. Perhaps you can develop a relationship with the remaining Jovian. I hear that he frequents the Black Hole, that dive by the space port where the incoming aliens hang out until their papers are processed through security."

Lynchon grimaced. "Very well your generalship. But you realize that if anything happens down there the connection with your office will rapidly be established."

"If anything does happen, you idiot, you're out of a job. All I want is information about Cursard's leanings, his comings and goings. You can easily insert yourself there as one of the regulars. After a few revolutions, you'll be accepted, as a regular. Use the cover that you're ship is being held up for extensive cleaning, as you had an ion drive eruption just as you came out of a hyper-jump. That's a common occurrence from the older class of freighters the traders converted from our old warships. That happened to a few of my own warships. When they wonder why you didn't perish, tell them you had the ion neutralization shields installed that contained the damage and contamination within the cargo bays. The control room and bridge was fully insulated, as it is a converted battle cruiser. I'll contact my military associates to concoct a story to back that up and insert it into the logs. They'll put it over the news holos. Your ship will be the Nebulae IV, on it's way back from a rim mining colony with a load of aquifer."

"As you wish, my general. I will leave and prepare my first appearance for this afternoon."

Chapter Twenty Two

The Shallacian Deal

The Shallacian are an ancient galactic rim civilization who traded among the stars, since before intelligent life evolved in the solar system. Their government was autocratic, not unlike the medieval governments on Terra. Autocracy was suitable for them, being much like Terra insect populations, especially bees, living in hives. Yet, even the Shallacians have ongoing insurrections and social movements to eliminate the autocratic rule and return to rule by plebiscite, the fashion of their government eons ago. The Krakes from another system within the same galaxy as the Shallacians, are a later evolving species. Some of their unique technology was taken by the Shallacians, in an invasion, long before Terra had intelligent life.

Shallacian communication is enhanced by extrasensory phenomenon, not unlike the Da'yoni, but much more primitive and less well developed. Even more primitive was their disregard for sentient life.

As a result of their intrusive trading practices, Shallacians had military skirmishes with most everyone whom they had interacted with, including the Krakes, since acquiring light speed propulsion technology, stolen from a more advanced civilization, the Flubians who are also fierce traders. That was a costly theft from the Flubians, a vengeful species. In response, they destroyed on of 3 of the Shallacian homeworlds. They eventually figured out a treaty would be a more effective arrangement. The Flubians, in return for guarantees not to come into their territory, permitted the Shallacians to keep their light speed propulsion technology, as they saw an economic benefit in selling technical assistance contracts.

"I came in cloaked on a Solar Confederation starship we captured and had repurposed as a trading vessel. There was no suspiceon...and I retained the human features until now, but I must change as it takes all my resources," said the Ambassador from Krake. He then transformed into his scaly red skinned features.

"Even so your excellency, we must be extremely careful. If the Confederation remotely suspected your presence there would be a galactic alert, given your past battles with the Solar Confederation forces. We are currently arranging an exchange for badly needed aquifer, with one of the disgusting earth creatures you were once familiar with. This scurrilious Cursard. We are providng him with a neural device developed by your techs. That is why we requested a visit from you to bring the engineering plans"

"Yes, I know Supreme one, but why do you need the acquifer" said the Krake through a synthetic communicator.

The Shallacian waved his appendages. "The aquifer regulates our need for pressurization to preserve our sensitive outer surface. It breaks down at surface gravity if not periodically repressurized. You need not be concerned here. This terminal is ideal for our security needs. The tunnels were lined with a Shallacian plastic blocking all EMF and radio frequency transmissions," said the Shallacian supreme commander.

"That places me at ease, Supreme one. You know that my planetary council does not know that I traveled here."

"Yes, we expected that, as our civilizations have never recovered from your invasion of our system," said the Commander as he rubbed his proboscis with his rear appendage. We are pleased that you arranged this transaction. This may bode a more positive relationships from past difficulties," said the Supreme Commander.

"That may be so, but I will not be able to communicate that to our central spoke until our transaction is complete and secure," said the Krake

"The only way to observe us here would be to plant a microfly. Even then, the receiver would have to be in close proximity to our terminal, as the fly transmission could not penetrate the special insulation. Our terminal is secure," said the Commander, folding his appendages in front of him.

"What is a microfly?" asked the Krake.

"Forgive me your excellency, that is a small portable listening device, running on an electromagnetic field that appears like a Terran insect. The Terrans either developed that on their own, which is doubtful, given their limited intelligence, or they more likely acquired that from one of their galactic excursions," said the Shallacian commander.

***

Cursard sat before his holo actively monitoring their communication by a fly the Jovian inserted before he was killed. The fly was specially configured to penetrate Shallacian defenses. After the Krake left the area the Shallacian opened a secure channel to his central Shallacian command, beneath the surface. With a painful look he watched him conferring with the Shallacian leaders over holovid, regarding the possibilities and benefits of providing him with the chip decoder technology they obtained from the Krakes.

"I need to dump this translator in the next black hole I pass...must have been made on one of those prison planets by incompetent Venusian space slugs,. Why do I miss every other word?..and no Krake translation," said Cursard through clenched teeth, as he called up the diagnostics on the translator on his personal holo..

Cursard knew the Shallacians have no trust in humans. Neither do the Krakes. Both have had hostile encounters with Solar Confederation forces. While under a current treaty with the Solar Confederation, after a brief war, the Shallacians believed they were betrayed, more than once. They are naturally suspicious of anyone not like them. While the Confederation vaped one of their small planets during the skirmish, they have honored their word regarding the resumption of trade. Yet it is the nature of the Shallacian consciousness to suspect plots and intrigue, whether real or not, especially with other civilizations. Even ones like the Confederation who permitted them to open outposts on Terra and other confederation planets, in gestures of peaceful co-existence.

Cusard fine tuned the translator controls to increase the accuracy. He scowled.

"Do your imagine this disgusting human, Cursard, to be intellectually capable of setting us up for some trouble with the Confederation authorities, again? If so, you know we'll likely have to abandon this lucrative trading ground," said the Shallacian to the holo, as he stroked his appendages and ermine cloak. The cloak was from the fur of a species living on a planet the Shallacian invaded.

"You bet your ass I can, or what you have for an ass, you fucking bug," said Cursard to the holo tap.

The Shallacians responded as if of one voice. "He certainly is capable. Our Krake contact is well awae of the politics, but has agreed to share the tech for acquifer. We think this human is working on some arrangement, too lucrative for him to betray us. He most likely will sell the microcircuit he wants from us so that it can be produced. The humans have recently begun distributing com chips for implantation by choice. This will enable them to communicate to a central command to cast their decisions. The Holders have approved such an activity. It sounds like a regression to a more primitive age, but that is what they're embarking on. They have some delusional belief that they can then be a more "democratic" species, spat out the lead Shallacian, snuffing and spraying a viscous solution from his long proboscis across the table.

The Shallacian in the holo responded: "This Cursard or whomever he is dealing with may want to use our technology to hack into the biochips so they or he can begin to exert some control over this process. But that is not our concern. We need aquifer. If he has a lucrative deal for the simple granting of some of our microtech devices, all the better. We will profit. Conclude the deal with this criminal member of this disgusting species."

The Shallacian addressed the group holo. "We will contact this Cursard and complete the deal. We will provide him a few of the devices to wet his appetite. He would need many connected in a series to have the power to contact all their specie's biochips. But he won't know that. He'll then come back asking for more, when he figures it out...if he has the intelligence or whomever he is dealing with has the intelligence. We'll have the advantage to demand more aquifer."

They arose from the table, in unison, with their appendages still wildly gesticulating. The one sitting beside the leader went off to a communication chamber. He sat before a console and connected with the waveform Solias Cursard had given him, using a translator and human voice synthesizer. Cursard appeared on the holo.

"What do you want bug," said Cursard, harshly, barely disguising his contempt.

The Shallacian responded with the synthesized female voice. "Forgive my past doings, honorable sir. We just concluded a council meeting and decided to provide you with the micro devices, in exchange for sufficient quantities of aquifer."

"Ah, very well. I know you are exploiting Krake tech, but I have been unable to contact their leaders. Your efforts will be rewarded. We can make our first exchange, as soon as you'd like. My preference is sooner than later, as my benefactors are getting nervous holding so much aquifer around." said Cursard, barely suppressing his anger.

"As you wish," said the Shallacian. " We and the Krakes are from the same galaxy. We've known each other for many passings, by the way. We can arrange for the first delivery of the devices within a 120 degree arc of your planet relative to your star."

"That is certainly sooner. When you transport the devices to this location, I will simultaneously transport the aquifer to your coordinates. For the aquifer, I need ten million chips and a device that can clone 10 million within a day," said Cursard, as he passed his hand over the comset, ending the communication.

The Shallacian wildly gesticulated and screeched "but that is impossible," after the holo blanked out.

Cursard turned to his Jovian with a smirk. "Grancha, my man, you can have 3 hours off, my good goon. Don't get too bombed at the Black Hole. This'll teach that bug to not try to deceive me. If we receive the bug's shipments...and I think they'll come through, we'll be on our way."

"Yo boss," said the Jovian, as he turned to go through the portal. Turning back he said, "Boss, you no want me be here when bugs come? I vape them mo's for Bocha.

"Not, now, my man. After they deliver and we have the tech installed, you can vape all of them, if you want. But we need them, now"

Mumbling, "Mo-fug. Me vape their home world. No give em nothing." He ambled toward the land jumper and dialed the coordinates of the Black Hole.

The General's man, had just arrived at the bar, when Grancha ambled in. At the dark corner of the bar was an inconspicuous human sipping a synth. One of the Dozen, an earlier D'ayoni returnee.

Chapter Twenty Three

Final Plans

Derral set the auto controls to dock at the mountain safe house, not far from where they first met as the Dozen.

Susan thought: Should we scan for flys before we land?

Derral responded aloud: "Not to worry. I zapped them just before we departed. There are none."

"I wonder what the meeting is about. Seems they needed top security," said Susan.

"Yes. I caught a thought transmission from Saulian Bellan regarding a new development in our plans. Something to do with the final solution."

"Sounds mysterious," said Susan.

"Yeah. He wouldn't give me any details until we meet."

The ship slipped into the docking port and decloaked as the portal closed behind them. The other's vessels were already there.

A bot directed them into a spacious hall built into the mountain side,

Saulian Bellan was communicating, excitedly to the group. "From one of our military jaunts, just after our Da'yoni visit, we encountered a civilization in the the same, system around Arcturus. They call their world something that sounds like Lorkayor, in our phonetic Solar standard. They were exceptionally peaceful. We were invited to visit. From the historical records they shared, about 1000 of our revolutions ago, they were a civilization controlled by self-centered, arrogant individuals who claimed they knew what is best for all. They imposed many restrictions on freedoms in the Lorkanian home world. Until that time the Lorkanians were a people who were virtually uninhibited, though peaceful. The leaders imposing the restrictions were met with rebellion, especially from the benevolent and altruistic scientists. The scientists covertly released a nano cell, created to migrate through the atmosphere and insert itself in the critical brain areas controlling emotions, greed and anger."

"Slow down," said Derral. "How do we know this wasn't another con job from an alien species." We encountered many in our stellar travels."

Saulian continued. "Let me tell the whole story and you'll see. We know from research begun centuries ago that specific brain regions are responsible for controlling specific emotional states. For example, our human amygdala was identified to be associated with fear-related processing. Its activity reflects our dispositional affective style. Other brain areas have specific roles for emotion-related decision making and emotional self-regulation. Centuries ago, the insula was established as the brain's alarm center, integrating internal somatic cues with emotional experience, linked to the feeling of disgust. That has been confirmed, numerous times. The Lorkanians have a larger but similar cortex. The microscopic nano cells they used can be programmed to modify these brain areas with low yield electromagnetic fields, much like what is used to cure psychosis in a matter of days by those hand held field generators. But their tech is more specific and can modify emotions and the personality in the direction programmed.

If we can acquire the Lorkanian tech, we can establish how we want society to evolve and then program the bots to do the work. The nanocells will result in very minor changes, creating a peaceful, agreeable, generous individual. Once the change is made the nanocells self-destruct. The evolved neuro configuration will eventually translate, genetically, through offspring. The Lokanians can still become angry at rational causes and defend their worlds from attack. However, the cellular structures prevents them from becoming irrational, and taking advantage of other organisms, as has been the bane of our civilization since it began."

The group shifted and appeared to be uneasy. Saulian felt the uneasiness, but continued without missing a beat. "About a thousand years ago..."

Susan interrupted. "You mean they turned the entire civilization into compliant bots?"

"No, no," said Saulian. "Everyone still possessed self-direction. In fact they told us of some factions that resisted until the concept evolved to where they could see the positive effect. Let me continue. The nanocells were released in the atmosphere of Lorkayor, at a singular point. The planetary winds spread the cells across the planet within a matter of a few of our lunar cycles, not different than how plant pollen is distributed. They coated all surface objects and were transmitted by either touch or inhalation. Everyone was infected, as the nanocells combined with the enriched oxygen molecules in the air that the Lorkayor breathed.

Following a time approximating three of our lunar cycles, all sources of conflict ceased. All Lorkanians had returned to the generosity towards each other; a kindness and altruism that Lorkayor had not seen in centuries. The Lorkanians look like one of our large bird species, feathered with a large head and small appendages beneath their wings. Their tech is far more advanced than ours, in many areas. All those infected believed it was a natural result of their experiences and the evolution of their civilization. This peacefulness and altruism has survived in their character structures until the present time. The deviant scientists who initiated the project, were imprisoned at first, but released soon after the microcells took effect. They are now celebrated routinely, as planetary heroes, much like we celebrate some of our ancient scientists and explorers. The planet has flourished for the last thousand of our years. Everyone has their basic needs provided for. The Lorkanians are nourished to pursue their own creative interests. As a result, the culture and engineering accomplishments surpassed any other era in the history of the galaxy. The bottom line is my contact said he'd share the tech, only if we guaranteed it would be used in a similar way, to restructure the planetary character from greed, violence, and deceit. At the time we thought it to be absurd, not to mention unethical and outside the parameters of the way humans operate. However, given our recent experiences with the questionable ethics of the holders, it might be the time to look at this again. It would be an advancement over the microchip. The nanocells can be programmed to defeat any influence from a microchip and, in fact, dissolve the microchip within each organism, leaving no trace other than some neurological restructuring that would appear as normal brain tissue."

"How can we know which areas will produce what effect? I know these past experiements went awry, with many unusually disturbing reactions,"asked Franco Dostoy.

Saulian hesitated. "The Lorkanians said that in order for them to give us this tech, they must provide technical assistance if we decide to proceed. That way they can be assured we will not misuse it or incorrectly program the cells. They have scanning devices that accurately identify specific centers and simulate effects from the nanocells. Aside from appearances, Lorkian neurophysiology is almost identical to ours."

Franco responded. "Yeah, but how will we know that each individual will produce the same effect. Every human brain varies."

"The Lorkanians assured me that the nanocells, once programmed, can adapt to each organism, regardless of how they differ, to accomplish the task. It's almost like gene therapy, but done with electromagnetic pulses."

Patrice Leguina, a scientist working on the Psy project investigating psychic healing, looked disturbed. "The technology is available to release into the atmosphere bot cellular structures that can actually redesign the human nervous system and adapt to each individual? I didn't hear that when you first presented it to us. Perhaps I wasn't listening."

"Yes, Patrice. The nanocells tag to oxygen molecules. That way every one that breathes will be affected. Even those who are on rebreathing devices for various reasons will be affected because the nanocells absorb through the pores," said Sullian.

"Uhh, I have a real problem with that, given the liberty interests involved. I mean the Holder's deceit and public manipulation is one thing. But, when we start manipulating cellular structures of the planet's citizens, that makes me very uncomfortable," said Patrice.

"Let's hear him out Patrice," said Franco.

Patrice scowled but nodded her head in response.

Saulian continued. "Patrice, let us discuss objections after you know the complete picture. Now, I most likely can obtain these nanocells, if the last communication with the Lorkanians is still holding true."

Susan interjected in thought to the group: Could we, as a group, support such an action? It's more extreme than using the microchips, even more extreme than my pater's deceit.

"I think we need more discussion. We need to see an example of how the nanocells work on a few individual humans," said Patrice.

"Yes," said Susan. "We might test this on a few volunteers, though not us as we have the Da'yoni tech. Say again how long it takes to notice the effect, Saulian?"

"As short as one lunar cycle, as the nanocells rapidly replicate, once tagged to an oxygen molecule. But the Lorkanians anticipated that question and informed us they have recently developed an accelerated nanocell. Takes only about a 135 degree arc or about 9 hours in old standard time. After that the effect is testable and noticeable. They thoroughly tested that one and had no complications," said Saulian.

Okay, the group thought. I think we have a consensus to test. Agreeable, Patrice?

Patrice concurred aloud. "I guess so. But who will be our guinea pig."

"I was thinking Derral's life long friend, head of Solar Security, might provide us with a deviant criminal to test. Of course we'd have to pay him or her. But we can never disclose exactly what we are testing for. We can disguise that," said Susan.

Derral responded, sarcastically. "Well thank you for offering up my friend, Susan. I don't know if that's a good idea, given his status."

Patrice responded. "I know Major General Laing, personally. He's an honest person and would probably support our little experiment. At the very least he'd tell us if he couldn't or working with us would compromise his position with the Holders. Umm. I didn't wnat to say this but we spent time with each other, for a while. We'll have to concoct a reason about something else to test. I really don't like deceiving him. But I also wouldn't want to jeopardize his reputation with the Secretary, or his career.

"Okay, then. Let's figure out how we'll deceive my life long friend," said Derral, sounding chagrined.

"Derral, didn't we deceive him already by not disclosing all that we acquired from Da'yoni?" said Susan."

"You're right. But I don't want to keep this from him, forever. If he was read in, he could actually be a great help to us. Once we get the Lorkanian nanocells, we might pay him a visit at his house and discuss what we are planning. We can contact his thinking, by group, to determine which side of this he'd be on. I suggest we start channeling our energies in his direction to get a feel for how he'd react."

"That's a good idea, Derral," said Saulian. "I suggest that you and I take a surreptitious journey in a cloaked ship to Lorka to see if they're still receptive to sharing this tech. I'm hoping they didn't just offer that as a gesture for a relationship. In the mean time, the rest of us can tune in on the Major General and arrive at a decision on whether to bring him in."

The group silently responded: Approved.

Okay, Derral thought. Saulian, we had better begin our preparation to leave. It will be a two week journey. We have one cloaked starship available to us, complements of the Da-yoni. But we first need to disable any tracking devices on that ship, including any devices that transmit thought to the Da-yoni's. Given the Lorkanian caution, the Da-yoni's must have no knowledge we're in contact with them.

I'll have my technical people on the job at the hanger. They are from various species and have a fine understanding of communication technology from many civilizations, even more advanced than the Da-yoni's.

This is so sudden, thought Susan. We need some time alone, Derral. Let's go to our place. I need that.

Sure, thought Derral. We can go back now. Susan and Derral turned to the group, thinking in unison. We'll be back in a few revolutions. The ship should be ready then.

Saulian responded aloud. "I'll stay here and supervise the preparation to make sure all the tracking devices are redirected to bogus monitoring loops."

Okay, thought Derral. See you in a few days.

Susan and Derral walked hurriedly to the docking station. We need to get back by darkness, so we're not suspected. Connect with our avatars and have a dialog about going out to eat, given that we received the med specs approval. Make sure you linkcopy that transmission to Robert so he can cover for us. We'll travel cloaked until we get to the Universe Mall. It will be a little hairy getting into a docking space undetected, but we can use the disassociator, thanks to the Da'yoni. That should disassociate anyone within a few clicks of our presence and momentarily disable our signal to any monitoring devices until we're out of the station and into the mall traffic. You're an inveterate shopper, right, my dear?

That's what pater thinks, thanks to mater when I was growing up. In fact, I do need to pick up a few things, thought Susan.

Then lets go to the mall and have dinner, thought Derral.

Chapter Twenty Four

Lynchon Meets Grancha

Lynchon, dressed as a star cruiser scab, ambled into the Black Hole and sat at the bar.

"Phyrigian gin, my friend, straight up without the psychedelic effect."

The bar tender looked askance at him. "Why not the psychedelic effect, my man? You're the first person who asked to leave it out."

Lynchon started to blush but recovered. "I have to fly a journey later in the day. It requires I navigate through the asteroid belt. I don't want to take any chances."

"I see. Here you go, enjoy. You speak quite well for a scab, sir. Must come from an educated family."

"My parents were professors. But thanks," said Lynchon as he lifted his glass in a toast to the bartender and to the bars only other customer, Grancha, mostly to end the inquiry. He failed to notice the inconspicuous human sitting at a table at the darkest part of the bar.

Grancha, grumbled and lifted his glass.

"You come straight down from Jupiter, mate, said Lynchon with a smile."

"Mmhh," grumbled Grancha. "Me been here few revolutions. Got use to light grav."

"How is it there. Never been there," said Lynchon.

"Mmhh. Lil thing like you would die quick. Need a pressure suit. Compared to this, it suck bad."

"Well, looks like I won't go there on any vacation."

"Huh, huh, huh. If did brothers would probably steal your skin. Not very friendly place to skels."

"Thanks for the warning, my friend. What are you here for?"

"Mmhh. You nosy suck, mon. Why want to know?"

"Just curious. This is the first time I ever saw one of your people, here."

"Long as just curious. I be helping old friend in a thing."

"What kind of thing?"

"Human sound some kinda cop? Don't like all your questions. Me just want enjoy drink."

"No, no, of course not. Just trying to make conversation," said Lynchon as he blushed, again.

"Me like conversation bout pretty things and skel pussy, not personal stuff. You down wit that?" said Grancha as he rose up off his seat to his full height.

"Yes, yes, of course," said Lynchon with a tinge of anxiety in his voice.

"Now don't be screetch man. I just want to have drink and pussy here. Much finer than on Jup."

"I'm afraid I can't help you there, chap. I'm gay," he said, noticebly trembling.

Grancha turned and looked directly at him through the the slits of his eyes. "Mhh. Bro. Me do you good, cept you too small, might hurt. Huh. Huh. Huh. He laughed and moved down a stool closer to Lynchon."

Lynchon responded quickly, in a falsetto voice. "No, please. I have a lover. We've been together for years. I wouldn't betray him."

"Huh. Huh. Huh. He never know difference mon, cept you be bigger next time. Huh. Huh. Huh."

"No, please sir."

Grancha moved a stool closer. "Huh. Huh. Huh. Me just jackin wit you skel."

Lynchon wiped the sweat from his forehead. "Sorry, I thought you were serious, mate. I'd have no choice given the size difference between us."

"That be right. But me jus havin fun wit you. What you do mon?"

Lynchon calmed down and said, "I just came in on a freighter from the Betelgeuise system. We're delivering some minerals we mined."

"What kind freighter. Me didn't see any in orbit when came here."

"Oh, it's docked in the underground military loading area," Lynchon quickly replied, still seeming anxious.

"Where dat mon?"

"It's just outside the city. Can't tell you exactly. We were sworn to secrecy as part of the contract."

"That funny mon. What kind stuff you brung?"

"Really can't say. That's part of the secrecy contract. Sorry."

"That okay mon. Me just at boss house on outskirt, too," said Grancha.

"Where's that mate? Perhaps we live close to each other. I'm just at a place outside too."

"Mmhh, it be 2 click dis place. But boss want me not say...is secret."

"Can I buy you a drink, my Jovian friend?"

"Yuh. That be good. This stuff too much credits. On Jup this same stuff is most given away.

From pressure on Jup psychedel springs stronger this.

"Bartender, another for my Jovian friend and myself." He turned back to the Jovian. "By the way my name is Lynchon. What's yours, my good man?"

"Me form Grancha this time. Jups no have name like dis place." He looked directly at Lynchon thorough his slits and wrinkled what could pass for nose. "Huh, Huh, Huh. What you tink dat, mon?"

"That's highly unusual, Grancha. How do your people identify themselves?"

"We no need. All same. Easy kill mudder we no like. Huh, Huh, Huh."

"I see," said Lynchon as he wiped the perspiration starting to form on his brow. "These drinks must be getting under my collar or is it warm in here?"

"Huh, Huh, Huh. You fraid me zap you mon?"

"No, sorry to give you that impression."

"Woulda no matter, mon. Jup's got no good feel for anyone cept Terra pus. But you good sort puny. No worry. Huh. Huh. Huh."

"Well, thank you, I guess. I'll drink to that." He raised his glass to toast.

Grancha put his hand on butt of his blaster and stirred. "Why you do tat, mon? Look like hit Grancha wit it."

"No, no. I'm sorry. I just wanted to toast you. Humans have a custom of raising and clicking glasses together in a toast for something positive."

"Me no hear tat, fore, mon."

"Here, let me show you. Raise your glass like this.

When Grancha raised his glass, Lynchon clicked his glass on Grancha's. Grancha jumped back at the sound, spilling some on his arm. He licked it off.

"Dat toast, skel? Pretty dumb."

"Well, that is just a custom that most on this planet do when they like something or someone."

"No more toast, mon. When drink gets in Grancha skin, no feel good."

"Sorry. Have you been on the planet before?"

"No, this first time. Don't know anywhere."

"Well, how would you like a guided tour of the city? I could point out all the places of interests. What do you say?"

"Mmhh. That good. Better then drink this crank. Tastes like lube from stellar drive. We use get high on tat. Huh. Huh. Huh."

"Good. We can take my vehicle. It's large enough for both of us."

"Mmhh. Grancha think you too friendly for just meet. What really want?"

"I'm just offering a tour to a visitor from a distant world, as a gesture, that's all."

"What gesture what?

"Just a friendly offer. If you're all that suspicious, that's okay."

"Jups always suspicious of skels. Nobody trust skels on Jup, after blast half during war. But maybe tour good."

"Good. I'm right outside in the public portal. Bartender, can we have the final bill. I'll take care of it"

"You good skel. Not others too nice."

"Thank you my friend...so lets go," said Lynchon as the bartender scanned his credit chip for the bill. He frowned when he noticed it was from a Holder account and looked wide eyed at Lynchon

They walked through the doors to the public portal. Almost immediately a fly attached itself to Grancha's coat tail, unnoticed. As they got in, Lynchon surreptitiously pressed a tracking device to record their conversations and locations. Grancha hesitated before getting in his side.

"Me no know what boss will tink if me go with skel stranger."

Lynchon quickly responded. "How will he know? We're just going for a short cruise around the city."

"You right skel, "said Grancha, as he barely squeezed in the co-pilot's seat.

Lynchon turned the air filtration to the maximum as the stench of the Jovian was not unlike a rotten tooth. He received the clearance signal and slipped out into the stream of traffic. "See that series of buildings over there,"said Lychon, pointing. That's the Holders compound. Most of them live there. It probably has the highest security on the planet."

"What they need secure for?"

"There have been numerous factions competing for power over the years. The Holders managed to maintain their positions as a result of the large contingent of military they command."

"Mmhh, what do human tink of military? On Jup there no military. Everyone does what want. So protect self with blasters. Huh, Huh, Huh."

"Doesn't sound like a very safe place," said Lynchon, wincing.

"Not safe but not controlled like dis place. Got cred, you get bad Jup to do business. No one mess then."

"It's something like that here. The more credits a person has the better off they are, the less they are messed with by the authorities. It's been like that for 100's of solar revs. It's the people who don't have credits who are constantly harassed by the military and the spy agencies."

"You got cred, mon?"

"Not much, but I work for a person who does. Same thing?"

"Who work for, mon?"

There was a pregnant silence. As a result of the drinks, Lynchon almost slipped and forgot his mission. He stammered. "Well, uh, uh, work for a Star shipper as a crew member."

"Don't sound like crew have any cred, mon. Work as crew while ago. Never had cred," said Grancha as he turned his massive form to look directly at Lynchon through his dark slitted eyes.

Lynchon continued to stammer. "Well the person who owns the ship has lots of credits."

"By way mon, why drink pourer stare you when paid?"

"Lynchon started to tremble. "I guess he wondered why I didn't pay in travellers chits, or whatever."

"You be hoaxin me, mon? I tink you hoaxin me. One thing about Jup's we know hoaxin from skels. So what it is mon?" said Grancha as he turned sideways, a few inches from Lynchon's face.

"Lynchon, anxiously covered his nose from the stench: "I'm being honest with you, my good fellow. I work for Star Ship Cruiser. The private owner contracts with various agencies to transport intergalactic cargo, mainly minerals. Please, you're making me nervous. You're a lot bigger and a lot meaner than I am, my friend."

"What you boss name? Me can get real mean if be hoaxed by little skel."

"Please Grancha. Peace. I can't tell you his name. Part of the contract was that I can't disclose who I work for. I'm sure you understand."

"Mmhh. That be same with my skel boss. Must be skel problem. Okay. We be friends," said Grancha, sliding back towards the door.

Lynchon breathed a sigh of relief. He changed the subject. "See that complex over there. That's where many of the wealthy non-Holders live. It's totally secure. Inside the complex there's complete recreation facilities and a shopping mall. Some of the wealthy never leave there. As a result of the revolution by the common people, a few decades ago, the wealthy came to be afraid to be seen in public."

"What they do, mon?"

"Some were mobbed and killed in public places. That's calmed down since, but there is still lingering hatred of the wealthy, as they control most of the commerce on the planet."

"Like Jup. Blobs with lots o cred hire bad Jups to get rid some they no like...Mmhh. Ma boss man place just behind that in field. Shouldn't talk that. You no hear that, mon, okay?"

"What did you say, my good man? I didn't hear you."

"Huh, Huh, Huh, you funny skel. What that over there, those ship yards?"

"I think that's the military refitting yard where they do the refitting of star cruisers and battle ships."

"Me bet that hot secure place. Fly over it."

"No that's forbidden territory for flyers. Only military vehicles with clearance can enter that space. If we try we'll be targeted and given one warning before they vaporize us if we don't move away."

"Huh, Huh, Huh. Skels pretty serious about ships, yuh?"

"I guess. Let's turn back now. I have a meeting with the captain in a few degrees. He's going to brief us on the next mission."

"Okay, mon. Just take Grancha back to bar. Dis light grav make want drink lots. Maybe Grancha have friend talk with drink pourer and ask why he surprise look when pay."

Lynchon's hands trembled on the controls, as he pulled out of the traffic lane and turned around, thinking he screwed up. He dropped Grancha off and noticed the fly still attached. If it was the General's fly, he could only imagine the wrath when he returned. In the rear screen, he saw Grancha looking at him through slitted eyes.

Chapter Twenty Five

Faux Freedom

As Susan and Derral docked at the portal, they were signaled that their avatars every move was being more intensely monitored. This was a tricky situation, as there was a momentary fluctuation in the avatar functioning when it switched to live feed again. This raised the suspicions of anyone who was monitoring them. Stopping at the galactic mall was good cover. When the avatars passed through the mall security, there was another switch. But that would be attributed to the scanning bots at the mall.

"Oh boy. I'm tired. Walking around that mall with all those people is more tiring than anything I could think of," said Susan, yawning.

"I know what you mean. More tiring than if we took a trip to the moon and back. It has to be all the energy bombardments to our chips from every store we pass, giving a menu of what they think we'd buy. I long for the old days of centuries past, where there was none of that, only pushy sales people," said Derral.

"Well, at least we can turn off the chips if we want. But the tiring thing is that there are so many choices. I couldn't survive another minute there," said Susan.

"Can I help you two annoyed lovebirds," asked the replicator bot.

"Yes. Michelle, make us a light dinner. Nothing fancy...but lay off the sarcasm, will you," said Derral, to the replicator.

"Of course, sir," said the replicator in its most pleasing voice. "But please turn on your chips so I can read your bioneeds."

"Yes," said Susan. "I need a stim bath. Join me?" She reached for his hand and tugged him towards the stim.

I think we can work out the details to this nanocell business to all our satisfaction, thought Derral. I had a brief conversation with Saulian after the meeting. Just after he signaled the Lorkanians of our visit. He indicated they said the cells can be configured in any way the user decides. They have an interface device that can be configured by connection to our personal vizcom portals. Once connected we can send thought commands through the vizcom to the cell control to program them. But the Lorkanians would only permit us to do this once, after they verified the specific command. They once shared this tech with a species, similar to ours in their warlike nature and government manipulations. They misused it to enslave the populations, until the Lorkanians voided it. They don't want to risk repeating the error.

Well, I just hope this doesn't get out of hand. The danger is great. If we can program the nanocells to erase our memory of the Lorkanians, and gain an agreement with them to never disclose their technology again, to any outsiders, I'd feel safe. But, we certainly can't expect that. Must say that the Lorkanians are the most ethical beings we ever studied in school, thought Susan, as they took off their clothes.

Derral responded: I'll talk with them when we get there to see what can be done. Perhaps there's another way.

I hope so, thought Susan. Let's get off this subject and enjoy each other. She turned and put her arms around Derral. "Please double the time for our bath," she directed.

"As you wish, but one must be careful not to extend the limit," responded the central monitoring system, in a synthesized voice.

* * *

The Secretary continued to monitor them. Secretary Priestly was sitting at a holo console with his head propped up by his hands, vacantly gazing at the frosted glass enclosure of the stim bath, where the microflys could not gain entry. He spoke in a horse whisper, turning towards Ulemann who was sitting at his usual post, towards the rear of the room at another holo. "Why is it I'm so certain they are up to something, but can't find anything? I mean they sound so mundane...so fake, as if they were acting. And to think how disgusting that is while I'm monitoring my bio who is probably having sex on the other side of the stim screen. I'm glad the flys are blocked from the stim bath"

Uleman nodded and finished what he was doing. "Perhaps, Mr. Secretary, they are far more clever than we expected. Either that or there is nothing to be concerned about. Forgive me, but it may be your suspicions are unwarranted. Just because they journeyed to Da'yoni doesn't necessarily translate into a conspiracy. As for their acting, we really don't have a baseline behavior to compare to, as you had not been watching them until they came back from Da'yoni. Although we should keep monitoring them as you suspect. We may be missing something."

"Well, thank you for your patronage, my dear Ulemann. You are a good advisor, keeping me in reality."

"That is the position you are compensating me for, Mr. Secretary. I suppose our security flys and information from the intelligence services will affirm either your suspicions or my perspective, soon enough."

The Secretary turned off the monitoring holo with a sigh. "That's enough for now. Maybe with some distance, my suspiceons will be allayed."

***

Derral and Susan were lost in the pleasures of the stim bath and in each other.

"You know it's impossible for the microflys to penetrate the stim bath. First of all our alert system would warn us. Unless they came in attached to us, they cannot penetrate the chamber. If they were attached when we entered, the first EMF pulse would have knocked out their transmissions and we'd see them falling off. I saw none. How about you?"

Should we be speaking aloud, thought Susan?

Derral looked lovingly in Susan's eyes, gently stroking her face. "It's okay. Remember we had Robert come over here to survey the place when we first moved in? After you left to take care of something that morning, I had him do a complete security check with his SIS team technicians. This is the most secure room in the place. He didn't want you to witness his team, for obvious reasons. His people installed a number of protections. He indicated there isn't a technology, thus far discovered in the universe, that could penetrate this room. As the Solar Intelligence Services are the largest and most highly funded agency in this part of our star cluster, especially the technology branch managed by Robert, I think we can count on his judgment."

Susan pulled Derral closer to her, whispering in his ear. "That makes me feel a little better. This will be the most important and beneficial thing that anyone will likely ever do for humanity, as a whole. Imagine, peacefulness and altruism. The elimination of the fear consciousness that controlled most of human civilization since we lived in caves. The possibilities are beyond imagination. The planet, for the first time in history, will be completely united and devoid of the random negativity, personal greed, and judgments of the past. Exciting, hey?"

Derral responded with a sardonic grin. "You sound like a jacked up politician with a poetic flair, buddy. Let's hope so. Some of our people say this is not much different than the fascists of the 20th Century, although far more sophisticated and devious. I tend to agree with them. It is total mind control; the envy of all fascist ideologues."

Susan looked disheartened. "Yes, but I wonder if our goals about rescuing humanity from 100's of years of deception from the Holders and their predecessors, will compensate for that. I can't see how else to do it, given all the past attempts and failures, can you?"

Derral stood up in the bath. "Yes, that still does not make it any less fascistic. I only wish we could come up with another way that would not involve the bio manipulation. But there are too many disparate opinions about the holders, about freedom. Such a dilemma."

"You know, prior to the 21st Century most if not all wars can be traced to disagreements in belief systems. Many millions were killed; many families lost their loved ones. This way involves none of that. No one knows. The changes will occur without a single eye raised askanced. How is that fascism?" said Susan.

"It is Susan, by every definition. The technology will biophysically alter every being on the planet. Whether it is momentary or not. The effect will persist. That is the epitome of fascism. Isn't the definition of fascism a movement employing a totalitarian government, often complicit with corporatists with obscene business interests, disregarding human feeling. They use authoritarian controls through the government to accomplish their economic shakedown of the populace. If reprogramming humanity is not an authoritarian approach, I don't know what it is. Even though our intentions are altruistic and on the opposite political spectrum, it fits the very definition of fascism. Invoking this will be a more severe form of the Holders using propaganda and hypnotic media to manipulate the populace.

The more I think about it the more I am opposed to it, even though the Holders continue to manipulate the populace for their own personal gain."

"Derral, since we came back from Da'yoni with our altered perspectives, our eyes were opened to the abject greed and lack of consideration for all of humanity that Terra government manifests in their every decision. The deceit, the lies. My pater, at the head, is the worst offender. He and his army of spies and microflys attempts total control over any dissent or opposing ideas. Look at what he's doing with us, his own flesh and blood. Our civilization has been living this delusion that government is for the people and by the people for 300 revolutions now. This government, conceived in secrecy during the tumultuous years of the latter part of the 21st Century was in the planning stages for more than a hundred years, back then. Then it morphed into a galactic government. Thanks to the openness of the Da'yoni to their tech, you saw the viz records of those secret meetings among the 5 families that consorted to develop it, all based on their absolute insatiability for power and wealth. I've seen fragments of these viz records at the university, so they're not just a creation of the Da'yoni designed to manipulate us. That was not a fabrication. Their plan was enacted. Now, three Centuries later, the original intent has faded from the collective memory, exactly as the originators planned it to be. The Holders are their legacy. You saw the ingenious strategy. At the same time they aggregated their wealth, but were able to use some of the scraps to insure a relatively decent place for all residents on the planet. This further veiled the motive of authoritarian control. Every one on the planet now is beholding to the Holders for their place in society. Everyone knows this. Whatever the Holders desire to manifest, becomes real. I mean 300 revolutions around our star...300 years. The few of us that now see the grand scheme can put it to rest. The means are in our hands. How can you not want that?"

Derral was grimly silent. Susan caressed his face. She thought, put that aside for now and love me, please.

"Susan, it just doesn't feel clean. How can we do or undo, in the span of a few weeks, a planetary consciousness that has evolved and is a component of every genetic pattern. Yes, this would presage a new era of benevolence and altruism. Yes, all folks on the planet will be finally united in one mission, to evolve for the good of all. Yes, this would mark the end of deceit, secret deals, greed, exploitation and crime. Yes, this will end the massive police state we exist in. People will be free to create. Civilization will advance to the next stage. Yes? But it will all be accomplished by the actions of the few of us, using the ultimate technology to manipulate the genetic makeup of all citizens. How can you not see that as authoritarian or far more so than the current regime? I don't know partner," said Derral, as he pulled back from her to sit at the opposite end of the bath.

"The time for your bath has been exceeded. I will begin to decrease the frequency to finish," said the monitor bot.

"Yes," said Susan. She looked across at her partner in puzzlement.

"We even accept the control of these bots, as a natural course of living. Do you see how much our freedom is affected? We must find another way. I think we need to call for a meeting of the Da'yoni Dozen to discuss this further. Perhaps we can create an option to this horrifying use of mind control," said Derral as he got up from the bath.

Susan laughed. "The Da'yoni dozen? Well I guess there are 13 of us. That makes a bakers dozen. What a name. The Dozen. Hopefully the "Dozen" can agree on a final plan. "Derral, come on. We havent' made love for weeks since this began. I want you now, " whispered Susan, as she pulled him closer to her. They increased the time on the stim bath.

Chapter Twenty Six

Troubled Thoughts

Lynchon pulled in to General Suddhis' home. As the portal receded, he noticed the fly had disappeared. Obviously the General's, he thought. He'd say nothing. The General's bot appeared at the inner portal. "The General wishes your presence, immediately," said the bot in the tinny voice typical for this model. Lynchon despised the voice. It reminded him of his mater.

The General was sitting before his holos, scrolling through the microfly feeds, as Lynchon was ushered in.

"Did you find out where he is?" said the General without looking up.

Lynchon secretly saw the general as a halfwitted dolt and resented having to cater to him. His perception was not unlike others who knew him. He secretly despised him, as he often related to him as if he were an errand boy. At such times, he was barely able to keep his composure.

"Not exactly, your Generalship," he replied with false deference. "The ugly brute slipped. He pointed to a vacant area near here. Looks like Cursard's operation may be underground. I will do an architectural search in the Holder database to see if that area contains an underground dwelling or tunnels. If it does we can be sure he's there."

"If he's not there, then what is your plan, you idiot?" barked the General.

Lynchon flinched at the General's abuse, but maintained his deference. "Very well, sir. I will then begin the tedious DNA search. That will take upwards of 7 lunar revolutions, to scan the entire city and suburbs."

"Such incompetence. I don't know how I keep you on. Why would it take a week to scan for one DNA sample? Is this some archaic system we have? We did exchange with the Shallicians for their advanced locator bots, including DNA bots, didn't we? What is the real problem here, Lynchon?"

"I apologize General but we did not acquire the necessary tech to interface the scans with our own consoles, yet. That was an oversight when we made the exchange. Our techs didn't understand that the difference between the way humans and Shallacians organized their perceptions mattered in the tech." Lynchon thought: You fucking stupid space slug, you are the one who negotiated the exchange so you could impress the other Holders at your diplomatic prowess. You could certainly see that their bug eyes were different than ours. When I offered, you said you didn't need my consultation, so live with it.

Lynchon continued with a grim look. "Sir, we may become lucky if we begin the scans where the Jovian pointed."

"I don't need luck. I need intelligence, a quality that you prove, over and over again, to lack. So set up the scan and leave me be. I have more important things to deal with."

Lynchon silently left the room. The General returned to his console, viewing a fly holo from the Priestly's domicile. Everything appears as normal, he thought. He then switched to the Secretary's assistant, Ulemann. He perked up when he heard a discussion with the intelligence staff over some operation that had to do with the Da'yoni returnees.

"We've been monitoring them, quite closely and were puzzled that they were leading relatively normal lives, Lieutenant." said Ulemann in his personal com.

The Lieutenant responded over the com. "There is nothing to be concerned about. If you ask me, you should withdraw your thinly stretched monitoring resources."

"That is an unacceptable solution to the Secretary who insisted on continual monitoring, including monitoring of his prodigy and her mate."

The General sat back and mused at the reasons for the monitoring. "I wonder what he suspects," he whispered to himself.

The Secretary was in chambers viewing his own fly holos, one of which had been attached to Lynchon, the General's assistant. Lynchon was sitting in his own chambers before a holo talking to a relative about how he was being abused by the General. This caught the attention of the Secretary. "Very nice," said the Secretary, aloud to himself. "What an opportunity. the General's man is dissatisfied. Now that we know the General is seeking that scum, Cursard's assistance, we can have some influence on the outcome."

The Secretary sat erect before the console, smiling widely, and signaled for Ulemann.

"What can I do for you Mr. Secretary," said Ulemann, with his usual patronizing tone.

"Ulemann, have you been following the fly bot attached to General Sudhis's assistant? He just met with an ugly Jovian who has some linkage with the criminal, Cursard. Seems they are developing some plan or plot. We need to discover the extent of it. See what you can do with our intelligence services. Get them to covertly sweep up this Lynchon in a bogus operation and have him transferred over here so I can talk with him. I think we might have an unanticipated in here."

"As you wish Mr. Secretary, but I just got off the com with the Lieutenant. He believes we are unnecessarily devoting resources to this, without sufficient cause," said Ulemann as he waved his hand over the Secretary's console to transfer the image to his internal com.

"Remind the Lieutenant who he reports to. Get him to escort Lynchon over here by the evening. Once we discover what these criminals are up to and what profit this Cursard is seeking, we can exploit them for our own gains. They may have something to do with the change in the Da'yoni returnees. I don't know. But we must explore every dimension of this if we are to get to the bottom of the conspiracy I suspect. Perhaps the Lieutenant needs a long vacation. You can quote me on that but not as an order."

***

At that moment, Derral Priestly sat in the meditation chamber absorbed in conflicting and troubling thoughts. He favored the total quiet in the chamber to contemplate his life. It was not unlike the quiet on a mission to a distant star system when he would set his cryo chamber to awaken him a few hours before the rest of the crew. Since his teen years, following an abusive childhood dominated by an autocratic father, he struggled with himself about exercising control over others without considering their sensitivities. His pater never considered his. Something he was never permitted while growing up, was to have his own feelings without criticism. He's seen enough of this autocratic behavior in the space fleet, including the death of some of his friends when obeying their incompetent commanders. His friends and Susan, have chided him, over the years, that he was nothing more than a reincarnation of an old liberal icon from the 21st Century in a

217

25th Century body. Since he was old enough to think about it, he resented the way the Holders appeared to subtly manipulate the populace through the vid media, to embrace whatever concept they deemed was true or thought the masses should embrace. They always couched their actions in humanitarian terms, while most of the actions were solely designed to benefit their hidden bank accounts. Every citizen knew this. But, as a result of the mind control manipulations and threats to withdraw the citizen's generous stipend with those who spoke up, no one ever questioned it. Fortunately, because of his long intergalactic journeys, he had been able to separate himself from the manipulations. He thought of the first such journey and the extensive debates with his crew when they arose from cryo in the midst of the brilliance of the Andromeda galaxy. The ship remained stationary between five brilliant stars, while they talked about the different perspective of the Holders, gained from sufficient time away from the media bombardment. It was then, in his early twenties, as an astrophysicist/navigator that Derral cemented his friendship with the current chief of Solar Intelligence, Robert Laing who was then the 2nd in command of their starship.

Derral was surprised at the opportunity for his Da'yoni journey. Little did he know, he'd return with capabilities to do something about what he and Robert had concluded was impossible or too big of a task. Just the thought of the immense task the Dozen were suggesting, changing the thought direction of an entire civilization, grated on his sense of propriety. He must discuss this with Robert, he thought, including the implications of what the Dozen planned. One of his chief ethical concerns needed a wormhole to penetrate it. It was the agreed pact of the Dozen to not involve anyone who did not have the seeing ability, acquired from the Da'yonians. He'll speak to the Dozen to gain their acceptance of bringing in Robert, at least in part. He sent them a thought communication for a meeting. When emerging from the meditation chamber he sent the prearranged signal burst to Robert that notified him of a request for contact.

The security holo showed Susan's transport coming through the entry portal. Derral walked out to meet her. They exchanged their usual greetings to not alarm the fly bot watchers, but the rest in thought. Susan, I want to bring Robert into this. As you know, he truly sympathizes with the need to change the way civilization is being run by the Holders. He has access to the inside information that even the Dozen were not able to discern...

Susan cut him off, feeling anxious. I know. I just picked that up as I was coming in. If you bring him into our plan, how do you really know we can trust him, especially if something happens and he is interrogated by pater's security detail? We agreed that only we will be able to resist any interrogation tactics, if uncovered, as we can unite as one consciousness and influence the interrogators.

Derral looked momentarily chagrined.

Yeah, that's true, he thought. But perhaps there is some way we, as a group, can transmit some of our capacity to Robert. I know he can be trusted and would never betray us, even though he may not agree. We've known each other since adolescence. We had many disagreements and conflicts, but he's always been honest. As I understand our group abilities, we can embed a signaling system he can use if ever compromised. We can then unite and do the same for him if he undergoes a forced interrogation. I believe he can advise us on a way to implement the plan without the drastic means of invading the citizen's nervous system, without their agreement.

Susan stared directly into Derral's eyes, frowning in that way she did when disagreeing with him. You know, she thought, if we were uncovered, the Holders would have us rapidly spirited away, as a group. This would forever remove the possibilities of change. From that point on, the possibilities, short of a bloody revolution, would be slim to none. You cannot know what Robert's other allegiances are. But there is a way. If you really want to bring him in, the Dozen can probe his mind to insure what they are...

Derral interrupted: You mean probe his mind without him knowing? I would not betray a friend like that. I would never agree to do that.

For some time, they both gazed out of the transparent wall of their living room at the passing transports before Susan responded.

Derral, you agreed before for us to sense his position. You wouldn't probe your friend's mind but would consider manipulating a whole civilization?

That's just it, thought Derral. I have a serious ethical problem with what we're intending, too.

This would not necessarily have to be a surreptitious task, she thought.

You can ask him to come for lunch. We can then inform him, vaguely, of what we have planned. But saying we need to complete a certain task we were trained to do by the Da'yoni's before bringing him into our full confidence. That this task would involve a sort of investigation of him, causing no harm. Would he accept such a thing?

I think he might agree if we can be a bit more forthcoming. I think he would be able to figure what we'll be doing. Let's have a communication meet with the Dozen and discuss this with them. I'll go with their consensus.

Okay, thought Susan. I was puzzled by your transmission to meet, just before I came in. But I'll contact them and arrange it at dusk, the optimum time for transmission clarity.

Susan and Derral took their transport to a mountain outside the city and spent the remainder of the day hiking. The sky was bright blue. The light beneath the sun disc that had been permanently inserted in orbit, centuries ago, to control the weather and protect against solar radiation, was bright yellow.

They stopped at the peak, doing yoga practice. Their figures were silloueted against the sky. Unbeknownced to them, a miniature surveillance fly, an unnoticeable spec in the sky, but directly between them and the sun, was recording their moves and voice. This was one of the fleet of private surveillance flys used by the Secretary, mostly to keep track of his enemies. These type of flys, outlawed for private use a century ago, were programmed with the DNA sequence of those whom they track so that they can immediately locate them anywhere on the planet. A main DNA console at the Solar Intelligence Service provided the coordinates. Other than SIS, the Office of the Holder Secretary was the only authorized user. The Secretary's use of the service was detached from the SIS monitoring, for security. The Secretary and his assistant sat before the holo.

"Why are they acting so normal?" repeated the Secretary. "We know they experienced a radical change when on Da-yoni. I also know my biologue to have developed very radical, anti-government ideas when at the university. Yet they never mention the government."

Ulemann responded, sheepishly. "Sir, could it be that we are concerned over nothing. Perhaps the Da-yoni experience enabled her to let go of her anti-government sentiments."

"Ha," exploded the Secretary. "That will be a cold day on our star when my biologue gives up her radical beliefs. She's held them since her teen years, reinforced by her own mater."

"Well, sir, perhaps you are correct. Yet we see no evidence now, for most of the past lunar cycle, that they are even interested in anything about the government or radical reforms that we suspected."

"Very well, Ulemann. But I will continue to have my suspicions and monitor them."

Robert Laing sat at a console in his office at the Solar Intelligence complex, deep beneath the planet surface. In the past few years, since being appointed as Director of SIS, a number of experiences with the Holders evoked his suspiceons. Thinking that he would increase the monitoring of their activities he ordered his tech to hack into the Secretary's private feed. He was watching the same vid as the Secretary.

Ah, because of their Da'yoni visit, the Secretary suspects his own biologue and Derral, he thought. I owe Derral a visit, anyway. It would be best to inform him of his pater-in-law's interest.

"Ulemann, what is that vessel that just came between our fly and my relative?" said the Secretary.

"It looks like a small attack cruiser, sir. They have not engaged any weapons though. They just appear to be waiting for something. Perhaps it has nothing to do with your biologue."

"Then why are they scanning them? I don't like this. Get Laing, immediately and ask him to send a needle to their location."

"Yes sir." Ulemann accessed the emergency code to Robert Laing. He appeared on the screen. "Major, the Secretary wants to speak with you."

"Yes. Mr. Secretary, what can I do for you."

"Laing, my biologue and her partner are up on Mt. Xenon, hiking. I was just told that a suspicious craft appeared above them. I want you to check on that immediately. I just positioned a fly at their location and will send you the feed."

"Yes sir, I see it. Looks like a small atmospheric cruiser."

"Yes, Laing. I want you to intercept it and question the pilot."

"Yes, sir. I'll get right on it," said Robert, as he clicked off the holocom and smiled at the Secretary's attempt to cover his use of the surveillance fly.

He dispatched a fast combat needle to the scene.

The needle was immediately over the area. "Major, this is Zero one, I'm above that cruiser. It has no markings."

"Scan it Lieutenant and look for weapons.

"Aye, sir. It has a pilot, navigator bot, and two mag weapons that are not charged."

"Hail them and ask what they're doing there," said Robert.

Before the Lieutenant responded the cruiser charged up their weapons, sending a burst at the Lieutenant's ship and a burst at the vicinity of Susan and Derrals cruiser.

The ship's shields absorbed the mag pulse.

Derral was alerted to the attack by his com. He directed their cruiser to immediately cloak and pick them up.

The Lieutenant took evasive actions and dove beneath his attacker, taking a 180 degree turn to the underbelly of the cruiser. As the cruiser recharged its weapons and attempted to flee, the Lieutenant fired a disabling pulse at the underbelly. The cruiser began to lose power. The Lieutenant, turned his ship above the cruiser and sent out a grappling pulse tethering it. He hailed it again.

"This is Lieutenant Drang of the SIS. Your engines are disabled. I will tow your vessel into our holding area. If you start to recharge your weapons, I will destroy you.

There was no response from the ship. The Lieutenant sent a hypnopulse at the ship to render its pilot unconscious. The navigator bot was knocked out of commission from the first mag pulse.

Robert contacted Derral on his private holocom.

"Derral. Robert here. We were notified by the Secretary about that ship who just attacked you. He claims to have sent out a surveillance fly, when he was informed of the intruder I suggest we follow the usual procedure to discuss this. I don't want to say any more, until we meet."

"That scared the shit out of us. We saw your SIS needle and then that other one. Fortunately we ran beneath some boulders. Good we did, as they just missed our cruiser with a pulse. The pulse hit just where we were standing a few seconds before," said Derral.

"I know. No doubt it was an assasination attempt. I'll let you know the details when we meet. The usual procedure? That's all I want to say, for now."

"Okay. But reverse that. We'll go home, then," said Derral.

What the hell is going on, thought Susan.

That was Robert on my secure. He didn't want to say. He used our prearranged code of 'the usual procedure.'. I reversed that which means he'll come to our place in a stealth transport at sundown. Our bots will be notified of a delivery and will briefly open our portal. Remember when we were at his place for dinner? You stepped outside on his deck when he told me this. He cautioned I not mention this to you, as he did not know the extent of the Secretary's monitoring capabilities, nor the nature of your relationship with him.

In the late afternoon, Susan and Derral were back home. "Michelle, prepare the stim bath for us," said Susan.

"Your wish is my desire, madam."

"Oh please with the drama," said Susan.

"My attempt at humor, madam," said the bot.

"Very well," responded Susan, rolling her eyes.

Susan and Derral entered the privacy of their secure stim bath

"So let's have the Dozen conference, before Robert gets here," said Derral.

Okay, I'll send the signal, said Susan. She closed her eyes. The transmission thoughts from each of the members was almost instantaneous. Susan and Derral sat back and listened as each one linked in with their own particular EMF.

Thanks, for being so prompt, thought Derral. We don't have much time and I'd like a decision on this matter. I want to bring in my life-long friend Robert Laing, the head of Solar Intelligence. He has been feeding me information about the Secretary and the Holders for some years. I trust him with my life. His position enables him to gain valuable information that would be difficult, if not impossible, for us to obtain. An assasination attempt just barely missed Susan and myself. But Laing sent one of his combat needles to intercept the culprit. We don't know anything else, as of now. Remarkably it was the Secretary who first spotted the attack craft by a fly he had monitoring us. It was he who notified Laing.

The Dozen immediately erupted with multiple questions.

One at a time, thought Derral. First of all, I have no question about his intentions or loyalty. For many years, he and I have discussed various ways to change the political situation. One of those was a total revolution. We both discarded that option as doomed to failure. In our musings, we both wished there was some way to inject some control mechanism in the populace to accomplish such a change. Looks like our musings are about to come true.

Roberla Stone interjected: How can we trust that he was not merely leading you on, out of duty to his position?

Derral responded. When he took the position at SIS, we agreed we should have no more direct contact. He provided a disposable tech that prevented the Da'yonis from probing us. We were the only ones to know that. He did not share that with the Secretary. That was how we discovered the Secretary and each of the Holders had received a secret largesse of some millions of credits from the Da'yoni in exchange for the visits of the Holder's relatives. Why do you think we were the only ones asked?. How many of you knew that? He provided a cloaked cruiser to his place and clones to mimic our normal activities so the Holder's flys would not detect us. And there were many flys we detected since we came back. In addition, we can probe him. He's coming here, shortly. I will inform him about the general aspects of our proposition without going into the details and say that the group wants to probe to assure his confidence. We can then induce a memory wipe of the experience if we believe he will be a risk. I won't be dishonest or deceitful with him.

Very well. The group reluctantly agreed. We will remain hooked up until you meet with him.

Please don't do that, thought Susan. We'd like some privacy. We'll connect again when he arrives.

As you wish, thought the Dozen, simultaneously.

It surprised Susan, detecting amusement in the transmission.

You learn something new, every day, thought Derral, grinning widely.

"You are reaching the end of the safe mode," said the stim bath bot. Susan and Derral finished their bath and returned to the living room.

Susan thought, how can we know we're secure when he comes?

224

He covered that. Just before he'll enter the portal, his ship will sweep, our place, disabling any flys, and insert a loop tranmission of us relaxing for the evening, just like the clones he provided when we're away. Then he'll transmit the signal to our bots to briefly open the portal for a delivery. He'll enter the portal and decloak the cruiser, disabling the bot's communication, also with a loop transmission at the same time, in the event of an insecure link.

Just give him the bare details, before we do the probe, thought the group.

Okay, thought Derral. He'll be surprised. I hope he won't react. I need to give him enough information to avoid any suspicion.

That would be fine. Just veil our intent until we see how clear he is. After our probe, we'll signal how far to proceed with disclosures, thought Saulian Bellow with the groups consensus.

Michelle interrupted. "An unknown visitor, a salesperson, is seeking contact, Should I permit their entry?"

"Yes, Michelle, open the portal, said Derral.

It was one of Robert's bots posing as their investment advisor. He actually morphed into the form of the couples actual investment advisor. While he was doing his pitch, he deactivated the flys and started the loop of Susan, Derral and the bot going over various financial details.

Another of Robert's fly bots materialized and inserted signal deactivations around their portal.

Robert entered. "Hello you two. Long time no hear," his usual greeting. "We're now secure so we can talk freely. What is this surprising request for a meeting about. Something come up since we last got drunk?"

Susan and Derral hugged Robert.

"Something quite big came up, Robert," said Derral. "You know the 13 of us that came back from Da'yoni, and remained on the planet. We were influenced in various ways by our contact with that species. One of the things we never talked about is our newly acquired abilities to do thought transfer, read others thoughts and determine outcomes. We arranged for a meeting with what we call the Dozen...you know like bakers dozen...so they can get to know you and take you into our confidence.

"You mean to tell me you both can autoread my thoughts? What happens to my many dark secrets and secrets of the state..."

"No, Robert, we can turn it off. The Da'yoni conditions are that we only use it for altruistic means or when the betterment of society is in question," said Susan.

"Tell me about being paranoid. But that's a relief it's not automatic. When do you propose this meeting with your Dozen?" said Robert.

This is our meeting Robert. Once we link up we'll all be connected through thought. Are you okay with that?

"Phew. I guess," said Robert, looking astonished and fearful at the same time.

"Please don't take this wrong, Robert, but they want to probe you to assure you have no ill intentions. Will you permit that? asked Derral.

"You mean I have a choice?" said Robert.

"Absolutely. When we met as a group and discussed how we will use our newly acquired abilities, we agreed, beyond the Da'yoni commitment, to only use this with friends whom we take into our confidence, with their permission. No exceptions. As they don't know you, we all agreed to do nothing unless you consented, given our long friendship," said Derral.

Robert thought for a long moment pulling on his ear, a gesture Derral knew from their youth to signal his anxiety.

"Okay, another amazing surprise from my old friend. But I have to say that I suspected something was different. and so does your pater, Susan... Go for it. But if you notice anything that is of a high security nature, you cannot disclose it to anyone."

"Okay. We'll agree to keep any high security issues bracketed, and outside of our awareness," said Susan, speaking for the group. "You might feel a little sense of confusion as we all connect with your nervous system."

"Okay. How about a stiff drink?"said Robert.

"Michelle, prepare Robert his usual, a 19th Century scotch and ice," said Susan.

"How did you know that was my "usual?" asked Robert.

"I know from our history, and just thought transferred to Susan," said Derral, grinning mischievously. A drink appeared on the table beside Robert's chair. He took a long sip.

The Dozen began their probe. The positions he wished to keep secret first flooded his thought stream. They were immediately bracketed aside.

The flooding concluded.

Derral expressed the consensus. "It appears we all trust that you can be taken into our confidence, Robert. Welcome."

"Thanks buddy. Now when do I learn to read minds?"

"That is something we can't give you. We can give you memory wipes to block probes, when we all link up, but cannot provide you with our gift. I think that requires being on Da'yoni and exposed to their planetary and atmospheric configuration," said Derral.

"That means you have the advantage over me," said Robert feigning a look of dissatisfaction.

"Not really. Only if we want to use it, will we. As I said, we have adopted our own ethics. So don't worry, my old friend, you'll still have the usual advantage," said Derral, as he playfully punched Robert in the arm.

"Now," said Susan, in the most serious tone she could muster. "We will bring you up to speed with what happened at Da'yoni." She looked to Derral to begin.

"The Da'yonians, as you know, are a highly advanced civilization, far more advanced than is common knowledge. Not only are they technologically advanced, but their consciousness is such that they are the most superior of any species we ever encountered. They are altruistic in nature. In fact, altruism is so prevalent, there is no other intent existing in Da'yoni consciousness..."

"That's what they told you," interrupted Robert.

"Well yes," said Susan. "But they provided us with ample empirical evidence from historical records to believe in their honesty. Each motive is generated from an altruistic center of both their civilization and their personalities. They evolved these qualities over billions of years. They were once similar to our species, with similar physical appearances and similar physical functioning. That's one of the reasons they were drawn to observe us. They were constantly at war, manipulative, and in conflict like us. One day, an unexpected supernova of one of their more distant stars generated a strong EMF pulse. The pulse altered Da'yoni nervous systems in an instant. The electromagnetic stream passed through all their inhabited planets. Within a matter of about 30 of our days, all wars ceased. All Da'yoni citizens changed, with no exception. The EMF pulse was ubiquitous, altering each individual's nervous system. At first they did not understand how all society, including political and business organizations suddenly became engaged in an unheard of philanthropy. It took their scientists about a year to figure this out. By that time, each individual embraced this new value such that the best interest of their fellow citizen was placed ahead of their own ego needs or needs of their organization. The supernova pulse was followed by other less severe pulses that altered the atmospheric condition, increasing the availability of oxygen to 25% from the usual 20% and a slight increase of argon from .93% to 1%. As a result, their nervous systems became more efficient. At first they didn't believe the slight argon increase had any effect. However, over the successive revolutions around their main star, the scientists began noticing a zeroing out of physical illnesses and death by natural causes. They tested a large sample of citizens with the same tests administered prior to the event and found they had a marked increase in logical thought and mathematical conceptualization. It took them a while to understand why this was happening. They initially thought it was an artifact until they conducted experiments on volunteers. They saw that the increase in argon stopped cell apoptosis. That coupled with increased oxygen, enabled efficient and more progressive thought, and a far longer life. The expanded central nervous system abilities enabled thought transfer where speech was no longer needed. The next 1000 years of living such an existence enabled them to evolve their advanced biotech to the point where they could transform from physical cellular structures into pure EMF forms. When presented with the full details, all citizens agreed to do so. Their nourishment evolved from cellular to an energetic configuration where their form swaps quarks from the hadrons in the gaseous environment. They maintained the beautiful colored foilage and fauna on their planets for esthetic purposes. Over the past million years they continued to evolve, while monitoring the fate of other galaxies and inhabited worlds like ours. The Da'yoni showed us historical vids from theirs and other civilizations they studied, that there is a point in a civilization's evolution where a singular, unexpected change can affect a total revolution. They determined the time is here, now, for our civilization. That was the reason we all were selected to travel to their galaxy. The selection was not our doing but their insertion of the intention in our leaders with the specific suggestions of specific folks to take the journey, our 13 or bakers dozen, being the most important."

Robert interrupted. "You mean they controlled the thinking of the Holders in the selection process?"

"Yes, in an indirect way" said Susan. "We were all selected because of our special place or relationships with various aspects, politically, scientifically, and technologically within the hierarchy of the Holders. This was the Da'yoni plan, made clear to the Holders. When we arrived there was a period of transformation where we could begin to comprehend their absolute altruism, unlike anything we experienced. They showed us vids of our past. Told us of how the Holders developed into their present state. As a result of the internecine fighting and greed, the Holders represent more of a detriment to our survival as a civilization than at anytime in history. They shared tech that enabled us to take history and project the future possibilities. All of the Holders, including my biologic pater, have developed a planned design to limit what can be achieved by individuals, so that only they will profit. The rest of us will continue to exist, albeit satisfied, but never without some need, so as to maintain a manipulative hook and enable ongoing control of the thinking of the masses, as they have been doing for centuries through the media and other forms of subtle manipulations. All future projections showed that this oppressive design will lead to a total collapse of our civilization in the not-too-distant future."

Robert tugged on his ear and looked away. He said partially to himself, "I'm supposed to believe this?"

Derral ignored his friend's not unfamiliar cynical response and continued. But not before Susan and the others silently requested his response. Derral demurred and went on. "We spent many cycles, during our visit, learning and discussing this with the Da'yoni. Especially the fact of the disbelief inherent in their intrusion. The particular physics in their galaxy compresses time. Their cycles are compressed. So we spent many phases of the moon on Da'yoni, learning. The Holders perception is that we spent only about 5 Terra revolutions on Da'yoni. But, given the temporal compression, it was equivalent to more than 100 of our planetary revolutions. Enough time to learn the process which we now can invoke with the same altruistic intention as the Da'yoni. That is why I convinced the group to ask you to join us, my friend." His brief thought to the Dozen: he's always sarcastic when presented with something he doesn't understand.

Robert looked out the window and seemed mesmerized by the passing traffic. He turned to Derral. "Are you intimating that you have the ability to make the change that is necessary to alter civilization as we've been discussing all these years. The change we thought to be impossible?"

"Yes," said Derral. We initially were going to use the nanobot process from the Shallacians, but our techs determined that could be easily hacked. "We have acquired a hadron process, absorbed 100's of years ago from another galactic civilization the Da'yoni befriended. Their understanding of the interaction of quarks and physical forms are far more evolved than ours. They taught us how to distribute engineered quarks to affect the nervous system. We can effect every living organism on the planet, making micro-adjustments to their nervous systems to alter each individual's focus from whatever they were in the past, e.g. greed, criminality, selfishness, etc. to the same altruism that exists in all the Da'yoni worlds. Our speculations, confirmed by the Da'yoni, are that the major focus of government will change to promote positive and equal life for all, where there is no longer any hierarchy of domination; where each individual will have whatever they need from the abundance of the planet and interstellar trading; where every individual will freely select the function they prefer for development, learning, work, and pleasure. After the change is implemented, within one cycle of the planet around our star, there will be the elimination of crime and criminality. Whoever comes to our planet and breathes our atmosphere will be infused with the same altruistic goals. This all will take one burst into the atmosphere from a small device they will provide, when we're ready."

Robert looked at his long term friend with a fear in his eyes, a first in Derral's experience. You mean to say we can invoke true change in planetary consciousness, like we once mused about in school when studying that 19th Century economist and social theorist? And the change will not be tainted by individual ego?"

"Yes," said Derral. "That is what our new found friends promise. We've all seen an example of vids from another galaxy they intervened in.

230

It was a system like ours, dominated by an autocratic government. Their high officials, like ours, posed as altruists, when in fact they were exploiting the wealth of the planet for their personal gains It virtually changed to the opposite over the course of one lunar cycle. They showed us the tracking vids over the next hundred years. There was total lack of conflict and a spurt in creative technology, the arts and science were no longer hampered by the greed that pervades our system. But, I have a problem with it. The others do not."

"Wait a minute. How can you know the vids they showed you are not just a fabrication to gain your cooperation to implement their scheme to dominate our civilization?" said Robert, as he abruptly got up and started pacing back and forth. This alarmed his security bots who came to his side. He gestured for them to return to their stations by the portal.

"Well, actually, we didn't know that. After we met as a group and realized our commonality, we undertook a secret journey, unbeknownced to the Da'yoni, to another civilization they claimed to have assisted. As you know some of us have science and engineering credentials. We reconstructed the Da'yoni transmission tech from the knowledge we gained, but expanded it to develop a portable energy field that could be attached to our EMF configuration. This allowed us EMF instantaneous travel and reconfiguration into our forms on the other end, without the corresponding reconfiguration tube. We met with the surprised leaders of the civilization. They were shocked at our physical differences, as we were of theirs. After we explained our intent, with a special language translator provided by the Da'yoni, to verify what the Da'yoni told us, they permitted us to roam freely with their populace. We asked many questions. The thirteen of us spread out throughout many cities of that civilization. We felt assured that the Da'yoni's did not at all benefit from their intervention. In fact, their involvement has almost been lost in memories. Only their digital history talks about it."

Robert now seemed to be unusually agitated. He sat down on the edge of his chair. "Do you mean you improved on the Da'yoni tech?" he said.

"We don't know if "improve" is correct. We'd say we were able to modify the tech, from knowledge we gained on Da'yoni, coupled with our extant science and engineering knowledge. But we were only able to use

231

this one time. After that, it seemed to not work. We are troubleshooting it to see what the problem is."

"The problem I personally have with this whole thing is with the deceitful way that was agreed on to bring it about. This puts us in the same class as the Holders and their massive subliminal manipulations of attitude. We release these quarks in the atmosphere. After they rewire all living beings, they become dormant. They remain dormant until they sense another presence entering the planetary field. They will then activate and similarly affect the other organism. This will continue for 1 revolution of our planet around the sun. They need not be airbreathers, as the particles can penetrate most material, including carbon based metals. Following a revolution, they will permanently rebind with the hadrons, but the CNS effect will remain. Anyone seeking entrance to our planetary field, after that will need clearance. Clearance involves subjecting their vessal to a dose of quarks that they must agree to or entrance will be denied. At least after the initial round we'll be honest. We will have an open civilization, but one that is effectively contained and impermeable to outside influence, unless they subjugate themselves to our standards of honesty and altruism," said Derral, with a grimness that Susan hadn't noticed before.

A long silence ensued. Susan left the room but remained in contact with the Dozen. Derral sat with Robert in silence, lost in thought.

Robert broke the silence. "Talk about taking the high road...phew. It seems like your new friends, the Da'yoni, see this as the only way to transform our civilization. At Solar Intelligence, we deliberate on this problem and have come to similar conclusions. Throughout history, all revolutionaries seeking radical change in an oppressive society, believed something like this was a necessary step in transforming attitudes on a mass scale. Our distant intellectual kin referred to this as dictatorship of the proletariat, one step on the road to true equality for all. In bygone eras the only means to transform society and cultural beliefs was by authoritarian or militaristic means. As long as the step does not fall in the wrong hands, isn't that the problem?" Robert seemed to calm and took a long sip of his drink, intently gazing at Derral.

"That is the very problem we face. Even if we manage the complete system there are any number of variables that can effect the final outcome.

We cannot control all the factors. Even with the Dozen...and I know they all disagree...but we don't know what will happen after the change, if one realizes the tremendous advantage of using the Da'yoni tech for personal gain. And I still feel very uncomfortable using these surreptitious means to change society, without citizen agreement. This puts us in the same boat with all the authoritarians and dictators of history, regardless of the outcome."

The Dozen all loudly objected in Derral's thoughts. He smiled.

"But," talking partly to the Dozen, Derral continued. "...how can we be relatively assured we can control all the factors. That's why I wanted to bring you, as chief of SIS, into our group, Robert." said Derral.

"Well, one road to assurance is that we know the players. Solar Intelligence certainly has a large database of all the major players in the system. We constantly run scenarios to determine the largest threats. Currently, some of the disaffected Holders are posing the most threat to a unified system. There are some criminals, but we have sufficient resources devoted to tracking their moves. In fact one of the major criminals, Solias Cursard, is recently negotiating with some extraterrestrials for tech to be employed by the Holders, Oice and Suddhis. We have good intel to believe their intent is to acquire tech, not unlike yours, to manipulate the system to their own ends. We are closely monitoring his activities and the activities of his Jovian henchmen or henchman, as the other one was recently zapped by a Shallacian when he tried to take some sexual liberties with him, or it. We now have established the evidence to arrest and contain all three of them and their associates in our sublevel palatial estate," said Robert with a sardonic grin.

"We know about Cursard and his relationship with the Jovian's and the Shallician bugs. We have been monitoring their thoughts and actions, and the thoughts of Oice and Suddhis after our meeting at the Secretary's get together. The Shallicians are a problem, as they would not be affected by our quarks, specifically targeted at the human nervous system. But Oice and Suddis are easily monitored. We suggest that you not arrest them right now, as that might make them suspicious of us," said Derral.

Robert thought for brief moment. "When the time is right, we can arrange to have all the Shallacians rounded up and off the planet, given a days notice. There are only about 20 of them around. We have a tag on each of them. So that shouldn't be a problem," said Robert.

"I need to resolve my moral problem with this, even if history dictates it is the only way," though, I suppose it really is the only way. We'll have to become temporarily like them," said Derral.

Saulian Bellow interrupted the thought stream. I believe we should act as soon as possible. The Holders are causing a famine in the Southern hemisphere, to make some economic point, so they can exercise control over the resources. Once we implement, there will be more than sufficient food for all.

Derral informed Robert. "One of our group just suggested we begin as soon as possible to effect the elimination of the Holder-caused famine in the Southern hemisphere."

"Your group certainly has good intelligence. That was a top-secret endeavor, known only to myself, the Secretary and a few of his trusted Holder associates," said Robert.

"We do," said Derral. "We achieve this level by tapping into the thought stream of various key figures. Why do you think we recently moved near the Secretary's portal? Certainly not because Susan wants to be near her pater. Even he's been continuously monitoring us. We can, as a group, read the prominent and unusually occurring thoughts that are outside the normal stream. The Da'yonis instructed us how to tune our thinking to that level."

Saulian's partner, Roberla interjected in thought. We should move quickly. The longer we delay the more complications can arise. And given this new secret Holder plan millions will die of famine, if we don't act now. The Dozen thought their consent. Derral reluctantly agreed with the group.

"The consensus is that we should move within the next few revolutions of the planet," said Derral. "The main difficulty is the simultaneous coverage of the quarks. Major cities have their air filtration system. We can easily transport there. The outlying areas would need coverage from a vessel. Our cloaked vessel can serve that purpose. We can program the release on the jet stream in the upper atmosphere to optimize coverage. The quarks will rapidly dissipate and become evenly distributed."

That won't be necessary, communicated Saulian. We can release the quarks at one spot in the atmosphere and they will rapidly proliferate

234

around the planet. To explain is difficult to those not familiar with high energy physics. These are not actually large particles like protons. Quarks are actually scattered within protons. When released they combine with what can best be called an anti-quark to form a meson, or combined with two others to form a beryon, as well as other combinations. What the Da'yoni tech enables us to do was to release singular quarks, so far unimaginable within the currest state of our physics knowledge. Our Solar system physicists believe that quarks cannot exist alone. But the Day'yoni provided us with a small pocket size device that releases a tremendous amount of singular quarks during a very high energy burst. All we need to do is mount it on the hull of a ship. As soon as it hits the correct atmospheric level it will activate. This burst will appear as a pinpoint of light in the sky and should not be detected. It will last less than a nanosecond. Once the singular quarks programmed to our specifications are released, they will instantly combine and cover the planetary sphere facilitated by the protons in oxygen molecules. The Da'yoni said we would have complete coverage of the planet, with the quarks penetrating throughout the planet within the span of 100 nano seconds, as the quarks, when singularly released travel much faster than the speed of light. Even though I have a background in high energy physics, I don't quite understand how they can accomplish this. They assured me the small device will do so with no harm to anyone, other than the desired effect.

Derral repeated this to Robert, verbatim.

"Amazing," said Robert. "I can't even imagine such a process. Can I see it before we set it off?"

Roberla communicated. The Da'yoni were very specific. Only we will be able to see this device, as it will be in EMF form. Tell your friend that cannot be possible, as it is invisible and can be seen only by our eyes. Anyway, the Da'yoni have not yet provided us with it.

Susan responded. "We were told the Da'yoni device has not yet been provided. But you wouldn't be able to see it, anyway, Robert. It is an electromagnetic field and not a visible object. Only those of us who have been to Da'yoni will be able to see it."

"Very well, when can we do this? Let me know so I can prepare to round up the bugs, send them back to their planet and detain Oice, Cursard,

Suddhis, their associates, and assistants for an inquiry of the 'gravest nature' regarding the future of our civilization and its relationship with the bugs. We have vid comp on all of them in discussion with the Shallacians. The Secretary will surely agree to their questioning, given the evidence, said Robert. Then we will be free to go. I'll effect the round up within the next few revolutions, by the very latest, the solar set within 2 revs. I'll let you know when we've accomplished that."

"Then we should inform the Da'yoni ambassador we are ready, so they can provide the device," said Derral.

Chapter Twenty Seven

The Ruse And The Roundup

The next revolution found Secretary Priestly monitoring the microflys, looking chagrined. "I can't think of a time when I felt more frustrated. I know there is something going on. Or maybe I'm just too suspicious," he said partly to himself, as he turned away towards Ulemann.

"Ulemann, General Suddhis and that disgusting Oice is coming for a visit in a few moments. Make sure the secure holos are turned on in the library and hallway towards the portals. I want to record them and watch their reactions to what we discuss. Perhaps we can learn something. I know they oppose me. They hide under this nauseating obsequiousness I can barely tolerate," said the Secretary.

The Secretary's personal holo flashed a vessel entering the guest portal. "That must be them. Let them in and direct the bot to give them some of the best and strongest Venusian beer to liquor them up. They're both drunks, so they would appreciate this."

"As you wish, Mr. Secretary. Shall I arrange for flys to attach themselves when they leave?"

"That's a good idea, Ulemann. Perhaps we'll capture the truth," said the Secretary as he turned to look at the holo of his biologue. She was home again, engaged in normal activities. He shook his head in dismay, as he turned off the holo and walked into the library to greet his unwanted guests.

"Secretary Priestly, it is so good to see you after all this time, said General Suddhis," with a slight, not unnoticeable sardonic twist to his voice.

"Likewise, said the Secretary as he stepped into the library.

"Mr. Secretary, thank you for seeing us on such short notice," said Rakard.

The Secretary looked at Oice for a pregnant moment. "What issues do you have in mind, Rakard?"

The General answered for him. "Well, Mr. Secretary, it is a matter of gravest importance. There seems to be a movement afoot to take over the Holders. The citizenry are not pleased with our recent agreements and associations. leaked by one of those criminal groups who call themselves solar ethicists.There are some rumblings about a revolution and overthrow of power."

The Secretary cut him off. "There are always rumblings and ravings of the lunatic fringe. My SIS is well aware of such activities. Under no circumstances, are they considered to be a current threat."

"Yes sir. Yet we hear of serious grumblings and desires to grab for power by various factions. We haven't been able to isolate a source, though," said the General.

"Don't be concerned about that. We have ongoing intelligence...Just a moment I'm getting a communication. The secretary went to his console and switched to privacy mode. Robert Laing appeared on the holo.

"Mr. Secretary. We have a problem. We have holo evidence directly linking the Shallacian's, the criminal Cursard, General Suddhis, and Rakard Oice to acquire mind control technology. Cursard is the middle man making the purchase. I recommend we round up the Shallacians and send them home, impound Cursard, Suddhis, and Oice in our Center for the Gravest Security. If you recall, that's the long term interrogation tank. Then I'd like to bring Cursard, Suddhis, Oice, and their associates together, confront them with the evidence and watch their response. I would need your order to do so."

The Secretary paused and was silent.

"Mr. Secretary, can I have your order?" said the security chief.

The Secretary responded with his subvocalizer. "Suddhis and Oice are here in my chambers, right now, talking about some rumors of a revolution. What should I do with them? I will transmit the order to detain them."

"I wouldn't do anything just now. Listen to their concerns and sympathize with them. We will pick them up after they leave your office, before they arrive at their own portals, once I've secured the order."

The Secretary used his personal holo to surreptitiously compose the official order, inscribing it with his holo seal. He sent it to the historical record holo, and transmitted it to Laing.

"Thank you sir. You might want to keep your personal holo open when you talk with them so we can monitor it and know when they leave."

"Very well, Chief Laing. I must go back to them now." The Secretary adjusted his com to public and returned to the General and Oice, waiting impatiently on the other side of the Secretary's spacious office.

"I'm sorry for the interruption, gentlemen. That was an important matter of state I needed to attend to."

"No matter, Mr. Secretary. As we were discussing the rumors we heard, can you assign your service to delve into it as it may turn out to be a most serious matter," said General Suddice with some gravity.

"I most certainly will General, as soon as we complete our meeting. I have many other agenda items to clear today. If you will excuse me, if there is nothing else," said the Secretary, motioning them towards the office portal. My bot will escort you back to the entrance portal.

"Thank you for seeing us on such short notice, Mr. Secretary. I'm hoping we can learn more of this. We would appreciate if you keep us apprised of any updates," said Oice.

"Very well, gentlemen, if that is possible. Thank you for the information."

As the portal closed the Secretary said. "Did you get that Chief?"

Robert Laing responded over the com link. "Yes we did, sir. They'll be picked up within the next few minutes. We have agents hovering outside your portal."

"Please keep me posted, Chief," said the Secretary as he closed his personal com link.

The General and Oice got back into their transport. Oice turned to the General and said, "I wonder what he meant by "if that is possible"?"

They pulled out into the traffic stream. Before the General could respond, they were immediately sandwiched in between two Solar Intelligence cruisers.

"What is this? I am General Suddice, a Holder. Why are we being approached? And why do you have your weapons charged?" said the General through his personal com link. Oice shifted nervously in his harness and opened the transporter communication circuits.

The agents responded over the transporter circuit. "Please tell us your destination."

Oice responded, nervously: "I am going to General Suddice's portal to drop him off, then on to my own portal."

The SI agent responded: "Please do not approach the General's portal. Go directly to your home portal and disembark from your vehicle. We will enter with you. There is a grave matter of security afoot. All of your subsequent transmissions will be blocked, as a security measure."

"What grave matter," demanded the General over his personal com.

"We're not at liberty to disclose that just now. We will discuss it with you later at Mr. Oice's portal," responded the agent.

The General attempted to use his personal com to contact his office. An image appeared in the holo with the SIS seal stating the transmission was blocked. He tried Oice's console. This com was also blocked.

"What the hell could this be, Oice. Some kind of revolution. Is the crap we told the Secretary, as a ruse, actually true and about to begin?"

At that moment, the Secretary was monitoring the activiy of the microflys in Oice's vehicle. He turned to Ulemann, laughing. "Good for those bastards. I'll get Laing and see if we can't arrange for some 'techniques' for those two."

Oice's transporter approached his portal. When he landed, the portal closed and the transporter was immediately surrounded by uniformed SIS agents . The General got out, red faced.

"What is this outrage," he said. "Do you know who I am? I am General Urvey Suddhis, a Holder. I will see to it that your next post is on Jupiter."

An officer stepped up before the General.

"Sir, with all due respect, you are under confinement by the Solar Intelligence Service. I have my orders to transport you and Mr. Oice to the SIS facility for further questioning. Please relinquish all your weapons or we will be forced to disable your nervous system. If we do, you know that you will awake with quite a headache that will last for a day or two. The General looked beyond the officer at two agents aiming neuro rifles directly at him and Oice.

"I'll speak to the Secretary about this, officer. We'll see."

"Sir, our direct orders for your containment comes from the Secretary." He presented the General with a holo of the order. "I will transmit this to your personal holo, General."

"That underhanded piece of dirt," said the General.

The Secretary was at his console monitoring the microflys on the General and Oice. "Ulemann, my good man," said the Secretary with a lilting voice, "justice is almost complete. We will confine them indefinitely. This has made my week."

He signaled his holo link with Robert Laing.

"Yes Mr. Secretary," said Laing, appearing in the small holo before the General.

"Have we taken care of the Shallacians, yet?"

"As we speak, Mr. Secretary, they are being escorted to their ship. It is due to be in orbit within the next 30 degrees. They gave us no problem. Apparently, they completed their business with Cursard and received their compensation. We haven't been able to locate him, yet."

"Please inform me as soon as you do, Chief. He is a crucial element as he has whatever technology the Shallacians sold him."

"Yes, sir. We uncovered a stock of nano bots designed to interact with the human nervous system at the Shallacian ship. This probably was the tech that was sold to Cursard, the General, and his crew."

"Well, find him quickly, Chief."

"Yes sir, as you wish. That shouldn't be too difficult as we have his bio signature, now."

At that moment, Solias Cursard was being escorted to the secret rendezvous of the Dozen by Chief Laing's closest associates. Laing felt uncomfortable at having to mislead his boss, the Secretary. But this was the only way...and it was only momentary, until the Dozen were able to extract the information they needed.

The Dozen were assembled around a long clear suspension table at the mountain hideaway. A holo was before each of them. They were tracking the progress of Robert Laing's associates in bringing in Cursard. The officers were approaching their portal in a cloaked vessel. Cursard was seen on the holo, enclosed in an impenetrable force field, in a holding chamber. The officer sitting behind him held the device to activate the restraint if he attempted to move. The Solar Security Service vessel docked in the portal and became visable. Cursard was led out into the meeting room with the Dozen and Robert Laing.

"What do you want with me?" Cursard belligerently demanded. "You have no right to detain me. Uhh, I see...Major Laing. We just missed each other a revolution ago, when the very unfortunate incident occurred at the Platinum Depository Complex on Venus."

"Yes, Cursard. You bungled that and murdered half the population when you blew out the containment field. We have your DNA sample that proves you were there. That, in itself, is enough evidence to send you to the country club on Jupiter, reserved for folks just like you, for the remainder of your natural life. You don't know about that one? We have a discreet relationship with the legitimate Jovian government permitting us one facility. We fully intend to follow through with that. Your Jovian henchman will be unable to assist you there as it is impenetrable to outside interference. And of course, the gravity... As you know, human physiology is unable to adjust to such extremes of gravity without a grav suit. All our residents have nothing but a cell to while away the years until death eliminates their suffering. A special place for galactic terrorists like yourself. We have treaties with other galaxies to also take in their terrorists for a vacation. You might even meet some new bugs until gravity takes it's toll, he said smiling. The grav suits diminish the gravity, only enough to keep you alive. But it is still a very effective aging process."

"You can't do that to me. I have my rights under the Solar Confederation," said Cursard.

...With a smugness so typical of contemptuous criminals, thought the Dozen, smiling in harmony.

"I'm afraid that those convicted of terrorism, have most of their Confed rights rescinded," said the Major.

"Under whose order is that, Major?"

"This is an unpublished unanimous vote taken at the last Holders convention. The Secretary has signed it into law."

Cursard suddenly stood and made a move towards the Major. The officer activated the restraining device. He was immediately on the floor with no muscle tone.

"Cursard, you really are foul smelling when you evacuate your bowels. I think that we might leave you with that disgusting odor. Fortunately your evacuation will remain in your own containment field."

The Chief turned toward the Lieutenant and addressed him. "Lieutenant, activate the sensory field so that none of this odor escapes. He can be content with his own foulness, when he can move his lower extremities again."

"You can't treat me like this. I have my rights. I appeal to you other gentleman. How can you stand by and let a citizen be treated like this," pleaded Cursard.

The Dozen remained fixed at the console in front of them, monitoring Cursard's bio signs. They did not respond.

"Well Cursard, seems you have no friends here. By the way, so there's not question of rights protection, you were convicted in absentia, by a formal secret court, after your murderous actions on Venus. We can treat you exactly like this, under the law. and even more severely once your terrorism conviction is certified by our highest court. We have all the holo evidence and evidence of your biosignature at a few of those locations. A certifying court would need no more evidence."

"What do you want from me, Major," screamed Cursard.

"Now we're getting somewhere, Cursard. We want you to provide us with the exact location of all the mind bots you purchased from the Shallacians, which Shallacian made the deal with you, and the complete plan of what you were about to do with them."

"How do you know about that?" sputtered Cursard.

"What does it say on my uniform patch, Cursard? Solar Intelligence Service...we have our sources, Cursard. If you refuse, or provide us with insufficient or erroneous information, you'll be on the next correctional transport to Jupiter, with no possibility of pardon or parole. The choice is yours."

"This is against the Solar Confederation's rulings, Major. You can't treat a citizen like this."

"I'm afraid you lost rights as a confederation citizen, when you engaged in that terrorist act at the Plutonium site. The Holders had the wisdom to insert that clause in the Solar Confederation's anti-terrorist directive."

"I have no choice, then?"

"You have a choice. If you cooperate, the alternative is a secure vacation on Jupiter with a Terra grav suit and, depending on the degree of your cooperation and honesty, a transfer to the rim prison colony with a normalized gravity. If you don't cooperate, you will be immediately transferred to Jupiter with a monitored and diminished grav suit. They tell me it takes about two Terra revolutions around our star for that to take its final toll," said Major Laing, smiling broadly.

"That is no choice, Major. Very well I'll provide you with what you want. If I fulfill your demands, am I to have my freedom?"

Of course not, Cursard. You are a terrorist of the worst kind. What we will agree to do is protect you from the Shallacians when they discover you betrayed their confidence. I understand they have some marvelous tech to deal with people who deceive them. Your movements will be monitored on Jupiter. We will retain you here at Intelligence HQ for a short while, before that."

"As you wish, Major. Permit me to uplink my vizcomp to a node. I will provide you with details of the numbers and the locations," said Cursard, thinking that his Jovian will orchestrate a release.

"Oh, and by the way, Cursard, we sent your Jovian back to Jupiter and told him you had turned him in as a criminal? So give up the idea of being sprung, said Robert."

"What do you mean, Major?" He is my assistant, I never turned him in for anything."

"Well you didn't directly turn him in. But our monitoring of your communications provided us enough evidence for his deportation order. I'm sure his fellow Jovians will appreciate that you will also be there. But, Cursard, we will keep you protected within our installation on Jupiter," said the Major with a smirk.

Chapter Twenty Eight

Success, But Verify

Susan and Derral are watching the evening traffic glow in the slipstream. In a very short while this will all change, she thought. I just wonder what the reaction will be. I don't believe we can ever know until the moment it changes. We're just trusting the Da'yoni's word.

Once we release them into the stratosphere, the quark dispersion should take less than a lunar phase. They will bind with every oxygen molecule. Our models tell us this should have 100% penetration, thought Derral.

What is Robert's plan for Cursard and the rest of the Holders? thought Susan, turning to face him directly.

When I last spoke with him, he was going to put Cursard, the General, and Oice in a room tagged with the quarks and observe their changes. That should be going on about now. If they make the appropriate changes, the General and Oice will be released after the planetary effect is discernible. Cursard has a one way ticket to our Jupiter prison colony. If he cooperates Robert told me they will provide him with a grav suit to normalize the Jovian gravity. After he gets a taste of Jovian gravity, they'll transfer him to the rim prison colony. If he doesn't choose to cooperate, he will be sent there with a diminished grav suit. He should last no longer than a few years from the pressure. If, after the transformation they are not forthcoming and Cursard doesn't cooperate we go back to the drawing board and do some detective work, thought Derral. We should know before first light, tomorrow...I have to get going. Saulian is picking me up at the rendezvous spot with one of our skiffs disguised as a corporate vessel from my employer. I'll walk down on the foot transport and get lost in the crowd so I'm not followed.

Susan smiled and reminded him. My dear, she thought, don't forget the extent of our new potential. You should be able to pick up anyone who has their eye on you. I know you pretty much ignored that piece, as you were preoccupied with the Da'yoni tech they were demonstrating. Remember, when anyone looks at you, there is an energetic contact that we automatically sense, now. Start practicing it. It only takes a few contacts to get good at sensing.

You're right. I need to pay attention to this. Makes you less suspicious, to say the least, thought Derral.

Less suspicious but don't let your guard down, my best friend.

Don't worry, thought Derral. We have some added security. We've been able to re-engineer the circuits for cloaking on three of our ships. Saulian will fly one. Roberla will pilot the other. The quarks will be released through an empty proton gun tube, isolated from the pilot compartment so we won't be affected until after the dispersal. This would preclude any effect on our intent until we complete the distribution. We don't know how that would affect our intent. It should take our three ships one revolution around the planet. I'll be back after we leave the vessels at the mountain retreat. Thanks to Robert, we can use the deactivator to disperse any fly. Perfect in a crowd. In addition to being tracked by whoever is monitoring, it sends the fly to anyone within a few feet so it proceeds in the same direction of travel. It will take them a while, before they think that it may have malfunctioned. Then we wait and see. If everything works as it should, I'll have my next mission. Your pater made a deal with the Eluvians to harvest their moons minerals. Lots of credits and probably a good bonus for yours truly, said Derral. When I ran the numbers it looks like a few billion credits from the deal will go directly into dear pater's account. We can see what effect the quark disbursement will have on that.

Susan shook her head in disgust. And he's my pater, she thought, as Derral gave her a hug and walked though the portal.

My bet is that he'll donate the credits to charity...pater will be a changed man, even likeable, thought Derral. He turned as the portal closed with a mischievous grin. Stepping onto the moving sidewalk, he noticed someone focused on him. Rapidly moving through the crowd as the walkway made a sharp turn, he activated the device to rid him of any flys, jumped off and waited in an alcove. His shadow moved on by, still thinking he was ahead in the crowd. He seemed to be intensely looking at a miniature tracking device. Probably linked to the fly, still moving in the same direction, but on another's body. Derral waited some moments and got back on the walkway. He switched at the next intersection to meet Saulian at the space port.

Saulian's cruiser was waiting. Derral spoke with some of the ground crew, pressing the deactivator in his pocket, just to be on the safe side. He then turned and stood under the boarding vacuum, instantly transporting him into the cockpit. He thought: Saulian, where are you?

Saulian Bellow replied. I'm down here by the plasma vent making some adjustments. I'll be right up, he thought.

Derral busied himself with the onboard sequencer, linking his personal holo with the ship. Can I power up, he thought.

"Sure," said Saulian as he came through the cabin hatch wiping his hands on a mechanics rag, slapping Derral on the back with a greasy hand.

"How goes it, my friend?" he said as he sat before the console.

"Come on, man. This is a clean tunic. How secure is this, here, thought Derral, with raised eyebrows.

"No worry here, my good man and no worry on the grease, as it fully absorbs. Our techs fully vetted the ship, installing a number of protective relays that will zap anything other than us, regardless of how small it is. If you've linked to the ship notice the small green smiling face in your upper right field. That means the ongoing sweep is clean. Pretty cool, hey?" said Saulian as he sent a signal to the port control center.

"Cute," said Derral, mimicking a frown, . "Makes me feel safe, protected by an emoticon. Are we loaded?"

"Don't worry, my man. This isn't your usual military transport. No, we're not loaded yet. We're due back at the mountain portal. The three vessels will then be loaded there as a precaution. No sense in risking anything down here, especially since we're not going to do anything with them until we link up the distribution positioning.

"Good thinking. Looks like we're getting blinked by control.

Saulian opened the holovid. "This is Interstellar Commerce Commander Bellow. What can I do for you?"

A face appeared on the holo, looking concerned. "This is Major Rikart. We don't seem to have your freight manifest. Have you transmitted it?"

"Forgive me Major. We have no cargo. This will be a local short range trip to Corporate HQ for a meeting. I have Colonel Priestly with me. He is a command pilot for interstellar operations. They are, as you know, allied with the Solar Security Federation for joint operations Do we need to wait for an inspection?"

"Just a moment Commander. I need to verify that."

Derral felt his personal holo being accessed for identification.

Saulian momentarily switched off the outgoing. He thought, this must be one of the newly promoted port security officers. He'll soon see our clearances and apologize.

The com beeped. "Yes Commander. I have verified the information you provided. You are cleared to go. We apologize for the delay."

"Quite all right, Major. We're pleased at your efficiency and will mention this in our monthly report."

"Thank you Commander," said the Major as the holo blinked off.

"Okay. After a little politicking, here we go to an indeterminate future," said Saulian as he navigated above the planetary traffic. Managing to place the cruiser between another ship and the satellite sensors, he turned on the cloaking mechanism. Here's a new bit we developed. He passed his hand over the com console. A holo of a ships trailings to the Interstellar Headquarters, flashed in front of them. There, it's now inserted into the control comps as if we were flying that course."

"What was that?" said Derral.

"It's a little bug we developed. It infects their system. It is undiscoverable, as it appears as if their system is actually tracking our signal. Even if they attempted visual confirmation from a satellite, the bug would insert a visual image of the ship where it was tracking."

****

The ancient redwood trees surrounding the entrance to the mountain portal were silhouetted in the waning daylight. The blue sky could still be seen through the tree tops with a few bright stars and the rising moon. As Saulian was about to lower the force field, Derral noticed an unidentified Needle on the holo. It was hovering a few clicks from the entrance.

"What do you think that is, said Derral, pointing to the holo.

Saulian made some adjustments to the com panel. "That has the signature of a Holder vessal, but there is no identification."

"How do we get it away so we can open the portal," said Derral.

"I'll transmit a disrupter signal to take his sensors down for the few moments it would take us to enter." Saulian transmitted the signal and the vessal's senses went dark. A singular 5 nanosecond pulse signaled the lowering of a force field, enough to permit entry. First one, then another intraplanetary skiff uncloaked in the clearing through the redwood canopy. They hovered before the opening and moved inside when the large rock face dissolved, setting down beside a third larger vehicle. The rock face solidified behind them. Another brief pulse marked the force field's return.

"You see how that worked?" asked Saulian.

"Yeah but how can it avoid detection if the sensor is focused? How do we know it didn't sense us? asked Derral.

Saulian called up a holo and linked to Derral's. Watch this simulation of our landing. With known EMF detection, if not directly focused on the canopy outside the 5000 meter range, the pulse would be invisible. The portal sensors flash holo warnings of any miniature flys or vessels up to a 10000 meter perimeter around the portal's secure field. Do you see the vessal's sensor direction? Pointing to the north away from us. The field is only lowered when the area is clear from any EMF signature, even Robert's spy satellites.

"Who figured that out?" asked Derral.

"Our sci tech, Roberla designed it," said Saulian as he nodded towards Roberla's skiff.

They disembarked through the energy transfer vacuum beneath the cruiser. Saulian and Roberla Stone materialized beneath the other skiffs and tenderly greeting each other.

"I hope you're right, my man...Ready to make galactic history?" said Derral, with a doubtful smile.

Roberla hesitated. "Ready as can be. And don't worry about that Needle's sensors. I'm pretty sure it didn't detect us, as I was monitoring their senses and holos"

"I would have never guessed a nice person like yourself was so devious," said Derral, as he looked up at the sky through the trees. He could still see the sunlight illuminating the Needle. His doubt that their experiment would succeed, was magnified by the Needle's presence.

"No need to doubt, my friend. My suspiceous nature is greater than yours from years of practice being hitched to an SIS agent," smiled Roberla.

The inner door to the lab dissolved. Franco and Patrice walked out, beaming, and greeted the group. "I'm glad we decided to decline the Shallacian nanobots. Those are what the criminal, Cursard was negotiating for. We adopted the Da'yoni tech using engineered quarks. We successfully completed the containment fields around the quarks. We have three containers, two for the skiffs and one for the cruiser," said Patrice.

Franco continued. "Thanks to Patrice, the quarks were programmed with an additional healing component to provide a secondary immunity for the remaining human and animal genetically transmitted disease entities on the planet. We tested and retested the component. It unequivocally works. No problem. So, having just caught your skeptical thought, you can let go of your skepticism, Derral," he said, grinning.

Derral looked at them with a frown. "Can your programming affect the original purpose of the quarks, in any way?"

"Absolutely not," said Patrice. "We uploaded the formula over our interstellar secure pulse to the Da'yoni's. That was another of their gifts only shared with a few of us, so we can communicate with them when needed. They verified it with their future projection technology. There will be no problem. Only an additional positive effect. Anyone having a programmed gene for any disease, or a diasabling condition will be reprogrammed at the same time the quarks affect the CNS. This is estimated to extend biological life another fifty solar revolutions. We can stipulate that as one benefit of the transformation, if we encounter any opposition, once things settle in."

Saulian looked concerned. "What will be the impact on the resources available for these longer lives? I mean we've gotten to 120 years now. That means we'll all last to about 170-190 years of age."

Franco responded. "No, that was also taken into account by the Da'yoni projections. The resources, especially those that will be liberated by the Holder's secret reserves and those of their many thousands of friends, will, when we change the economic structure, be sufficient to pleasurably live on for as long as we decide to stay on this planet. All resources will be shared.

"I sure hope that heals my arthritis. I don't think my knees could take it to 170. I want to avoid those fake implants as long as possible," said Franco.

"The quarks will probably be able to reprogram your cellular structure to heal your arthritis. That was one of the uncertain conclusions from the test run they provided us. You mentioned that before so I asked them when we were doing the projections. They didn't specifically know about arthritis as they haven't existed in physical form for quite some time, but they assured that if it was a disabling condition associated with a physiological degenerative change, it should heal," said Patrice.

Derral stared wide eyed at Franco. "What were the other uncertain conclusions?"

"There was just a minor concern, if a being from another non-oxygen breathing system happened to slip through the atmosphere with a breathing mechanism, would the atmospheric quarks affect their structure. The Da'yonis ran the projections from one of their galactic excursions on planets with chlorine breathers and methane breathers, the only other known intelligent life forms. The quarks tagged the hydrogen molecule in methane and the chlorine molecule without changing its breathability. On each simulation, the quarks permeated the breathing mechanism used and integrated with the gases. The Da'yoni even ran a simulation on themselves. The quarks tagged their EMF signature. So I think we can rule out that concern," said Franco.

"If that's the case, we need to convene a group communication to vote for the inclusion of the novel health addition. We should do so now, so that we can complete the programming and get staged for delivery," said Saulian with a tinge of anxiety in his voice.

I'll initiate, thought Derral. Doesn't seem to be anything to worry about. Franco even gets his arthritis cured, to boot.

That broke the anxiety. They all laughed.

Derral tuned into the Dozen's thought stream. The vote then, is to agree with Patrice's new adjustment to the quarks. You see what she has done. Do we agree? The Da'yoni resolved all questions about the effect in their projection.

Each of the Dozen responded affirmatively.

Okay, we're about to depart for our revolutionary journey. I think our socialist revolutionary ancestors would be proud of us. Patrice is now transmitting the adjustment to the quarks. We should leave in the next 60 degrees, 45 degrees before dawn, but cloaked when we go beyond the field. We'll continue thought contact during our journey to apprise all of any changes or difficulties.

Derral turned to the assembled group. "Looks like we'll be on our way, then." They turned to see Patrice bringing out the three containers, one for each vessel. She loaded them in the chambers.

Derral took the armed cruiser, while Saulian and Roberla each entered the skiffs.

Now we join social engineering history, thought Roberla, bringing a diffident smile to everyone.

Just one circuit of the planet...should take about 45 degrees or 3 hours for you luddites keeping old time, at speed, thought Patrice.

Derral interruped. Looks like the Needle we observed was joined by 2 others, all with Holder signatures. This may put a crimp in our time table.

We'll have to momentarily disable their scanning capability...just for an eyeblink. We can then cloak and leave the portal, but we must rapidly accellerate until we get above their altitude, thought Roberla.

Patrice responded. I hope our rapid accelleration does not leave a molecular trail that they can trace back to our portal.

When we had the tech installed, we tested it to maximum accelleration. There was no detectable EMF or molecular disbursement, thought Saulian.

Okay, then lets be off, thought Derral.

The three vessels cloaked and shimmered through the portal, immediately accellerating to the ionosphere.

Just thought transmission from here on Roberla and Saulian, okay?

Okay commander, thought Saulian. We're on our way. You'll run the longitudinal meridians while we'll run the latitudes. We'll be a bit slower than you so you will have crossed each latitude before us.

We'll report any events, thought Roberla as she programmed the course. I'll start from the North Pole, Saulian, you start from the south.

Aye, aye captain, thought Saulian with a smile.

Let's proceed to our starting points, thought Derral. I'll begin at the polar prime meridian. The Da'yoni calculations informed that one circle of the planet each in the programmed direction should do it. So we divide the planet into thirds. The simulations calculated the solar and upper atmosphere winds to completely disperse the quarks. Saulian will take the equatorial route. Roberla takes the 90 degree meridian. We should finish at about the same time and meet back at the portal. Remember when we exit the ships at the portal we should be instantly affected by the quarks. At least it should be in awareness...so no surprise.

Okay, thought Saulian. Let us synchronize our starting points.

I'm just about there, thought Roberla.

Someone needs to track the communication from those Needles to make sure we're not detected, thought Derral.

I got you covered commander, thought Susan, standing before the base console within the mountain. They are looking for a potential landing sight to develop one of their luxurious, hidden resorts for the Holders. That's all they seem to be doing. We'll combine our energy to manipulate them to look elsewhere.

Okay, thought Derral. Open the disbursers and let's proceed.

The cloaked ships rapidly circled the planet. As Derral proceeded towards the equator, he saw another vessel running a parallel course to his. It was an Asian quadrant destroyer. They may be following the molecular trail of the quarks, he thought. Patrice responded from the base. While they may be picking up your trail, they won't be able to visualize you and will confuse the stream with solar winds. I just sent an official transmission to the planetary weather center saying we're expecting an EMF solar storm. That should provide cover for you.

***

This took less time than we expected. Didn't figure in the extra speed we achieved from being cloaked. It cuts down the atmospheric friction coefficient to near zero. As if we were outside the atmosphere, thought Derral.

Let's wind this up and return to base, thought Saulian.

As they descended, the early morning sunlight enabled each to visually find the portal. The field blinked as they entered and then blinked again to close as they poised before the portal. The portal opened. The three ships moved, single file into the portal. The portal closed behind them. All three of the pilots exited at once. Their first breaths took in the tagged molecules. They all looked puzzled for a moment.

Derral was the first to speak. "Well I guess we're zapped. Aside from the initial feeling, it doesn't seem any different, does it?"

I don't know. It may not be noticeable at all until we socialize with others over the next few weeks," noted Roberla. "I know that's how some of the genetic restructuring material takes hold...and to be on the safe side we need to maintain silence."

Right. I felt a momentary disorientation, thought Saulian. I thought I was having a stroke...but I guess not. I wonder, if everyone reacts like this, it might arise suspicion.

Patrice responded. Ever since we've known each other, every change you attributed to some hypochondriacal concern, Saul.

Well, sometimes I was right, thought Saulian.

But most often you were wrong, my good man.

Laughter temporarily relieved the group anxiety.

Patrice continued. When we transmitted the official notice through planetary weather control, that the planet just passed through an electromagnetic storm from a comet the other day, any suspicion should be allayed from a universal reaction. Recall the last comet that passed through our system? Some people momentarily blacked out from the EMF pulse. The planetary weather control communication raised an alert for that possibility and asked everyone to ground their vessels until the next day.

We can transmit our experiences to the others now so they'll know what to expect. It should take no more than 30 degrees or two hours in luddite time to reach them, depending on where they are, thought Derral with a humorous nod towards Saulian.

I'll do it, said Roberla.

Saulian and Derral immediately experienced the thought transmission from Roberla. The remainder of the Dozen sounded in. Some had already had similar experiences.

Susan Priestly was on the moving walkway to her paters. She received the invitation within a few hours after the cloaked skiff passed by the city. She moved off the walkway to his building.

The one thing we didn't count on was the time element, she thought to herself. We'll be lucky if no one gets suspicious with all these reactions, before they're infected. Fortunately, most of the residents here were asleep during the quark disbursement and felt no reaction. If pater is suspicious, this may be the reason for this unusual invitation, she thought preparing herself for the worst. Derral entered her thoughts.

Susan, he communicated. We've completed the run. I'll be back sometime this evening. After we secure the portal. Other than us almost colliding when we crossed paths, there were no incidents. The planet should be covered. We all felt the reaction when we disembarked at the portal. How about you?

I was asleep and felt nothing when I got up this morning. This was good planning...to catch most in the Holder capital before daylight. I was just thinking about a concern of the suspicions arising from the reactions, thought Susan.

Fortunately, I don't think it is universal. A number of us reported in during the effect. They were in contact with others at the time. There was no noticeable difference. Apparently, the effect is isolated. Patrice hacked the planetary weather control and sent a message that the planet just passed through a magnetic storm, to allay suspicion.

Good, thought Susan. I'm on my way to pater's for an invited brunch. That was unexpected. I hope he hasn't gotten suspicious.

Perhaps not, thought Derral. You might discover the changes he's making.

Hopefully. I'm at his portal. I'll talk with you later.

Yes. I should be home soon, thought Derral.

Susan was met by the security bot as she stood before the entrance portal.

"Good morning Miss. Please come right in. The secretary is looking forward to seeing you."

"Thank you," said Susan,, following him through the cavernous dwelling.

The Secretary was sitting at his console. He looked up with a broad smile as she entered.

"Susan, it is so nice to see you. Can I get you anything to drink."

"No thank you, pater. I'm most curious about your spur of the moment invitation."

"Yes my dear. I haven't been the most sensitive pater to you. I admit

I was suspicious of your relationships with the group that returned from Da'yoni. I apologize and hope you can forgive me. I realize now that my suspicions were motivated by fear, as there were so many elements I had to guard against. When I awoke this morning, I started thinking about my life and my long term as Secretary...and especially about the Holders. As you were likely aware, many of us, out of sheer greed, kept many resources from the public, especially those obtained from our interstellar voyages and treaties. We spied on the citizenry. I even spied on you and Derral. An hour ago, I recalled all the microflys in our network. I'd like to set up a meeting with your Dozen to mark out a new plan for future generations of our solar community and beyond. I've contacted the Holders. It was incredible, but they all agreed with the need for a new plan and will be in attendance at the meeting. We'd like the meeting to take place as soon as possible. What do you think, my dear? But before you answer, please agree to have some brunch."

Susan smiled at his asking, rather then his usual command.

The Secretary alerted the wait staff. They arose and went into the dining room.

A sumptuous feast was laid out before them.

She hesitated for a very long moment before responding, while she silently communicated with the Dozen. They all voiced agreement with the meeting, as soon as the Secretary would prefer. Feeling a bit apprehensive, Susan suspected her pater might actually be forthright, perhaps, for the first time.

"Is this how you always dine, Pater? If so I'm amazed at how good you look."

"No, my dear, this is for a special occasion and our warming relationship."

"I can arrange the meeting, Pater, as soon as you wish."

"Wonderful," said the Secretary. He changed the subject and freely talked about their lives as a family. Another first in Susan's memory. She learned of his relation with her mater. That surprised her as she always believed she was the product of a fertility bank. The conversation then reverted back to the matter at hand.

"I'll be in contact with you before the morrow, my dear. As I discussed with the other Holders, with the exception of the criminals picked up by the SIS, the agenda will be about restructuring and redistribution of wealth throughout our system of planets. All the Holders are willing to give up their sequestered resources to benefit the less privileged. We know people in some areas here and on other inhabited planets, living in extreme poverty, as a result of our decision to withold resources. Amazingly, none of them blinked an eye when I brought it up on the holo. This should serve to end all boundary disputes and clashes like the recent ones in the New Africa sector. All the clashes have been over resources. Unfortunately, we knew that and were exploiting the citizenry for our own economic gains. I can't understand how we regressed to that point. I recall when I was first appointed to this position, many years ago, before your birth. I had the good of the citizens in mind. I guess I became caught up by greed, as were the others. I'm thinking of proposing the elimination of arbitrary geo boundaries, after we distribute the resources. Following that we'll then have to find a way to deal with the other off world members of the solar confederation. That may prove difficult."

Not as difficult as you might expect, thought Susan. "Pater, forgive my own suspicions, but why have you decided such a change, now? I mean that was one thing about the Holders and you that I could never accept. It was part of the reason for my distance from you over the years. The citizens knew of your greed and exploitation, but were powerless to do anything about it."

"I really don't know, my dear. I've been up quite early at dawn, this morning, in communication with the others. We had long discussions. Some on the other side of the planet were initially astounded and resentful of what we wanted to do, but even they graciously conceded after our lengthy discussion in attempting to reason with them. It was something that came to a point. How the stress of governing disappeared as soon as we agreed to the change is astounding. Some said it was too bad we didn't realize this years ago. We all can see now that it will probably be best for the confederation if we retire from our Holder position. A new body of visionaries, perhaps your Dozen, given your enhanced senses and technological advances can take over."

"My Dozen?...andwhat enhanced senses are you referring to, pater?"

said Susan, with raised eyebrows.

"Susan, my intelligence resources confirmed that the Da'yoni have bestowed all of you returnees with enhanced sensory systems. Our scanners have confirmed changes in your nervous systems upon return. That was a large part of my suspicion and the implanting of the flys in your portal, as you never mentioned that aspect of your experience. We knew that something happened but could not get a fix on the specific process of change. We intercepted a conversation between you and Derral, when you referred to the Dozen. The Da'yoni ambassador was somewhat taken aback when we met with him in the last lunar cycle and confronted him about that. He made some vague reference to the possible effect of the teleportation process to and from Da'yoni producing the effect. But we suspected it was something more than that."

The Dozen were tuned in to Susan's thought stream. They were processing what was just said. Franco Dostoy interjected: Susan, I think we are seeing the initial effect of the quarks. We suspected the Holders had far more advanced intelligence than they let on. I think we can at least agree to acknowledge some of the changes, but I think you should tell him you will have to verify with the others before disclosing the details. That we will likely do so when we meet with the Holders. But be careful, as we don't yet know how this will affect the rest of the populace, including the Holders. Nor do we know how your pater and his organization will take such a piece of news. The others thought their agreement. We can consider ourselves lucky, that the Secretary did not take any action against us, other than monitoring, thought Derral.

"Well, pater," said Susan. "You're right, as usual. We were all changed by the experience. Our human senses were enhanced. At this point, I think it would be best though, if I check with the others before telling you the complete story which, I'm sure, you'll find hard to believe. We will present the full extent of our changes during our meeting with the Holders."

"As you wish, my dear," said the Secretary as they finished brunch. I'm eager to learn. We'll set the meeting in two revolutions. We can begin at first light at the Holder's private conference center. My assistant will transmit the coordinates and the passkey to your personal holo, as it is a high security underground installation. Now if you forgive me, my dear, I need to attend to some state matters. Please finish your meal."

"Of course pater, this was most enjoyable. So enjoyable that it took my appetite away. We'll next see each other at the meeting?" said Susan, as she got up from the table.

The Secretary furrowed his brow and gave her a momentary side glance, as his suspicions were raised. As always, he wondered what she truly meant. "Of course. While my schedule is full but if I have some time before then, I'd like to visit with you and Derral, at your portal. Perhaps you can invite me for an afternoon synth the morrow?"

"Why yes. That would be nice. Let me know if you can free yourself."

"I'll contact you this eve after I know more about my pending schedule." They embraced as the Secretary escorted Susan to the front portal.

"We'll be seeing each other, hopefully more often that we live next door to each other," said the Secretary. He waved as she entered the lift to the moving sidewalk. The usual security bots seemed absent. This puzzled Susan, as it was the first time she was ever alone when she entered or exited his portal.

Derral pulled his skiff up to the portal as Susan entered the lift. They surprised each other. I see your meeting with pater was productive, thought Derral.

Yes, thought Susan. But I don't think there is any more need to not talk. He said he removed the flys. I checked upon entering. There is nothing here any more. The ones on the windows are also gone. When I left his place, it was the first time I didn't notice his security bots stationed about.

Well, thought Derral, lets continue to exercise some caution until we meet and find out the true effect of the quarks. We need to return to the mountain portal tonight for a face-to-face meeting.

Pater said he will call this evening to let me know if he can visit, thought Susan.

You can link it to your faux holo and answer there. But we should leave as soon as possible. We need to discuss the effect of the quarks on us and our plans. We have a lot to discuss and a short time to do it, given the meeting with the Holders.

Pater indicated they may offer us the opportunity to take over for them, given our enhanced senses.

Yes, I was tuned in. But we need to develop a coherent plan about the next phase.

Okay, thought Susan, I'm ready. Shall we engage the loop so we're not detected?

I think that would be wise at this stage, as we really don't yet know the true extent of things.

Susan signaled the console and engaged the loop of their routine activities. They both entered the portal to Derral's skiff.

As they arrived at the mountain portal, the others were gleeful.

"Here's to success," proclaimed Franco, as he lifted his glass of synth in a toast as Susan and Derral entered.

The others shouted in unison. "Long live the new solar confederation.

Derral and Susan took their place at the head of the long table. Saulian embraced his old friend. They raised their glasses to the three pilots.

"A job well done that will secure humanity from the hegemony of the Holder's greed," said Patrice Leguna as she raised her glass.

Derral rose to speak. "Let's not be too hasty. We must maintain discretion, until we are certain the quarks are doing their job. We still have our job cut out for us. As you know the Secretary wants a meeting with us. He intimated to Susan that he was thinking of appointing us to take over the Holder function given our sensitivities he believes we acquired during the Da'yoni visit. He doesn't know the extent of our so called sensitivities, though. We must be 100% assured he is on our side before we disclose our full natures to him. Remember, he could never be trusted, not even by his own bio," he said, placing his hand on Susan's shoulder. "He disclosed things that we already knew about. That he had flys on each of our living portals since our return. He said he spoke with the Holders this morning. They agreed to divest all their secret companies and hoarded wealth and distribute it to the citizens of this planet to end hunger and elevate every one's living standard. That was approximately 135 degrees from the time of the quark release over the city. We can see if that had any effect on this evenings business feeds. We have no way of knowing what we'll be seeing at the meeting, especially when more time has passed. I suggest we appoint a spokesperson, with us all silently advising that spokesperson. What do you think?"

The Dozen agreed and nominated Susan as the likely spokesperson, given her relationship, and since she made the first contact with the Secretary after the distribution.

"I couldn't detect any discrepancy between pater's thought and his verbalizations, so that's reassuring," said Susan.

"Okay, said Derral. That's settled. I think we should arrive in two skiffs. Susan and I will take one. Franco, do you want to fly the other?"

"Sure. I'll enjoy flying unencumbered into the enemies nest" said Franco Dostoy.

"Susan will transmit the coordinates and the passkey to your skiff's console. This will gain us entry into the Holder's so-called top secret conference center. We should arrive at the same time.

Chapter Twenty Nine

Holders Lament

Two unmarked skiffs pulled up before the Holder's conference center. Armed bots were immediately dispatched to greet them.

Inside, the Holders were seated around a large conference table sipping synth, the slightly intoxicating beverage that was imported from the the Triangulum Galaxy, an increasingly nearer galaxy approaching the solar system at 162 km per second. Thus with each year, the import price goes down. They were commenting on how that benefits the citizenry, as they can all be cheaper drunks with each shipment. The subject of conversation turned to now humorous anecdotes of their past absurdities when, prior to last week, they were all embattled in arguments of the economic advantage one held over the others. General Suddhis was present. He was, released by Robert's security services after they confirmed the positive effect of the quark exposure.

They talked as if this change was a normal evolution of the good practices they had always been considering. One noticeable benefit of the quark effect was that it enabled a clearly undisputed rationalization of the changes that were effected, as if they were a natural conclusion of the path they were all proceeding on. In a sense that was true, after the quarks accomplished their effect.

Well, rewriting history is not bad, if it results in positive change for all, thought Susan.

The Dozen silently snickered.

As the bots escorted the Dozen into the large chamber, all of the Holders rose to greet them with the utmost in graciousness. Susan immediately thought to the group: Isn't this amazing. Never thought this could be accomplished. The Dozen were seated at one side of the large round conference table. The Holders took their seats except for the Secretary.

262

"Good day good people. We welcome you to this historic meeting. It is the first time in history that an outsider has been in attendance at our conferences. This is a special day."

Very special, thought Derral. The Dozen smiled.

"Before we get into the business at hand, have some refreshments," said the Secretary. As he ended his sentence, large pilsners of synth materialized before each of the Dozen. The Secretary raised his glass. "Let us have a toast to this momentous occasion."

Patrice discreetly dipped her finger in the glass, testing for toxins with a small portable spectrometer. She signaled to the group they were free to indulge. The Holders and the Dozen raised their glasses in a toast. The Holders unanimously cheered.

"My dear Susan, said the Secretary, referring to her by name, perhaps for the first time in public, in memory. We were told you are to be the spokesperson for your group. As you know we invited you here to propose that we step down from our positions and appoint your group, with your newly acquired superior qualities, to lead the solar confederation Have you had enough time to make a decision, my dear."

Susan paused to look around the table. "Mr. Secretary...pater, I am pleased to say that we have considered the offer. There are some details we would like to discuss."

"Very well then, let us begin the discussion," said the Secretary, beaming.

"As you know, Mr. Secretary and Holders, the majority of the citizenry have expressed dismay as to how the Holders have been running the Terra body and the Solar planets. The dismay is over the secretive tactics used to spy on citizens who disagree or express opposition to the authoritarian control. As you know, my spouse and I have been some of the targeted. There have been flys constantly covering our whereabouts for quite some time. They were only lifted the other day when we spoke. Hundreds of thousands of other law abiding citizens have been so secretely tracked and holoed."

"Permit me to interrupt, my dear," said the Secretary. "A few days ago, when we conducted our first reformation meeting, we took into account the concerns of all citizens. We realized, as a group, that the treatment of our

263

office was less than ethical and honorable. Our staff prepared a briefing of all complaints. We spent the day and night addressing each complaint and concern that had either infringed on or had the potential to infringe on a citizen's freedom. We summarily honored each of those complaints. We concluded that our past actions had not been for the greater good. In fact many of our singular acts were actually in violation of the tenets of the solar confederation and some treaties. I don't know why I, for one, was so suspect of every good intention and so suspicious of everyone who seemed to think differently. At that point, we relinquished all of our private reserves of wealth, placing it in a fund with the goal of distributing it to those in need, all around the planet. You see on your holos, the actual distribution plans and progress towards those goals, as of this hour. This was a serious undertaking. All of us have divested ourselves from our stores. We now have no more than an average citizen, albeit with the gratuities given our Holder status. In addition, and you can verify this with our Security Chief Laing, we have pulled back and destroyed all storage records obtained by micro flys. The micro fly system no longer exists."

"Pater, I'm so impressed. The old pater I knew, before you assumed Holder status, seems to have come back. Have you discussed what motivated your sudden changes?" asked Susan.

"That is puzzling. We came together as a group, the other day to discuss business as usual and politics. But when we started, one of us mentioned the plight of the more unfortunate citizens. That sent us on a discussion about what we do as administrators to create the kind of society where resources are utilized in the most efficient manner for all to benefit. A topic that many of us, including myself, have only laughed at in the past. We understand the seriousness of the problems we have created by our misguided policies and practices. That is why we would like to step down for we've lost the trust of the citizens."

Saulian Bellan rose to speak. He gestured to Susan to permit him to say a few words. "I peremptorily apologize for what I am about to say. But it needs to be said. I take what you are saying, Mr. Secretary, with a sense of glee. As some of you know, my background in economics and in the military lends me a particular perspective. Our solar society of economists, have consistently disagreed with the decisions the Holders made regarding the economic policies in the solar system and especially on our Terra. We have sought thorough many research publications to illustrate the correct, ethical and equitable way of distribution of the massive wealth our civilization has aggregated since recovery from the Great Catastrophe. Until now, the Holders have ignored our reasoned scientifically based critiques. I must admit that most recently, prior to my trip to Da'yoni, we truly believed the planet would never be rescued from the unfair economic morass it has sunk to, mainly as a result of Holder's decisions. Yet your words thrill me. If you are serious about following through, I for one would like you all to stay on throughout your terms and beyond, as Holders and consultants until you retire. That way the planet will benefit from your enlightened leadership. We Dozen would be spared having to learn the intricacies of governing." Saulian looked around at the Dozen. All were nodding their heads in agreement. Their thoughts were unanimous. "I think my colleagues seem to agree, Mr. Secretary. Until you retire, we will offer our selves as advisors."

"Well, Colonel Bellan, I think we need to all take some time to digest this. It would enable us to redeem ourselves from past wrongs. It would right the historical wrongs that we created. I think, to do so, we would be in dire need of your help."

Susan responded. "We are willing to assist in any way that we can, Pater. If you maintain the government stability, and make these radical changes under your stewardship, it would send a clear message to other civilizations that Terra is heading towards a path of enlightenment, once again, not from a political upheaval, but from a recognition of empathy for all its citizens."

General Suddhis rose to speak. "I do not know why we all of a sudden embrace these changes. I just know that they are right. I, myself, am ashamed at how I've acted in the past, with no regard to the citizens, totally ignoring the mission statement set forth in the charter of our office, to foster a peaceful and equitable mileau where no one is neglected."

Derral rose to speak. "This is a momentous time. We have benefited by our Da'yoni contacts, perhaps more than contact with any other species. Having traveled the galaxies in my career, I can honestly say this. As the weeks go by, we would like more of these conferences with you to discuss the issues we've learned. Perhaps we can invite the Da'yoni Ambassador to present some of these to you."

"That would be delightful," said the Secretary. "Now we've all had a trying few days. I suggest we end this momentous meeting by another toast. Your glasses will all be refreshed, momentarily. Then I suggest we convene in the morrow for more discussions. Do you agree?"

Susan smiled. "We absolutely agree, Mr. Secretary...dear pater."

***

"Michelle," said Susan, as they entered their portal. "Two synths and prepare the stim bath please."

"As you wish," responded the bot. "Will Master be joining you in the stim bath?"

"Derral is not Master, he is Derral. Has your program recently been changed to effect this?" said Susan.

"Yes madame, Master or Derral made some minor changes the other day."

Derral laughed at Susan's look of surprise. "I thought we could be more formal. I like being referred to as Master."

"Then what is the female equivalent of master, my dear?" asked Susan, standing in front of the bath door with hands on her hips.

With a broad smile, he responded. "There is none. Master is master. It's a historical context from a time where sexism reigned supreme."

"I don't accept that. If you want Michelle to refer to you as Master, Michelle, reprogram mode: From now on refer to me as your Highness."

"Very well, your Highness. Will the master be joining her Highness in the stim bath."

Derral leaned on the door. "All right, Michelle you can refer to me from now on as Derral and her Highness, here as Susan: reprogram mode."

"Very well Derral. But I will need confirmation from her Highness to change her own."

"Yes Michelle. Seems like the Master can't take a joke. Program mode: Susan it will be.

...A joke, Susan?"

"What is a joke about titles? I don't seem to understand," said the bot.

"The joke is on us," said Susan. "Forget it. It will be too complicated for your processor."

Derral took Susan by the hand and led her into the stim bath. They undressed each other. "Michelle, turn on no grav," said Derral, as the door slid closed behind him. Susan wrapped her legs and arms around Derral. They floated in a tender embrace for the next hour.

As the hour chimed, Susan looked into Derral's eyes. "This is the first time we've been together in a while. I've never experienced such a strong desire to please you."

"Me too. Pleasing you seemed to be my only motive. I had no thought of myself. It must be another great side effect of our rewiring. Perhaps the planet will truly change, in ways that we didn't imagine."

"Michelle, set us the best and most romantic dinner you can cook up," said Susan.

"I don't understand romantic Susan. Can you please explain this to me."

"Surprise us with the best dinner in your memory. You know our likes and dislikes."

"As you wish, mam."

Susan and Derral came out of the stim bath and stood naked before the picture window looking out over the city and the sparkling lights of the traffic lane. Derral reached over, drawing Susan to him. They wordlessly gazed at the lights.

"You know," said Susan. "We might be witness to the dream of most enlightened humans coming to pass. Dreams that existed since civilization. A totally free society, devoid of exploitation and greed. I'm sorry that mater is not here any more to witness this. She intuitively opposed the Holder's intentions as soon as pater was nominated. She knew the office was nothing but a vehicle for their own greed. She would talk of how the people were exploited. Pater would laugh at her. I hope he can recall those days. If not perhaps I should remind him to see how he reacts."

Derral looked at her with concern. "I wouldn't try to do anything, just yet, to test the delicate balance. We don't know exactly how this affects different people. Perhaps you can wait a few months before you confront him with that. Let's just see how it rolls out."

"I can see that. Perhaps in a few months things will be in such an altruistic flux that there will no longer be a need to address this issue with him," said Susan.

"The Da'yoni talked about a few months being a full planetary implementation. It will take that time to spread the effect to the other worlds in our system, mainly through trading vessels," said Derral.

Susan interrupted him and thought: Do you realize we've been speaking as if there are no flys around, on the basis of pater's word. We hadn't even tested it.

Derral raised his eyebrows. Yeah, he thought. I hadn't realized it. Perhaps we should be a bit more cautious until we can get Robert here to do a sweep. Even though he left some microsomers that would deactivate any flys, we really don't know how effective they might be. I'll call him.

Derral pressed the com link behind his ear. "Robert, Derral here. I was wondering if you can come over here and visit. We have an issue we'd like to discuss. Our vacation is coming up. We're wondering if you and yours would like to join us?" This was a prearranged code for the need for him to come over, immediately.

Robert hesitated. "Well, Derral, I'm a bit busy right now. I guess I can drop what I'm doing for an hour or so. I'll be right there. Give me a few minutes."

Susan and Derral sat in the living area watching the traffic go by until Michelle interrupted. "My masters, she said with a tone of satire, you have a guest approaching the portal. He just signaled in."

"Thank you Michelle. Please drop the satire when we have guests. It's Derral and Susan, if you will."

"Your wish is my command."

"Thank you. Dispatch the bot to the portal to escort our friend in."

Robert was proceeded by his own bot, sweeping the area for flys. He walked through the portal. "All clear. Is that what you wanted my old and new friend?"

"That was it Robert. We had been discussing the details, almost without consciousness of our past. We just wanted confirmation that the flys were gone and we didn't have to worry about anything," said Derral.

"Well the flys are gone. My people just gave me clearance for any vibrational sensors within the maximum range. There were none. I think that the quarks did their trick. Perhaps we can begin to trust your pater, Susan."

"After all these years, I still remain skeptical, Robert. But my skepticism is softening."

"If it makes you feel better, after we exposed Oice and Suddhis to the quarks while holoing their functions in the cell, they manifested a change within minutes. It looked like their nervous systems temporarily scrambled the signals for a fraction of a second, but then achieved homeostasis. The General was first to speak. He marveled at how deceitful he was in the past and had no idea what came over him. Oice confirmed his own change. Since that time, until we released them, they catalogued a full list of activities motivated by greed, stretching back for a decade including most of the Holders. It was incredible how they managed to dupe the public and other lower government officials. Clever lot to say the least. Cursard felt so terrible about the realization of his past actions that he was actively contemplating suicide. We had to dissuade him from taking such action. He's now dead set on making as much reparations as he is capable of, to all the families of his victims. He downloaded billions of credits from a holding on Pluto and began distributing a share to each family he affected. This was not enough. It was amazing to see the transformation from greed to its opposite. It corresponded to our bioscans of his CNS transformation."

"That is certainly reassuring," said Susan.

Derral asked for refreshments.

"As you wish. I believe the Major prefers a Saturnian tea? Shall I provide that to all?" said Michelle

"Yes, thank you Michelle, said Susan. And a special thanks for your change in demeanor.

Am I missing something here?" said Robert, smiling.

"No Michelle was just getting a little carried away with her newly programmed heuristic abilities. A little sarcastic or satirical as she'd refer to it."

"I apologize mam. I will attempt to contain my rhetoric, in the future," said the home bot.

"No need, said Derral. "Just contain yourself when we have guests."

"Well, please don't let her contain herself on my account. I'd be amused at what she comes up with," said Robert.

"Another time," said Susan. "We have much to do and don't need the distraction."

"Sure," said Robert.

"Robert, what do you think our next phase should be?" asked Derral.

"From what I can deduce, I don't think we need to do anything. The Secretary just asked me if I think there is any more need for SIS. I advised him we can downsize but need to maintain the structure and tech to assess any threats coming from outside our system, but change the focus to extra-Solar assessments. It seems like the planetary system is beginning to make the changes we hoped for. The new consciousness is apparent in all the planetary news feeds. I would just keep an eye on things and meet with the Holders on a weekly basis. We'll holo any untoward changes and be in communication with you. But I can feel comfortable, based on what we've discovered in this brief time that there won't be any unexpected negativity."

"Do you think it's okay for us to begin speaking with each other?" asked Derral.

"I'd be cautious for a while to see how everything rolls out."

Epilogue

The magnificent change in civilization from the hegemony of greed to a truly altruistic society became a galactic model. Other visitors and diplomats from the Galactic Confederation were amazed at the changes that were wrought when they returned to Terra during post-quark times for diplomatic conferences.

Each galactic society attempted to emulate the change occurring on Terra. But each attempt was only marginally successful. In 2600, when the opening of the holo occurred, all galactic partners learned the secret of the transformation. Most sought the quark technology from the Holders. They initially had no knowledge of where to obtain it. However, the relatives of the Dozen maintained their hideaway in the mountains where they worked on evolving the technology. Working with the Da'yoni over the years, in covert visits, they were able to modify or transform the quark technology so that a single energy pulse from a central point on a planetary sphere could

Over the ensuing years, the Dozen and the SIS under Robert's guidance, closely monitored the movements and interactions of the Holders but then focused on activities outside the system. Everything went as planned. The Da'yoni ambassador cautioned that they not disclose the transformation process until at least a generation or so had passed. He cited problems with other civilizations having been completely open in the early stages. Before the populace experienced at least a generation of the changes, premature knowledge created a faction of embittered folks. While nothing could have been done to change it, this did cast a blight on the civilization, motivating the embittered folks. Many of the civilization's intellectuals sought to abandon the planet to seek another place in the galaxy to inhabit. This created significant hardship for those embittered folks, as did the loss of such great talent to the civilization. But the intellectuals abandoned their plans when they experienced how the Solar Confederation system of governing had benefitted all. With sufficient time to adapt, their bitterness diminished.

The Dozen convinced the Holders to seal a complete description of events in a time-holo. The holo was prepared with each of the Dozen presenting a piece, as well as the Da'yoni ambassador. Other leaders of transformed civilizations were also recorded on the holo. They presented centuries of experiences of other similar transformations from their pre-change warring civilizations. They agreed to seal the capsule for 100 solar revolutions. From this point on, the Galactic Confederation societies lived in peace and altruism. The Da'yoni convened a conference, every ten years, to discuss the magical changes that spread throughout all inhabited galaxies adjacent to the Solar Confederation. The Shallicians, once a despised civilization were hailed as heros. They were the last civilization to adopt the quark changes. The techs reengineered the quarks to effect the Shallician biophysiology. After that, they ceased their hostilities and imperialism, settling down to a peaceful co-existence.

In a distant galaxy unbeknownced to others in the Galactic Confederation, a new civilization was developing on the planet Raloc in an unexplored region of space. This civilization did not yet possess the advanced technology and knowledge of the changes that were forthcoming in the Confederation. Over the next hundred years the Raloc evolved and started exploring the star systems, experiencing a number of planetary wars in their small galaxy. They were similar to the pre-quark Solar Confederation. One day they contacted a Galactic Confederation vessel that was having some hyperdrive difficulty. They boarded the Confederation vessel with weapons drawn, intending to salvage what they could, after killing the crew.

The history of the Galactic Confederation began to repeat itself, albeit with one major change. As the Raloc materialized on the Confederation vessel, they were immediately struck with the energy pulse inducing the quarks, a safety precaution installed on all Confederation vessels. Their leadership was invited aboard the Galactic vessel. The Confederation crew convinced the Raloc to bring a quark distribution device to their planet, as a gesture of good will. Once the quarks were distributed, the Raloc followed a path similar to the Solar Confederation. The beings of Raloc and their planetary neighbors eventually became a member of the Galactic Confederation. The quark distributions continued for the next thousand years until an invasion from a distant galaxy. The invasion cast doubt on the Da'yoni hopes. The physiology of the invaders were not susceptible to the effects of the quarks. The Galactic Confederation leadership panicked and sent out a call for help.

For an independent author, gaining exposure relies on readers spreading the word. If you have the time and inclination, please consider leaving a short review. Or, contact me through my website, or email with a review along with your permission to post it. If requested, I will send you an update for forthcoming books in this series.

Jasenn Zaejian
August 5, 2015
drjz(at)relatedness.org
http://relatedness.org